MEN OF DANGER

MEN OF DANGER

Lora Leigh

Red Garnier

Alexis Grant

Lorie O'Clare

St. Martin's Paperbacks

This is a work of fiction. All of the characters, organizations, and events portrayed in this novel are either products of the author's imagination or are used fictitiously.

MEN OF DANGER

"Hannah's Luck" copyright © 2010 by Lora Leigh.
"Reckless and Yours" copyright © 2010 by Red Garnier.
"Tempt Me" copyright © 2010 by Alexis Grant.
"Love Me 'Til Death" copyright © 2010 by Lorie O'Clare.

Cover photograph © Shirley Green

For information address St. Martin's Press, 175 Fifth Avenue, New York, NY 10010.

ISBN: 978-0-312-57636-3

Printed in the United States of America

St. Martin's Paperbacks edition / May 2010

St. Martin's Paperbacks are published by St. Martin's Press, 175 Fifth Avenue, New York, NY 10010.

10 9 8 7 6 5 4 3 2 1

CONTENTS

"Hannah's Luck" by Lora Leigh   1

"Reckless and Yours" by Red Garnier   85

"Tempt Me" by Alexis Grant   179

"Love Me 'Til Death" by Lorie O'Clare   291

HANNAH'S LUCK

Lora Leigh

PROLOGUE

RICK GRAYSON stared into the casket as it sat atop the raised dais in the funeral parlor. Mourners milled around the room, stopped by the casket, whispered their condolences to him and then moved off, uncertain, hesitant in the face of his silence.

Everyone mourned the lovely, vivacious Sienna Grayson, except her husband and the friend she had betrayed.

She was as beautiful now as she had ever been, perhaps more beautiful in death than ever before. Her long dark brown hair curled around her shoulders, contrasting with surprising warmth against the white dress her family had picked out for her to wear through eternity.

Her brown eyes were closed, long lashes feathering against her cheeks. The makeup artist the funeral home employed had done an excellent job. Her skin wasn't death-white, but instead had been given a warm golden glow. The bullet that had exited the front of her neck and torn off half her face was nowhere in sight. There was not so much as a glimpse of the damage that had been done to her.

The damage he had done.

He stared at her. His cheating, lying wife. The woman who had sold out her friends, her family, her husband, and her son, for drugs. For the thrill, the high, God only knew what other reasons she had had.

How could he have not known?

He stared at her now, realizing that all the clues had been there, and he had overlooked them.

He had known someone was betraying the agents sent to Alpine, Texas, to track down a homeland terrorist group. He had suspected it originated from his office, and he had been investigating it for years, but he had never known the extent of it.

His wife and his deputy had betrayed him.

How had he lived with such evil and not known it? he wondered. How had something so vile mothered the child that now lay sleeping in a chair in the corner of the room? Their son, Kent.

Rick glanced over at him, seeing the peace on the boy's face, and realized, not for the first time, that his mother's death had barely affected him.

He turned back to his wife. Sienna. Lovely, lying, murderous Sienna. The county mourned her now as they would have a fallen hero. The truth about her death, and the kidnapping of another woman, had been hidden so deeply that even he wondered exactly what had happened at times.

Only a handful of people knew the truth. Knew that his wife and his deputy Hershel Jenkins had been involved with a militia group so bloodthirsty and powerful that even America's law enforcement agencies hadn't been able to get to them. It had taken a team of dead men to catch them.

He continued to stand there, to stare at her. Tried to figure out why she would turn into nothing more than a camp whore for a small group of powerful men who thought they could determine who was and who was not American.

A group of men that kidnapped, hunted, raped, and murdered those they targeted, and his wife had helped them.

He couldn't believe it. He couldn't believe that he hadn't suspected her. That he couldn't have known. That somehow it had slipped by him.

A cocaine whore. That was what had been written in the report by one of the federal agents who had wrapped up the paperwork in the case.

His wife had been a cocaine whore.

He wanted to shake his head. He wanted to deny it. He didn't want to accept that he hadn't seen it. He couldn't believe that the years of training, that his years as a sheriff, had taught him so little that he hadn't even suspected her.

Or had he?

Had he even been surprised the day a bleeding, nearly hysterical Rory Malone had given him and that team of "dead" men the information that tied it all together? He hadn't wanted to believe it, but he realized now that despite his horror, his shock, he hadn't disbelieved it.

Some part of his mind had already accepted that something was wrong with Sienna. Something was lacking. She hadn't been a wife in years but she had refused to divorce him. She had threatened more than once to take their son, and to make certain Kent's life was hell, if Rick ever divorced her.

He'd convinced himself at one time that it was an empty threat. That she wouldn't hurt Kent. Now he knew what a monster she truly was, and he thanked God that his sister had done more to raise the child than Sienna.

But it didn't ease his guilt. Six federal agents had died over the years because of information she had given the militia. One had been a young woman. She had been hunted like an animal, brutalized, tortured. Raped.

His soul felt as though it were being ripped from his body at the thought of what had happened to her. Her and other young women. Wives. Mothers. Sisters. Women whose only crime had been the color of their skin. They had been Mexican or of Mexican descent. And they had been punished for it in the worst ways. By his wife.

He could still feel the hollow, brutal shame that seared his guts like a brand. He may as well have killed those women himself. He should be as liable for their deaths as she was, yet he had been cleared.

"Daddy, I'm hungry." He stared down at where Kent now stood by his side.

At five, the boy was still small for his age, and still incredibly innocent. Rick thanked his sister for that.

Mona had kept him through the years as he worked,

because Sienna was always busy. She had things to do, events to plan, hair appointments or lunch or dinner with her friends. She hadn't had time for their child any more than she had had time for her husband over the years.

He thanked God again.

"Come on." He reached out his hand to his boy, gripped his little fingers, and moved to the door of the funeral parlor.

"Is Mommy coming back?" Kent asked as they left the funeral home.

"Mommy's not coming back, son," he told him as they walked to the truck parked on the other side of the parking lot.

Kent didn't say anything, though Rick hadn't expected him to. As he opened the door to the truck and lifted the child into his car seat Kent looked up at him solemnly.

"Daddy," he said softly.

"Yeah, son?" Rick clipped the seat belt around the car seat.

"I'm glad."

"What?" Rick looked back at him, shock welling inside him once again. "You're glad of what, Kent?"

Kent stared back at him, his brown eyes, so like Rick's, somber and suddenly too grown-up.

"I'm glad Mommy's not coming back."

Rick could feel the blood draining from his face, felt something in his stomach curdle in fear. What the hell had Sienna done to their child?

"Why?" Rick touched the boy's thick hair, hoping to dispel whatever memories would have made Kent say such a thing.

"Because she was gonna hurt Miss Brookes," he said quietly. "I heard her on the phone, Daddy. She said she hated Miss Brookes and wanted her dead and that she was going to strangle her. Just like she strangled my puppy."

He was going to throw up. Rick swallowed back the bile that boiled in his stomach and rose to his throat.

"Your puppy ran away, Kent," he told his son.

Or had it? Sienna had hated the dog he had bought Kent last year. Had she done something to it?

Kent shook his head. "She said on the phone, 'I'm going to strangle her like I did that damned dog.'"

Rick didn't correct the profanity. He could only stare back at his son in horror.

"You didn't tell me," he whispered. "Why, Kent? Why didn't you tell me?"

Why hadn't his son trusted him enough to tell him, to bring his fears to him?

"Because, Daddy," he said quietly. "Mommy sent me to Aunt Mona's, and Aunt Mona promised she wouldn't strangle anyone. Now she won't strangle no more puppies, will she?"

There was an edge of fear in Kent's voice, in his eyes. Rick wanted to howl in fury, and in rage. God help him. Sweet, merciful God, forgive him for letting that monster touch his child after his birth.

"She can't hurt any more puppies, Kent." He clasped the little head in his hand, unclipped the seat belt, and gathered him into his embrace. "Never again, Kent. Never again."

And now, he would have to make damned certain she hadn't hurt Hannah Brookes, either. Because if she had, that guilt would rest on his shoulders, as well. Because Sienna would have never hated her, would have never focused on her, if it hadn't been for him.

If he hadn't watched her when he shouldn't have, and if he hadn't been so careless in doing so that Sienna had caught him.

It was his guilt. It was his shame. He just prayed no one else had paid for it.

CHAPTER I

Two Years Later

HANNAH BROOKES pulled into the parking lot of the Brewster County sheriff's office and sat staring at the glass entry door.

Texas heat shimmered off the pavement in waves as a hot desert sun beamed down with all its fierce summer rays. She could literally feel the warmth outside the air-conditioned comfort of the car and hesitated once again before shutting off the car engine and stepping out into it.

It was a typical summer day, she reminded herself. It shouldn't bother her now any more than it ever had. But it did. Because that heat on the outside reminded her of what was awaiting her once she entered that building and walked into Rick Grayson's office.

She breathed out heavily at the thought, wishing there was a way to buy an AC that could counter the effects that man had on her. He made her, a normally confident, self-assured teacher, feel like a teenager with her first crush.

She was thirty years old. She wasn't a teenager anymore, and she damned sure shouldn't feel like one. Her hands shouldn't be shaking and her heart shouldn't be racing.

She'd been married. Her virgin days were long behind her. She'd had a lover or two since her divorce. So why was she sitting here like a ninny that had no idea how to talk to a man like Rick Grayson?

Probably because she didn't know how to talk to a man

who made her heart race and her hands shake, she reminded herself. It had never happened before, even when she had been young and inexperienced.

"Dumb," she muttered as she shut the car off, pulled the key from the ignition, and pushed the door open.

Standing to her full five feet three and three-quarter inches, she hit the remote lock on the door, clutched her handbag tighter, and strode to the door.

She was not a ninny. Her heart might race, her hands might shake, but she could come up with a very, very good reason for it this morning.

Pushing through the door, she strode, shoulders straight, head high, to the receptionist's desk.

"Carl Dee, how are you doing?" she greeted the officer standing behind the desk with a smile.

Carl Dee had always been Carl Dee. No one called him Carl or Dee, it was always both, and he was quick to remind anyone that called him otherwise.

"Hey, Miz Brookes." His wide grin was slightly awry as he ran his hand over his frizzled red hair and glanced at the computer he'd been typing on. "Sheriff's making me learn a new program here. Save me, please."

She laughed at the playful teasing in his expression. His five-year-old daughter looked just like him. The same grin, the same playfulness.

"It looks pretty complicated." She shook her head with mock seriousness. "I don't know, I might mess it up for you, then the sheriff will lock us both up."

"The mood he's in this week, I wouldn't doubt it. He's grouchy as a sore-tailed bear coming out of hibernation," Carl Dee grumped, shaking his head. "What can I do for you?"

Hannah grimaced. "Well, I need to talk to the bear, if you think he'd see me?"

"Poor Miz Brookes." Carl Dee chuckled. "Let's hope you're not here to yell at him. He yelled back at the last pretty girl that stomped in here on him."

Her lips twitched. "Mona was here today?"

Mona was the sheriff's sister. Those two had been arguing and yelling at each other since they were kids, from what she had heard.

"In the flesh, pretty as she can be, and raging hell and brimstone down on his head again." He picked up the phone on the desk. "Give me a sec here and I'll see if he's calmed down some." Carl Dee winked at her, his brown eyes twinkling in laughter as he punched the line into the sheriff's office.

Hannah turned and surveyed the lobby of the new sheriff's offices as he talked. Slate-gray tile floors blended nicely with the pale cream walls. Photographs of the county were displayed on the walls, and the chairs in the waiting area looked reasonably comfortable.

Arrangements of dried desert flowers filled pots on metal and glass tables, while a television droned quietly in the background.

"Miz Brookes, the sheriff's secretary will be out in a minute to get you." Carl Dee drew her attention back to him. "Just give her time to bring him fresh coffee so he'll be sure to be nice and polite."

Hannah laughed at the aside. She remembered a time, though, when Sheriff Grayson's good humor had been the norm. When he had smiled, even laughed some. A time before his wife had been murdered by homeland terrorists who had been friends.

"Hannah, how good to see you again." Mae Livingston came down the hall, immaculate as always in black dress slacks and a light gray cotton shirt and two-inch heels.

She envied the other woman's svelte figure. Short blond hair brushed against her neck and jaw and framed a heart-shaped face and gray eyes.

Hannah had had all three of her children in school. They were just as easygoing, and as frighteningly self-confident, as their mother.

"Hello, Mae." The hazards of a small town, Hannah thought. She knew just about everyone.

"Come on back, dear," Mae hooked her arm with her

own and began leading her back. "Are you enjoying the summer without all those kids yelling back and forth?"

Summer vacation had just started the week before.

"I'm still missing them." Hannah shook her head with a laugh. "Those are my kids, too, Mae. Their parents have all taken them away from me for the summer."

In part, it was the truth. There were days she prayed for summer vacation, but once it arrived, she missed all those young minds and amazingly adept personalities.

"Lord, child, you should remarry and have your own kids," Mae told her as they reached the sheriff's office. "You'll change your tune."

They were still laughing as Mae opened the door and they stepped in. Hannah almost came to a hard, pulse-pounding stop at the sight of the sheriff, dressed in his customary jeans and dark gray shirt as he laid a file on Mae's desk.

He had a brooding, wary look as his eyes narrowed on Hannah. The golden-brown gaze was disconcerting, probing, and she often feared it saw more than she ever wanted it to see.

"Hannah." He nodded shortly.

"Good morning, Sheriff." She clutched her purse tighter. "How's Kent doing?"

Kent had been in her class two years before, just after his mother's death. He'd been well adjusted, happy, laughing. He hadn't acted like a child that had just lost his mother.

"Doing fine," he answered as he leaned against Mae's desk, his gaze intent. "Mona browbeat me into letting him take another of those summer trips with her. Stole him right away from me about an hour ago."

There was an attempt at humor, but she could sense the vein of discontent, as well. He hadn't wanted to lose his son for the summer, but evidently Mona and Kent had outvoted him. Kent, charmer that he was, was good at getting his way.

"I hope he enjoys himself," she stated as she drew in a long, slow breath and glanced at Mae. "Could I speak to you a moment alone, Sheriff? I promise not to take up much of your time."

She didn't dare.

He glared at her, his eyes narrowing as though she were indeed putting him out.

"Come on." He nodded toward the office. "Would you like coffee or a soft drink?"

"Nothing." She shook her head and entered the office.

The door closed forcefully behind her, causing her to jump and turn in surprise to face the glare that had turned into brooding anger.

"Since when the hell do you call me sheriff, Hannah?" he growled as he stalked to his desk before turning back to her, his expression dark.

"Well, you are the sheriff." She hooked the strap of her purse over her shoulder before crossing her arms mutinously over her breasts. Mostly to hide the fact that her nipples were hardening in his presence.

His frown deepened. "You didn't call me sheriff last summer."

"Last summer we had two dinner dates and I never heard back from you." She smiled sweetly to cover the fact that it bothered her. A lot. He hadn't even kissed her. Two wasted evenings, two wasted weeks waiting, hoping, fantasizing. For nothing.

The bastard.

"So we're strangers because I never took you out again?" If anything he seemed angrier.

Hannah sighed wearily. "No, Rick, I'm not here because of a dinner date or as a friend. I'm here because I need your advice in an official capacity."

He didn't move, he didn't even seem to breathe. He turned to ice. She watched the transformation in fascination. Pure ice. Icy golden eyes, expressionless face, stone-cold.

"In what manner?" Even his tone was cold.

"Can I sit down?" She moved to the chair anyway, wishing her knees didn't shake and that her clit didn't ache. Jeeze, she had it bad here.

"What kind of trouble are you in?" He answered her question with one of his own.

Hannah sat back in her chair and regarded him silently for a long moment before she let a wry grin touch her lips. "Hopefully none at all, Sheriff Grayson, unless it's breaking the law to have prowlers attempting to break into my house."

His expression slowly thawed until he was staring back at her in surprise. "When?"

"Last night." She sighed. "I called nine-one-one and they sent out two patrol officers, but as soon as whoever it was heard the sirens they ran. They were nearly inside the house."

She could still feel the shaky terror that had assailed her the night before when she had been awakened by her Pomeranian, Chilli's, growls. He hadn't barked, which had been her first clue there was trouble, because Chilli was a barker. Unless he was scared. Then he growled. Low and deep, and not a single bark escaped.

"I called nine-one-one when I heard someone at the back door," she explained. "They were turning the doorknob when the patrol cars came down the street, sirens wailing."

"You have a security system?" he asked.

Hannah nodded. "I do, and I set it before I went to bed. But it took the police nearly ten minutes to get to the house. They were almost in the house before the patrol cars arrived. I need to know what else I can do to keep them out of my home if they try it again."

She was scared. Rick could see it in her pretty green eyes. About as scared as a woman could be of what might happen. And he didn't blame her one damned bit.

"Do you have a gun?" he asked.

She nodded slowly. "It was Dad's. I know how to shoot it, but I'd like to keep it from coming to that. And I have to be awake to use it. If they get in while I'm asleep, and Chilli doesn't hear them, then anything could happen."

Rick thought about the red Pom and doubted a breeze could get past that temperamental pooch without it knowing.

The thought that someone was trying to break into her home had the hairs at the back of his neck standing up in alarm, though.

"I just need some advice." She leaned forward, the scooped

neckline of her navy blue shirt giving a hint of cleavage that would make any man's mouth water. "Tell me what to buy, what to do, to make the house safer and I'll do it."

He had to drag his gaze from the top of her breasts and force himself to focus on the sincere, rounded little face.

Damn, she was pretty. She wasn't beautiful, but she was pretty. Unique. Dark wavy brown hair fell below her shoulders. Wide green eyes watched the world with a hint of innocence. White, slightly uneven teeth nibbled at a plump lower lip that tempted a man to taste.

She tempted him and therefore he stayed way the hell away. She tempted him bad, so he stayed far, far away.

As he rubbed at his jaw he considered her thoughtfully, his guts tightening at the thought of what could have happened if a prowler had managed to get into the house. She could have been raped, murdered. That bright smile and brighter gaze could have been gone forever.

"Why don't I stop by the house on my way home this evening and check things over, see what we can do?" The words were out of his mouth before he even realized what the hell he was saying.

Where had that come from? And what the fuck was he supposed to do with the hard-on pounding beneath his jeans now? His cock was tight, erect, throbbing and pushing against the zipper as though trying to burst free to get to her.

Just what he needed. Son of a bitch, was he crazy? Had he managed to lose his mind somewhere since he woke up that morning?

Then that incredible smile of hers transformed her face from pretty, to alluring. Mysterious. Her green eyes brightened with relief and she took what appeared to be a fortifying breath. It lifted her breasts and left his mouth dry.

Hell. He liked that smile.

"Are you sure you don't mind?" She rose to her feet, drawing his gaze to the perfect fit of her jeans. Not too snug, not too loose. Just enough to show the rounded hips and gentle silhouette of her body.

Out of politeness, he rose as well, when he would have preferred to sit and stare like a hungry dog.

"I'm sure I don't mind," he promised her, standing still as she moved from the chair and prepared to turn for the door. He wanted to be behind her when she walked away.

"Thanks, Rick," she said softly, her voice as filled with relief as her smile had been. "I've worried myself sick since last night. I haven't slept a wink."

"I'll be there around seven, then," he promised.

"I . . . I could fix you dinner?" Her voice was hesitant as though she wasn't certain she should offer.

"Fried chicken?" Hannah Brookes could fry some killer chicken. He'd had the pleasure of sampling it at a school dinner when Kent had been in kindergarten. It was damned good.

Her smile lit up the office. "Done deal," she promised. "I'll see you this evening, then."

Stupid. Stupid. He cursed himself for his wayward tongue and his stubborn hard-on. But he still waited until she turned before moving from his desk.

He watched her walk. The bunch and clench of her rear beneath those jeans made his jaw tighten.

He reached past her as they got to the door, and opened it for her, watching as she turned back to him.

"Thank you again," she said softly.

"You're welcome, Hannah." He closed the door on that bright smile before he did something really foolish. Something dumb like jerking her back inside his office and pushing her across his desk.

Damn, it had been too long since he'd been with a woman, he told himself. More than four years. Two years before Sienna died, give or take a few months. He hadn't had sex with his wife, and he hadn't cheated on her. And after her death, he had been too wary, too filled with a darkness that didn't make sense to him.

Hannah had brought out that darkness. The two dinner dates they'd had, he'd been tense, hungry for something that had nothing to do with food, and had had him off balance just enough to cause him to draw away.

Besides that, he knew Hannah Brookes. He'd known her all her life, and she wasn't a one-night stand. Rick wasn't looking for anything more than a few hot nights and a fond farewell.

No more marriage, no more betrayals, he'd promised himself. He'd known Sienna all her life too, but he'd never known who she really was on the inside.

He'd risked his son once already, he wasn't going to do it again. Sienna may have been Kent's mother, but the monster that dwelled inside her had been anything but maternal.

Shaking his head at the situation he had suddenly placed himself in, he paced back to the desk and threw himself into the chair as he stared at the door once again.

He couldn't get it out of his mind. Someone had tried to break in on her. She was a schoolteacher; a burglar wasn't going to make much from breaking into her home. There were a hell of a lot better hits on that street than her little house. That left other motives for trying to get to her. Those motives sent a chill racing up his spine.

He might not trust his instincts with women anymore, but he couldn't get past the suspicion that if that prowler had managed to get in, then Hannah might not have survived the experience.

He could handle one evening and one fried chicken dinner, he assured himself as he pushed his fingers wearily through his hair. Hell, he'd survived two dinner dates last summer, hadn't he? He hadn't even kissed her, despite the nearly overwhelming urge to feast on that slightly full lower lip.

He had the self-control to resist. He'd resisted temptation for four years. Two years during his marriage, two years after his wife's death. Sienna had taught him the hazards of giving in, and he promised himself he'd never make that mistake again.

CHAPTER 2

RICK ARRIVED at Hannah's just a few minutes after seven and had to consciously steel himself against the woman that opened the door to his firm knock.

She was a kindergarten teacher, for God's sake, he kept telling himself as he stared down at her, dressed in a soft summer dress. Shoulders bared, tan leather sandals on her feet. He expected polish, a bright red or maroon; instead, it was a soft pale pink that made him wonder if it was the same color as her nipples.

The thought had his cock harder, if possible, as he stepped into the house. There was matching polish on her fingernails. That creamy dark flesh pink that was driving him insane.

The dress was an added stimulation. It bared her softly tanned, shimmering skin. Thin straps and just a little hint of cleavage then it flowed like a whisper to below her knees. It wasn't short, tight, or seductive, and all the more destructive for it.

It was feminine, just shy of innocent, with just a touch of flirty.

Damn, she was good.

"I'll check the doors and windows, see what you need," he said, barely managing to get the words past his throat. "I brought some locks and a few other things in case you need them."

He'd brought a toolbox and bought enough damned dead bolts and security locks to reinforce Fort Knox.

"Thank you," she murmured behind him as he headed to the back door. "Dinner will be in about an hour."

He nodded, but didn't dare look at her again.

"Did they dust for prints?" he asked as he walked through the kitchen.

"Yes, but I haven't heard anything." She was behind him. He could smell the scent of woman and a flirty, spicy fragrance that tempted his senses.

"I'll see what I can find out tomorrow." He unlocked the back door and went to work. The quicker he was finished, the quicker he could get the hell out of here. Get away from her. Before he messed up. And when Rick Grayson messed up, he really messed up.

WELL, HER LUCK was about as dismal as normal, Hannah thought as she watched Rick from beneath her lashes. The chicken was perfect, the mashed potatoes creamy and delicate, the fresh green beans and biscuits the perfect complement.

He was still stiff as a board and talking in monosyllables. As though he hated being there. And the tension was so damned thick she could have cut it with a knife.

He'd replaced her dead bolts and her locks, drilled out deeper anchors for the bolts, installed additional window locks, and instructed her to keep her cell phone by the bed and her bedroom door locked at night.

She promised to do it. He had nodded stiffly and sat down to dinner.

It reminded her of the two dates they'd had the summer before. Stiff, stilted, and filled with tension.

Yep, that was her luck. She hadn't had a decent date in years, and it had been even longer since she'd actually had a lover.

"I'm sorry I kept you so long." She moved to her feet and began to whisk the remainder of the dinner from the table before returning for the dirty dishes.

He was still sitting there, nursing that cup of coffee between his fingers as though it were a lifeline of some sort.

"The chicken was delicious, Hannah. Thank you." He watched her, his gaze shuttered as she returned to the dining room.

"You're welcome." Okay, so her voice was a little crisp, but it wasn't nasty. She wasn't being impolite, she was just eager to have this failure of an evening over, as well.

She picked up the side dishes and went back to the kitchen. Dumping them in the sink, she turned to return to the dining room when she suddenly ran into a broad, hard, wide chest.

Rick's hard body. His hands settled on her hips as though to steady her, and she might have needed the help because suddenly her knees were weak, her head spinning.

Her head lifted, tilting back to stare up at him. He was a foot taller than she was, wider, stronger, so masculine he stole her breath and made her so wet she was certain to have to change panties once he left.

She'd been wet before they ever sat down to dinner. She should have excused herself during the meal.

And now, she could feel the slick wetness increasing, her sex flexing, clenching in need.

What was it about this one man? What made her body ache for him, her imagination dream of him? Why was she so fascinated with a man that didn't want . . .

Her eyes widened as she felt the hard wedge of flesh against her stomach. His erection behind the denim of his jeans.

"Why look so surprised?" he growled, his voice deeper, rougher. "Surely you knew what the hell you do to me?"

Her mouth went dry. Shaking her head slowly, Hannah let her fingers curl tighter around his wrists, felt the tough flesh beneath her fingertips, and wondered how his fingers would feel against her.

"You never seemed interested." She swallowed tightly.

"Not interested?" His hands tightened at her hips. "I think we just ruled that one out."

Her lips parted as his head lowered slowly. His gaze locked

with hers, and it seemed to Hannah that the world suddenly moved in slow motion as she waited for this kiss. Waited to feel his lips against hers, to touch him, to taste him.

It was happening too slowly, and it was happening too fast. Something seemed off balance, not quite what she had expected from him.

One hand moved from her hip to cup her face, tilt her head. She suddenly felt incredibly small and feminine, helpless against him, as her hands fluttered uncertainly before landing on his chest.

"Rick?" She whispered his name as his lips brushed against hers, light as a feather, heated, firm.

"Yeah, baby." Suddenly she was floating, lifting against him, until she felt her rear meet the counter as he moved between her thighs and his lips settled hungrily over hers.

This was no introductory kiss. There was no initial exploration. It was an explosion through her senses. His lips settled over hers as his tongue licked, stroked the seam of her lips until they parted.

Then he was taking what he wanted. Hannah found herself helpless against the pleasure, her hands clenching on his shoulders as she fought against the dizzying waves of sensation that shot through her body.

She could feel his erection pressing between her thighs. His hands were on her hips again, moving her against him, sliding around until he was cupping her rear, the throbbing heat of his cock penetrating his jeans and her panties to stroke liquid fire through the core of her.

It was so much, so fast. It was a sudden maelstrom of near ecstasy that stole her breath and left her gasping. Fighting for balance as his lust, her hunger, raged through her, burning across her nerve endings and sending her senses spinning.

She became lost in it. Pulled into a vortex that she couldn't stop, that she didn't want to stop. Her fingers threaded through his hair, longer than it had ever been, thick and cool to the touch as she held him to her.

His lips slanted over hers as she licked at his tongue. He sipped at her lips as she fought for that deeper caress again.

His hands ground her against him, the hard wedge of his erection pressing into her clit and sending rioting waves of pleasure tearing through her.

Rick couldn't believe the maddening hunger that flared between them. Just that fast. Just the touch of his lips against hers and the raging hunger took control, stripped him down to the need that burned like wildfire in the pit of his belly, and left him helpless against his desire for her.

He'd never known a kiss like this. Brutally hot, starving, as though this kiss were feeding a part of his senses that he'd never known existed.

It cut past the distrust, burned to the core of him. A distant part of his brain was snidely informing him it had just been too long since he'd fucked. Another part of him, a part he didn't recognize, a part as unfamiliar as the dark lust tempting him, urged him to take, to relish, to push into the shadowed realms of lust with this woman. The ones he'd always avoided before. The ones he'd never even been tempted to know with Sienna.

The thought of Sienna. The thought of where he was going with Hannah, of the hunger she unleashed that he couldn't control, was like throwing ice on fire.

He jerked back from the kiss, his breathing harsh, heavy, his vision almost blurry as he stared back at her. If he thought his vision was blurred, then her face had passed that point.

Confusion and hunger marked her expression as she stared back at him, her lips parted and damp, that full lower lip swollen more, reddened, tempting him to sip from it again. Bringing to mind images so fucking carnal he was about to come in his jeans.

His hands still gripped her ass, his cock was still pressed as tight against her pussy as it could go with the layers of clothing between them.

"Rick?" She whispered his name again, her hand lifting to touch his lips, the caress like a fiery blast of renewed hunger striking at his gut.

What the hell was he doing? He'd known this was a mistake. Knew it. Now that he'd kissed her, tasted those tempting lips, how the hell was he supposed to just walk away?

"I could stay." There he went again, letting his dick take control over his brain.

She blinked back at him as though in surprise. What surprise? She should have known where this was heading, just as he had known.

"Tonight?" She was still breathing hard, heavy.

His hands tightened on her rear as he moved against her again, feeling the heat of her through the denim, wondering if she was as wet as she was hot.

"Tonight," he answered, his hands sliding from her rear to her legs.

He pushed the material of her dress up her legs, feeling the silky flesh as he watched her gaze become cloudy with desire again, her face flushing with it.

Sliding his palms to her thighs, his thumbs were within inches of the heated folds of her pussy when she jumped, her fingers suddenly closing over his wrists just as he was a hairbreadth from his goal.

He stared at the innocence, the uncertainty in her eyes. She wasn't a damned teenager, she had to know what he wanted from her.

"Isn't this going a little fast?" Her breathing was still rough, ragged.

"We're not teenagers, Hannah," he told her, his voice rough. He could feel the situation rapidly spinning out of control. "Adults don't sugarcoat sex. We're adults."

She blinked back at him. "Oh wow. Really?"

His eyes narrowed. That wasn't innocence in her tone, it was pure mocking disbelief.

"Hannah," he said, warning in his voice. He would not allow her to have the upper hand. "We're both about to burn out of control here. There's no sense in denying it."

"Am I denying anything?"

No, she wasn't, but she was no longer the sex kitten she had been beneath his kiss. She was withdrawing, he could feel it, tensing in his arms, and that wasn't what he wanted.

"This isn't what you want?" He stepped back, expecting her to stop him. To wrap her legs around his waist and hold her to him, to protest the sudden chill that he could feel wrapping around his own body. Surely it was wrapping around hers, as well.

He made the mistake then of glancing down, seeing the hard little nipples poking against the thin bra beneath her dress. He almost went to his knees with a plea to just let him see them. Touch them. Suck them into his mouth and snack on them like the ripe little fruits he knew they would be.

She slid from the counter. A flush covered her cheeks, her neck. Arousal and a hint of anger burned in her gaze.

"Thank you very much for the locks on my doors and windows." Her breathing was rough, and there was an edge of hurt in her voice.

"Hannah, what did you expect?" Exasperation filled him now. He wanted her so much he was about to burn alive with the lust.

She tilted her head and stared up at him, her gaze solemn despite the arousal that still darkened her bright green eyes.

"Why, I don't know, Sheriff, a little romance maybe." She waved her hand as though uncertain what to say or do. "A pretense of it anyway." She shook her head as he stared back at her, confused. "Forget it. Maybe you're just too old to remember what that means."

Too old?

"How old do you think I am?" he growled, his gaze narrowing on her at the insult.

"I know exactly how old you are." Her arms went over her breasts again, hiding the pert imprint of those hard little nipples. "I didn't think thirty-seven was really that old until now. But if you've forgotten that the way to a woman's bed is through her heart, then you're older than I imagined."

"Who the hell said I wanted your heart? What does that have to do with sex?"

Fuck.

Now, he knew better than that. He knew the instant the words left his lips that he'd just fucked himself right out of her bed.

"Good night, Sheriff." Woodenly, chillingly polite, she moved past him to the kitchen doorway. "It was very nice seeing you again, and I do appreciate everything you've done tonight. But I need to wash my hair now."

Wash her hair? The little minx. She was blatantly lying to him, using one of the oldest mocking excuses in the book just to piss him off.

Gritting his teeth, he moved past her, stalked through the house only to pause at the front door as she moved behind him.

"If you change your mind . . ."

"If I decide I want a cold, lonely fuck rather than a flesh-and-blood man, then I'll make sure I call you first," she promised sarcastically, her smile falsely bright as she opened the door, inviting him to leave. "But don't hold your breath. It hasn't happened once in my entire life, and I rather doubt it's going to happen now."

His lips thinned.

He had half a mind to jerk her to him, kiss her again, experience that heady, heated gut punch of pleasure, just to see if it was as damned good as he remembered.

Instead, he gave his head a hard shake and left, as she invited him to do.

For good, he told himself. He wanted her. He'd wanted her longer than he should have, but he'd be damned if he'd let her lead him around by the cock.

"Good night, Hannah." He left, ignoring the ache in his cock, and the unfamiliar ache in his chest.

"Good night, Rick." Her voice was soft, and a second later he heard the door close behind him.

He should have known better, he told himself. Damned kindergarten teacher, she was probably as immature as her students were. He was better off. He should have known better. He'd make sure he didn't make the same mistake twice.

* * *

HANNAH LISTENED until she heard Rick's truck reverse out of the drive and head down the quiet street she lived on.

Head lowered, eyes closed, she sighed heavily before forcing herself from the door. Locking it securely, she headed back to the kitchen and the dishes that had to be done.

She should have known better, she told herself. She should have remembered her luck with men and called this one quits before she ever offered him dinner, before she ever took him up on his offer to check out the house.

She should have saved herself the trouble of getting the best kiss of her life, only to realize that Rick Grayson wanted nothing more than a one-night stand.

Funny, she hadn't thought him the type. He was steady, a little irritable sometimes since his wife's death two years before, but that was to be expected. Right?

He seemed like a family man. Upstanding. Honorable. Those were the qualities she'd always seen in him. It hurt like hell to realize she was wrong.

It hurt like hell to realize that she had been pinning her hopes on being right about him.

He fascinated her. He drew her like a moth to a flame, and she couldn't help but want to touch all that incredible, masculine heat.

The letdown was incredibly disappointing. The memory of his kiss would haunt her. The hunger for him would take a long time to abate, she knew that for a fact. She had just gotten over that need from those two cold little dates last summer. Now this. How long would it take her to get over the kiss, the memory of his hands on her ass, his cock pressing tight and hot against her clit?

A little groan escaped her lips as she let her hand trail down her stomach to touch the sensitive mound between her thighs. Her fingertips pressed against the swollen knot of her clit as a heated surge of longing tore through her again.

It was going to be another long, lonely night, she thought. She hoped she had enough batteries to see her through. Because one thing was damned sure. She wasn't going to sleep again until she managed to relieve the pressure he had built inside her.

Yep, this was just her luck, she thought, jerking her hand back and attacking the dishes. She was the one left cold and lonely. He was probably out finding someone else to fill his night.

The person filling his night wouldn't be her. Not tonight. Not ever under those conditions. Just her luck. What was that saying? Unlucky in love . . .

Maybe she should take up gambling . . .

CHAPTER 3

TWO DAYS LATER Rick turned down Hannah's street, his gaze brooding, his mind in turmoil, as he still fought to make sense of what had happened the other night.

Had it been so long since he'd had a woman that he didn't know how to talk to one any longer? He'd spent the better part of the evening tongue-tied. He hadn't been able to think, to speak, to make sense of anything but the need that had crawled through his system.

Now he was back again, doing something just as stupid as he'd done the other night. Perhaps more stupid.

He was dying for a woman, but he'd found in the past two nights that not just any woman was going to do for him.

He'd gone out both nights, his sole aim to find a woman for the night. And he could have had one. Hell, he could have had twenty if he'd wanted them. There had been no shortage of offers at the bars he'd gone to.

He'd had every intention, both nights, of leaving with a willing female and filling his night with hot, nasty sex.

Instead he'd left alone, gone home, and jacked off to the thought of one woman. It was scaring the hell out of him. All his self-preservation instincts were rioting even as he pulled into the drive behind her little sedan.

He didn't have to force himself from the truck. Before the truck was even in gear he was throwing the door open.

Striding to the front door, he knocked firmly and waited.

She was home. He could hear the television droning inside and her car was here.

Knocking again he frowned at the thought that maybe she just wasn't opening the door for him. Not that he could blame her, he'd been an ass the other night. He would probably be an ass tonight.

He didn't want a love affair with her. He didn't want a relationship. He wanted this hunger for her out of his system, plain and simple. Something inside him warned him, though, that Hannah wasn't nearly that easy.

The door opened as his hand lifted, his fingers curling to a fist to knock again.

Hannah stared back at him in irritation and he swore in that second his cock went spike hard, drawing up tight as his blood began to heat in his veins.

A woman shouldn't be able to affect a man like this. To make his head fill with the memory of her kiss, the feel of her ass in his hands.

"What do you want, Sheriff?" She leaned against the door frame negligently, as though his being there didn't affect her in the least.

He admired her for the attempt, though he saw right through it. Hard little nipples poked against the material of her tan T-shirt and the bra beneath it.

Her face had that intriguing little flush again and her gaze was darkening as she shoved her hands into the pockets of her shorts and crossed her ankles. Clenched her thighs.

She was wet. She had to be wet. Hot and sweet, ready for him.

"I thought I'd check and see how you were doing." He ran his hand over his hair as he glanced around the house. "Can I come in?"

She seemed to think about the request way too long before she pulled back from the door and opened it wider.

Stepping into the house, he turned back to her, and watched as she closed the door and turned back to him hesitantly.

He could move against her right now, he thought.

Before he could stop himself, he was doing just that.

Within a second her back was against the door, her palms against his chest as his heart began to race out of control.

"What are you trying to pull on me, Rick?" She was breathless, hungry.

He could feel the hunger between them as hot and brutally destructive as wildfire.

"The hell if I know." His fingers flexed at her waist as he held her and admitted to himself that he couldn't figure it out. "You make me crazy, Hannah, do you know that?"

He watched as the lush waves of her hair rippled against her shoulders as she shook her head.

"Yeah, I can tell." Her tone was sarcastic. "You're so attentive, Rick."

He grimaced as he fought not to lower his lips to hers.

"Look, I came to see if you wanted to go out." He didn't want to go anywhere except her bedroom. "Dinner. Maybe some dancing."

Her eyes narrowed on him as her breasts moved hard and fast against his chest. He swore he could feel the imprint of her nipples through their clothes.

"Dinner and dancing?" she asked slowly. "Are you going to speak to me while we're out? Are you going to act like we're not together and that I've forced you unwillingly out in public?"

She was pushing him, tempting him. There was a challenge and defiance in her gaze that had every muscle in his body tightening as his dick demanded action.

Too long. It had been too long since he'd been with a woman, that was all there was to it. That was what was causing this. It wasn't the woman, it couldn't be the woman. It was the need for a woman and the fact that he had been intrigued by Hannah for years.

"I'll talk." He forced the words past his lips. "We'll dance."

He moved against her, pulled her closer, or at least tried to pull her closer. She was already as close to him as he could get her.

"Kiss me, Hannah." He lowered his head and brushed his

lips across hers, forcing back the tremors that wanted to attack his body at the thought of tasting her again.

"Rick." Her lips parted against his.

She didn't say no, though. She might not have said yes, but she didn't say no.

His lips parted over her, his head slanting as he settled into a kiss that began to burn through his senses.

Oh hell yes.

Her arms curled around his neck as she lifted to him, her lips moved under his, her tongue stroked against his.

Sweet, burning flames engulfed his senses as he let himself sink into the fire, into Hannah. He needed this. God help him, he needed this kiss, this touch, her fingers in his hair, her belly rubbing against his erection.

He needed the touch of her like he needed air to breathe. If he could just touch her for a little while, taste her enough to sate his senses, then maybe the long, lonely nights he had known for far too long would cease to torment him.

Maybe he could fill a few of those long lonely nights with Hannah.

"Rick." She whispered his name against his lips. The caress of it had his eyes closing as he fought to keep from taking what he needed from her.

Pulling back, he rested his head against hers, his eyes opening as he let a self-mocking smile tug at his lips.

"Come out with me," he whispered. "Or I may not be able to leave without making a fool of myself."

He stroked up her side then down again, feeling the little shudder that worked through her at the caress.

She breathed out heavily. "Are you going to break my heart, Rick?" she asked then.

He breathed in slowly, almost regretfully. "Only if you let me, Hannah. Please don't let me."

She stared back at him for long moments before nodding and moving away from him.

"I'll be back in a few minutes." She glanced back at him, her gaze somber, thoughtful. "I need to get ready."

"I'll wait right here," he promised. He wasn't going any-where, not yet, not without her.

HOW DO YOU stop a man that you're completely fascinated with from breaking your heart? Hannah wondered as dinner drew to a close and she sat back in her chair to enjoy the glass of wine she had ordered.

Rick sat across from her, his golden-brown gaze hooded, sensual, watching as she sipped at the wine.

He had talked. They'd discussed his son, Kent, and the camping trip the boy had taken with Rick's sister Mona.

"Have you been camping this summer?" Rick asked as he sipped at his coffee and watched her with those dark, hungry eyes.

"Not yet." Hannah shook her head. "My brothers haven't decided yet if they can make the trip in from Dallas with their families."

Camping was a family thing for Hannah. Her parents, three brothers, and their families usually managed to get away several times through the summer and fall months.

"Your brothers are doing well?" Two of her brothers were his age, the third was close enough that they had been friends when they lived in Alpine.

"Good." She nodded. "They stay busy."

"Don't we all," he breathed out roughly.

"They talk about you often." She smiled then. "The older they get the more I get to hear about how wild they were. You're usually included somehow."

"Dragging their butts out of trouble," he said, chuckling, the sound a dark rasp of pleasure against her senses.

And it had been true. He'd usually been the one covering for them or watching out for them.

"Are you ready to go?" He glanced at his watch before turning his gaze back to her. "I thought we'd go dancing for a while."

There was a slight shift to his expression, a nuance that assured her that Rick wanted any excuse he could to get his hands on her.

He had warned her not to let him break her heart. She had a feeling that was a foregone conclusion.

"I'm ready." She finished the last bit of wine as he rose from his chair and moved to her.

His hand settled on her lower back as they moved through the dining room. The feel of his fingers there, faintly caressing her through the thin material of her summer dress, sent the blood racing through her body and dampness spilling from her sex.

She was so damned wet now she should have made her excuses to go to the ladies' room. But she'd already been twice. He'd catch on fast if she went again.

Walking out into the sultry night air, Hannah had to take a fierce grip on her own control to keep from suggesting that perhaps they could return to her house. Or to his. To a bed. She didn't care where.

Sweet heaven, but this man had an effect on her that wasn't easy to combat. There wasn't a doubt in her mind that he was going to break her heart, because she knew she would end up falling in love with him. She was already half-way there. She had been for more years than she wanted to count. She should break this off now. She should go home and forget that he had kissed her, touched her. Forget that she wanted him as desperately as she wanted her next breath.

Instead, she let him help her into the truck and stared back at him as she settled on the seat, her legs still hanging out, his hands on her knees, holding her in place.

"I've wanted you a long time, Hannah."

She stared back at him in shock.

"You never knew?" He brushed back a strand of hair from her face.

"No." She could barely speak past the tightening of her throat and the need rising inside her. His hand cupped her cheek, his thumb brushed over her lips.

"I have." His voice was soft, edged with some emotion she couldn't put her finger on. "I've wanted for so long, and I felt guilty as hell."

Surprise shot through her. Guilt. He'd felt guilty because

he'd wanted her before Sienna had died. She understood what he meant. Even though she just told him she hadn't known, she had sensed it then, two years before Sienna's death when Rick had brought Kent into school for registration.

They had lived in the same town most of their lives, but that night, she had really seen Rick. His smile, his dark chuckle, the feel of his hand as he shook hers.

Sienna had been cold, brittle. Hannah had had several run-ins with Sienna over the years. Little things that really hadn't mattered.

"Why haven't you said anything? Why were you so cold last summer?" she asked. He hadn't seemed the least bit interested in her when they had gone out the summer before.

"You make me crazy." The hand on her knee slid beneath the material of her dress, pushing it up her leg as he moved his palm to her thigh. "You make me want you until I can't think about anything else."

He meant it. Hannah stared up at him, seeing the faintly confused, intent look on his face and realized that he meant it. He wanted her that bad.

He was going to break her heart. That was her luck, it was horrible when it came to men. She had yet to choose one that wanted a relationship. Even her husband.

Would it be better to go ahead and just get it over with? If she slept with him now, maybe all those pesky emotional issues wouldn't come into play. Maybe she could actually have the pleasure, have a sense of caring at least, and be able to watch him leave without the repercussions that had come with her divorce.

As she stared up at him, she felt his hand moving higher, watched his head lower further. He was kissing her slow and easy, lengthy sips of her lips that had her hands sliding up his chest again to his hair. They clenched in the strands to hold him to her.

Her lips parted beneath his as his tongue stroked over them. He licked them, a hard male groan leaving his lips, and her breath caught from the pleasure.

Heated, liquid need was pouring through her system. Her pussy clenched with the need for touch, her clit swelling in desperate desire as his fingers flexed against her thighs.

Hannah felt her legs falling apart involuntarily. It had nothing to do with the feel of his hands pressing against her inner thighs and the knowledge of the touch to come if she just let him in.

She forgot where she was, what she should be doing, and the hazards of loving any man. All she could think about was this touch, this kiss. His hands as they slid higher, as his fingers touched the silk of her panties and pulled them aside.

The pad of his thumb ran up the closed slit of her sex, the feel of it, the glance of his flesh brushing over her clit, had her jerking in reaction, a stilted moan falling from her lips.

God, they were in the middle of a parking lot, her legs spread, his finger pressing against her clit and she was so hot she was about to go up in flames.

"Jesus, you're wet," he growled against her lips.

The sound was rough, deep, and hungry. It sent a shiver racing up her spine and more dampness spilling from her pussy.

"Come here." With an arm wrapped around her hips, he pulled her closer to the edge of the seat, giving him greater access to the damp folds he was caressing.

"There," he crooned in that rough voice as his thumb stroked through the wet flesh once more and Hannah shuddered against him.

Her head tipped back, giving his lips access to her neck as his thumb rubbed and probed and sent heat coursing through her body.

"Rick." She sighed his name again. "Someone's going to see."

She wondered if she even cared if they saw. She was sitting there, and she sure as hell wasn't protesting a damn thing he was doing to her. She was on the verge of begging for more.

"Not yet." His lips slid against her neck before he let his

teeth rake over it. The stinging little pleasure was like a rush of heat attacking her nerve endings.

Hannah fought for breath as his strokes between her thighs intensified. He parted the slick flesh, groaned against her neck, and a heartbeat later she felt the slow, firm penetration of two fingers.

Her breath caught, her eyes opening drowsily to stare back at him as she fought to breathe. It was exquisite. It was the most pleasure she had ever known, had ever thought she could know.

"It's so good," she breathed out roughly as he pressed deeper, retreated, only to return again, his fingers stretching her erotically as she tried to hold her eyes open, to watch his face, to revel in the hunger burning in his eyes.

"It could be better, Hannah," he told her softly. "So much better."

His fingers slid deeper, punctuating his words as she fought to hold back a strangled cry of pleasure.

"Ruining another good woman, Grayson?"

Angry, almost childish, the accusation had Rick freezing in her arms, his fingers sliding slowly from her wet heat as he pushed her skirt back down her legs.

Hannah looked past him, barely recognizing the furious face of Rick's brother-in-law, Jay Martinez.

"We should go," she whispered to Rick, recognizing the fury that began to sizzle between the two men.

"We are." Rick's tone was hard, cold. The sensual man of seconds before was replaced by the dangerous, well-trained warrior she knew he was.

He closed the door to the truck, moved around the front, all the while followed by Jay.

"You killed Sienna," he yelled at Rick's ramrod-straight back. "You murdered her, and we both know it."

"Go home, Jay." Rick jerked his truck door open and slid inside.

"He'll kill you too, Hannah," Jay rapped out at her, his dark eyes glaring. "You can't say you weren't warned. Unlike Sienna. She never saw the bullet coming."

Rick slammed the door closed, gunned the motor, and pulled out of the parking place with more restraint than she would have expected.

"Hannah, he'll kill you," Jay's voice echoed behind her.

Turning to Rick, she stared at him and saw the harsh, savage lines etched into his expression now. The lover was gone. He was hard, remote now. Withdrawn.

"He blames you?" she asked, thinking of Sienna's death at the hands of the militia that had kidnapped her and one of her friends two years before.

"He blames me." Rick's hands clenched on the steering wheel.

"Jay and Sienna were close," she said softly. She had gone to school with Jay, she knew he'd adored his older sister, despite the fact that she had been adopted before he was born.

"Yes."

They were back to monosyllables again.

Hannah restrained her sigh and watched as they drove through town, moving ever closer to her home. She hadn't wanted the night to end this way. She had hoped it would end on a much more pleasant note. A much more pleasurable note.

It looked like, once again, Hannah Brookes was doomed to spend the night alone.

CHAPTER 4

SIENNA HAD BEEN killed by members of a homeland terrorist group that preyed on Mexican illegal immigrants as well as those who had immigrated legally and were born in the States.

They were a white supremacist militia that had on several occasions kidnapped their victims, hunted them, then killed them with such torturous means that Hannah had actually had nightmares after reading about the events in the newspapers two years ago.

Many of those militia members had been known and trusted members of the community. A sheriff's deputy, the mayor, a bank president, the owner of a local ranch. She had taught the children of several of those men in school, and she had watched how their families' lives were destroyed once the news hit.

Sienna Grayson and Sabella Malone had been kidnapped by the group when the terrorists found out that Sabella's lover had discovered evidence against them in one of the trucks that had been in the garage, and had turned it over to authorities.

In retaliation, the militia had kidnapped her and the sheriff's wife. Sienna hadn't survived. When federal agents had moved in on the group Sienna had been killed.

It had been tragic. The community had turned out in force to mourn with Rick. Though many of them had disliked Sienna personally, it seemed everyone had cared for their sheriff.

He was a good man, Hannah thought as they drove through town. He was a good sheriff. In all the years he had held the post there had never been a whiff of scandal attached to his office.

He kept his life, both private and public, squeaky clean. If Rick Grayson had skeletons, and she was certain he did, then they were buried so deep in the proverbial closet that she doubted anyone would find them.

To call him private was an understatement. Even before his wife's death, Rick hadn't been a whiner or the type of man that told everyone his business. After her death, he seemed to have closed up even further. Though Hannah would have been surprised if he hadn't.

"I'm sorry about that, Hannah." His voice was a black velvet whisper through the night as he spoke. "Jay has things set in his head and there's no convincing him otherwise."

"Things like the rumor that you shot your wife?" she asked, catching the little flinch her words evoked.

"Yeah, things like that." He shifted his shoulders as though the weight of them were a burden.

"Jay was always fiercely protective of Sienna," she stated. "I went to school with him. He would never let anybody say anything bad about her."

But there was plenty said. Jay had gotten a reputation as a gutter fighter at a young age because of his defense of his sister. It was too bad she hadn't been equally protective of her reputation. Not that Hannah could say that to Rick.

"No, he wouldn't," Rick agreed with a heavy sigh as he glanced back at her. "It didn't do anything for the mood though, did it?"

The wry smile that tugged at his lips surprised her. He was obviously trying to brush off the encounter, to recapture the heat and sensuality that had been there earlier.

"We could talk about it over a cup of coffee if you like?" She smiled as she turned away from him, a flash of light catching her eyes.

She heard Rick curse as her eyes widened and fear clenched her chest tight. Leaning forward, she peered out the window, her throat tightening.

"Oh God," she whispered. "Is that my house?"

There were police cars in her front yard, several in the street in front of her house. Her front door was hanging open and several officers were talking to neighbors.

"Hang on, Hannah," Rick commanded as he drew the truck to a stop and reached out for her, grabbing her arm as she moved to exit the truck. "Let's see what happened first. Stay put."

The ring of authority in his tone made her remain still and silent for several precious moments as he jumped out of the truck and rushed around to the door.

She had already thrown the door open and was in the process of getting out of the high cab when he gripped her waist and helped her to the sidewalk.

"Let's see what's going on before we jump to conclusions," he warned her.

Hannah nodded, grateful for his arm as it reached around her back, pulling her to him.

The sense of safety that wrapped around her stilled the shudders that had begun racing through her, but nothing could still the fear that tightened her chest and her throat.

"Sheriff, you found her." A young officer moved from the front yard toward them, his expression concerned as Rick stopped, holding her back.

"She was with me all along, Officer Johnson," Rick informed him as Hannah's hand lifted to her throat, her chest tightening further as she stared at her house.

It was small. It wasn't roomy, but it was hers. It held her possessions, her life. It was her refuge, and now strangers were walking through it?

"What happened here, Officer Johnson?" Rick asked, his tone becoming commanding.

"Sorry, sir." The officer jumped to attention. "At approximately nine o' clock this evening we received notification from her security company that her alarm had gone off and they couldn't reach her." He turned to Hannah. "Did you have your cell phone on you, ma'am?"

Hannah's gaze jerked back to him as she shook her head. "I noticed it missing this morning. I haven't found it yet."

"Well," he continued, "when the security company couldn't reach you we were called out. Your car was in the drive, your parents hadn't heard from you, so we entered the house to make certain you weren't in trouble." He waved toward the broken door as he grimaced. "Sorry, ma'am. It was the only way in."

"Find anything?" Rick asked as he began to draw Hannah toward the house.

As the two men talked Hannah felt the overwhelming urge to run. She didn't want to go into her home when all these people were milling around in it. She wanted them to leave. She wanted to lock herself in and make certain the few things she had were still safe.

"Nothing was stolen that we can tell," the officer was saying. "The back door was kicked in. They didn't even try to keep from setting off the alarm. The uhh . . ." He glanced at Hannah. "The bedroom is the only room that appears to have any damage."

"Hannah!" Rick's voice was sharp as she broke away from him and ran for the house.

She pushed past the officer at the front door, knees shaking, her heart in her throat, and rushed upstairs to her bedroom, aware that Rick was following close behind.

Damage to her bedroom? Her sanctuary?

She ran into the room then came to a hard, dead stop.

Rick cursed harshly behind her, his voice dangerous, icy, but all Hannah could do was stare in humiliated horror.

Okay, she didn't have an active sex life. She had a few toys. Well, several adult toys actually. A vibrator, a soft gel dildo, and a little egg-shaped clitoral vibrator.

The clitoral vibrator hung from the fan over her bed, twirling lazily as she stared at it in agonized humiliation for long seconds.

The gel penis-shaped toy was stuck to her dresser mirror

where the words WHORE had been printed in block letters with red lipstick. And her vibrator? It had been shoved into the ripped lips of the huge teddy bear that sat in a chair beside her bed. A gift from one of her brothers.

There were police officers in her bedroom. They stared with her, their gazes shifting from her as she stared around the room, shame burning through her.

"How did someone have time to do this?" Rick asked, his voice so icy, so stone cold that even Hannah flinched.

"Sheriff Grayson." An older man dressed in a rumpled suit stepped forward.

"Detective Dickerson, how the hell did someone have time to do this before your men arrived?"

"Response time between break-in and our arrival was fifteen minutes," the detective stated. "The security attempted to call Ms. Brookes's contact number and when she didn't answer they alerted us. According to the security logs, her pass code was punched into the alarm an hour before the break-in, though. How long has she been with you?"

"Longer than that," Rick stated as Hannah turned to the detective in shock.

"No one has my code." She shook her head in confusion. "No one. Not even my brothers or parents."

The detective shook his head, his lips flattening as he rubbed at his temple for a second.

"Someone knew what the hell they were doing, then," he said. "There are devices that can get past this system, but your normal burglar doesn't have them. Who wants to get at you that bad, Ms. Brookes? Bad enough to do this when they found you weren't here." He turned and looked around the room before returning his gaze to her.

"I'm just a teacher," she whispered.

"Any parents threatened you? Harassed you?"

"Nothing." She shook her head fiercely.

The questions didn't stop. They were insistent, probing. Hannah couldn't take her eyes off her bedroom as the detective interrogated her.

Other than the toys that had been displayed, nothing else

seemed to have been disturbed. They had found the most humiliating things and used them to hurt her.

But why?

As she answered the detective's questions she fought to understand. As far as she knew she didn't have any enemies, she told the detective. No, she hadn't argued with anyone lately. No, she wasn't dating anyone and hadn't in more than a year. Until tonight, Rick injected.

It went on and on until she felt as though she were going to scream in frustration. She just wanted them to leave. She wanted everyone out of her home so she could hide the evidence of her loneliness and lick her wounds in peace.

"Well, we've dusted for prints." The detective finally rubbed at his nose as he stared around the room again. "If we find out anything, we'll let you know. But honestly." He shook his head again. "I doubt we're going to. Someone was pretty thorough here."

"Thanks, Will," Rick was saying. "Could you let me know what you find, as well?"

"Sure thing. I'd suggest you get her out of here for a while. Get the doors fixed and install some additional security."

Hannah shook her head. She wasn't going anywhere.

"She'll be at my place," Rick stated.

"No." She tried to inject a measure of strength in her voice, but she heard it shake, heard the tremor in it herself.

"Like hell." Rick's tone was gentle but firm. "You can't stay here, Hannah, and you know it. You can come back tomorrow, do what you have to do. Tonight, you can stay at my place."

She didn't want to leave.

"I have to clean . . ." She could feel the tears building in her voice.

She wanted to wipe away the embarrassment. She needed to hide her personal items, needed to get them out of sight.

"It can wait until tomorrow." His voice lowered. "The police officers will secure the doors for tonight and tomorrow I can come over with you and replace the doors."

"But . . ."

"No buts. It can wait till tomorrow."

She felt like a child, uncertain, frightened. She couldn't believe someone had done this to her. She couldn't understand why they would want to.

She let Rick draw her away from the bedroom, her eyes going once again to the toys that were laid out for the world to see.

"This is so humiliating," she whispered as they left the house, his hand at her back as he led her down the steps. "Why would anyone do that?"

She wrapped her arms around herself, staring at the crowd outside her home, wondering how many of them knew what her room displayed. There were no secrets on a street with neighbors like hers. They were good people, kind, caring, and nosy as hell.

Everyone probably knew she had toys and were speculating about them. Poor Miss Brookes. She couldn't get a man so she bought toys instead.

Shame flooded her face once again.

And who would call her a whore? She had toys for a reason. She hadn't even had a date in forever, let alone actual sex. Tonight was the closest she had come in years.

"Come on." Rick bundled her back into the truck before loping to the driver's side and stepping in. Slamming the door behind him, he was pulling from the street within seconds and reaching across the console to grip her hand with his. "It's going to be okay, Hannah."

She rubbed at her forehead with her free hand before staring out the window in confusion.

"It doesn't make sense," she said again. "Why do that?" She turned to stare at him, unable to comprehend the reason behind such maliciousness.

"We'll find out why," he stated, and she actually believed he might do it. He seemed more angry than she was. Anger hadn't hit her yet, though. She was still in shock, uncertain and confused.

Rick continued to stare out the windshield, glaring into the night. He had a feeling that what had happened tonight had nothing to do with Hannah, and everything to do with him.

He should have stayed away from her last summer. Some instinct had warned him last summer that he was making a mistake. What if those two dates, seemingly innocent and going nowhere, had made her a target because of him?

"We'll figure it out, Hannah," he promised her, feeling her hand tremble beneath his as he drove through the night to his ranch. "Until we do, I promise you'll be safe."

He couldn't let anything happen to her. Sienna had done enough to destroy his life; he wasn't going to allow her ghost to finish him off.

Making the turn up the paved road to his home several miles from the main road, he kept his gaze roving through the night, searching for anomalies, or anything out of the ordinary.

He knew his home like the back of his hand. For several months after the militia had been disbanded he'd had a few problems on the ranch. Cattle that were killed senselessly, a few attempted break-ins, nothing serious. Harassments, little else.

This wasn't harassment. He would consider this war, and he would let the few remaining members of the terrorist group who hadn't been arrested know it. Hannah wasn't going to be a target for their revenge.

"Here we are." Using the automatic garage door opener, he pulled the truck inside and turned it off. Closing the doors from the control inside the truck, he opened his door and stepped out quickly to open Hannah's.

She already had her door open. Gripping her waist he helped her from the truck, realizing how small she was, how delicate, as he set her on her feet before him.

He deactivated his alarm with the control on his key ring before opening the door and leading her into the kitchen.

His security system was more advanced than most, installed by a team of agents so deep cover that most in the government didn't know they existed. The men who had helped round up the militia two years before; one of them was still a resident of Alpine and married to the wife he'd had before his "death."

That one still amazed him.

"Come on, I'll get you something to wear and you can take a hot shower." Gripping her hand he led her to his bedroom. "I'll fix you some hot chocolate or something. That always helps Kent sleep."

Thank God he'd relented and allowed Mona to take his son camping with her. If someone was targeting him over the destruction of the militia two years before, then he didn't want his son involved in it.

"Rick, you don't have to do this," she protested as they entered the bedroom.

At least he'd thought to make the bed this morning. The bedroom was in fairly good shape. There was dust on the furniture, the wood floors a little dull. He'd stacked his clothes on the dresser rather than putting them away after Mona had returned them to him.

He didn't always have time to clean house.

Moving to the stack of clothes, he removed a t-shirt and brought it back to her.

"This should be long enough for you." His lips twitched with humor as he surveyed her. "You're a short little thing, aren't you?"

For a second the fear evaporated from her eyes, to be replaced by a narrow-eyed warning.

"No short jokes, please," she ordered him with what he imagined was her "teacher voice."

"I wasn't joking," he assured her. "I was simply making an observation. You're cute, though."

If anything, that steely glint in her eyes got brighter.

"Great, I'm cute," she muttered. "Puppies are cute. Squirrels are cute."

"You're cuter?" He almost grinned as the pouty curve of her lip tightened.

She had to look up at him. If he wanted to kiss her without straining his neck, then he'd have to grip the curves of her ass and lift her to him. He liked doing that. He liked the delicacy and feminine allure of her stature.

"I'm not cute," she bit out, obviously put out by the description. "Now where's the bathroom? I need that shower."

He hid a grin as he turned and led her to the bathroom door. "You can take a nice, long Jacuzzi bath or a hot shower," he said. "I'll be in the kitchen when you're done."

He left her alone, closed the door behind him, and blew out a breath.

Hell, he wished he could stay. He'd like to sink into that big bathtub with her and wash her from head to toe. Or take her in the shower, watch the water stream around her as he lifted her to him and took her against the wall.

He could feel beads of sweat popping out on his forehead at the thought. His cock pounded in approval. The blood rushed through his veins in excitement.

So the night hadn't ended as he had envisioned, but he could work with this. Before the night was out, he might even have her in his bed. That was even better.

He could handle that. For one night, he assured himself. Just one night. One morning. To awaken beside a woman that wanted him. To greet the day with pleasure rather than an empty bed. A soft, passionate woman rather than the memory of the dreams that haunted him at night.

One night. That was it. Then things would go back to normal. Whether he wanted them to or not.

CHAPTER 5

HE SHOULD HAVE known better than to put that sexy, rounded little body in one of his T-shirts. He had quite a height advantage at six three, since she was barely five feet four. The T-shirt, he'd imagined, would fall nearly to her knees.

There were things he hadn't taken into account. Full, rounded breasts that lifted the shirt several inches, as it fell over the pert flesh and revealed the hardened points of tight little nipples beneath the loose fabric. Rounded hips that gave the material new shape and form, and gorgeous lightly tanned legs that he was damned sure would fit perfectly around his lower back if he was stretched between them.

The sensual vision that emerged from his bedroom an hour later was properly covered, no question. The shirt reached below her thighs, not quite to her knees. Totally respectable. It covered more than some of the short dresses he'd seen other women wearing in town.

But there was this line, almost invisible, between totally respectable and lushly sensual. Hannah was lushly sensual and she gave a whole new look to the dark T-shirt that he knew he would never wear again without a hard-on from the very thought of how she looked in it now.

"I need to get back to the house in the morning," she was saying as she pulled on another of his shirts, obviously one she had confiscated from his closet.

The long-sleeved, button-front black shirt hung on her like a loose robe, but still, it did nothing to hide the lush little body beneath.

"I'm off duty the next few days." He managed to force the words past his lips. "I'll take you myself."

She pushed her fingers through her hair and went over to the bar, lifting herself to the stool across from him and finally meeting his gaze.

"That was so humiliating." She sighed. "I bet everyone on that street knows exactly what was done. Length, width, and color of each toy I owned are probably being discussed and gossiped over as we speak."

His thighs tightened at the thought of the toys and their various uses. Hell, he couldn't get the image of it out of his mind. Hannah spread out on the light lavender print of the quilt that covered her bed, her head thrown back, legs spread as she fucked herself with that dildo.

Sweat popped out on his brow. His cock thickened to the point that he was in agony.

"They'll find something else to gossip over tomorrow." He cleared his throat as he checked the coffeepot out of sheer desperation to see if the coffee had finished.

Pouring both of them a cup, he placed hers in front of her along with a spoon before pushing the sugar and creamer toward her.

"Thanks." Her smile was a little absent as she fixed her coffee to taste.

He sipped at his, barely tasting it as that image teased at his mind again.

"Why would anyone want to just embarrass me?" She stirred her coffee before glancing up at him again. "Kindergarten teachers don't exactly make enemies, you know. I could understand it if it were the high school. I mean, teenagers can be mischievous, but kindergarteners? When was the last time you heard of a five-year-old with the ability to do what was done tonight?"

"Their parents perhaps?" He knew better, just as she did.

She stared back at him knowingly. "Last summer, my car was egged just after that last date we had," she said. "Little things happened that I brushed off as pranks by the local kids. They get a little bored sometimes."

He sipped his coffee as he watched her broodingly.

"Now, it's escalated," she pointed out.

"What else happened last year?" He put down his coffee and watched her intently. "And why didn't you report it?"

"As I said, I assumed it was the work of some bored teenagers. I never imagined anyone could actually want to frighten me. A car with egg on it, flowers unearthed from my garden, along the fence in the back. It was just little things." She watched him closely. "This is because of you, isn't it? Someone is trying to hurt you and they're using me to do it."

She was smart, he had to give her credit for that, and suspicious. Just as suspicious as he was.

"You didn't tell Detective Dickerson about those events," he stated. "Why not?"

She looked down at the countertop as her nail rubbed against it for a long moment, before lifting her head.

"I wanted to talk to you first. After what happened with Sienna's brother tonight, I've pretty much pieced most of it together. I'd just like to know why."

How was he supposed to answer that one? Oh, sorry, Hannah baby, I think someone knows I blew my wife's fucking head off when she tried to kill her best friend. She was a cocaine junkie and a killer.

Yeah, he could see that one going over really well.

"I'm not sure why," he finally answered instead. "But I'll find out."

He was lying to her. Hannah could feel it, she swore she could see the darkening of his eyes when he spoke, the betraying little tic of a muscle at his jaw.

Why would he lie to her?

"What happened when Sienna was kidnapped, Rick?" she asked instead. "The president of one of our largest banks, our mayor, your deputy, Galen Patrick—one of our biggest land owners—and a U.S. Marshal were killed that night along with Sienna. Some people say she was involved with them."

She had never been one to beat around the bush, and she wasn't going to now. She had a pretty good feeling that tonight was going to end with her in his bed. She at least wanted to know what she was getting herself into.

"I don't know what she was involved in, Hannah," he stated as he turned from her to refill his coffee cup. "She was kidnapped together with Sabella Malone. When the smoke cleared from the rescue attempt, Sienna was dead and a lot of men that everyone trusted were implicated."

"That was a perfect nonanswer if I've ever heard one," she told him, realizing he wasn't going to tell her anything. She pretty much had it figured out, though.

Rick had been a part of that rescue attempt. Knowing him, he would have gone after his wife and her friend first. And everyone knew Sienna and Mike Conrad were a little too close. Rumors had been swirling about her and her flings for years; she was just surprised that Rick hadn't suspected.

Or had he?

"Does it matter what she was involved in?" he asked her then. "Does that have anything to do with us?"

She shook her head slowly. "If there was an 'us,' then it wouldn't have anything to do with it."

"Oh, there's definitely an 'us,'" he growled as he moved around his bar, his expression shifting from emotionless to lusty in a heartbeat.

Savage features were suddenly stark with the hunger that exploded in the air around them. Hannah stared at him in fascination as he swung the bar seat on its swivel base until he could push between her thighs.

That easy. She was too easy, she thought distantly as his hand curved around her neck to hold her head in place as he lowered his head. She should protest somehow. She should do something except part her lips and consume him like chocolate.

She couldn't help it. He tasted of rich, dark coffee and hungry male. It was an aphrodisiac she didn't want to resist.

A drug like this could entrance every woman in the world and create addicts in no time.

Pleasure suffused her from head to toe, wrapping along her nerve endings, as her arms lifted and curled around his neck, pulling him close to her.

He held her tightly for long seconds before pulling back, and lifting her against him, his lips never leaving hers.

His kisses were dizzying, intoxicating. She felt as though she were flying, twirling, in time and space as his head slanted and he deepened the kiss.

Her rear met what she assumed was the top of the small island counter, allowing her to press herself tighter to him. His hips were wedged between her thighs, his cock, a hard thick wedge beneath his jeans, was pressed against the mound of her pussy, rubbing the material of her panties against her clit.

There wasn't enough clothing between them to protect her against the sensations. She wondered if there could ever be. Because nothing had ever been this good, this hot. Sexual intensity built inside her, wound through her system and centered in her womb, as he ground his cock against her, his hands gripping her hips, holding her to him.

Arcs of sizzling sensation raced through her bloodstream as she moaned into the kiss. She wanted more, needed more, and yet she wanted other things, as well. She wanted to taste more than his lips. She wanted to feel more than his hard erection through his jeans. She wanted to feel it hot and bare, sinking inside her, stroking her to ecstasy.

Skin to skin. That was what she wanted. His flesh stroking against hers, inside her. His lips all over her body, her lips all over his. She wanted to eat him like candy.

She licked at his lips and moaned at the rich male taste of his kiss. She felt him nip hers, and nearly whimpered at the incredible pleasure that whipped through her at the stinging caress. A second later he licked over the curve, sending another heated caress through her senses.

She had always known that Rick Grayson could affect her this way. That knowledge had just been there, for as long as she could remember, tempting her fantasies and her hunger.

"Damn, I love your taste," he growled as his lips moved from hers to her jaw, her neck, while sliding the shirt she'd borrowed off her shoulders.

"Taste me some more," she panted, lowering her arms to push them free of the material.

His hands gripped the hem of her T-shirt, lifted it, and he drew back, pulled it over her head.

Oh God.

She was all but naked in front of him now. Her breasts were rising and falling rapidly, her nipples pebble hard and so sensitive that even the cool air of the room was a caress to them.

"Sweet Lord have mercy," he whispered as his hands lifted, his palms cupping the round curves, his thumb raking over the hard tips slowly, his gaze darkening as he stared at the flushed contours of her breasts.

Hannah's lashes fluttered in pleasure at the feel of the callused pads of his thumbs against her nipples. It was exciting, just a little naughty. It was the most sensual experience of her life.

"Feel good?" he whispered as he raked his thumbs over them again.

"Good," she gasped, her lashes opening to stare back at him teasingly. "It could be better."

"Better?" His lips quirked with a hint of a smile. "How could it be better, baby?"

She was sexy as hell, her green eyes staring back at him with a glimmer of fun and pleasure that was more than just physical.

"Maybe you need to kiss them?" Her tone was wicked, her voice almost innocent. "I bet I'd really like that." She was breathless.

"Think you would?"

Rick bent his head, his gaze lifting to watch her face as he pressed his lips against the gentle curve of one breast.

He watched her eyes darken, her lashes flutter.

"Like that?" He realized in that instant that he loved playing with her.

"That's a little bit better," she breathed out as she braced her hands on the counter behind her. "Maybe a little bit more."

He wanted a nipple in his mouth so bad he couldn't stand it. But he wanted to play with her, too. He loved watching her face flush, the way she bit at her lower lip, the way sensuality suffused her features.

He wouldn't last long, but he'd enjoy it while he could stand it.

"Little bit more?" He licked over the area he had kissed. He kissed another spot, just beside the cute little mole at the side of her breast, before he licked there, as well.

"Oh yeah." She sighed roughly, one hand lifting to the back of his head, her fingers sifting through his hair. "God, Rick. This is so good."

As though she had never played before, either.

He kissed again, moving closer to the tight peak of her breast, coming ever closer to the dark pink areola.

"Yeah," she whispered, her breathing as ragged as his own as her hand tightened in his hair. "There."

"Here?" He kissed the beginning of the darker flesh then licked over it. Around it.

He didn't touch the sensitive nipple, but moved closer, then away, closer and back. He licked and kissed until she was straining closer to him and his mouth was watering for the taste of the tight flesh.

"You're a very good tease," she accused him roughly.

"You're better." He almost grinned. "You've been teasing me for two years. Every time I've seen you."

Her breath caught as he breathed over the tight tip.

"So you noticed after all?" She almost whimpered when he brought his mouth closer, barely brushing his lips against the hard flesh.

"Every time." He licked the hard tip.

Hannah jerked in his arms, a fragile cry falling from her lips as he licked her nipple, tasted her. And she was sweet.

So damned sweet that he wondered if he'd ever be able to pull himself away from her.

He couldn't deny the need any longer. He licked her nipple, tasted it, laved it, as hunger rose inside him like a ravenous beast.

It had been too long. Four years without a woman was too damned long, and his sexuality had always been high on his list of priorities.

And this woman. He'd wanted her for far too long. She had been a part of his fantasies for too many years.

As he drew the hard tip of her nipple into his mouth and felt her hands on the snap of his jeans, his balls drew up tight, his cock throbbed with need.

The hunger pummeled him, raced through him like a fiery storm, and centered on the taste and touch of her.

"I dream about you," she gasped as he sucked at first one nipple, then the next. "For so long, Rick. I've dreamed of you."

She was pushing him to the brink. Her voice caressed his senses while her hands tugged at his jeans.

A desperate groan tore from his lips as he pushed her back, urging her to recline against the counter as his lips swept down her belly. Pushing her thighs apart, he had to clench his teeth to hold back the need raging inside him to take her now.

To release the violently throbbing flesh between his thighs and take her, to sink inside the silken, wet folds his eyes were devouring.

Soft curls shielded the upper curves of the mound, but the lower curves, the sweetly plump lower lips, were pink and bare and glistening with her juices.

If he'd known what was awaiting him here, he might not have been able to hold back as long as he had. Spreading her legs further, her soft cry echoing in his mind, he lowered his head.

He licked through the narrow slit, groaning at the sweet, feminine taste of her. Sweet heaven, she was hot, her juices heavy and slick like the sweetest syrup.

Pushing her legs even farther apart, he was only distantly aware of her small feet bracing against the edge of the counter. Her hips lifted for him as he parted the folds with the fingers of one hand, and licked deeper, more firmly.

He was dying for the taste of her, and here she was. A banquet. A sweet delicate offering that he didn't have the strength to resist any longer.

That he couldn't resist.

Hannah curled her fingers in Rick's hair and fought to hold back the cries that threatened to pour from her lips. She felt his fingers caressing the opening of her sex as his tongue licked along the folds, circled her clit and lowered again.

He was licking her like candy, taking her with his mouth and tongue until she wondered if she could bear the sensations, even as she craved more.

The teasing was over, and she didn't regret it. She needed more of him. Needed him until she was arching against him and calling out his name even though she tried to hold back the desperate sounds.

"God, you're sweet." His tongue sank inside her pussy, stealing her breath for a long, dazed second as she nearly exploded with the intensity of the pleasure.

She'd never had that before. She'd never had a man fuck her with his tongue, and feeling Rick doing it was the most sensual thing she had ever experienced.

He thrust his tongue inside her, retreated, took her again. Hannah could feel herself panting for breath, dying for more. It was exquisite. Hot and wicked and sexy.

When he pulled back, he didn't leave her wanting. His head lifted until he was kissing her clit, drawing it between his lips briefly as he kissed it deeply. Two expert fingers pressed inside the greedy entrance, working into her as she gasped, her hands tightening in his hair, perspiration dampening her flesh.

"More," she gasped desperately. "Oh God, Rick. Please."

Next he drew her clit between his lips, licked it with his tongue, while stroking his fingers inside her.

She was so close. She could feel the desperation clawing

inside her now, clenching in her womb and spilling more of her juices to his fingers.

As he sucked at her clit, his tongue flicked over it, worked it with sensual mastery as his fingers fucked into her, stroking her past sanity and into a whirlwind that overtook her.

She felt the explosion tearing through her. Her orgasm raced through her senses, tearing his name from her lips and lifting her upper body. He worked her orgasm, lengthening it, caressing her through it and driving the pleasure higher.

Collapsing back against the counter, she fought to find her breath, to clear her head as she felt him move between her thighs.

When she forced her eyes open and looked down her body, she saw the head of his sheathed cock nudging against the flushed folds of her pussy.

Hannah watched, her breath suspended in her throat, as the broad, blunt crest pressed against her, stroked fire against the sensitive nerve endings, and began to part the tender entrance to her body.

"Rick." She breathed out his name, suspended in pleasure now, watching, feeling, locked in a vortex of such sensation that she wondered if she would ever completely escape it.

The heavy flesh parted hers, worked in, stretching her, burning the tender tissue erotically as it gave beneath the blunt force. The exquisite sensations whipped through her, tightening her body as she fought to hold on to her control just another moment. Just one more second. She wanted to watch, wanted to memorize this moment so she could hold it inside her forever.

Looking up at him, she saw the hard, brutally tight features of his face, his golden gaze narrowed as he watched as well, his cheeks flushed, lips slightly parted. Pleasure suffused his expression with the same intensity that it suffused her body.

He worked his cock inside her slowly. Back and forth, sinking in inch by slow inch until they were both groaning with the pleasure of it, desperate for more.

Her hands curled around his wrists as his hands gripped

her hips, holding her still as he gave a final thrust and buried himself to the hilt inside her.

Hannah stared at where they merged, mesmerized, locked in a sensual, erotic fantasy that she couldn't believe was real.

"Damn," he breathed out roughly, his gaze finally lifting to hers. "You're tight, Hannah. So sweet and hot, and so tight around me."

She felt her pussy spasm around his cock then, tightening, gripping him in reflex as he grimaced with the pleasure.

"Hold on to me," he whispered, blinking against the sweat that dampened his face. "God, Hannah. I don't think I can hold on here."

She shook her head desperately, fighting just to breathe. "Don't hold on," she whispered, needing him with the same hunger that he seemed to need her. "Take me, Rick. Please God." Her voice broke on a cry. "More. I need more now."

Something inside him seemed to break. Rick lost control in that instant, and he prayed he wouldn't regret it. Gripping her hips tighter, he began to move, fucking her as she wanted, giving her more, stroking inside her with a hunger he couldn't still.

Each thrust sent shards of burning pleasure racing up his cock. She was tight and hot and the condom did nothing to restrict the heated caress of her pussy. It gripped him, the snug tissue flexed and convulsed as he thrust inside her, stroking his cock until he was fighting, dying as he fought to hold back his release.

He wanted to feel her coming around him. He wanted to feel that tight little pussy exploding around his cock, sucking him deeper inside her, convulsing around him.

Leaning forward, his hips working harder, faster, stretching her, burning them both, he covered her lips in a quick, hard kiss. Another. Another. He couldn't breathe, could barely see. He pumped inside her, felt her tightening and knew she was close.

His lips traveled to her neck, to the tight, flushed tips of her breasts. He licked one nipple, another. Then drew one of the exquisite nubs into his lips and sucked it as he thrust inside her, harder, hungrier.

Her body tightened. She cried out his name as his head jerked back, his thrusts slamming into her as her pussy clasped him tighter, the heat of it intensifying until he felt her explode in his arms.

The tightened muscles seemed to erupt with tiny convulsive jerks along his dick. They fluttered around him, heated, held him, and sent him flying into a release he swore he might not survive.

Groaning her name he felt his balls jerk, his semen exploding from the tip of his cock and his world centering on this single moment in time and pleasure so brutal it marked his soul.

She was writhing beneath him, twisting, locked in her own pleasure like nothing he had never known. In his arms, Hannah Brookes was losing herself to him, and no other woman had ever done that. He had never seen it, never known it. And it broke through a wall of reserve he hadn't realized he'd put between them.

It made his own release sharper, brighter. The pleasure so intense that his knees felt weak, his head seemed to spin with it.

As he collapsed over her, fighting for the strength to get them both to his bed, he wondered if he would ever be the same.

This was what he had fought against for the past two years, he realized. This sensation, this knowledge, this pleasure. A pleasure he wasn't certain he wanted to live without now. A woman he knew damned good and well that he didn't want to lose.

CHAPTER 6

HANNAH WAS FLOATING on a cloud three days later. Even the mortification she had felt at the violation of her home couldn't penetrate it.

As one night had led to days, she found a sense of balance, and an excitement to each day that she hadn't really expected. She had put off returning to her own house as long as she could, though. She was running out of clothes to wear, and she needed to make certain the house was back in shape.

She was hoping for an invitation to stay with Rick longer, but one hadn't come and she had cheerfully ignored that fact. She'd take what she could get now; it was more than she had expected to begin with.

With Rick at her side she returned to the house, and he helped her wipe away the evidence that someone had been determined to humiliate her in the worst possible way.

"Tell me." Rick came up behind her as she cleaned the red lipstick off the mirror, standing head and shoulders above her, his arms wrapping around her waist as he met her mirror gaze. "How often did you use your toys?"

There was a hint of playful humor in his eyes, in the quirk of his lips, as he settled his chin against the top of her head and watched her closely.

"Oh, only about every time I saw you." She grinned, and it was no less than the truth.

His brows lifted as he brushed her hair back from her

neck and leaned down to kiss the tender skin. Continuing to watch her, he asked, "And how often did you see me?"

Hannah cleared her throat and couldn't help but smile. "I made sure I saw you somewhere, about once a week."

His eyes narrowed. "Once a week, huh?"

"At least." She tilted her head to the side, allowing him greater access to her neck. "You always looked really hot, too. I had some really good fantasies."

"Oh yeah?" His hands moved beneath the hem of her shirt to stroke the bare flesh of her stomach. "What kind of fantasies?"

"All kinds of fantasies." Her voice lowered, her gaze becoming dreamy as she remembered many of those fantasies. Fantasies she might have a chance of living out now.

"You could show them to me," he suggested, his hands moving higher until he was cupping her breasts, watching his hands in the mirror as his fingers rasped over her nipples.

"I could do that," she answered breathlessly, watching her nipples harden beneath his touch as pleasure tore through her body.

It wasn't a gentle pleasure, not yet. It was rapid, fiery, it was a desperation, a hunger that she wondered if she would ever get used to.

As she tipped her head back against Rick's chest to enjoy the journey of pleasure, there was a hard series of knocks at the front door. Her head jerked up, a frown pulling at her brow.

Behind her, Rick cursed and reluctantly released her to lead her out of bathroom.

She was aware of him walking ahead of her protectively, and a shiver of pleasure raced through her at the realization. No one had ever done that before. Even her brothers had tended to push her toward self-protection as she grew up rather than attempting to soften the battles for her.

At the front door Rick glanced out the side windows, then looked back at her with a grimace. "It's Detective Dickerson."

She felt like grimacing herself. Dickerson was the last

person she wanted to see today. She would love to know who had broken into the house, but Dickerson hadn't seemed too interested in figuring it out when she had talked to him on the phone earlier.

Opening the door, Rick stood back and allowed the detective in.

His craggy features were set into stern lines, his lips turned down in a natural scowl as he glanced between them.

"Afternoon, Sheriff." He nodded toward Rick.

"Detective." Rick nodded back as he drew Hannah against him. "Have you learned anything more since this morning?"

Hannah could hear the underlying question in Rick's tone. The demand to know the reason for the detective's visit now.

"Nothing at all, Sheriff." Not a smile cracked the detective's face. "I thought perhaps you might know something about it, instead?"

Hannah felt Rick tense behind her as the air suddenly thickened with tension.

"Why would I know anything about it?" Rick asked carefully. She could hear the deliberation in his voice, feel it in his body.

Detective Dickerson's expression became sterner. "There are a lot of rumors still milling around about your wife, Sheriff Grayson. Sienna didn't have the best reputation, and maybe some people thought you should have figured out what she was before she was killed."

"Whoa, that's enough." Hannnah stepped forward as she felt the anger suddenly filling the air, placing herself between the detective and Rick. "I think you're way out of line, Detective. And I think it's time you leave."

Dickerson glared down at her. "Miss Brookes, you should consider what could really be going on here," he warned her. "You could be targeted because of your relationship with Grayson, and that could get dangerous."

"And you should get your ass out of here and do your job rather than poking at shadows, Detective." Rick's voice was a hard, dark command behind her. "When you have some proof of your accusations then you can bring them to me personally. Until then, try looking for the person or persons responsible for this rather than pissing me off."

And there was no doubt Rick was pissed off.

"Good-bye, Detective Dickerson." Hannah opened the door wider. "Let me know when you have something concrete. I'll be willing to listen then."

Dickerson's lips quirked. "You were seeing the sheriff last year, and you had problems then, Miss Brookes," he reminded her. "Think about what I said."

He turned and left, but Hannah couldn't help but consider it. She had had the same thoughts the night before, thoughts she had expressed to Rick.

When she closed the door behind him, she turned back to Rick.

"What's going on?" she asked him, wishing she could see behind the tight, closed expression on his face. "Why would anyone want to strike out at me because of Sienna, or because of my relationship with you?"

Most people liked Rick, even when they hadn't liked Sienna. She was sure that Rick hadn't known about the games his wife was rumored to have been playing before her death. The rumors hadn't started until after her funeral. Before that, there hadn't been so much as a whisper about her infidelity, simply talk that she and Mike Conrad appeared to be close. But there had been no evidence, no sightings, nothing that anyone could point to to say that she had been cheating on her husband.

And if Sienna had been unfaithful, why would anyone want to punish Rick for it?

"I don't know what's going on," he said as he looked around the entryway of her house. "But I don't want you staying here alone." He brought his gaze back to her. "Pack a bag, you're coming home with me."

Dominance filled his tone, instantly triggering the independent streak that her brothers swore was a mile wide.

"I'll be perfectly safe right here." She crossed her arms over her breasts and glared back at him. "I don't need a knight in shining armor, Rick, and I sure as hell don't need a keeper."

"Maybe you don't, but by God I need to know my lover's safe." He jerked her to him, that alpha streak that she suspected was stronger than her stubborn streak darkening his expression. "Don't fight me, Hannah. I won't leave you here alone, and you'll be safer at my house, in my bed. We both know it."

His security system was state-of-the-art. His bed was warm, his arms were secure. She stared up at him, knowing that was exactly where she wanted to be.

"I don't like being ordered around," she informed him firmly. "Ask me, Rick. Speak to me reasonably. Don't order me."

He frowned down at her before grimacing in regret, though his gaze never lost that commanding glitter. "You'll be safer with me, Hannah." He seemed to grit out the words. "Stay with me."

The command was softer, but it was still there. She felt a grin tug at her lips as she shook her head at him in a gesture of helpless amusement.

"You're definitely not used to asking for anything," she told him, relaxing just enough so that he also relaxed a little.

"It's not something I do often," he agreed. "Let's get you a bag packed. Whoever seems to want to get to you won't be expecting the security system I have in place. We'll catch him."

He was taking over her protection, but she was smart enough to know that someone had to. She sure as hell had no idea what to do at this point.

"Fine," she breathed out roughly as she turned and stared around her little house. "I'll stay with you. For a while."

No commitment yet. She wasn't going to rush this. She wasn't going to do anything to make him feel as though she were trying to.

They were lovers, that was enough for now, she told herself.

He followed her upstairs as she packed her bag, then accompanied her to her car.

"I need to stop by the office for a few minutes." He leaned down to the window as she rolled it down. "Follow me there and you can visit with Mae until I'm done."

Evidently he had no intention of letting her out of his sight. The thought of that sent a ray of hope winging through her.

She was already falling in love with him. She knew it, felt it inside her. He fascinated her as no man ever had. Pleasured her as she had never known pleasure in her life.

The chance to be with him, to know him, to love him, just for a little while was more than she had hoped for before now.

He kissed her quickly before striding to his truck, giving her another little edge of hope. As she followed him back to the sheriff's office, she forced herself to pull back, not to make plans for a future that might not be. Enjoy the present, she warned herself. Enjoy what she had now.

It was more than she had expected.

Parking next to his truck at the sheriff's office, she smiled as she locked her car, feeling him behind her.

His hand rode low on her back as they walked to his office and entered Mae Livingston's domain.

"Mae, Hannah's going to visit with you for a bit," he told the other woman as he headed to his office door.

"I'll make sure she's taken care of, Rick." Mae's smile was welcoming and warm as Rick kissed Hannah, on the cheek this time, and disappeared into his office.

"My my my." Mae lifted her brows as Hannah felt a light flush suffuse her face. "Now this is a development."

"You're no more surprised than I am," Hannah told her with a light laugh.

"But happy as hell," Mae mused, her gray eyes thoughtful as she stared back at Hannah. "And I do believe I saw our sheriff smile. Do you know how long it's been since he smiled, Hannah?"

She shook her head, her heart racing in her chest at the next small reason to hope.

"I'd guess it's been way too long." Mae sighed. "Even years before Sienna's death. They didn't get along well at all in the last years before she was kidnapped."

Hannah lowered her head before glancing at Rick's office door.

"Yeah, he'd be pissed if he caught me talking about it." Mae agreed with Hannah's unspoken thought, her voice sober. "But it's good to see him smile. And it's nice to know he's with you, Hannah. Sienna didn't do much to make that man happy, no matter how faithful he was to her." She shook her head sadly. "She was a strange one."

"The detective on the case believes he's the reason someone targeted me," she told the secretary. "Because of Sienna or something she was involved in."

Mae frowned at that. "There are a lot of rumors going around," she finally said. "You know how crazy some people can be."

"Unfortunately, I do," Hannah admitted.

"Rick wouldn't be happy if that were true," Mae stated. "He'd be damned guilt-ridden, Hannah. You'll have a hell of a time getting past that guilt if it's true."

In other words, she could lose him. Hannah started to ask the other woman's advice on how to keep that from happening when the door to the hallway opened and another man entered.

Shawn Grayson. Hannah barely recognized Rick's older brother. He was the same height as Rick, the same dark blond hair, but his eyes were blue rather than golden brown, and his body leaner, not as broad or as commanding as Rick's. He was also not nearly as likable.

He came to a stop as he saw her, his gaze filling with amusement.

"Hannah Brookes," he murmured as he moved closer to her chair. "It's been a while."

"Hello, Shawn." She nodded as he sat on the corner of Mae's desk and gazed down at her.

"I hear you're seeing our good sheriff." He grinned. "Are you having fun?"

"That bit of information traveled fast," she stated.

"Good gossip usually does." He chuckled, his full lips curling good-naturedly before turning somber. "I hear you've had some trouble at the house, too? Is Rick checking that out?"

"Talk about supersonic speed." Mae's tone was caustic. "That piece of gossip really traveled."

Shawn turned back with a mocking glare toward the secretary. "I've been home three days and everyone just loves filling me in on my little brother's news." He chuckled. "Whether I want to hear about it or not."

"No doubt," Mae harrumphed. "Do you need to see Rick or you just here to see what's true and what's not?"

He laughed at that, rising to his feet. "I just need a minute of his time, but it can wait."

"Good," Mae muttered. "He's never in a happy mood after you visit."

"Yeah, well, it's how we get along," he said, laughing, before turning back to Hannah. "Rick's not always the most easygoing person in the world, you know. He drove Sienna crazy with his possessiveness."

Now that was a surprise, because it wasn't what she had heard over the years. Sienna had driven Rick crazy with her possessiveness and her refusal to settle down. Sienna hadn't been the home-and-hearth type.

"I'm sure I can handle him," she assured him as Rick opened the door to his office and stepped out.

His expression lightened at the sight of his brother. "When did you get in?"

"A few days ago." Shawn grinned back at him. "Just need a moment of your time if you don't mind, bro. Then you can get back to your girlfriend."

Rick nodded, winked at Hannah, and closed the door behind him after Shawn had gone in.

"Let's hope he doesn't piss Rick off." Mae sighed. "Shawn has a habit of it."

"Brothers." Hannah laughed. "Mine manage to piss me off every chance they get."

Mae smiled. "I have sisters, so I never had that problem."

Despite Mae's prediction, Rick was still smiling when he and his brother came out of Rick's office. Shawn left with a final good-bye and Rick turned back to her, his brow lifting.

"Ready?"

Hannah nodded as she rose from her chair.

"See you later, Hannah." Mae smiled in farewell as they took off.

"That's the first time I've seen Shawn in years," Hannah commented as they moved along the hallway.

"He comes here a few times a year." Rick shrugged. "Manages to stir everyone up then he leaves again."

She laughed at the statement. That sounded like Shawn.

He escorted her to her car and within minutes Hannah was following his truck out of town and toward the small ranch he owned. It wasn't a large working ranch. A few head of cattle, a couple of horses. The single-story ranch house sat beneath towering, sheltering trees and created an idyllic settling.

As they entered the house, Hannah found herself back in his arms, his lips on hers, his kiss fueling a fire that had begun simmering inside her when he had touched her in her bedroom.

There was something about Rick's kiss that fueled a heady, sensual hunger inside her that she hadn't known she possessed. A hunger that seemed to rise from the very core of her, and set fire to her senses, making her realize how little pleasure she had experienced before.

Her arms twined around his neck, her lips parted beneath his, and she melted into him, just as she had always dreamed of doing. There was a dominance, a strength, a sureness in each touch of his hands, each stroke of his tongue.

When he lifted her closer to him, there was a feeling of security in his arms that she had lacked. With him, she knew she would always be sheltered, always safe. He might prick at her independence, but if he loved her, then she had no doubt that she would never have to fear him or anyone else.

When he finally lifted his head, his gaze was somber, despite the arousal filling it.

"What if I don't want to let you go when this is over, Hannah?" he suddenly asked her. "What if I don't want you to leave?"

She reached up, touched his cheek, and let her lips curve into a smile that she knew held too much hope.

"What if I don't want to leave?" she asked him instead. "When this is over, Rick, what if I want to stay?"

CHAPTER 7

HE WAS FALLING in love with her.

As they made a light dinner, shared the cooking, laughed, touched, Rick began realizing that there had been more missing in his marriage to Sienna than he had known.

The simple intimacies that he was already sharing with Hannah had never been present between himself and his wife. She hadn't wanted to cook from the first week they had been together, and it was something Rick had never thought he would enjoy with her. He'd been used to cooking for himself, so he had never thought to ask her to cook until after Kent had been born. And by then, he'd known Sienna would never agree to it.

He and Hannah cleaned the kitchen together. Another small thing, and yet something else he hadn't shared with woman.

It was simple things. Laughing when she flicked suds at him, kissing her cheek, or simply touching her as he put the dishes away.

There was a sense of companionship beneath the arousal, a knowledge that he could touch her as he pleased, that he could be comfortable with her.

He'd known last year. Two dates with her, a week of sporadic phone calls, and he'd known that she had already started to touch him. He'd run. Like a fucking coward, he'd forced himself out of her life because he knew he couldn't face telling her the truth about his marriage to Sienna.

They'd lived a lie for over eight years. From the moment they were married until he'd realized that she'd been involved with the Black Collar Militia and the deaths that had plagued the area for years.

His wife had been the mole in the office. She had been the one who had given the militia the information when agents and investigations had been centered in the area.

Not that he'd ever told her, but she'd had access to his office, his computers, and his notes. And Sienna, despite the rest of her faults, had been perceptive. She had known what to look for in a person, their weaknesses and their strengths, and she'd known an agent when she saw one.

And she'd known how to fool him, despite the distrust that had built up between them.

He'd suspected for years that she was cheating on him, but he'd never caught her. It had simply been an intuition, something that he couldn't put his finger on.

As Hannah went out to the barn with him to feed the horses, she worked beside him. She didn't ask what she needed to do to help, she knew what to do. She didn't care if she got her hands dirty, and she didn't mind laughing at herself.

And Rick realized why he had run from her the year before. Because he had known that he was falling in love. He had known that resisting her was something he just couldn't do.

And even now, that scared the hell out of him.

After they returned to the house, he locked up, set the alarm, while Hannah pulled her sneakers off and headed for the kitchen.

Night was falling. The soft muted colors of the setting sun blazed through the windows of the kitchen, bathing her in a golden hue.

He'd noticed that a lot over the past few days. Sunlight loved Hannah, it caressed her features, seemed to sink into her skin and light her from within.

Moving to her, he wrapped his arms around her and pulled her against him. He was still hard for her. He'd taken her so many times that he knew the need should have eased by now. It hadn't. It seemed to have settled into his guts to stay, and the wariness he had expected to feel wasn't there.

"I need to shower," she murmured as his lips caressed her neck.

Hannah wasn't moving away from him, though. She never moved away from him. No matter how often he touched her, or how, she was always ready for him.

"I could wash your back." He bit at her neck, loving the wild, sweet taste of her flesh.

"You could do that." He heard the smile in her voice and he loved it.

Hell, she was sinking claws into his heart that he knew he was never going to be free of.

Taking her hand in his, he pulled her into the bedroom, then straight to the bathroom. The thought of having her in the shower was more than he could handle. His cock was already straining at his zipper, demanding action.

In the bathroom he adjusted the water to the shower before turning to her. He undressed her slowly, like unwrapping a present. His very own present. Just for him. Revealing each soft silky inch of her body as he dropped the clothes on the floor.

Once Hannah was naked he had to get her into the shower, beneath the spray of water, before he could strip his own clothes. He practically tore them off, tossed them aside, then stepped under the spray with her.

Steam collected in the enclosed space, filling it with an erotic sensuality that wrapped around them and nearly destroyed him with need.

"I've dreamed of having you here, just like this," Rick told her, the words slipping unbidden from his lips.

"I've dreamed of being here with you," Hannah admitted as he worked shampoo into her hair and washed it slowly.

Suds collected and rolled down her body as he spread the luxuriant shampoo through her hair before rinsing it and doing the same with a soft conditioner she had brought with her. When he was finished, Hannah pushed him away, then surprised him by doing the same for him. He bent to her, watching her as she washed his hair, her hands working the strands of hair as though she loved them.

They bathed each other. As Rick washed her, he kissed her. He worked the lather over her breasts, down her belly, and between her thighs. As he rubbed the tender folds of her pussy with the soft washcloth, he gloried in her moans.

Then he was moaning himself when she insisted on doing the same for him. The caressing motions were nearly his undoing when she moved to his dick and washed it as though she couldn't afford to miss a single spot.

Showering with her was an adventure. It was one Rick knew he was going to want, to need, to repeat, over and again.

By the time they were scrubbed from head to toe the laughter had died to strangled moans, sudsy strokes were replaced by the soft spray of the water rinsing their bodies, and he had her in his arms.

His lips were devouring hers as though he had never kissed before, never caressed a woman's body. He was so hungry for her that it could have been four lifetimes rather than four years since he had touched a woman.

But then, he had never touched Hannah's body. The past days had been like a dream he didn't want to awaken from.

His lips moved to her swollen breasts, covered a hard nipple, and sucked it inside. He stared up at her as he drew on the tight little point, watching her face flush, her eyes darken.

He groped along the small shelf to the side, gripped the opened condom he had laid there earlier, and hurriedly rolled it over his erection. He wasn't going to last long and he knew it. He needed her too bad now.

Hannah's hands speared into his hair to hold him closer as she arched toward him, moaning as he lifted her so she could wrap her legs around his waist.

She was so sweet, so delicate in his arms. It was like holding a live fire, one that warmed him from the inside out.

As he licked at first one nipple, then the other, he lifted

her, allowed the head of his cock to tuck against the soft folds between her thighs before stilling against her.

Lifting his head he stared into her dazed eyes.

"What's wrong?" She was panting with pleasure as she stared back at him, her nails biting into his shoulders as her thighs tightened around him.

"I want to watch," he whispered. "I want to see your eyes as I take you, Hannah. Don't close them."

She was breathing harshly, heavily, a little whimper breaking from her lips as he penetrated her the slightest degree, stretching the entrance open as her eyes darkened further.

"I love watching you," Rick admitted. "Watching your face flush, your eyes growing drowsy and dark as I fuck you."

Her long hair, slick and wet with water, spread around her shoulders like a dark cape that contrasted with the silky smoothness of her pale skin.

He pressed in further, feeling the muscles of her pussy clamp around the head of his cock. He felt the pressure of it wrap around his balls as the need to come nearly broke his will.

He'd barely remembered to slip a condom on, and wished he could take her without one. He wanted to feel her holding him, gripping him, flesh on flesh, and promised himself that one day soon he would do just that.

The tight, hot grip of her sheath was ecstasy itself. It fluttered around his cock as he worked inside her, stretching her, feeling her burn around him.

This was like no other experience he had ever had. It was like nothing he had ever known before. He wanted more. He wanted it to last forever. He wanted to come inside her, sate the hunger, and hold her close as he slept.

"Rick." She cried his name, her lips moving over his shoulders, his neck, his jaw. "Oh God. It's so good."

It was too good. It was paradise. It was heat and life and he had no idea how he could ever survive without her now. He couldn't imagine letting her go. Couldn't imagine never touching her again. He couldn't envision a day that he didn't have her kiss, her laughter, or her smiles.

Or this. Her legs tight around his waist, her lips at his shoulder, teeth raking, nipping, as he thrust inside her, filling her with his cock. And when she came, she would bite him as she tried and failed to hold back her screams.

"Yeah," he groaned, feeling her pussy clamp around his cock like a hot little vise, trying to hold him inside. "So sweet, baby. So sweet."

Hannah cried out his name as he moved harder, faster, shafting into her with a hunger so desperate it shocked him, even now. It shocked him every time, the well of desperation, the aching need and satisfaction she could inspire inside him.

That need was tightening inside him now. Rick could feel the heated grip of her pussy intensifying around his dick as she grew closer to her own release. Her nails were digging into his arms as those sharp little teeth pressed into his shoulder.

God, she was going to come. He could feel the muscles of her pussy growing tighter around him, flexing, fluttering, until with a hoarse cry she gave in to the pleasure. Her teeth locked into his flesh, her body arched into him, thighs tightening, pussy milking him until he had no choice but to follow her over the edge.

His hand slapped against the shower wall as he fought for the strength to hold them both upright. His release pumped from him, sending lightning-hot surges of ecstasy racing from his balls to the base of his spine where they exploded in a feeling so intense it weakened his knees.

He became lost in her. He poured a part of his soul into hers, and swore he felt a part of hers enter him. They were locked together more than just physically. Something more bound them now, and that something more was so unfamiliar, and yet so satisfying, that he couldn't fight it. He didn't want to fight it. He wanted to stand there with this pleasure flowing between them forever.

And he might have, but the hot water began to grow cooler, warning him that soon their heated flesh would receive a chill they didn't want.

Easing his drowsy lover to her feet, Rick supported her as he shut off the shower then disposed of his condom.

Pulling two fluffy towels from the towel holder outside the shower, he dried her off gently. He took his time to make certain the sheen of water was gone before he exposed her to the cooler air outside the shower. Wrapping her hair in another towel, he drew in a deep, satisfied breath as she leaned against the bathroom wall and watched as he dried himself off quickly.

"One fantasy down," Hannah murmured, her gaze roaming his body as he pulled on clean jeans.

"A shower fantasy, huh?" Rick grinned. He couldn't help grinning. Damn, but she made him happy. He hadn't smiled in more years than he could remember.

"Well, I have to admit, you were definitely better than the fantasy, but yes. A shower fantasy."

Hannah looked like a tempting pixie standing there teasing him with nothing but a towel wrapped around her.

Zipping his jeans, he reached for the heavy robe hanging behind the door when he suddenly froze, his gaze focusing on the cell phone he had laid on the bathroom counter.

Before Hannah could process what was going on, he plunged the bathroom into darkness, flipping off the lights and jerking her back, his hand over her lips in a warning to be silent.

"The alarm," Rick whispered at her ear as he hurriedly began helping her into her robe. "Someone's in the house."

Hannah stared back at him in horror. Someone had managed to break into his house?

"Help will be on the way." He pushed her farther back along the wall. "Stay here. Stay quiet."

Help? On the way? He was depending on someone to get out here, from town, to help them? She looked at him, fighting the fear for him that was suddenly overwhelming her now.

She couldn't lose him. She had just gotten him. She had fought for two years to make him see her, to finally find the emotion in his eyes that she had the past few days. And now, someone was going to try to take him away from her.

Hannah shook her head desperately. "I can help." She kept her voice as low as possible. "I can use a gun, Rick. Don't leave me here."

She couldn't handle the thought of it. That he would face danger alone.

"Stay." Rick's voice was hard, brutal, as he pushed her back into the shower stall. "Please, Hannah. Let me do this. Don't let me lose you, baby." He cupped her cheek, his eyes shadowed as he stared back at her. "Please, God. Don't let me lose you now that I have you."

She watched, her heart in her throat, fear racing through her system now, as he backed out of the shower and disappeared into the darkness.

Crouching down, Hannah listened, trying to hear over the pounding of her heart and promising herself, swearing, once this was over she was stripping a piece of hide off his ass for leaving her like this, for not taking her with him. As though she were helpless. How many damned times did she have to remind him? That she had three brothers. Older brothers. Marine-trained brothers. She was not a helpless little debutante that didn't know how to shoot a gun.

Hannah might not know how to deal with stalkers while her brothers were away on a mission, but she did know how to shoot one when he showed his ugly little face.

She'd wanted an excuse to see Rick. A reason to come to him. The attempted break-in had served that purpose. But now, he thought she was as helpless as a child.

Biting her lip she listened intently, sure the pounding of her heart was loud enough for a deaf stalker to hear.

She couldn't hear a damned thing. Not the creak of a floorboard, a breath, or a struggle. Hannah was in the dark in more ways than one and her nerves were ready to jump out of her skin.

God help her if she lost him. If Rick thought it would hurt him to lose her, then he had no idea what it would do to her, to lose him.

* * *

RICK MOVED THROUGH the dark house, his weapon held steady at the side of his head as he searched for the intruder that had managed to get in.

He could feel the cell phone in his pocket, a series of silent vibrations assuring him that help was on its way. He'd expected this for two years now, lived in fear of it happening while Kent was home, and now his heart was in his throat because Hannah was here, in the middle of the danger he was responsible for bringing to her doorstep.

A few people might have been capable of getting into his home without setting off the main alarm. But no one could have suspected the silent backup alarm. Its installation was so precise, so well hidden behind the main system, that it would have taken someone who was aware of it to trip it.

And only Rick and the Elite Ops were aware of that system.

His chest ached with the knowledge that only a few people he knew could have gotten past the unique code word he used for that main system. Only one other person knew it. And it was the person he had suspected, the one he had prayed he was wrong about.

He had prayed that Hershel, his former deputy, and Sienna had been the only ones close to him who had betrayed him. He had tried to convince himself during the past two years that the lack of action was proof that they were the only ones.

But now, he knew he was wrong.

At least Kent wasn't here, he told himself, grieving at the betrayal. His son would have been terrified.

Slipping silently into the living room, he caught the slight shift of movement at the doorway into the kitchen. Tall, lean. The intruder slipped out of the room, heading for the bedroom as Rick followed quickly, silently.

He was almost on the intruder. He could see the slope of the profile, the dark mask that covered the face to hide it from the camera that activated when the alarm went off.

He didn't have to see the face. He knew who it was.

CHAPTER 8

STEPPING INTO the bedroom just behind the intruder, Rick flipped the lights on, jumping to the side as the pop of a silenced gun went off.

He moved just in time. His own weapon came up but, before he could fire, the figure jumped for the bathroom and horror sliced through his soul.

He raced to the doorway, fear tearing through him as he heard Hannah's enraged little cry. Rather than fear it sounded like horrified fury as she cursed viciously.

The light flipped on, and he was met with the sight of her being used as a shield for the intruder behind her, her beautiful green eyes glaring at him angrily.

"I told you to leave me a gun!" She struggled against the hand wrapped in the strands of her wet hair until the muzzle of the silencer was jammed beneath her neck in warning, and he stared behind her into Mae's triumphant gray eyes.

"You almost had me," she drawled as she drew the mask off and tossed it to the floor of the tub. "How did you know I was here?"

"Because he's smarter than you are?" Hannah cracked out sarcastically.

"She's a bitch, Rick." Mae laughed before jerking viciously at Hannah's hair and drawing a surprised cry from her lips as she jammed the gun tighter into her neck.

"Why?" he asked her, keeping his gun carefully along his thigh as she stared into his eyes. "Why, Mae? I trusted you."

She laughed at that. It was no more than he had expected of her.

"You trusted me?" she questioned him in amusement. "That was your first mistake, Rick. Trusting me. After what your father did to me, you should have known better."

His father. He'd married Rick's mother rather than Mae. He'd had a short fling with her, and decided, as his father told Rick later, that Mae's temper was more than he could handle. Weeks later Rick senior had met the half-Mexican Maria Lopez and within months had married her.

Mae had seemed to let the past go easily. She married Aaron Livingston, raised a son of her own, and buried them several years before Sienna's death. The son was killed in Iraq; his father had had a heart attack a year later.

He shook his head wearily. "This isn't about Dad," Rick said sadly. "We both know better."

"He married a dirty fucking Mexican," she said, sneering. "He couldn't even fuck something decent, he had to screw that Mexican bitch instead, didn't he?"

His mother had been no bitch. She had been kind, filled with laughter. Just as his father had been.

"You're a part of the militia," he stated, watching Hannah's face from his peripheral vision. He knew what was coming. He could feel it. He could see the triumph and the maliciousness in Mae's face, and he knew.

"Just as Sienna was." She snickered. "We used to laugh about you, you know. We were good, weren't we, Rick? We fooled you all along."

"You fooled me," he admitted. He'd known all along that whoever the mole was in the department was good, damned good. If it had been Sienna herself, alone, then he could have understood it. She was his wife, she had access to parts of his life and his job that others wouldn't have had. She and Mae, together, it would have been incredibly easy to fool him.

"And you killed Sienna," Mae said.

He barely held back the flinch that would have shook his body at the vicious statement.

He stared back at her silently as she laughed with pure pleasure.

"Did he tell you that he killed his wife?" Mae asked Hannah, jerking at her hair again. "His sweet, loving wife. He blew the back of her head off. Did he tell you that? Did he tell you how easily she fooled him? That she was a plaything for the militia? A little camp whore with a taste for cocaine. God, she was so good at fooling him, it was incredible. And so amusing."

Hannah stared back at him, her gaze desperate, her eyes filled with demand, almost a warning, as he watched her. As though the information Mae was giving her didn't matter. That Hannah didn't care that he had killed his wife. That she didn't care that his wife had been addicted to cocaine, and had betrayed her husband, her friends, her community.

"I'm glad you were amused," Rick said quietly.

"Was amused." Mae breathed out with an air of boredom as the gun pressed deeper against Hannah's neck. "I'm no longer amused. You betrayed Sienna, Rick, and the BCM takes care of their own. They avenge their own. Tonight, you'll get to watch your new lover die. Then I'll kill you."

There was that look in Hannah's eyes again. The warning.

She had three brothers. That thought hit his mind suddenly. Three brothers that were in the marines. Had they taught her to protect herself?

Rick's jaw tightened as he fought the fiercely protective instincts rising inside him now. He had to trust her. That was what she was telling him with her eyes. She wanted his trust.

"Tell her good-bye nice and sweet, Rick," Mae suggested, her smile demented, her gaze filled with fury and malicious hatred.

"Hannah." He whispered her name, giving a tiny imperceptible nod.

Mae moved the gun a fraction away from her neck, just enough that she could swallow, lift her head the slightest degree. He watched her eyes, saw the acknowledgment in her gaze. And then she went into action.

She jerked, kicked, her elbow went back, and at the same time she managed to surprise Mae enough to push her head forward.

Mae hadn't expected her to make a move. Had she thought they would just die? Go like lambs to the slaughter?

As Hannah fought, the bathroom seemed to explode. Rick's arm came up and he fired, just as the bathroom windows shattered, dark figures flying through the openings. Rick grabbed Hannah, jerking her into his arms and pulling her to the floor with him.

He'd hit Mae, he knew he had. The men coming through the windows weren't the enemy, they were friends.

The Elite Ops rushed through the room, as silent as the night after the crash of the windows. Some grabbed Mae, restraining her, checked her wound, while others raced to secure the house.

It was surreal. Relief washed through Rick with a force that left him weak as he quickly got to his knees, turned Hannah onto her back, and stared down at her in shock.

She was laughing. Her green eyes were lit with life and love and adventure. And she was laughing.

"Three brothers." She raised her arms, looped them around his neck as her head lifted and her lips pressed against his in a quick, hard kiss. "Remember, Rick. Three brothers."

Three brothers. He felt a grin tugging at his lips, felt the lifting of the fear and the pain that had tightened his chest, just enough to allow him to breathe.

"I love you," he whispered, his hands framing her face as he stared down at her, felt her inside him as he had never felt anything in his life. "I love you, Hannah."

Her expression lit up his soul. All the love, all the life he could have ever imagined, ever dreamed of.

"You finally saw me," she whispered.

Rick shook his head at her slowly. "I've always seen you, Hannah."

"No." She cupped his jaw with her palm, love shining in

her eyes, in her face. "You didn't before, but you have now. Now you have, Rick." Her thumb brushed over his lips. "I love you."

She loved him. She had loved him last year. She was going to love him next year. He could feel it, he knew it.

"My luck's changing," she said softly. "It's changing, right?"

"Mine definitely has," he stated, helping her to her feet. "I finally got lucky." He wrapped his arms around her, held her to him, and glanced away to see Mae being hustled quickly from the house. "We both got lucky."

And they had.

Mae was still alive and she wouldn't see the inside of a jail. At least not a traditional one. She had information the Ops needed. So she'd be taken care of. Her disappearance would be explained away. In the meantime, he had Hannah. If her luck had changed, then his sure as hell had.

He had Hannah, and having her, loving her, was what mattered. His luck had definitely changed.

RECKLESS AND YOURS

Red Garnier

ACKNOWLEDGMENTS

MY HEARTFELT thanks to Monique Patterson, to her awesome assistant Holly Blanck, and to Roberta Brown who brought us together.

AND THANK YOU to Sierra Dafoe, Wylie Kinson, Robin L. Rotham, Sheryl Carpenter, and Georgia Woods, for your amazing support and enthusiasm. You're so much better than chocolate.

THIS ONE'S FOR you, Mr. Red. And to our reckless moments.

PROLOGUE

PAIGE.

Her name was Paige.

So sleepy. She could not open her eyes. Her arms felt as though a building sat on top of them, and an insectlike sensation crawled up her legs under the sheets.

But the sounds . . . The rhythm was strangely soothing, like a lullaby. A nice, sweet lullaby. Keeping company in the quiet.

Beep. Beep. Beep.

"Mrs. Avery! They said Paige was in a trauma and we had to come—"

"Ohmigod, we're so sorry about the judge! But what happened? What's wrong with her—"

"Shhh! Francine, can't you see she's sleeping?"

A voice rose above the others—ringing with maturity, authority. "Girls! Please. You can't all be in here at once! Out in the hall, please."

Again quiet.

Sleep called to her, drew her deeper into its spell even as she fought for consciousness. She didn't want to sleep. She wanted . . . she wanted . . . she didn't know what she wanted. Maybe she wanted to die.

Beep. Beep. Beep.

A knock came. "Mrs. Avery, I'd like a word with your daughter."

Mrs. Avery. Poor Mrs. Avery was everywhere. Doctors called her name. Nurses. People. Friends. *I'm so sorry, we heard, this is awful . . .*

Mrs. Avery's voice was tired now. Was she angry? She sounded strained and far away, shuffling to the door. "Officer, this is not a good time . . ."

The voices faded into the hall, still audible to some degree. ". . . shock . . . head trauma . . . doesn't remember . . ."

They were talking about her. Weren't they? But she did remember. Didn't she?

Her name was Paige.

Her mother said to pack. They would leave soon. No one would bother them again. But Father . . . Father was . . .

". . . accident . . . autopsy . . . funeral . . ."

Father was dead?

Paige heard more murmurs out in the hall before she sensed the presence in the room. The unmistakable breathing of someone—and not her. She could hardly believe the sneer in the man's words the instant they registered.

"I hear Daddy's dead."

Her nostrils flared at the pungent scent coming off his body. He leaned over her. The bed creaked with the weight of his arms, and a tendril of fear took hold in the pit of her belly. He thrust his next words into her ear, words that chilled down to the marrow of her bones.

"Remember what I told you, hmm? Be a good, good girl, Paige, and stay very, very quiet. If you dare open your mouth I swear to God I'm going to break your boyfriend into tiny little pieces. And then I'm going to break you."

A sound welled in the back of her throat, a cry for help, but it died when he squeezed her upper arm hard enough to cut off her blood supply. He released her. "Good girl. Don't forget."

She tossed her head and moaned. *Mother.* Seconds passed, minutes. Hours?

He was gone—and she did not want to lie here. Felt restless. She needed to do something. Something *important.* Something she should run to, far and fast and hard, but her stupid legs—

"Paige?"

The voice. It struck her like lightning. She fell utterly still, stiller than still. Her lungs froze in her chest and her ears strained for more of that hoarse, male rasp. First she heard footsteps.

Her body tensed at each of the five steps that brought the speaker closer, and her mind went blank while she frantically waited to listen. Her world narrowed down to that one whisper he uttered—

"Paige, it's me."

Me.

Unexpectedly, as though this voice were all she needed to set loose a well of emotion, her lips began to tremble. A hot fat tear leaked from the corner of her eye.

A second followed down her cheek, and the moment a flat, callused thumb gently began to swipe it, she impulsively turned her face into that hand. She ached to weep into it. Let "me" catch all her tears.

She began to sob in earnest, and a second hand engulfed her left cheek. She heard a gruff "fuck," while he furiously tried to wipe the tears away. He seemed as desperate to stop them as she ached to set them free. "Oh, fuck." Long fingers spread open to hold her, heels of his palms cradling her jaw. His hands shook.

She willed her eyes to open but they stung. Her lashes felt stuck together with Super Glue and she hated that they would not obey her mind. A sound full of distress and frustration burst from her lips. He tilted her head back a fraction and his warm, ragged breath misted across her forehead. Soft dry lips brushed across one closed eyelid, then the other. *"Shhhh. I'm here."*

When the hot, moist flick of his tongue lapped the tears from the corner of one eye, her stomach exploded with emotion. The breath shuddered out of her.

His mouth trailed down the other cheek while he rained kisses on her.

A powerful tremor shook her body; that same shudder seemed to run through him, too. His hands tightened reflexively on her face and he lowered his head, grazing the shell of her ear with his lips, whispering, "I'll make it better. Whatever it takes, anything I need to—"

Her mother's voice sliced through the room like an ice pick.

"Take your hands off her."

A feeble protest tore out of her as she tossed her head in negation. *No.* But the hands slowly, hesitantly, left her. She could no longer smell the sun on his skin, the masculine aroma of sand and trees clinging to his clothing; instead the scent of medicine and plastic prevailed.

"I ask you to get out now."

Her heart thundered in her breast. She could not move. She could not scream. Could not say, *No no no. Don't go, don't go.*

Beeeeeeeeeeeeeeeeeep!

"You're distressing her, leave *now*!"

His footsteps echoed on the tile floor. Leaving. Leaving *now.* And she could not do anything but lie there, afraid, in the darkness, with his fleeting touch imprinted somewhere deep and lonely inside her.

Her name was Paige.

CHAPTER I

Phoenix, Arizona, March 4
Seven Years Later . . .

PHONE RINGING.

Damn phone *ringing.*

Lying prone on the bed, Zach flung an arm out and groped around for the receiver, lifting it just in time to catch the familiar boom on the other end.

"Rivers?" Fellow PPD detective Cody Nordstrom. Friend. Pain in the ass. Gossip *girl.*

Rolling onto his side, phone to his ear, he glared at the clock on the nightstand. Four forty-three P.M. Sunday. Fuck it.

After the all-nighter he'd pulled—bringing in some sick shit who'd beaten his teenage daughter to death—and a one-hour shower at noon, he'd been asleep exactly four hours.

"I'm awake," he grumbled as he climbed off the bed and picked his jeans up from the floor. "What's up?"

"Your pigeon's home."

One thought slammed him like a torpedo. *Paige.*

"There's a 459R reported there. Patrol's already dispatched. Apparently she's unharmed." A dramatic sigh. "So here I sat, thinking, *figuring,* 'Man, this would really ruffle Zach's feathers.'"

On his feet, fully alert, Zach grabbed his Glock, his backup, and his badge, shoving them all in place. "Robbery, my ass." The house had been empty for seven years and the day she came home they decided to rob it?

"I hear you, I hear you. So then I wonder if maybe you

can find something there that'll persuade the lieutenant to reopen that old case you have a hard-on for."

The judge's case. Paige's father's case. The case every cop in town knew Zach was itching to nail. He plunged his head into his T-shirt and brought the phone back up. "I will."

"Or hey. Perhaps her failing memory has returned and you'll have yourself a witness?"

Charging outside, Zach yanked his car door open, resolute. "I'm on my way."

"Rivers?"

The engine of his SUV roared to life. "Yeah."

"There's a little Las Vegas going on here. Mia's got a twenty on you getting the girl and the bad guy."

"Against?"

"My twenty that you only get the bad guy."

He smiled a fuck-you-too smile. "Thanks, asshole."

"Wait a sec. It's kind of dull down here. Mind if I come over and take a peek?"

"I'll meet you there." Zach flapped the cell shut, tearing the SUV onto the street.

Paige was home.

God help him, his chest felt ready to burst. Thoughts, memories, feelings, bolted through his body, working up a storm.

A storm called Paige. Avery.

By the time Zach pulled over in front of 106 Dominion Drive, his heart was thudding like a beast unleashed.

Paige was back, and apparently he wasn't the only one with his nuts in a twist about it. Someone was alarmed, panicked, determined to frighten her off, or all of the above.

The judge's old residence sat in sprawling splendor atop a flat stretch of land; six thousand square feet of Spanish Colonial, burnt-tile rooftops and arched windows. The cacti flourished along the walkway that led up to its wide front doors, and the scent of fresh paint clung to the warm spring air.

Stepping to the sidewalk, his hunter's instinct simmering inside him, Zach narrowed his eyes against the glaring afternoon sun and focused on his surroundings, sweeping the area with one sharp, calculating look.

Evidence. Damned if he wouldn't find it. He knew this house like the back of his hand. He'd driven past it mornings and nights, rain and shine. He knew every plant, every rock, every bit of grass on its lawns, he knew every window. The top west window. *Her* window.

He passed a glaring FOR SALE sign that jutted out of the ground. This, for one, was new. Hell, Zach actually *entering* the house was new.

"Well, well, well, Stalker's here. Our very own *detective* now."

City cops were already on the scene, well-trained officers in most capacities. Vance Dean, whom Zach had patrolled with before he'd made Homicide at the VCB, looked up from an old gold clock he was dusting for prints.

"Welcome to the party, sweetheart. Though I've yet to see the dead guy?" he added with a lift of his eyebrows.

Zach panned across the room, noting the havoc the perps had wreaked. Overturned sofas. Torn lampshades. Crystal chandeliers in tatters. Photos, dozens and dozens of broken photos, of her as a child, of her parents.

The Averys' living room looked like the anteroom of hell.

He tamped down his anger. "Forced entry?"

"Nope."

"Hairs? Blood?"

"On my wish list."

"Stolen articles?"

"Victim says everything's here. Just a B and E so far."

"Victim," Zach tersely repeated. "She all right?"

"Pale. We secured her in an area adjoining." Vance pointed down the hall. "Found nothing upstairs, but you might want to check it. Miles is on the south of the house."

Zach pulled out his Sony camcorder and began to record, taking in everything with his eyes first, then with his camera. *Give me something, asshole, so we can finally meet, me and you.*

Upstairs, the bedrooms were undisturbed, the master and guest bedrooms clean and luxurious. Paige's bedroom . . . smelled nice. Like lavender, hell, he didn't know. Like *her*.

Bracing himself against the deep, dark stirrings that sultry scent caused, he moved the camcorder and tried not to think this was her room. Where she'd slept. While he'd been thinking of sleeping with her.

Hundreds of books, perfectly arranged, lined the bookshelves. A row of cosmetics occupied the left-hand side of the bathroom sink. All perfectly neat. All Paige.

When he finished recording and descended the stairs, Zach felt like someone had just set off a bomb inside his chest.

A tall, bulky blond waited on the first floor, hands in his suit pockets. Cody Nordstrom and his crimson tie. "Quite a mess you got here, Detective," he said conversationally.

He pocketed his camera. "You've seen her?"

"Introduced myself. I handed her my card." He shot him a long, dry smile. "Though I suspect she'd rather take yours."

"Where is she?"

His friend stuck his thumb past his shoulder. "Study. She's a quiet one."

And when Zach turned to the adjoining room, he saw her.

How could he not? How could he *not* see Paige? She was beautiful, and fragile, and she was real. So real his eyes hurt.

He took a step into the room, and another, feeling as if he were expanding under his skin like a helium balloon. He had hoped, and imagined, and if he was truthful, he might have even prayed, but still he had never expected to see her again.

But now Paige Avery was home. And she was breathing the same air he was. And her lips—*dear God, just finish me off*—were still the stuff of heaven. Plush and pouty, shimmering pink.

She sat on a green wing-backed chair by a floor lamp, a business card in one hand, her cell phone in the other as she busily punched in some numbers. A pretty white blouse with a lacy collar contoured her small waist and discreetly dipped between breasts he'd kissed a thousand times in his mind and a precious few for real. Her hair was a deeper shade of red than he remembered, cut attractively into bangs that fell across her forehead and curled behind her ears, and her features were sleeker, more refined. Still so lovely. So damned lovely, all of her.

His hand settled on the grip of the Glock at his hip, then he realized he did not know why he grasped it. He did it when he got an uneasy crawling up his spine, or a tingling in his stomach, and he did it now when he felt . . . open. Vulnerable.

"Maybe she'll talk to you," Cody said at his side.

Zach nodded, indicating he would speak with her, and his teammate left the room. It had been years, and it had been hell, and he still dreamed of her face seven years after he'd last seen it. Had dreamed of *this* moment.

For two thousand and six hundred days.

Strange, all the things he'd thought he'd do—haul her into his arms and kiss her until her toes curled, promise to never let anyone hurt her, threaten to make her regret it if she ever, *ever* thought of leaving again—he did none of that. Just sought her eyes for something. Recognition. Remembrance. For her to look at him.

Look up, baby, look into my eyes and know who I am.

And then she turned. Her gaze was like a spear slammed straight through his heart. There was nothing on her face. No fear. No excitement. No smile of welcome. Nothing at all.

She stored away her phone in a small brown purse, and her eyes ventured down his body, skimming the T-shirt, the jeans, lingering slightly on the gun, and at last returning to meet his gaze.

He held his breath, waiting for . . . just waiting. For a smile perhaps. A whisper that said all he craved to know. His name, God, let her say *Zachary*.

But still she stared.

And he stared.

Sucker punched by those eyes. A light, worn blue, no

longer shining with innocence, but wide and lost and killing him.

"Paige." His throat closed around his words. "I need to ask you a few questions."

She sat up straighter, her eyes flaring wider, shoulders tensing. As if he were a giant mastiff without a leash, she warily watched as he pulled up a chair across from hers and lowered his body onto the seat.

A thousand questions tumbled inside him, questions from the cop and questions from the man and questions from the boy who'd loved her.

He propped his elbows on his knees, leaning forward, gentling his voice. "Where were you when this happened?"

She stared at his lips, then seemed to catch herself and went rigid. "I was out," she said, her voice a bare wisp. "Buying boxes to pack some of my mom's belongings."

"You were alone?"

She nodded.

He told himself he wouldn't remember, not now, dammit. But he could still taste Paige inside his mouth. He could feel the weight of those little breasts in his hands, could hear her gasps as she suckled hungrily on his tongue and he sucked on hers.

Paige Avery had come home . . . and Zach was dying to come home to her.

She used to pass him with her eyes downcast in the school halls, and would not glance across the cafeteria, and when her friends talked to her she smiled and very rarely stole a glance at him. But when no one was looking, Zachary would touch her with his shoulders or his elbows or his hands or his fingers, and she would shyly touch back. And they would find a nook or a closet or a place to kiss and kiss and kiss each other's heart out. Then the twenty-four hours before Zach had her lips on his again he spent replaying Paige's gasps and how they tumbled down his throat and he would moan every night at the sheer agony of wanting her like he did.

"Detective . . . ?"

Zachary's brows rose the moment he registered her softly spoken words.

"Your name. It's . . ." She trailed off and signaled at his clothes. "You're not wearing a tag. Your colleagues call you 'Stalker'?"

He watched her carefully as he told her. "Rivers. Zachary Rivers."

She cocked her head and regarded him. Her hands began to wring on her lap. "We've met before?"

"You could say that." Fuck.

Fuck fuck fuck *fuck*.

He had wondered, assumed, she would remember *some* about him. He'd imagined she would lie in her bed like he did in his, and . . . well, shit. Clearly, she didn't. She did not remember Zachary Rivers. At all.

He numbed himself against the wrenching in his stomach and barely remembered to tape their interview. He felt like the biggest fool. Biggest fucking fool that ever lived.

She had not only forgotten the crime scene, as he'd read about, as was usual in the case of trauma-induced amnesia. She had forgotten *everything*. Everything Zach could not forget. Not their fights, not their kisses, their secrets, or the dozen times they'd been close to making love.

Clenching his jaw, he drew out his tape recorder and set it on his thigh. *Get the job done and fucking stop with this bullshit—Detective.*

"Taking it from the top again," he said.

She smiled. It was a weak smile, and it made his gut twist with longing.

"How do we know each other? We were friends?"

She seemed baffled by this. Zach thought it best not to elaborate and simply nodded. But no. She had not been his friend. She had been Paige Avery and he had been in love with her.

Desperately in love.

With Paige.

Who had loved him back with every ounce of her heart and soul.

They'd been more than friends, more than lovers, more than a secret.

Aware of the other officers' tomblike silence in the adjoining room, Zach pushed to his feet and abruptly cleared his throat. "Tell me more."

"Detective." By the way she dropped her voice to a whisper, they could've been alone somewhere. Necking. "I just got here," she said. "To the city, I mean." He could hear the rest of her unspoken thoughts. *Why would anyone do this to me? Why aren't you out there catching this bastard?*

He stared into her eyes, still not believing he had them this close.

"I know, Paige. And I'm sorry about your mother. I heard."

Her eyes shimmered, and her voice cracked around the edges. "I'm sorry, too."

"So, Stalker. We found your bird, didn't we?"

He stiffened at the voice from the doorway. Miles Perrini had a twisted sense of humor. Okay when you were having beers but definitely not okay here.

"Get to work, Miles," Zach said softly.

But Miles called out, "Hey, Vance, we found Stalker's birdy. Come have a look."

The guys were such assholes. Couldn't stop laughing over Zach's "little dove who got away . . ."

"You mean the little dove who got away?" he heard Vance's approaching voice ask.

Zach swore under his breath, and to her, he murmured, "Excuse me."

THEY WERE RIBBING him.

The two patrol officers who had appeared soon after she'd made the 911 call were ribbing the detective.

Paige stared at the domed ceiling, pretending to be engrossed in the wood beams as the officers walked around. The house's oppressive ambience was shattered with their laughter.

They kept whispering things. Saying, "Damn, that's got to hurt, man."

Paige settled deeper into the leather chair and forced her gaze out the window. Neighbors peeked over the top of the police car.

And she desperately wished she'd stayed in Seattle. At her studio. With her cat, who'd been grudgingly checked into a pet motel and must not be enjoying it at all. She should, she thought for the twentieth time, have let the Realtor handle everything. Hired help to settle the estate. But ahh, no. She'd wanted to come back to . . . to *what*?

See pictures? Try to *remember* what for seven years she had not? Finally know the place Mom had pretended did not exist on the map?

A neighbor made a questioning gesture from the sidewalk, and having no idea if she'd once met this worried-looking old man or not, Paige gave a little wave that hopefully transmitted the message: it's all fine, you can go back to your life now and leave me to mine.

The old man ducked his head formally and went around a parked black Cherokee. The *detective*'s black Cherokee: there was no doubt in her mind it was his.

Now that the shock was fading, now that the anger was tightly on a leash, and Paige was gradually returning to her senses, she began to register this darkly attractive officer. Really register him. God, she could not stop stealing glances. He was tall, muscled; a suppressed strength and authority radiated off his athletic body.

She'd never seen such a virile thing in her life.

He was dressed in jeans and a solid crewneck T-shirt. A gun rested at his hip as he bent over a broken chair and pointed something out to the other officer. He spoke in low, hushed tones, and his voice made her stomach sink in her body, then fly up to her throat.

When his lazy, dreamy smile spread over something the other said, it hit Paige like a blow, left her struggling for air and staring so stupidly at him that his smile faded the second he straightened and noticed. His expression transformed, became serious, his eyes intent. He seemed to be done with his search and plunged a hand through his hair as he strode forward.

He had a face from her dreams. Hard boned and square, with a direct stare that trapped you. His eyes were amazing, green as a Colorado forest, candid, thick lashed. His body was lean and sinewy, the kind that moved with the grace and coiled strength of an animal of prey. His hair reached his collar, the color a dark sable, just a shade under black.

Paige couldn't *breathe*. She could not tear her eyes away, stop staring, stop *ogling* him. God, this was so not the moment.

Time seemed to come to a standstill when he halted within arm's length of her. The two officers weaving around the living room lifted their heads to catch Paige's reaction as he spoke. "With your permission, I'd like you to accompany me upstairs."

Someone coughed.

Paige frowned, wondering why a muffled laugh followed that cough.

"Please ignore them."

His voice was deep and rich, like something rumbling out from a bottomless, magical well. Hearing it appeased her, but at the same time, made her core ache and tighten. Her legs, and remarkably the rest of her, felt unsteady as she rose to her feet.

He stepped back to let her pass, then noiselessly followed her up the stairs.

She could feel his eyes on her nape. His body close to hers. Felt aware of his every step in the wake of hers. Up the landing . . . down the hall . . .

Why was her heart pounding like this? Because she feared what he'd find or because she feared the directions her thoughts were taking?

"I don't like this house all that much," she said shakily as she entered her bedroom.

When he passed, his arm brushed her shoulder, triggering a tense, fiery frisson down her spine.

"You never did."

He delivered the remark with no inflection as he surveyed her mirrored nightstands, and Paige couldn't conceal her startled, "Oh."

He walked past her vanity, his presence a shock of testosterone in such a girly room. The white comforter, the lacy pillows, the canopy, all seemed to fade into the background, flimsy and insubstantial compared to the primal magnetic force, the realness, of *him*.

Facing her, he crossed his arms and assumed a wide-legged stance that made her feel utterly small. "Were you in this room previously today?"

A shaft of unease spiked through her stomach. She'd not only been in this room today, she'd been screaming at the walls. *You son of a bitch! I won't forget forever, I won't give you the satisfaction!* "Yes," she admitted.

"Can you retrace what you did for me?"

For me . . .

Flushing at how utterly personal that last sounded, she sailed over to the door. "I only came in and . . . sat on the bed for a bit."

She promptly demonstrated, bouncing slightly as she did.

He didn't smile, didn't move; he was so intimidating. "You sat."

His gaze drifted down her neck, lingered on her chest for a heart-stopping moment. Then his fingers curled into his hands and his jaw bunched as he dragged his eyes back up.

His voice rumbled up his chest, an octave lower than before. "Did you do some reading?"

She exhaled slowly and forced herself to focus on his question, but she was loath to admit to him what had just happened. What she'd done.

He'd think her crazy. Reckless.

"I straightened up," she improvised, then winced and tried

to appear contrite. "I shouldn't have? I'm sorry, I'm afraid it's a terrible habit of mine."

He nodded toward the bookshelf and signaled at the bottom. "Do you recall which of these books you moved?"

Note: he didn't ask if she'd moved them, but stated it as fact. She'd tampered with evidence. She might very well be in deep shit.

"I . . ." It took a second for her to register her folly. The yearbook she'd haphazardly stuck among the others was standing *upside down*. The rest of her books were lined up perfectly *and* in alphabetical order.

Cheeks flaming bright red, she rose to point at it, careful not to touch now that he was watching. "This one."

She heard the snap of a glove and almost jumped out of her skin.

Swallowing a lump the size of a golf ball, she mentally calmed herself down and remained in place as he plucked out the yearbook with one gloved hand. Suddenly her every inhale of air was scented of him. He smelled natural and clean and terribly *good*.

Only inches away, she regarded him in confusion and awe as he bent his head. A lock of hair fell on his forehead as he thumbed through the pages.

Something in that visual made her breathless. She had a vivid image of his lips fusing with hers, of her hands in his hair, and insanely thought of sun and warmth and mint and apple juice. Her mouth began to burn so badly, she brought three fingertips to fleetingly feel her lips.

His head jerked up, his eyes flashing a bright, fiery green, and the startling move made her drop her hand. "Were you aware of a page missing?"

"I . . ." She nervously moved away and said, "Yes."

He set the book down, and she became the sole focus of his attention. She struggled not to squirm under his brutally intense regard. "If you don't trust me, I can't help you, Paige."

Help. Someone was offering to help her. She had denied that she needed help for years, but what if she did? What if this stranger *helped* her?

Gathering her courage, she confided, "He left a note. A message."

A black brow rose. "He?"

"Or she."

"Do you still have it?"

She fished the torn page piece by piece out of her pocket, holding them out while seeing herself as she'd been less than an hour ago, hissing through her teeth and tearing the page like a mad person. "Son of a bitch! You . . ." She had ripped the paper into shreds just as the bastard had her family's precious pictures downstairs, gritting her teeth until she thought they'd crack. "I won't stay quiet, I won't . . . forget forever, I won't give you the satisfaction!"

She'd destroyed evidence! God, how sick was that!

"You tore it," he said.

She thought she'd burst from the embarrassment. "I'm sorry," she rushed to say. "I shouldn't have done that. It just made me so angry."

A restless muscle jumped in the back of his jaw as he fixed his attention on the small pieces she'd handed him.

She could see him sorting them out in his mind. The image was branded in hers. Mocking. Twisted. Infuriating and . . . frightening.

In the yearbook photo, she'd been a smiling, glimmery-eyed senior. Her pet peeve? Natural disasters. And there, under "goals," where the true goals of an innocent eighteen-year-old—"world peace and no hunger"—had been scratched off, bright red words replaced them.

MEET DADDY IN HELL.
SOON, MY DEAR.

"I didn't mean to destroy it," she said meekly.

He looked up and, somehow, into her.

"I understand," he said quietly.

He understood.

While Paige could not understand the balm his voice

spread inside her, the medicine his simple words provided; he *understood*. He stood close enough to touch, and as she stared into those solid, riveting eyes, he could've been holding her, the moment felt so profoundly intimate.

She was the first to break eye contact, unsettled to her core. Who was this man? The detective cleared his throat and within minutes he'd called up one of his team—the stocky blond who'd earlier introduced himself as Detective Nordstrom—who efficiently bagged both the torn page and her yearbook. Then Paige was once again alone with him.

Stalker. She did not even want to know the reason he was called "Stalker."

His relentless green eyes skimmed the walls of her room, studied the window overlooking the street, covered the length of the plush bone-colored carpet, and Paige found herself examining the tall, lithe man while he assessed her room. She could not remember ever stroking a man's hair. She couldn't remember ever *wanting* to feel someone's breath, or skin, or . . . God, his hands. As he tugged off the latex gloves, the sight of his large bronzed hands and the long, skillful fingers made her womb clench.

"Do you have someone to stay with tonight?" he asked.

Paige hesitated.

How sad to admit she had no one to call. Then she reasoned that whether or not she should find a room in a nearby hotel wasn't this officer's problem. She would clean up the mess downstairs, let the Realtor earn her commission and *sell* the house, book her return flight to Seattle for perhaps sooner than later, and all would be perfect. All would be *perfect*.

"I'm okay," she assured, smiling with a confidence she didn't feel.

She must have convinced him, though, for he just nodded.

On his way out, he set a business card down on the vanity. "I'll keep you apprised of anything we find."

"Thank you, Detective."

When he left, Paige stared at the empty doorway for the longest time, then crossed the room to lift his card.

Zachary Rivers.

ZACH SLID INTO the front seat of the SUV and shut the door. *Okay. Breathe, motherfucker,* breathe!

Instead, he grabbed the steering wheel with both hands and dropped his forehead until it banged.

Ahh, fuck. He was shaking with a need so violent, so pent-up, so festered, he thought he would break apart. The sight of her sitting on the edge of her mattress, her little breasts heaving, her pretty mouth slightly parted as she realized he could damned well *see* the tiny pink tips of her nipples poking out, had made him want to cover her body with his, delve his hands under her blouse, and suck her nipples until she cried out "Zach!"

She'd cried out for him before. Oh hell, she had *screamed* for him. Every Friday night she was not at Francine's, he would kiss her until she was writhing in his arms, moaning his name into his marauding mouth, their bodies grinding and rubbing and so damned hungry for each other they'd—

A knock had him straightening. He pressed the window button.

"All bags are going to the lab." It was Cody.

Zach rubbed his face with both hands, struggling to clear his mind. "Yeah. I'll call and ask how much backlog they have, see if there's a chance to do this fast."

"Before the little miss decides to hightail it again?"

Gritting his teeth at the thought of her leaving, Zach climbed out and headed for the back of his Jeep. He rammed his camcorder into the duffel that contained everything from handcuffs to crime scene tape and plastic bags for evidence gathering. Zipping it shut, he frowned up at Cody, who was leaning against the fender, watching him in speculation.

"She's pretty."

"Fuck, stop it."

"Hell, I admit I've been curious."

"Not a *word,* Cody."

Silence. Then a long, put-out sigh. "So you think it's the judge's murderer?"

Zach did not respond to that at first, but instead assessed a passing sedan until it disappeared around the corner. "I don't know," he said after his friend gave up the wait and started for his vehicle, "but I want the bastard!"

The murderer . . .

Dozens and dozens had been questioned. Zach, of course, had been questioned.

You and the girl have a little forbidden romance going on, don't you? You want the father dead. He sentenced your father. Put him behind bars. Why not kill him? Get the girl, get revenge.

The bastard who'd interrogated him was now Zach's CO. Needless to say, he had no love for Zach—and vice versa.

Zach had had no alibi. That fateful month his life had fallen apart at the seams; his only living parent had been sentenced to twelve years in prison, his car—the one he'd been working so hard to pay off—had been stolen, and then Paige . . .

He'd been alone that evening, in his small apartment next to the arcade business, and he'd been waiting for her, just like every Friday for the past months.

He'd worked at Dixie's Fun and Games for less than a year—first at the miniature golf outside, then inside where the game room was packed with arcade games and teenagers eager to play them during the weekends. Zach did everything from ramming out the stuck coins to mopping the soda from the floor.

His ears would be ringing by nine P.M. and his heart would be kicking into his ribs, wild with anticipation. By ten P.M. the lively place would be cloaked in shadows, broken only by a rainbow of tiny twinkling arcade lights. The smell of popcorn would linger. And Zach would walk to his apartment to shower, and he'd change into a fresh set of clothes, and he'd wait for Paige, long for Paige, *ache* for Paige.

Sometimes she came early and would step into Dixie's

to watch him. Sometimes she helped power off the lights, grabbed some popcorn for herself, or threw hoops. Other times she would pull him under an arcade game, or lie on the bed of an inflatable kiddie game; then all he would hear was the wet, slippery sounds of them kissing, the rustling of clothes as they touched, the sounds of them breathing raggedly and wanting each other. But that night Paige never showed. Not at his place, not at Dixie's. Investigators insinuated no one had a better motive to kill the judge than Zach.

Nothing could ever be proved.

He'd stayed away from her until the interrogations stopped and he was cleared, but by then Paige and her mother had disappeared.

Zach remained. And every morning he'd wonder if this was the day Paige would come back to him. *I'll make it better. Whatever it takes, anything I need to do . . .*

He realized now, as he slammed the cargo door shut and climbed back into the driver's seat of the Cherokee, that Paige might not even remember his vow. She'd been lying so still in that hospital bed, weeping her little heart out. Zach had wanted to tear his own flesh out, it hurt so much.

And it hurt to see her now. Wounded. Afraid. Alone.

No surprise that he still wanted, with the same fervor as he had yesterday and every day for the past seven years, to make it better for her. *Would* make it better for her, fuck it.

He'd worked the streets for two years, training like he didn't have anything to live for—which, maybe, at the time he'd believed to be true. He'd gotten punched in the gut and in the face, blasted with pepper spray until he was sure he'd be blinded for the rest of his life. Then he'd moved up . . . and up . . .

And now he wouldn't drive off, goddammit. He shut off the engine only a second after he'd powered it up, got out of the car, and slammed the door shut as his cell began vibrating at his hip.

He slapped it to his ear. "Rivers."

The silence, the breathing behind it, had his body tightening in instant response.

"Um. Detective Rivers?"

The pink hue of sunset was creeping across the skies as he glanced up at her window, noting the sheer drapes were drawn. "Zach," he said quietly.

"Ah, Zach . . ."

She seemed to be searching for words. Zach gradually followed the walkway up to her house. "Open your door, Paige. I'm here."

"Oh."

She hung up.

When the door opened, Paige stood wide-eyed and breathless, staring at him with the look of a woman who'd sold her soul to the devil and somehow feared he'd come to collect.

Zach braced a hand on the door frame, his heart ramming against his rib cage. He hadn't felt like this in seven. *Years.*

He ached to grab fistfuls of her hair and draw her up against his body, to take her lips with his, to slide his tongue into her sweet, warm mouth and remind her what she had felt for him, to do with her everything they'd done before and everything they hadn't.

Instead he said softly, so softly, "Did you want to talk to me?"

"No." One nervous hand briskly tucked a strand of wayward strawberry hair behind her ear. "I mean . . . no, I don't have anyone to stay with tonight."

It took Zach one full heartbeat to absorb this.

She could've called Cody. Who was older, friendlier even. But she'd called him.

Reeling with this, Zach jerked his chin toward the house. "Go get your things."

CHAPTER 2

THEY'D BEEN DRIVING for a couple of minutes. Minutes Paige had spent stealing covert glances at the detective. Minutes she'd been inhaling the intensely masculine aroma of his intoxicating person and his leathery car. *Minutes* that felt like hours she spent suffering in baffled silence.

He'd been on the phone—first with someone at the lab, then with his lieutenant, who got a very thorough brief on the "situation." The silence, when he hung up and simultaneously powered off the police radio, had her scrambling to speak.

"I'm sorry," she began uncomfortably, facing the window as they passed a gas station. "I didn't know who else to call and suddenly I felt . . ."

"That's all right."

Biting her lower lip, she chanced a look at him and fairly dissolved to putty in her seat. His shoulders were broad, his biceps bulging as he maneuvered the wheel, stretching his T-shirt to capacity. Awareness of him as an excruciatingly handsome man brought forth an awareness of herself—being a woman. Not dead. Not in a coma. Very much in her five senses.

All of which he stirred.

"I realize I grew up here," she admitted. "I should have a friend to call."

He shot her a sidelong glance, giving her a full view of

that fantastically somber face for a heart-stopping second. "Again. It's all right, Paige."

His husky timbre had her suppressing a shiver. Who *was* he?

She shifted uncomfortably in her seat and tried distracting herself with the buildings outside. None seemed familiar—not the modern glass structures, not the weathered brick office buildings—and her failure to recognize them increased her discomfort. Having a big black hole in your brain was incredibly frustrating.

"Want to talk about it?" he asked.

He sounded so ready to listen, Paige actually blinked. "Talk about . . . ?"

He shrugged his big shoulders. "You." He gazed out the windshield. "Your life."

An uninvited sadness crept into her voice. "I can't remember most my life. I have frighteningly little to tell."

She had never spoken about this openly. Not even with Mom. Paige had tried to stay cheerful and positive with the grieving woman, and kept to herself how unsettling her lack of memory was.

The detective hardly reacted to her powerful words. Still as a granite sculpture, he seemed to be waiting for her to offer more.

"Well," she ventured sheepishly. "What would you like to hear?"

"I don't know. That you're happy."

A rueful smile appeared. "Happy. What does that even mean?" Since he did not enlighten her, she lifted a challenging brow. "Are *you*?"

"We're not talking about me, we're talking about you."

"Aha! So you're not happy, either."

His teeth shone blinding white, his smile so charming it brought the light out in his eyes. A shaft of yearning pierced through her, and Paige dropped her head and drew circles on her thighs, biting her lower lip. Who *was* he? "I left the city several years ago with my mother," she told her lap. "My father was, well, he was . . . um . . ."

"Murdered."

A breath she hadn't realized she'd been holding left her in a whoosh. "Yes." Of course. Everyone in town must be acquainted with the happening. "And I lost my memory."

He braked at a stoplight, and their gazes held. A sensation that he was trying to see beyond the surface, that those intense green eyes were searching for Paige Avery, spread through her entire being. With his scrutiny came an unexpected feeling of discovery . . . as though for the first time in her life, another human being could *see* her.

"What do the doctors say?"

His question was feathery, undemanding, but it made her twine her fingers into a knot on her lap. Because she'd asked herself a similar question every morning and night, but hers started with "why."

Why can't I remember?

"I'm sick of doctors," she confessed, rubbing her thumbs together. "And cops. Not . . . not you, of course. I'm just sick of their questions. And feeling so frustrated. Sometimes it was as though the entire case depended on me. The harder I tried to remember the more physically ill I became. Mother had to take me away. A second chance, she said. Start over." But how could she?

She was an emotional cripple, damaged and deeply affected by events she couldn't even remember. On more than one noisy, rainy Seattle night, she had awakened in hysterics to shake her mother awake. *I have to go back, I have to go back . . . Mom, we have to go back!*

Paige, calm down! Calm down, you're dreaming.

But she'd been wide awake and struggling to grasp the barest hint of a memory teasing at the fringes of her mind. Her mother couldn't understand her ramblings. Paige could never give her a reason to return. She only knew that there was this big hole inside her. That she felt lost. That at night she felt anxious to visit the same place she didn't want to face, either: her past. She craved to know everything her mind had forgotten.

A faint streak of sunlight lingered on the horizon, casting

an orange hue across the evening skies. Poignant somehow. She had never expected Phoenix to suddenly feel . . . welcoming.

Zach parked at an abandoned parking lot spread out before an old, one-story building. A weathered sign that read DIXIE'S leaned against the dusty windows. The land surrounding the building seemed to have once been a miniature golf course. Despite the puddles of sooty soil scattered here and there, it still boasted a few hills covered with synthetic grass, and a wall of jutting rocks decorated its perimeter.

"Ohmigod, I know this place," she gasped.

Out of the car more quickly than he in her excitement, she rushed toward the side entrance, one that seemed somehow separated from the rest of the building. She ran her fingers up the weathered dark wood of the small door, then one long suntanned arm reached out to unlock and push it open for her.

An apartment. It was small, but cozy and inviting. The essentials—sofa, TV, coffee table littered with magazines—sparsely furnished the area, and the air smelled clean and potently masculine.

Unable to resist the tug of the room at the far end of the narrow hall, Paige peered inside. A large bed, one nightstand, one lamp, one pillow. So odd, the magnetic draw of it, the way it called to her most basic, instinctive self.

Walking inside, she whirled around with a smile that stretched from ear to ear. "I've *been* here."

His broad shoulders filled up the doorway, and he nodded, and his face just . . . broke. His aloof, detached expression transformed, his brow became marked with lines, and he closed his eyes tight enough to make her think it was paining him to do so.

Paige splayed a hand across her midriff. "I have this sensation. I can't explain it."

Their eyes met. His pupils dilated, merging with the liquid green irises. He stood there—large, taciturn, stunning. She could think of nothing but how attractive he was. His jaw spoke of character, and his mouth was lush and succulent. His top lip flared into a bow, and the bottom was plump and she desperately wanted to taste it. To . . . to . . . *suck* it.

She grew wet between her legs. "I'm . . . shaky." Breathless, full of puzzled wonder, she whispered, "And I feel like I . . ." *Belong.*

She could feel his weight on top of hers, could feel . . . God, his lips dragging over her shoulder, her neck, her cheeks, her temple, could hear the echo of her name murmured in her ear. *Paige.*

A tremor of excitement melted her knees. "This is your place . . . ?" Her throat cramped around his name, preventing her from saying it.

"Zach." Violently tender green eyes scanned her features. "My name is Zach. Paige."

"Zach." Her hushed whisper feathered into the silence, leaving her with the sensation of having done something illicit. Her entire body twittered like a wanton's with the inexplicable eroticism of having spoken his name.

Friends. He said they'd been friends. *Only* friends? she wondered. And how could a woman, ever, in her life, forget *him*?

He gestured toward the bed, saying thickly, "You can sleep in my bed."

Her stomach gripped as he pulled the drapes shut. "Oh, no . . . I couldn't. Impose."

"No. No imposing."

He covered the threshold once more and stared into her eyes, stroking a large, restless hand up and down the wood frame. The air felt so thick with awareness that his strong, splayed hand could have been sliding intimately up her thigh.

"Do you need anything?" he rasped. "Food or . . . anything?"

Stomach squeezing as a thousand—indecent—suggestions sprang to mind, she shook her head and forced herself to stay put the moment he left even when her legs wanted to follow him.

Too restless to settle down, Paige absently glanced through

the books stacked atop the TV. *Cold Case Files. Hidden Evidence.* Then she walked over to the window and plucked the drapes apart to reveal the quiet moonlit street outside. But no. Her heart continued beating abnormally fast.

After a moment's hesitation, she gave in to the impulse and went to peer into the living room through the slit in the door. She eyed the small stainless steel kitchen from afar and spotted him—a sleek, mysterious feline, a weary feline, checking the windows, the door. Then he removed the gun at his hip, clearly at ease with the weapon, and set it on top of a nearby desk.

He sank into the chair, stretched his legs out far, and examined some clippings for a while.

He was going to find her father's killer. Paige had no doubt, could sense it in the way he concentrated, surveyed, studied. He was beautiful. Sinewy, seething with restrained power. He was a quiet one, wasn't he? Kind of *shy.*

A deep, fierce throb built inside of her as she watched him rise, large and gorgeous and lonely. Or maybe it was she who felt lonely.

He moved to a sofa. The soft glow of a nearby lamp gleamed richly on his hair, dusting across his face and his taut, corded forearms like gold.

In a single fluid move, he wrenched his shirt off, and Paige's tummy tumbled. Her lips tingled, suddenly aching to . . . to . . . trace all that bronzed flesh? Press heated kisses against his sinful mouth?

He lowered himself to the couch and her breasts pricked. His abdomen was carved with slabs of muscle, his ribs perfectly delineated—scattered with scars.

He extracted another gun, a smaller one, from his ankle, and let it drop on a side table. Then his silky dark head fell back on the couch, and he groaned. The long, drawn-out sound reverberated in her bones, and Paige sealed her eyes shut, wanting to moan, too. Stop this!

Gathering her wits, she sat on the foot of his bed, stiffly at first. She removed her shoes and began to scoot up and up until her head was nicely cushioned. His room was . . .

simple. His pillow . . . She rolled her head and took a whiff. Clean and masculine. Yummy, actually. She began to snuggle, arranging the pillow just so, hitting it equally on either side, lifting it to manually plump it up. Her eyes widened at the sight of a picture lying on the sheets.

It was her senior picture.

Heart stopping, she studied her own smiling face and fingered the worn edges, guessing that once, the photo had been tucked in someone's pocket.

She didn't know why she flipped it over, but she did—to find the shockingly familiar sight of her own neat handwriting.

So you'll think of me.
Every second of the day, I think of you.
Paige.

Her hand flew to her mouth, and she said, "Oh."

ZACHARY, TELL me again you love me.
I love you, Paige.
Eyes closed as he stood in her embrace, Zach groaned heatedly, feeding from the sweet, scalding nectar of her mouth, sliding his hands under her snug T-shirt. Her breasts filled his hands, firm and round, the tiny nipples poking into his palms. He slanted his head, searching feverishly into her mouth as she curled her tongue around his.

With trembling hands, he eased the fabric of her bra aside and squeezed both those little pearls at the same time. Her hold firmed around his neck, and she squirmed against him, gasping. *Everything . . . everything hurts.*

He slowed down. Slid his palms down her torso, her ribs, and held her waist. He kissed her temple. Her cheek. Held her body against his and struggled to breathe as he tenderly nibbled her ear. *We hurt because we want each other.*

Up on tiptoe, breasts pressing into his chest, she tongued his jawline and chin, letting her hands roam up his chest. *Do you think . . .* her voice quivered, her tongue sought his . . .

we could...she shivered; he groaned; their mouths opened... *kiss like this, but with our clothes off?*

Damn.

Zach pushed the memory aside and glared up at the ceiling, refusing to think of how close she was, how warm and good and right she would feel. Only an asshole would make a move on her at a time like this. Only a sick, twisted fuck would try.

"You asleep?"

His head shot up. Paige stepped into the shadowed living room, barefoot and heart-stoppingly beautiful.

Years ago, after his father—a quiet, reserved man, much like Zach—had done something stupid, Zach had been warned to stay away from Paige. Judge Avery had taken matters into his hands, and the entire school faculty, the principal, guards, and teachers, were on a high state of warning. Dozens of pairs of eyes followed her, and him, to make sure Zach didn't come within three feet of Paige.

Zach didn't crave that kind of trouble, so he had stayed away. But his eyes, damn them, would always find her. His hands would brush hers. His heart would pound like something mad every time he saw her. When she spoke in class, in that calm, clear voice of hers, his thoughts would scramble. He'd shift in his seat, uncomfortably aroused, and the instant their gazes met and held, it was as though his entire world revolved around her big, thick-lashed blue eyes. Eyes of a girl screaming to be kissed.

By Zach.

And he'd picture running his thumb across that heart-shaped, coral-pink mouth, sliding all ten fingers into that silky fiery hair, and drawing her close for him to smell a little, feel a little, pet and taste and lick a little. And want her so damned much.

But tonight, nobody was watching.

Zach could hear only the rustle of her movements as she skirted the sofa. His heart kicked, an animal trapped in his rib cage, as he fought the urge to engulf her with his arms. He could, Christ, he could draw her gently to his lap and say,

Paige, baby, as long as I live, no one will hurt you, not again, not ever . . . He could kiss her softly, or hard, God, *hard,* and he could coax his name out of her lips . . . and Paige would know, she'd *have* to know, know that she was wanted and needed and loved . . . by Zach Rivers . . .

His stomach gripped as she approached. She searched his features one by one, somehow dissecting his thoughts and *tearing* him open, until he said, "No, not asleep. Thinking," and rubbed his face with his hands.

She smiled. Venturing forward, she lifted a magazine from the floor and set it on the coffee table. "Why do they call you 'Stalker'?"

He couldn't understand why she felt the impulse to chat now. At eight p.m. after a draining day. When he was shirtless. When he'd been this close—*this* close—to storming into his bedroom, climbing into his bed, and kissing the hell out of . . . his girl. "Just a bad joke."

Her soft smile made his stomach tighten. "You stalk all the pretty girls?"

"Just looking for one."

Her eyes sparkled and her smile spread even wider. "Have you found her yet?"

He cocked a brow, disconcerted by her interest.

Then she held something out, and her voice dropped to a shaky whisper. "Is this her, Zach?"

Paige's picture.

His eyes flew to hers, his breath stopping halfway down his throat.

His stomach caved in on itself, his gut twisted, and he felt . . . violated. Revealed.

"Did I give this to you?" she asked softly.

Climbing gradually to his feet, neck and cheeks flaming hot, he grasped the picture and stared at a spot past her shoulder. "We were kids." He said it with a tinge of self-mockery, a smile of contempt. "We were kids, we didn't have a clue about anything."

She craned her neck to fully face him, her smile fading. "But you're a man now. And I found it under your pillow."

He set his jaw, disgusted with himself. "Here." He nudged her arm with the photo. "You want it back?"

She recoiled when he attempted to give it to her, folding her arms back. "No."

"Take it," he insisted.

"I don't want it."

"Take it."

"I said I don't want it!"

He could smell her, a scent unique to her, of soap and skin and flowers. Zach inhaled her like a caveman, an animal, desperate to cling to her aroma and even more desperate to find where it came from.

Swallowing with difficulty, he lowered the picture, and with a little sound of despair, Paige wrapped her arms around herself. "But maybe *you* don't want it anymore," she said in a tattered whisper.

Her chest labored. Her breasts rose and fell, rose and fell, stretching the white fabric of her blouse, begging Zach's starving eyes and aching hands and every living, breathing part of him to notice those perfect, perky, thrusting globes.

Wrenching his eyes away, he set the picture aside and moved to the window. He didn't answer her. Couldn't talk. He wanted to kiss her for hours and hours and hours until they ended up naked. Until they ended up spent.

But no. It had taken weeks—no, months—of tenderly pillaging Paige's sensual mouth to graduate to fondling her breasts. And he'd done that slowly, too. First just grazing the firm tips with his knuckles, smiling when she blushed, chuckling when she squeaked "we shouldn't" while eagerly pushing those nipples out for him to do more.

"Did we have sex, Zach?"

Oh Christ. He was burning under his skin. He was dying here. And she mentioned—

"Were you my boyfriend?"

Had he been? What had he been? Zach gazed out the window, automatically absorbing the moonlit landscape as he wondered. What to tell her. How to define the way they'd wanted, needed, cared for each other, all the reckless things they did just to steal a few hours to be alone.

"But if you *were* my boyfriend," she continued, "you would have looked for me. You would have . . . found me."

He planted a hand on the wall next to the window, his face hardening at the painful reminder. "I did. Find you. Ask your mom, Paige."

"My mother isn't here anymore."

The fragile note in her words made him curse himself in silence. He plunged a hand into his jeans and fisted it inside his pocket. "You're right, I'm sorry."

Silence fell. He could feel her frustration rising like a wind slapping around the room. "Please *tell me* something."

Zach pinched the bridge of his nose, slowly emptying his lungs. What could he tell her? Why in Christ's last day did you have to tell someone she'd *loved you* even though the world had warned her not to?

Paige felt robbed of her memories but he felt robbed of . . . damn it, of her.

He could *tell her* that he was tortured every day of his life, wondering if he should've fought harder for her. He could *tell her* the man whose blood ran in his veins was in prison for killing an entire family while driving intoxicated, and he could also *tell her* that the police force had rarely seen a man so driven to be a cop, so damned desperate to atone for what one of his had done. When he looked at Paige Avery again, he'd wanted nothing more than to have nailed her father's killer to the ground so that he would never again be told—would never again believe—that a Rivers wasn't fit for an Avery.

Then again. He could just *tell her* she'd been his girl. She'd think they'd gone for pizzas and held hands in the cafeteria and smooched at the movies.

None of which they'd done. Because he was Zach Fucking Rivers.

"Maybe I should go." Within minutes, he heard, rather than saw, that she was wearing her shoes. Leadenly, almost grudgingly, she crossed the room. There was anger in her voice, even though it quavered. "I thought I could find some answers in Phoenix but I see I'm not getting any from you. And you've already gone above and beyond the call of duty."

The front door clicked shut and Zach stiffened, ready to bolt after her, when through the farthest corner of his eye, he caught sight of the car outside. The headlights flared on, illuminating the vacant street. He saw red.

"Ahh, fuck." He charged for his shirt, his guns, and stormed after her. "Paige!"

CHAPTER 3

SHE IGNORED HIS voice the first two times he called, striding down the warm moonlit sidewalk, feeling brittle inside.

"PAIGE!"

The third time her name tore through the darkness, she actually felt fear. The blatant alarm in that familiar voice sent a surge of adrenaline through her, spiking up her awareness. Awareness of tires over gravel, of headlights blistering her back, a car speeding . . . and Paige began to run.

Tires screeched behind her.

Suddenly all she could hear was that motor roaring in closer. Zach calling out behind her. What was he saying? What was he—oh!

The rocks! The rocks!

Her heart jumped to her throat and she let out a silent, wrenching scream as she twisted her head just a fraction and saw the car, speeding closer still. Finally registering the piles of landscape rocks scattered to her right, she flung herself over one, arms stretched out. A gunshot exploded. Tires squealed, and one popped loudly like a balloon. Poof. She landed on her side, hitting the rich, moist soil with a yelp.

"PAIGE!"

Going flaccid, she rolled to her stomach, digging the heels of her palms into the sandy earth as she struggled to rise. But her elbows buckled, and she fell flat. She heard the car's slow, noisy escape; an invalid limping for cover. Then she heard nothing but thundering footsteps.

She quaked all over, adrenaline coursing through her body, when Zach dropped beside her and urged her onto her back.

"Christ." His pulse fluttered wildly at the base of his neck, his breath striking her face in hot, fast gusts as he frantically surveyed her.

Stunned by what had happened, Paige clutched his shoulders with cramped fingers, soiling his shirt with a coating of mud on her palms. Her blood was rushing like a roller coaster thrill inside of her, threaded with fear and shock. The car was no longer in sight.

And he detonated. "If that wasn't the most stupid, asinine thing to—"

"Oh shut up." She glared at him, but she didn't let go of him, her nails gouging into his skin.

"You've got a lunatic on your back and you leave me with some *bullshit* line." Frowning darkly, he began to feel her, and his voice went hoarse. "Are you hurt?" His hands were invasive, shockingly delicious, running along her sides, checking everywhere. She felt electrified. "I asked—"

"I'm fine."

She almost sobbed in despair when she had to release him, wanted to cling, touch something, touch *him,* but he fell onto his back at her side and plopped an arm across his forehead. "Son of a bitch just tried to kill you."

I'M ALIVE.

Gripped by another, more potent feeling than fear, she saw his chest rise and fall heavily. His magnificent body sprawled on the ground, vibrating with strength. The gleaming streetlights caressed his firm jaw and mouth.

The night had gone deathly still, but her body burst into chaos. An overwhelming need ripped through her, staggering her, tearing his name out of her in a cragged whisper. "Zach?"

He dropped his arm, his eyes flashing with intent. "He's not getting to you."

He jolted into action, snatching up her small shoulder purse from where she didn't recall dropping it, shoving his gun into his waistband at the small of his back, then half carrying and dragging her across the synthetic-grass hills and back to his apartment. He slammed the door behind them. "We're leaving." A black duffel fell at her feet. He got busy and shoved items inside the black bag. A laptop, cords, a manila folder.

All the while, she watched him. Blood sizzled in her body as if her veins were gas-soaked ropes lit by a torch.

Punching some numbers into his cell phone, he called in the license plate while he yanked out a pad and pencil from the desk and briskly jotted down something. He hung up fast, then frowned in concentration as he made more notes, his lips compressed; an avenging angel seething with protective instincts and testosterone. "We have to get out of here. Nordstrom will—"

"Zach?"

He glanced up at her, incensed and agitated.

Paige couldn't help it. She flung herself at him and—oh, God. She set her lips on his. Recklessly kissing the warm flesh, spreading one hand across his locked, strong jaw.

He made a tormented sound from somewhere deep in his chest. The pad and pen crashed against the floor. He cupped her cheeks with two hands, tilted her head, and seized her lips like a man possessed, thrusting his tongue so deep and hard into her mouth she felt the sizzling, satiny lick down . . . there.

She cried out, and he growled, greedily suckling her tongue, suddenly unleashed.

"Jesus." He fisted handfuls of her hair, drawing her closer to his tasting mouth, cocking his head. "Jesus, Paige, Jesus."

Butterflies exploded in her stomach. She made an odd little sound of pleasure as he started plunging in and out, in and out, tasting, tasting more.

Driven by an urgency and thirst she hadn't known, she looped her arms around his neck and melded to him. His tongue was strong, moist, and powerful as he twirled it around hers. She sipped from him with embarrassing vigor, as if trying to suck his essence into her body, so much so that she drew back all of a sudden, startled by her hunger.

Zach growled and backed her up, pinned her against the door with his weight, and ruthlessly dove for her lips once more. "Give me your mouth, Paige."

Gasping, Paige grabbed handfuls of his hair and let him have it.

An odd gurgling sound rose up in her throat as their thirsty tongues explored. His hands clamped on her waist, holding her still as he intensified the kiss until she thought she'd drown. He searched so far inside her she was certain he was out for her heart.

The biting bulge of his erection scraped against her stomach. Her breasts throbbed where they pressed against his chest. And she thought she would seize this moment, because she was crazy, because she wanted him like she'd never wanted anything in her life. Her pelvis began to move, craving more of him, all of this man, this hunk, this protector.

She bit at his lip and he bit harder, devouring her damp lower lip, whispering, "Sweet, thirsty baby."

His endearment spilled through her in a lust wave. She whimpered softly when he eased back a fraction, leaving her empty, in agony, in *pain*.

When he spoke again, running unsteady fingers down her cheek, his breath blew over her face, misty and warm and fragrant. "You want me."

His eyes. They burned with a passion beyond desire, beyond longing, beyond anything physical or passing.

The wise thing to do would be to disentangle her shivering body from his, but instead she gripped his taut shoulders and fought for an explanation. "Must be the . . . shock."

His heat singed her, made her yearn to feel it up close, to be burned to a million ashes.

"Shock. Right. *Hell*."

Neither of them moved.

She didn't know whose breath was shallower. Whose body felt tighter, hotter, against the other's. But she didn't want to stop, didn't want to start thinking that *no no no* she shouldn't be kissing a man right now, shouldn't be squirming against him, but nothing had ever felt as good as he did. His mouth. The voracious, unchecked way he kissed her.

Blood thrilling in her veins, spiced with adrenaline, lust, and something indecipherable, she slid her shaking hands down the solid wall of his chest. He inhaled sharply, nostrils flaring, as he watched her with wild, flaming green eyes.

"Paige?"

He sounded puzzled. And he was firm and long and he was pulsing against her stomach. He smelled of sex and wanting. Darkly, avidly gazing down at her as no man, ever, in her life, had looked at her before.

The taut, bunched muscles of his body against hers sent dabs of fire across her belly, little devils of temptation licking her to sin.

She couldn't voice what was happening to her. "I just . . . want . . . to . . . to kiss you more."

As though losing some kind of internal battle, he tangled his fingers in her hair. "Christ, come here."

Positively melting, Paige obeyed. Their lips latched, and they kissed. He groaned. She moaned.

Caressing the back of her head with his fingers, he took a breather for less than a second, realigned their heads, then covered her lips and they kissed some more. Kissed until she didn't know if days had passed or minutes. Kissed until her mouth was hot and burning from his kiss and the rest of her body rivaled it.

His hands cupped her waist and then didn't move, only held her still as his mouth did everything. His head moved, his lips moved, his tongue moved. Paige burned to bare her breast to him and ask him to lick it, burned to bare her soul to him and ask him to take it.

"Need to go." His chest heaved roughly as he spoke. "Need

to make you safe." Setting his forehead against hers, he reluctantly rolled his head. "Just . . . give me a sec." He took two, three, four breaths releasing another sound of frustration as he pushed away. "Argh. Okay. Let's go."

Even minutes later, when they were in his car, Paige couldn't stop shaking. Zach was speaking to Nordstrom at police headquarters, briefing him on the happenings. Driver wore a black mask, widely built, definitely male, he said.

Paige hadn't been able to see one whit, had been blinded by the headlights, the fear.

He'd barely hung up with Nordstrom, who was supposed to call if he knew anything else, when his phone vibrated at his hip. "Rivers," he snapped. And went on to relate the same to another caller.

A wave of possessiveness rushed through her at the sight of his plush, stern, moving mouth glistening with the remains of her gloss. He wiped the back of his hand across it as though he could feel it—and it made her want to smear her gloss across his lips once more.

Trying to distract herself, she checked her own cell phone. Five missed calls from the real estate agent. Not the time to call the chatty woman and not in the mood for anything except more of what she'd recklessly started, she tucked the phone away.

Zach was wrapping up, listening to his superior now, his expression severe. Paige could feel the anger coming off him, and more than that, was aware of something else. The air between them pulsed, felt dense and charged with lightning. His eyes kept seeking hers as he spoke; the look in them was heated and probing and as personal as his kiss.

"Yeah, Lieutenant, I got her," he finally said, and flipped his cell phone shut.

He gazed broodingly at her red, swollen, thoroughly kissed lips, one hand on the wheel, the other casting aside his phone and coming to rest on his knee.

Silence.

A light smattering of mud she'd smeared across his hard cheeks still blackened bits of his skin.

His thumb tapped restlessly against his muscular thigh as he stared out at the sea of lights ahead. "Do I owe you an apology?" She only stared, reacting to his voice with a quiet inner frenzy. Promptly he added, "For what happened back there?"

Somewhat despaired he'd even ask that, she shook her head. "I'm the one who started."

"You're on a high." He shot her a pointed look that seemed to arrow down to her nipples. "Endorphins."

No. She was high on *him*. Zachary Rivers.

Who made her heart flutter.

And suddenly, excitingly, the thought that he could be high on her too sent even more adrenaline pumping through her veins, gripping around her tummy, stimulating her nerves. He'd been so excruciatingly, torturously rigid. So excited to grope her. So hungry for her. God!

Yes. He had her all right. May his lieutenant and his colleagues and the entire world know.

Zach totally, completely, had her.

"You know what, Zach?" She stared outside, her mind turning bleak as she thought about the message, the car, that heartless, motherless *bastard*.

"Hmm."

He sounded contemplative, and the minute she caught the grim expression on his face and noted his strong, jutting knuckles as he gripped the wheel, Paige knew he wasn't far behind with his thoughts.

"I'm not going back to Seattle until we find him."

CHAPTER 4

HE RENTED A ROOM.

Small, cheaply furnished. It was the kind of place you could rent for an hour. Hardly the kind of place one would look for an Avery. Zach could picture her staying in a hotel room with fresh-cut flowers and complimentary mints. This place had complimentary condoms. And the only flowers to be seen were the ones on the label of the plastic air freshener by the nightstand.

Loathing having had to bring her here, he secured the locks, searched the small bathroom, and went to the window to examine the pitch-dark alley below. Escape route, if necessary. He closed the blinds, and at the same time, he closed his eyes for a minute. *Get a grip, Rivers.*

But damn. He was reeling.

Paige running away from him . . . Paige running for her life . . . Paige clinging to him.

Some twisted bastard was after her and Zach burned with the need to protect her in ways he hadn't been able to before. But he couldn't think, dammit, couldn't find his cool head.

Because she'd kissed him. *Kissed* him.

She'd slipped her tongue into his mouth, had held his face in her hands and—dammit, his hands tingled at his sides. He was trying, and not very effectively, to keep from reaching out for her. He was thrumming with a raving need to take her body with his, lick every inch of her skin, spill days and weeks and years of wanting inside her.

"We're spending the night here?"

Abruptly, he turned. "Yeah. You're safe now."

And there she was, gazing at him across the room with glimmering blue eyes and lips that were pink and glistening. It had been nothing, he reminded himself. The kiss. Nothing.

Paige had been euphoric to be alive, had felt a need for intimacy, and Zach had been on hand. He'd been willing, and able, and more.

She was curiously examining the room, and it was too damn bad the sparse furniture provided no such distraction for him. He could not drag his eyes away from her. Yeah, she was safe now. But not from him. Not from the past so quickly catching up with them.

She'd never looked so bedraggled—hair tousled, cheeks bright red, shirt rumpled. Just . . . adorable.

With some difficulty, he cleared his throat. "Cody ran the license plate. The SUV was reported stolen forty-eight hours ago." Would that the owner had better luck finding it than Zach had his Camaro all those years ago. Damn, but these things made a man feel impotent.

He sank down on the only chair in the room, rubbed his face in his hands. "Lieutenant O'Neill wants to meet with you tomorrow. He suggests you go under hypnosis. You know something, and we need to know what that is."

"Hypnosis?"

He dropped his hands. "O'Neill's wife, Sue Ellen," he explained. "She's a master hypnotist. We don't usually require her services, but he believes that in your case, she could be of some help."

Paige's fingers opened on her stomach. "Mom always refused to go that route, she said we shouldn't trust our minds to anyone." Her smile was sad. "But I guess I must try. To remember. Sometimes I get a thought and I push it away, my stomach hurts."

He curled his fingers into fists over his knees, wanting to

reach out to her, hold her, say—God, so many things. "I'm sorry, Paige."

She nodded. "I'm sorry, too. And thank you for . . . what you did."

He could not tame his heartbeat, find calm, even if on the outside his voice was strangely disembodied. "No thanks necessary."

He shifted in his chair, uncomfortable in his jeans. They were stretched to their limits. He hauled in a calming breath, but he could still feel her rubbing against him. He could still see the car screeching by inches away from her, could still feel the panic and terror clawing his gut.

He wanted someone's blood. He wanted sex. He wanted . . .

Paige.

Needed her.

Long ago, he'd envisioned roses, wine, the best for Paige Avery—now he just wanted. Nothing mattered. She was here. If he never saw her again, if she never remembered him or felt again what she once had for him, she was here. Right now. In the shadowed little motel room. Where he could keep her safe from anyone but him.

Zach, touch me, touch me there . . .

Here? Where it's wet and tight and hot for me?

Zach!

"What is this place anyway?" Paige glanced around the room with increasing curiosity. She studied the mirror behind the bed. The mirror above the bed. The basket of condoms on the nightstand. It was all so tacky and, in her fine eyes, probably not too clean.

"Somewhere he won't look for you," Zach said curtly.

Her eyes widened as though a thought just socked her. "Is this where people come to . . . to . . ."

"Fuck?" She gaped in shock, and Zach spread out his arms apologetically. "Depends. On whether or not they feel like a fuck."

She went statuesque, like a Venus about to be beheaded. A panting Venus.

A queen bed occupied most of the room. It was more than they'd ever had before. And Zach wanted her more than he'd ever wanted her.

A year of foreplay—months of holding back, being gentle, being patient—and a week of torture knowing it would happen Friday, a week anticipating, panting, sweating, wanting . . . He'd known their lives would change that Friday—and their lives had changed, all right.

She'd never come back to him.

Restless, he rose and propped a shoulder against the wall. His eyes, traitors, kept falling to her chest. Her blouse was damp, the lace collar soiled, and two soaked circles delineated her breasts. It was a trial not to stare at the creamy rise of flesh visible through the moistness, *impossible* not to notice the faint dusky hue of a nipple. Christ.

"Get in the bed, Paige. Catch some sleep."

She offered a shaky smile. "Oh, I'm not tired." By the nightstand, head bent so that the tips of her hair tucked under her chin, she seemed inordinately interested in the bountiful condom basket. "Can you believe some of these are flavored?"

God. Zach crossed his arms and tucked his hands into his armpits, trapping his fingers. "Your shirt is wet."

She tensed in surprise, glanced down at herself, then up with a gasp.

He signaled with one unsteady hand. "I can see your . . ." Pink, stiff, beautiful nipples. The blood rushed up to his head, dizzying him. "Get in the bed. Cover yourself."

She didn't move. Stared with a look so familiar, so full of longing, his heart hurt.

"Get in the bed, please, Paige."

Flushing, ignoring his comments, she nervously rummaged through the condom basket. "Apple. Strawberry. Peach."

He swallowed, yanked his shirt off, feeling just a hair away from insane. A breath away from begging for her, begging for tenderness, for an opportunity to feel her skin under his fingertips. "Here. Put this on."

She caught the garment in the air. The whites of her eyes were evident around her pupils as she clutched the shirt tight, passing her tongue between her lips at the sight of his chest. Her wandering gaze was a palpable caress, feathering across his shoulders, pecs, abdomen, setting his skin on fire.

"Put it on," he said softly.

Gnawing her lower lip, she briskly set his shirt aside and studied the basket contents once more. Her outstretched arm shook. "But now I can see *your* nipples."

"And?"

Her cheeks flared with color. "And I think you're the sexiest thing walking the planet."

Shock, sudden and total, made it difficult to speak. "No," he said, dumbfounded. "No, no, that would be you."

Her lashes dropped as though it pained her to listen, and she made a little sound in her throat. Zach could feel a groan surge up his chest, more like a growl, a howl of hunger.

And then her fingers delved into the basket, and Zach felt like she was carving into his heart. "There's raspberry, too."

Her hand trembled, her voice trembled. *He* trembled.

Hoarsely, his voice thick with the arousal flaring through his body, he reached for his weapons and set them on the chair he'd occupied, murmuring, "Pick one."

"Me?" Flustered, Paige kept investigating the basket, the color rising up her throat. "But . . . you're the one who's supposed to wear it."

The thought of him sliding something on, sliding inside her, nearly drove him to his knees. "Pick one . . . for me." *For my cock. For me to make love to you until morning.*

He didn't know what she would do, didn't know what he was doing, only knew his heart was pounding in his chest, his groin, his head.

She lifted a foil packet. Thrust out her chin. Her throat worked, but for a moment, no words came. "This one? A . . . natural one." Her timid smile was like a kick in the heart, familiar and heart-wrenching, and the thought that she could be playing around knocked him cold.

"Don't tease me."

Her smile faded. "I'm not—not teasing." She stared into his eyes, her little tongue darting out to moisten her lips. "Please don't tease me, either."

"God, no, never."

And then he couldn't take it, couldn't take the look in her eyes, couldn't take her nearness. He started for her. "Make love with me."

It was a plea.

Jolting in surprise, she backed away, around the bed, and Zach followed. "Put me out of my misery." His voice hoarsened even more. "I want you. I've wanted you every day. I've been with you a thousand times in my mind. Every night, every single night, in my bed, I make you mine."

With a noise of distress, she flattened against the wall, opening her hands behind her. Her eyes shone with lust and worry. "It's just that I . . . I've never done this before."

Zach planted his hands on the wall beside her, leaning in. "Do it with me now."

DO IT WITH ME now . . .

A spasm shook her at that decadently provocative suggestion.

Her breasts throbbed, felt full and heavy, hurting. Hurting at his words, at the physical ache of *wanting* him, at the thought of having that bronzed, unyielding body inside of hers.

A warm moistness kept pooling between her legs. "Zach."

Eyes alight with heat, he engulfed her face with large, dry palms, as though somehow he could hold her scrambling thoughts together.

"Zach what? What? Tell me."

She could find no words to describe what she needed. She felt starved. Greedy.

Her stomach tumbled as he bent his head to hers. "Do you want to be touched?" he rasped. Their noses grazed, and he inhaled deeply. "Do you want to be kissed, baby?" The words he whispered as he aligned their mouths were the most erotic sound she remembered hearing. "Do you want Zach?"

"Oh God, yes." She framed his face with quavering hands the same instant he swept down. They made a sound of craving and took each other's mouths—and they went wild.

A fire ignited as their lips pressed. Their breaths met as they opened wide. His tongue plowed inside, swift and sure. She moaned from the taste of him, his cool, unique flavor flooding her senses.

His arms snaked around her waist, hands boldly cupping her buttocks and drawing her brusquely up against his length. "God, you're so sweet. Feel so . . ." Heads slanted, their tongues sought, found, tangled. "So right."

His fingers bit into her ass as he dragged his tongue across the seam of her open lips. His size dwarfed hers, his big shoulders hunched. Agonizing ecstasy ripped through her, and as she gave up her mouth to his passion, she knew not who he was, not who she was, but who he had been to her.

He'd been music, he'd been chocolate, he'd been beaches and puppies and treasure hunt stories and everything she adored.

She shuddered with emotion, slid her fingers into his silky black hair and greedily trailed her lips across his square jaw, her wheezing breaths puffing across his skin. "I want you," she sobbed, "I'm dying with wanting you."

He put breathing distance between them, and the hooded eyes and the heavy lids and the flare of his nostrils rendered him even sexier. "Get naked."

She could only pant.

"Naked, Paige. For me. Now."

Her heart froze with alarm. But he would see her. And he was so virile and magnificent, and she was so scarred and so . . . scarred.

Roughly, he hooked a hand into the waistband of her slacks, unsnapping them with two fingers while Paige, suddenly spurred to action, frantically turned around and undid the row of buttons of her shirt.

She braced her hands on the wall when he pulled her

slacks down her hips, leaving her in her plain white panties. "All of you against all of me," he said gruffly.

"Yes."

Paige jerked her arms out of her shirt, tossing the garment aside as he unhooked her bra. Her breasts tumbled free, and Zach cupped one globe with one hand and swept her hair aside with the other, heatedly kissing her nape. "Me inside you."

"Yes."

"Fuck, *come here*."

She shrieked in surprise when he scooped her up wearing nothing but her panties, and carried her to the bed, him in his jeans.

The mattress creaked as he climbed over and gently settled her on the bed. Propping up on one elbow, he took a long, thorough assessment of her nakedness. It took less than a second for his attention to catch on the slash cutting across her hips and abdomen; and it stayed there for a heart-stopping moment.

A ball of humiliation settled in her throat.

She didn't know what crossed his mind as he absorbed the sight of her scars—the long gash across her hips, the dulled centipede slashes running up each of her thighs—but she knew if he stopped touching her she'd weep. She'd weep from the need for him; she burned from inside out, could feel her heart pulsing between her legs, her very soul screaming for closeness.

His eyes flashed with unmistakable fury as he visibly strained to get himself under control. Mortified, Paige sat up, folding her legs to her chest. "I'm ugly."

"No, baby, no!"

Reacting fast, he firmly urged her back down and slid a gentling palm up her thigh, around her hip, and stroked the scar running side to side with his thumb.

"You're not . . . not ugly. Never."

She might have been hesitant to believe his words, but he'd ducked his head and was eating at her neck with his mouth, sounding so aroused, sliding his fingers across her waist as he brought his whisper to her ear. "The thought of you in pain makes me want to kill." He made a fist over her stomach, then loosened his hand. "Sweetheart, you're lovely. Look at me. Look at me, Paige."

When she did, his stare felt like a bonfire in her chest.

"You're lovely."

The denim of his jeans chafed parts of her legs as he pressed into her side. His hands began roaming, igniting the skin they touched.

And now she wanted to weep not because he didn't touch, but because he did. And he touched her as though his whole life he'd been waiting to touch her. Whispering over and over again that she was lovely, felt amazing . . . that she was his.

His words rendered her even more vulnerable than her nakedness. She had an urge to brace herself, felt her body set protectively against how fragile she felt.

"Shh. Relax." Zach cradled the underside of one breast with his hand and kneaded out the tip. "God." He nuzzled her with his nose. Gave a lick. "Delicious."

Her nerves jumped when his hand slid downward. With skillful ease, his middle finger traced the elastic of her panties. They were both making sounds, half-starved pants that echoed in the room. The ones he made—long, drawn-out immersed sounds—made her shake on the inside.

"Let's see"—he caressed through the soaked fabric, using three fingers to expertly stroke the tenderized flesh lying desperately in wait under panties—"if I remember what to do."

He shifted slightly above her, and, gasping as he whisked the pad of his thumb across that little sensitive place, she clutched his shoulders with ironclad hands. "Zachary." A ray of a memory played in the depths of her mind. Of crying out his name.

She closed her eyes, helplessly rotating her head when he drowned the peak of one exposed breast with his mouth. His groan, a low and famished sound, vibrated against her flesh. His mouth was a scorching vortex. His tongue swiped. Over and over. Lapping, circling, licking. *Suckling.*

Her head tossed, her hips circled instinctively, and she gasped in pleasure.

"That's it." He suckled. "That's it, enjoy it."

His finger. Oh God. It was sliding down her panties. Down down down. He tugged the cotton aside and drew back to watch as he revealed the curls at the apex of her thighs, glistening with moisture.

"Wet for me," he rumbled.

Holding the fabric aside with his middle finger, he stroked the pad of his thumb across the slickened entry. Up and down. Teasing her clit. Rolling it under his thumb. Then he pushed into her sheath. "*Hot* for me."

Screaming, she wadded handfuls of the comforter into knots. She opened her mouth to beg, to say "please, goddammit, take me!" when he came up.

He nipped her lower lip, feeling his way across her mouth with gentle bites and strokes and nibbles. "Do you want more here?" He exchanged his thumb with his longest finger and plunged into her depths, that one stroke so delicious she spread her thighs wider, curving her body to take it all in. "Do you?"

Wildly she groped between their bodies to hook two fingers into the waistband of his jeans. "Please hurry!" Sitting up for best maneuvering, she fumbled with his snap, making a frustrated noise.

Chuckling, he said, "Shh, I'll get it," and leisurely went up on his knees to work off his jeans.

She pulled off her panties, watching his biceps bulge as he unbuttoned and unzipped. He too was laboring to breathe, the air soughing in and out of his muscled chest as he undressed.

The sight of his erection popping out made Paige's stomach grip. Zach's body was all taut, long muscles and smooth, tanned, lickable skin. A path of silky hairs started at his navel, leading down to his jutting cock. He was thick and long, the balls high and firm, the stalk flushed with wanting.

Wanting to be in *her.*

Blushing, Paige glanced at the far wall, then briskly at him when he said, "Don't turn away."

He wanted acknowledgment. He wanted her eyes. And God, they wanted him. Her inner muscles rippled at his visual, clenching lustily as a stream of moisture trickled down her thigh.

"I'm hard," he said in a low, guttural sound. "And wet. For you."

He was beautiful. All flushed, aroused male on his knees on the bed, his shoulders high, his glistening penis at its fullest length.

Melting inside, Paige rose to her knees with him. For a blind second, she didn't know what to do. Then tentatively she fingered the plum-shaped tip of his shaft. It bobbed at her touch and jerked higher against his flat stomach.

He let go a groan, grimacing with pleasure. "Pet me."

Sucking in an excited gust of air, she curled her hand around the thick width and slid her fist down the pulsing flesh. Setting her lips on his straining throat, she flattened her tongue against his collarbone, tasted the thin film of dampness coating his taut, square shoulder. "You're beautiful, Zach."

She thought he purred, like a lion being "petted."

She had never held something like him in her hand. So . . . vigorous. Her wandering thumb encountered a silky wetness at the tip of his staff as she circled her tongue around a small, delicious brown nipple.

His hips began an agitated swivel, the moves sliding his cock inside her grasp, and almost collapsing from arousal, Paige moved her hips suggestively, too, responding to him by instinct, murmuring, "Please."

In a startlingly quick move, he flattened her on the bed. His weight bore down on hers as he smoothed his tongue into her ear, feverishly licking, going out of control, his voice demanding and utterly sexy.

"Want this." He fondled her weeping sex with his fingers, both teasing and tantalizing her with quick little plunges of the middle one. "Want this like I do."

A splayed hand skimmed down her side to slide into the

small of her back and crush one buttock in his grip, hauling her up against him.

His large, demanding penis ground into the apex of her thighs, and she sobbed with need. He was so hot everywhere, his hands burning, his mouth rough and delicious on her face.

Cupping both her ass cheeks now, he began a soothing massage that ground her against his pulsing length, electrifying her senses. "I could do this all night," he ground out.

"Oh, please don't!" Gasping, she clasped his hair and feverishly ran her tongue up his neck.

He chuckled—deeply, excitingly.

His hands continued to mold her, goading her with the biting press of his hardness, and when he lifted his head to stare into her eyes, he looked very hot and very bothered. She'd never imagined she could incite a man to such bleak hunger.

"Tell me what you want from me, Paige." As he spoke, his hips gave a tantalizing nudge to hers. "Tell me and I'll give it to you."

Her answer lodged up in her throat as she opened her legs wider and twined them around his body, a move that locked him between her thighs.

Panting, she clung to his neck and said, "I want you."

"All of me?" He purposely rolled his hips against hers, prodding her sopping, oversensitized sex with what he could give her. "All of me? Say you want all of me."

He was enormous.

"Yes," she gasped, "yes. All of you."

For three wild, debilitating seconds, he held her hips in his hands and only rubbed against her, his cock glossing across her tender slick folds, and they moaned in unison.

"This, too?" he asked gruffly, darkly. "You want this part of me, too?" He bent and bit the shell of her ear. "I want inside you."

"Yes. Now. Please!"

He lunged in the direction of the condom basket, tore at

the first foil packet he found, and before Paige could even determine which kind of rubber he'd slipped on, he returned.

His sinewy, sweat-coated body blocked out all sights, his haggard breaths all sounds. Reaching down, he snared her ankles and hooked her legs around him, settling between them. "Don't," he said, "for the love of God close your eyes."

She kept them open, helplessly clinging to his famished green gaze. He thrust once.

"Paige."

Relief ripped through her, and with it came the staggering pressure of having his hot, wide length buried inside her. She purred from beyond her throat, fighting against the urge to toss her head, swim in the sensation.

He thrust twice.

"Baby."

Her body undulated. She mewled with bliss.

On his third thrust—one that was overwhelmingly deep and made her catch back a sob—it was Zach who closed his eyes, gritting his teeth, saying, "God."

ZACH DIDN'T KNOW who took whom here. He only knew their bellies pressed, their chests pressed, she was soft and warm and quivering, his cock was buried to the hilt inside of her, and he was ready to detonate.

He struggled to control the urge to pump, thrust, ram harder and deeper until they passed out, and instead sucked in big gulps of air in an effort to regain his control. They'd been masochists as teens. Had loved drawing out the pleasure, loved wanting each other until their pleasure coated each other's hands.

This was her *first* time. Hell if he would let himself shatter this fast.

"This feels wonderful." Her clouded, lust-filled eyes searched his face with amazement.

This. Flesh to flesh. Naked. Like they used to be. But this time, he was embedded inside her.

"I can feel you beating in me," she murmured.

Swamped by the sweet pain of her confession, Zach latched onto her mouth for sustenance, to anchor himself, to stop his world from spinning.

"And I can feel you." He kissed the tip of her nose. "Tight and warm and wrapped around me." Realizing he could be crushing her, he eased some of his weight off her without breaking contact, shifting to his side a bit. "You relished getting naked with me. Every time I touched you, you came for me."

She shuddered. Her middle finger stroked his glistening bottom lip. "And you? For me?"

His cock jerked inside her. "God, yes, always for you."

Tentatively she curved her hand behind his ear and tunneled all five fingers through his hair. God, she used to do that. Run her hands all over his hair, his neck, his nape.

His lids drifted shut. Her warm, gliding skin slid along his shoulders, her seeking fingers venturing down his damp back muscles. And he kept his eyes closed, shaken by the gift of her caress, because nothing, ever, had come close to the bliss of Paige loving him.

Only Paige could make a touch, a feathery kiss . . . Rock. His. World. Like this.

"You're shaking."

He swallowed thickly, his erection pulsing madly inside of her, his muscles taut and quivering for release. "No."

"You are. Why are you shaking?"

He locked his arms more firmly around her, hating his body, hating that it wouldn't stop vibrating. "I don't know: you feel good."

She set both hands on his chest and kissed his neck, his ear, his jaw. Sweetly. So sweetly. Her breath fanned out across his flesh, her lips moving softly, her tongue lapping at his sweat-coated flesh.

Into his ear, as she lay there, utterly still, utterly possessed, she breathed, "Move in me."

He almost choked on his breath as he did—his orgasm there, there, threatening to splinter him to the bones.

He slid in deep, fighting the seductive pull of her inner muscles and the delicate torture of those fluttering hands.

He manacled her wrists and forced her arms above her head, ramming into her with mind-jarring force. She cried out, her legs tightening around his hips.

"Every little part of you that you disliked," he said in a rumble, bending his head to take a good, hard look at her, "I will take with my mouth until you love it again."

How did she feel? Seeing those beautiful marred legs, those beautiful thighs, those hips, abused and marked with her pain. He stroked the scar between their bodies, tenderly fingered its raised edges.

She responded with a mewl, not embarrassed now, but aroused by his touch, her sweet, juicy little sex muscles clenching and unclenching around his cock. Her skin was dewy with sweat, tendrils of hair clinging to her temples. She was tight, so wet, so hot, driving him so crazy. He thrust into her again. Both their moans tore into the silence, filling it with ecstasy.

Extracting himself from her and stretching up on one arm to gain leverage, he trailed one hand up the inside of her arm until their palms met. Their fingers laced. "I'll lick every inch of you so you'll know what I think of your body. There will be no doubt in your mind what I think of it, how sexy I think you are." He ducked his head to her heaving breasts and roughly, hungrily, with lips and teeth and tongue, gorged on one puckered, red-swollen nipple.

She let out a whimper that tickled down his spine as he suckled and gasped when he lightly bit. "Don't ever hide from me, ever," he growled.

She wiggled restlessly against his body, goading him with her hips and sending a bolt of lust straight up to his head. "Fill me up again."

He buried his face between the rising curves of her breasts, dreading he was perilously close to losing control. His cock was a burning torch and Paige fit him like a glove, her sexy little pussy excruciatingly snug and welcome.

"Zach. Do it. I beg you."

"I won't last."

He cocked his head to soak the tip of her other breast, swirling his tongue across the rigid pink pearl. He suctioned, the tension in the center of his body heightening at the way she thrust her chest up to him.

"Don't. Don't last." Her sobbing gasps made him impossibly harder. "I'm so excited, I'm hurting."

Everything . . . everything hurts . . .

We hurt because we want each other, Paige.

Groaning, he tested the tender folds between her legs with his fingers, found the channel drenched. His balls contracted with need. A low mewling sound exited her lips when he withdrew from inside her.

Panting, she folded her knees until the heels of her feet were firmly planted on the mattress, opening her up even more. She looped her arms around his neck, holding him to her. "Zach," she urged.

Setting his teeth and striving for control, he established himself in the clinch of her thighs, bracing his weight up on his elbows. Their chests heaved as he gazed into her lust-filled blue eyes.

"You wanted this?" He forced half of his thickened length into the gripping heat of her pussy, inch by inch being tugged and swallowed by her. "Paige? Did you?"

"More."

He thrust fully into her. They cried out together. The pleasure was beyond anything in this realm, intense, consuming.

Aroused to the point of madness, he began to pump for real, losing the battle, losing himself. "Give yourself to me," he pleaded. He kissed the arching column of her neck, using his tongue, his teeth. "Let go, Paige. Let go."

Her nails bit into his shoulders as she held on, the bed creaking faster, her body moving wildly to keep up with his. "Zach."

"Yes, God, yes. Give me everything."

"Zach!" Her exclamation carried to his ears.

And still he pumped. "Am I too big for you, am I hurting you?"

"No, no, don't stop." Her hips swiveled, allowing deeper access, intensifying the pleasure of his long, penetrating entries. "Oh, oh."

She raked her fingers down his back, her nails biting into his ass, urging him farther into the titillating clenches of her pussy, drawing out his pleasure with compact, delicious milking motions.

Zach opened his mouth over hers, delivering a mind-blowing kiss, all the while knowing he wasn't taking her. Paige was taking him. Oh, damn, she was.

Sliding and sliding into her silken heat, he was gone, past the point of stopping. He trailed his lips across her temple and plunged his tongue into her ear, his voice rough and commanding. "Say . . . my name."

"Zachary."

He groaned, pumped. Bliss surged through him, pulsing, fiery, twitching him taut. "Paige."

"Zach."

"You have no idea, *no* idea."

Her head rolled restlessly over the pillow and her back arched. The way her body thrust with his demolished him like an avalanche.

"Ahh, God!" He wrapped her in his arms and increased his pace, fucking together, fucking deeper, faster, harder. "Come with me. Come to heaven with me."

She screamed. He bucked. And they came in a long, sweeping, exhausting orgasm.

CHAPTER 5

PAIGE FELT POWERFUL. Like she could do anything, lift a building or sing opera or fly.

Tucking herself under the covers, she eyed the reason her toes were still tingling and her heart was soaring, appreciating the sight of Zach's glossy tanned backside as he went to clean up. Her nerves quivered at the strong flex of his buttocks as he walked.

Zach.

She felt light-headed and weak, and her hands itched with anxiousness to feel him again. As he emerged from the bathroom and fetched his guns from the chair, he plucked up his jeans from where they'd fallen, as well.

For a moment, she dreaded he'd slip them on—ergo, she must dress, too—but instead he draped them across the back of a chair. A bevy of butterflies fluttered inside her as he returned to her naked. Somber, almost shy, and gloriously, toe-tinglingly naked.

She sat up a little, committing his face to memory; his inky hair rumpled from her hands, his lips fattened and reddened from her mouth, the hint of a beard shadowing his jaw.

He set his guns on the nightstand and plopped down next to her, and her mind raced with wishes and thoughts. Would he kiss her again? Lick her? Bite her? Cuddle?

Aww, he cuddled. And kissed her forehead, her nose,

lingered on her lips as one arm encircled her shoulders. "Sweet. You're so sweet, Paige."

Suppressing a sigh, Paige went willingly as he propped his head against the mirror and pinned her to his side. "So we'd never done that before?" she whispered up at him, feeling exquisite and wonderful.

Smiling tenderly, he swiped the pad of his thumb across the bridge of her nose. "In my dreams."

Hers was a wistful smile. She couldn't resist touching him, couldn't help but notice how *he* couldn't resist trailing his fingers down her arm, either. "Why do you carry two guns?"

He used his free hand to lift one, then the other. "Your baby. Your backup."

She reached out to stroke the cool, hard metal of the one he held out. The smaller gun, not quite black but obscure and gleaming. "Is it . . . loaded?"

"Yeah. But the safety's on, see?" He showed her the little catch, then bounced the gun in one big hand. "Here. You're curious?" She nodded, curled her hand around the grip as Zach trailed her onto his lap. She said, "It's heavy."

His arms enveloped her from behind. He seemed fascinated by a spot behind her ear and teased it lightly with his lips. "Do you want to know how to use one? I could teach you."

She thought of how safe she felt with him, and of how unsafe she would feel tomorrow . . . next week . . . without him. And nodded. "Teach me." *Teach me to kill if I need to.* She glanced past her shoulder as he gently pried the gun away. "I'm a photographer, I should have good aim," she said.

His brows rose—his smile so utterly charming, she felt it tickle the bottom of her feet. He set the gun aside. "A photographer."

She shifted on his lap and stroked his hard face with her fingertips, smiling in return. "And why is that amusing, may I ask?"

Her thumb stroked the plump flesh of his bottom lip first,

and when his smile faded, she leaned in and kissed him. Kissed him as though that firm, ardent mouth were hers. He clamped a hand on her nape and held her to him, making the kiss longer, drawing it out more. "It's not," he rasped. "Amusing. It's perfect. You always had an eye for spotting beauty in things."

An eye for him, she was sure, and goodness, her camera would love him. Would capture the strength in his jawline, the striking black of his eyebrows and lashes. She swung more fully to face him and leisurely traced the scars at his ribs. Even those seemed beautiful, poignant somehow, sleek and pale against his sun-kissed skin. "Ever been shot?"

One large hand heavily petted the top of her head, his fingers leisurely untangling her hair. "Not yet."

She wrinkled her nose at him. "You sound like you expect to be."

He smiled a slow, languorous smile, one that said *It's my job*.

"And this?" She fingered the longer scar, felt him stir against her at her caress.

Both his hands delved into her hair, fingers stroking her scalp. "Unfortunate encounter when I patrolled. Stab wounds, five of them, punctured a lung, it was hell."

A string of goose bumps rushed down the length of her arms. "I'm sorry."

He shrugged. "I wanted it."

Her eyes widened in outrage. "You *wanted* it?"

"I was fucked up."

Touched by his frankness, she ran two fingertips across that mobile mouth as he spoke, her eyes becoming heavy. "Talk to me." She filled her hands with his taut jaw and leaned closer, inhaled the mist of his breath. "Your voice." *I want to take it in me, wrap it around my body, I want to . . . to hear.*

He was quiet at first, no sound audible in the room but the rustle of the sheets as their bodies adjusted. They snuggled deeper under the covers, her body sliding down the length of his until they touched head to toe.

Then he spoke, his voice a velvet wave, rolling thick and dense across her nerves, sending a melting sensation down her legs. "The first time I saw you, it had been raining. I'd just been admitted and was coming out of the principal's office, and you were rushing down the hall, trying not to be late."

His hands caressed along her body and his voice, his words, reached a thirsty, intricate part of her that seemed to greedily cling to each one. "You were soaked, your books almost slipping from your grasp. And then you saw me. And you stopped. For the longest time you just stared at me. And I stared back and thought, 'God, is there a prettier sight than this girl?'" There was a soft silence, then his hot, wet tongue stroked heatedly into her ear. "I wanted to lick you dry."

Lying against six feet two inches of this man, Paige could too easily picture the devastating eighteen-year-old Zach must have been, standing tall and gorgeous in the middle of a school hall, staring at her with those weakening eyes of his. She quietly marveled, "I must have thought, 'God, please let me have this gorgeous green-eyed boy all to myself.'"

He chuckled, and it was a throaty, humming sound that wrapped around her like a blanket. "You had me at 'Oh. You must be the new transfer.'"

She smiled against him, but she did not want him to stop, wanted his words in her ears. His voice was all the things you would hush to hear—a whispering breeze, a soothing creek, a haunting black thunderstorm . . .

Snuggling closer, she laid her ear on his chest, just over the steady, provocative pounding of his heartbeat. "Tell me more about me and you."

He stroked her back as he did, his words resonating in his chest under her ear. "Fridays you used to stay over at your friend Francine's . . ." Her entry felt sensitive after the sex, and even then, she was teeming wet, felt his hardness surge against her tummy as he remembered. And his voice, richer still, darker, deeper. "But you weren't really with Francine—you were sleeping with me."

The thick, long staff between their bodies began to pulse with heat, and a dense arousal coated his speech. "We kissed for hours. Until the sun came up. We touched, ate, talked, didn't sleep. We parted every Saturday morning, trembling with wanting each other."

She shivered. Her breasts throbbed. She sought out his mouth, blindly, and he gave it to her. They caught, burned, blended. Then his words misted across her face, and his voice. God, his rich, delicious *voice*.

"Every time, we kissed a little longer. Touched more, petted heavier." He stroked a finger along the back of her arm, his voice changing, becoming terser and gruffer with longing. "I lived for those moments, when you were in my arms and I was drinking from your lips, filling my hands with your breasts, your little hands all over me." He fisted her hair in his hand, heaved her up, and kissed her firmly, possessively. "We kissed at school, but it drove me insane not to talk to you. I couldn't touch you, couldn't hold you, couldn't be with you."

Her voice broke. "Why?"

"My father. Your father." A thousand questions tumbled in her mind. She wanted to know everything and at the same time, she *didn't*. "We were watched at school, and I was ordered to stay away. But there was old Mel's closet—Mel was the janitor. And we hid between classes and kissed until our mouths were swollen." He seized and enjoyed her lips until her chest felt like exploding, too. "Nothing, *nobody* could keep me away from you."

Her lashes rose, and his incandescent green eyes trapped her, sucking her into their depths, spinning her within the whirlpool of her needs. *His* needs. He lowered his hand, scraped his knuckles across a breast that had become accessible when she shifted.

"Any time, *every* time you'd let me, I'd latch on to this little peak until you were writhing with pleasure, screaming 'Zachary.'"

She shivered, got wetter, hotter, her rising temperature

causing her to desperately press her breast into his hand. "I wanted you," she whispered. *I still want you.*

The look he leveled on her blazed with heat. "You loved me, Paige." The words buffeted her with a blow of searing pain, mingled with yearning and longing and regrets. That someone remembered what she couldn't drove the sharpest, longest dagger into her chest.

Because she should remember this, too.

A choked noise darted out of her as his hand turned, engulfing her flesh. His fingers teased, tweaked, plucked the nipple, and his timbre dropped another notch. "We wanted to make love."

She could picture the eighteen-year-old girl in the picture, a good girl, full of hesitation, and too easily conjured up the isolated, enigmatic new boy who'd been patient with her. "And?" she softly prodded.

In a startlingly easy move, he flipped her onto her back and slid down her length, easing her knees apart. "And I waited."

Moisture pooled between her legs. He knew her. She knew him. Somehow it was as if she'd been born for those hands whisking up the inside of her knees, for his hands to trek across her skin.

God. What had she found here? What had she *missed* her whole life?

His palm stroked languorously up her left thigh. Deliciously callused, the hands of a man who used them. Paige had forgotten about her scars, but at his gentle handling, she burned bright red with embarrassment. "Please come back here."

"Shh. Baby, shh."

He nuzzled her stomach, both hands kneading her thighs. They weren't lovely, her scars. Despite what he'd said. They were painful to see and had been painful to wear, but suddenly they knew his lips, and they became another part of her body. Another part he could kiss.

"Poor baby." He kissed her scars from tip to tip, side to side, one at a time. "Poor baby."

His hands slipped under her body and cradled her cheeks as he ducked his head. His nose nuzzled the tender fluff between her legs. Then he expertly parted her folds open with his thumbs. "Poor"—his tongue sampled—"wet"—he licked again—"baby."

Pleasure jolted up her spine. "Zach!"

"I'd tasted only what had coated my fingers all those years ago, but this . . ." He made a pass across the swollen glistening lips and, eyes closing, repeated several passes until he stopped at her center, lapped, and melded his mouth with that part of her. "I could drink you up, Paige. I could live on you, eat and eat and eat your sweetness all day."

She arched her head in delirium, gasping, "Oh God, when you speak I go crazy." Sexy, sexy voice. Wicked, wicked tongue. Dirty, dirty words.

Her hips moved to his mouth, her hands grasping his head, plucking and pulling at his satiny hair. "Zach. I want you up here." As he came up, he kissed the tip of each breast before he readied himself, his cock glowing pink, his bronzed skin coated with perspiration.

Her mouth watered. "Strawberry," she said, and spread her legs apart as he lowered himself above her. What did Zach taste like under the strawberry? What did his skin taste like there, and the moisture that came from him?

His hips sank between her thighs. As their heated flesh collided, her thoughts scattered. He smiled down at her, caressing her face with one hand as he trapped her ankle with the other and guided her leg around his hips.

She cried out anxiously, going rigid with anticipation, her leg tightening reflexively around him. "Oh God!"

He rolled his hips, prodding her with his cock. "Shh. Ease up. It's just me here."

He entered slowly, his hand opening on her cheek, pushing his thumb past her lips and beyond. She made a sound of relief as he filled her, latching on to his thumb, tasting it with the same fervor she'd wanted to taste that larger, more mesmerizing part of him, and eagerly swiveled her hips to take more of him inside of her.

He bent and caught her earlobe between his lips, savoring that little tidbit as he began to move. "Just me, Paige."

Me.

Me . . .

Me!

CHAPTER 6

"THE EVENING of the accident, Paige."

The day had come. Sooner than she'd wanted. Or perhaps later than it should have.

Her mother had had her reservations about "this kind of assistance," but Paige hoped now she'd understand. That Mom would know she had to do this, that she owed it to herself, to her dad, to try.

She lay woodenly in a lounge chair—the sort you'd find at a psychiatrist's office—inside the O'Neills' home, where Sue Ellen had her practice. Their house was a small castle, in Paige's opinion, furnished so tastefully, with sweeping draperies and artworks gracing each and every wall, that she'd at first been taken aback by such a lavish setting. How much would this woman charge?

Now she stared up at the crystal chandelier suspended from the ceiling. The crystals sparkled prettily with the light. Both her hands were fisted over her stomach; which, by the way, didn't stop churning. "Not yet," she gently pleaded to the middle-aged woman.

Relaxation seemed impossible at this point. Her senses were on high alert. She was aware of everything, aware of Zach in the other room, of Zach *listening*, Zach watching through the cameras . . .

Over a long console behind the hypnotist, a trio of incense sticks burned. The room smelled faintly of cedarwood.

"You aren't allowing yourself to relax, Paige, you must let *go*."

Paige nodded listlessly.

The lieutenant's wife, Sue Ellen, had the pinched look of someone with little patience, or of someone working under dire stress. Her voice was perplexingly flat, and this somehow increased Paige's anxiety.

"Close your eyes now," the woman said evenly, crossing her legs and linking her hands. "We will try this again."

"Again. Yes."

Paige tried easing her muscles. Zach had explained that the "procedure" had to take place with her in the room alone with the hypnotist.

The moment she had been guided into the room, Zach—strong, armed, delicious Zach—had been dialoguing outside with Lieutenant O'Neill, a bald, stocky man who looked to have spent the last couple of years without sleep.

"My husband has checked the perimeter," Sue Ellen had soothed. "This is a safe neighborhood. And don't worry, the men will be watching next door. Both rooms are set up specifically to enable forensic hypnosis. There are cameras in ours, and a monitor in the other. This allows the detectives to watch and tape your testimony."

"O-okay," she'd said.

Paige, you don't have to do this . . .

Zach's words this morning danced in her head. She'd answered, *I want to.*

And she did! But goodness, she was nervous.

"Ready, Paige?"

Next door, she told herself. He was next door.

"Ready," she breathed.

ZACH SAT SO STILL before the TV screen he could be just another of the sculptures in the room.

On a chair next to his, O'Neill lowered his soda can, clearing his throat. "Rivers, perhaps it's better if you—"

Zach lifted one hand that effectively silenced him. "No, no, no. I need to hear this."

He needed to hear what she'd been through. He needed to hear her remember him and know that he had not made her up, that his entire life was not centered on something that could never be. He needed to know what had happened—how, when, and why *the fuck* he hadn't been able to protect her.

He ran a palm down his hot face, then clasped his hands together in front of him and leaned on his elbows. Had she seen the bastard? What had he said to her? Done to her? Fuck.

"All right, Paige, so relax."

"Is Zach . . . is Detective Rivers listening?"

Oh, baby. Oh, *sweetheart, I'm here.*

"Yes. And Lieutenant O'Neill."

Zach schooled his expression into one of detachment, aware of O'Neill scrutinizing his profile. Damned if he'd let the ruthless bastard see what Paige did to him. Damned if he'd let himself tear apart in front of *him*.

"Let's start again, shall we?"

START AGAIN, YES. Paige nodded, appeased, and shifted on the old chair, trying not to notice that it felt as if the soft seat were swallowing her. Her eyes kept sailing across the room, distracted by all the adornments on the wall.

"Eyes closed, Paige."

Swallowing, Paige stretched her legs out until her toes rested at the very edge of the chaise, and attempted to concentrate.

Sue Ellen told her—no, she ordered, really—to get comfortable. So she "did."

They started with her breath. Paige inhaled. Paige exhaled. *Releasing tension and anxiety. Allowing your body and your mind to relax.* Her mind whirled and whirled.

All around making love with Zach.

The memory of his taut, strained face as he came made her weak inside. Zach probably hadn't realized as he drove here—deeply immersed in his own thoughts—that as Paige sat unspeaking beside him, she'd been kissing his lips and his hot, hard mouth had been pillaging hers, and that huge, thrusting part of his had been pushing and pushing into the depths of her.

Zachary Rivers, I am addicted to you!

In a solid, monotone voice, Sue Ellen began to count down. She started at ten . . . *Feeling your muscles relaxing . . . welcoming a deep sleep . . .*

I want you to visualize looking across a deep blue ocean. Above the water the fishes form a number ten . . . then skim apart to form a nine . . .

Release your fears, Paige . . . You are free . . .

Release your thoughts . . .

When you hear the words "deep sleep," you will come to this place of relaxation and open your mind . . .

Out of respect for the process, Paige kept her eyes firmly shut, but inwardly resisted opening her mind to . . . to her. To a videotape.

But she wanted, oh, how dearly she wanted, to give Zach what he must need. A name. A *lead*. Find this evil bastard. Give justice to a man who'd dedicated his life to it.

Sue Ellen began to question her, and finally opening her hands on her tummy, Paige relaxed a little, trying unaccountably to open her mind to herself only.

"Deep sleep . . . deep sleep . . . Think back, Paige," the balmy voice urged, but Paige now only half listened to what she said. Her body singularly limp and heavy, she was delving into that big black nothingness, surprised to no longer feel the accompanying anxiety. "First, let us go back to a moment of your life you remember fondly."

Hmm. So easy. Lying awake last night. Feeling wonderful. With her body tucked into the immense, sculptured form of Zachary's.

"Deep sleep, Paige . . ."

And he had lain awake with her. With those large, safe arms around her waist. Every once in a while resting his lips on her temple, her cheek, her shoulder.

For the longest time you just stared at me. And I stared back and thought, "God, is there a prettier sight than this girl . . ."

Wondrously, magically, a thought fluttered down on her in response to his. It was like being hit by a raindrop, wet and spreading across your skin until you were soaked.

In that instant she knew exactly what she'd thought as she stared across the hall at that bronzed, dark-haired boy. And then dozens of thoughts were raining down on her. Her mind was giving her these gifts, beautiful, surreal, so incredibly vivid she gasped with the wonder of reliving them.

Her first kiss. Her first real kiss. *Zach's* kiss.

She'd been robbed of it, too. Now it was hers. Her kiss once more.

Fiery. Passionate. A kiss after days and days of wanting, days of covert glances, of brushing shoulders as they passed the halls, of catching each other watching.

She'd been on a hall pass and the corridor had been empty when he appeared, coming the opposite way. They stared. Their paces slowed. They halted. Then he grabbed her wrists, pinned her against Penny Morgan's locker, and kissed her heart out.

Her eyes stung at the memory. Her throat worked to dislodge the clog of emotion in her trachea, because God, yes, she remembered it all. She remembered love. Being loved by him. Loving him innocently. Completely.

"Tell us where you are, Paige. Tell us . . ."

Paige scarcely heard, because it had been years since her memories talked to her, and the sound of them was the sweetest thing she'd ever heard.

This was not the reason she was here. She knew they wanted something else from her, and yet she was drowning in her own memories, thoughts and thoughts swirling in places that had been empty before.

"Zachary Rivers is staring at you, Paige."

"Well, well, look at that blush when you tell her!"

"What are you guys talking about? Paige can't even talk to Zach Rivers, Francine."

"Trista, seriously. Get real. And Paige, swear to God, if Zach bumps your shoulder one more time as some lame

excuse to touch you and straighten you up and you go all blushy like you do I'm going to slap the both of you!"

Her friends, Paige thought tenderly. What were they doing now? She hadn't told them then that every day, she and Zach kissed their mouths red. She couldn't tell them that Zach was everything—everything—to her.

And she'd just about had it with hiding.

The halls were bustling with students, but suddenly determined, Paige squared her shoulders and walked up to Zach as he shut his locker. To his broad back, she whispered, "I love you."

He stiffened. It took him forever to turn around, and then he stared at her as though she were a bizarre creature from another planet. It seemed that everyone else stared, too.

"What are you doing?" he asked. Just a whisper. In his eyes, she could see storms, she could see he wanted to grab her and say the words back to her. But he was far more careful lately than she.

The bell rang.

As soon as the halls were clearing, he dragged her down the hall and into the tiny, shaded interior of the janitor's closet, and shut the door. "That was reckless, baby, reckless." But he grabbed her ass, boosted her up and against him, and pushed her lips open with his, plowing greedily into her mouth. "Christ, what am I going to do with you?"

She cupped his strong cheek. "Love me." Her smile faltered on her face. "I've been waiting and hoping and praying for you to say it, so then I thought—"

"I love you." He braced her against the door and kissed her with such rampant passion she quaked. "I love you, Paige. I'm crazy about you. Crazy. Crazy. Crazy."

They kissed crazy crazy crazily, and when he tore free, Paige said tearfully, "I don't care what my father says. I don't care what anyone says, I want to—"

A sound out in the halls broke them apart.

Zach set her on her feet, briskly kissed her upturned

forehead and smoothed her hair down her shoulders. "But-ton up your sweater."

She frowned and looked down. "I'm not wearing a sweater."

Ahh! she realized. He was teasing. Because sometimes she was *wearing a sweater, and "button up your sweater" meant "people are coming, they could see us, they could catch us. Beware."*

The story of their young lives: Paige "buttoning up her sweater."

She sighed dejectedly at that, suddenly wanting to have a good, long cry, she felt so frustrated. "Zach, I don't want to button up my sweater anymore."

"Tell us what you see, Paige, where are you? What are you doing?"

Her heart thundered in her breast as a marvelous exhila-ration swept over her.

"I remember," she said hoarsely, aware that her cheeks were getting wet, that her voice was highly unstable, "I re-member a boy." *What she was really saying was, Zach, I re-member you.*

"Who is this boy, Paige?"

She ached to see his face. That stern, chiseled face with those steady green eyes. Was he listening? Was his heart pounding as hard as hers? "His name is Zachary Rivers."

Zachary Rivers, are you listening to me?

SHE WAS TEARING *him apart with her words.*

Do you know what last night with you meant to me?

Oh, fuck, he could tear down the walls just to crush her against him.

"YOU GAVE ME my first kiss," Paige whispered, unaware that she'd begun talking to him as she wiped away her tears. "And when we were crammed into the projection room to watch the JFK assassination, you stood that whole hour beside me, and the backs of our hands touched. You stood so still, and I stood so still, so that nobody noticed when you hooked your pinky around mine."

And you smelled so damned good, I couldn't breathe.

"PAIGE. PAIGE, I must ask. The day . . ."

"And," Paige added, laughing between her tears, "when I visited the arcade, you thrust me up on your shoulders and taught me how to slam-dunk. And . . . you're a horrible, horrible liar, Zach. Because I didn't slam-dunk that ball at all. But you always were so gentle, always said nice things to me."

Nah, you dunked it for sure. I remember.

Zach remembered all of it.

"Paige baby, throw the ball."

"Don't drop me!"

"I got you. Now throw the ball, just slam it in there, into the hoop."

"O-okay." Straddling his shoulders and clutching the sides of his neck with the insides of her slim, firm thighs, Paige raised her arms and shoved the ball, all delicate and femininelike, into the hoop.

The ball bounced at his feet. Chuckling to himself, Zach lifted her from his shoulders and, in one clean swoop, set her on her feet.

"That's a slam dunk?" she asked.

At the risk of every basketball player in the country lynching him, Zach said, "Yeah. You slam-dunked that one."

And then, because Zach couldn't resist those wide, cobalt-blue eyes, because he'd been thinking of her night, and morning, and afternoon, and because these stolen moments were all Zach had, all he was allowed, to be with her, he hauled her up against his body, whispered, "I adore you," and covered her lips with his.

And then they were kissing in a way nobody, in school or out of it, would ever suspect Zach and Paige kissed.

* * *

"PAIGE. ABOUT the accident."

"You hated when I cried," she said hoarsely. "You'd start cursing and at the same time getting all cuddly on me."

No, sweetheart, I don't hate it . . . well shit, maybe I do.

"PAIGE. THE DAY your father died," Sue Ellen tried. And for the first time Paige realized the hypnotist's voice wasn't steady anymore.

Fear skewered into her heart. Daddy.

"Tell us about the accident."

The accident that killed her strong, upstanding, stern dad, who rarely gave hugs but loved to give lectures.

The horrifying scene darted past her mind all of a sudden, stumbling forth in flashes. Red Camaro . . . forcing us off the road . . . herself screaming, screaming, screaming, and then . . .

A stillness.

Daddy gulping for air. Talking to her.

"There's a false back in his bookshelf," Paige rushed, "in his study. Behind Oscar Wilde's *The Picture of Dorian Gray.* The driver was driving a red Camaro. He threw us off the road. Daddy said—" She broke off, Dad's words distressing to remember. He'd been sputtering blood. Dying beside her. Saying he loved her. He was sorry. He'd been wrong. Oh, Daddy.

"A red Camaro, you say? Whose red Camaro?"

Paige went numb, her mind stopping blank.

"Whose red Camaro, do you recognize this car?"

Her heart seemed to wilt inside her. Her stomach caved in on itself, and as a wave of nausea struck her, she brokenly, wretchedly admitted, "Zach's."

THE REVELATION slammed him with the force of a bazooka.

"Zach's?" Zach dumbly repeated.

"She said Zach's," O'Neill stated.

Bewildered, Zach put his head in his hands, swamped with confusion, torn by the memory of her, broken, weeping, in that little hospital bed, and suddenly he was shaking to his knees with a rampant need for violence. A red Camaro. His old Camaro. *"Fuck."*

He was beyond speaking, beyond pissed, beyond anything human.

Someone. Some asshole. Had used his car. To kill the judge. To nearly kill Paige.

The rage was fulminating, eating at his liver.

Zach wanted to *kill*.

He wanted to find this bastard, take his gun out, and ram it down his throat so hard and fast, the guy would eat each and every bullet he spewed into his mouth. He'd gotten glimpses of this man inside him—one with a death wish, one with a streak of rebelliousness, one that was his father's *son*, and now he was afraid of him.

Of what he would do if he came face-to-face with this bastard who'd ruined his life, taken Paige away from him, killed her father.

FUCK!

Regarding Zach in distaste as he crushed his empty soda can against his chest, O'Neill raised one eyebrow. "You always did have a motive, didn't you?"

Zach scowled, his gut twisting so violently he was sure inside of him, deep where it most hurt a man, he was bleeding. "The car was reported stolen," he ground out, rising to his feet. "Check your goddamn files."

"Her mother once took out a restraining order against you, Detective," he pointed out, and tossed the can into the wastebasket. "Or should I say, Stalker?"

His blood curdled in his veins. For a moment he wanted to smack his CO's face in.

Clinging onto the few threads of control he had left, he said, "I'd never hurt her. All I did was try to see her."

"It was Zach's red Camaro. And was Zach driving his Camaro?" Sue Ellen asked through the screen, more demanding. "Was he the driver, Paige? Is he the killer? Is Zachary Rivers the killer?"

Paige covered her ears, releasing a low, anxious sound.

Wide-eyed, Zach watched her. Her sudden silence, her hesitation to deny this, was so wrenching he could barely stand on his feet.

"Is he the killer, Paige?"

She spoke in a hiss, "I don't know!"

Floored, Zach fell into the chair.

She didn't know. She wasn't sure. Did she think it was *him*? Had her memories been distorted? Corrupted? Did she believe he would ever, ever, do anything but want to love and cherish and protect her?

"Paige," Sue Ellen soothed. "Don't be afraid. You're safe here. I know it may hurt to remember because you trusted him. Didn't you? You loved him?"

Her head jerked up and down in a mockery of a "yes," her hands cradling herself as if her brain were bursting. She was weeping so hard Zach became enraged. He wanted to slam his fists into a wall, tear into that room, and demand that this charade stop.

And then she broke through his anger, his sanity, his already-shattering composure, and whispered, as though she only meant for him to hear, "Zach." More like a plea, like when she'd called him last night, when he was inside her, their bodies entwined.

An awful suspicion took hold of him—and the back of his neck pricked with alarm. He approached the monitor with a harsh, ominous scowl. His chest felt crammed with foreboding even as his heart began to pound. *Protect, protect, protect.*

"Your wife has taken this a little too far, Lieutenant." His hands opened at his sides, and his fingers tingled, for her, for his guns. "Want to tell me why?"

Lips thinning in distaste, O'Neill stopped recording. "Not looking so good for you, Detective," he said with asphalt-dull eyes.

"SO IT WAS ZACHARY Rivers who killed your father?"

Paige couldn't stand it. The woman's words were ringing in her head, deafening her ears, robbing her eyes . . .

Her stomach recoiled in protest, and her skin crawled in denial. *No.* It wasn't Zach. Couldn't, wouldn't be, *wasn't.* Why did she ask? Why did she insist?

If she weren't writhing in her own pain she'd be flinging herself at the woman, screeching out, *Liar!*

"It was him, Paige?"

God, would she shut up!

She scrambled in her mind to get a look at the driver, saw his face only feet away as the car rammed into them, and then raised her voice until she yelled at the hypnotist in return. "No!" she cried. "It's not Zach. It's not! It's . . ." Who was it? "The driver was . . . he wore a stocking over his face but he was bald. And Dad said there was evidence in an envelope, and that I should get it to the district attorney. He said that . . ." *O'Neill is dirty.*

Her body tensed. Her entire system jolted back to full consciousness. O'Neill.

Bald. Stone-faced O'Neill.

If you dare open your mouth I swear to God I'm going to break your boyfriend into little pieces. And then I'm going to break you.

Zach was with him.

"What does your father say, Paige? Who did you see?"

Emergency alarm bells clanged inside her head. She'd lost Zach once. She'd lost him once to this man. She would not do it again. No no no *no!*

The camera. It was honed in on her. Zach could see her. But O'Neill watched, too. How could she signal? Let him know the danger? Oh God oh God oh *God.*

Her mind raced. Her blood was rushing so fast inside her she thought she'd collapse. She could barely hear her own words through the cacophony of her roaring heartbeat. Striving to appear dazed when in fact she had never felt more alert, all she could think of saying was, "I should button up my sweater." A heartbeat. Two. God, he didn't remember, he didn't understand. "I should button up—"

Wood splintered as the door came crashing down.

Zach filled the doorway, gun drawn, and Paige would never forget the wild, love-filled look in his eyes.

She wanted to fling herself at him, say, "I love you! I've been quietly fighting to come back to you!" but she was paralyzed by her terror.

Sob catching in her throat, she pointed toward the figure of O'Neill looming behind him, now raising something gloomy and glinting to Zach's head. "It's him."

CHAPTER 7

THE MELLOW OVERHEAD lights dimmed in Zach's eyes as if a cloud had passed over them. Dread, ice-freaking-cold and paralyzing dread, slammed over him.

O'Neill.

Lieutenant O'Neill.

Every face he'd seen that day in the hospital seven years ago flashed across Zach's mind—mocking him.

He had seen Paige's friends. Her mother. The doctors. Nurses. The cops. The old lead investigator, Lieutenant O'Neill, who'd interrogated Leticia Avery that day along with two other detectives, had been there.

Son of a bitch! No wonder O'Neill had never allowed him to reopen the case. He'd never let *anyone* reopen it because he'd killed the judge.

And he'd tried to kill Paige.

Her skin had lost all color, and her eyes were wide and pleading on his. "Zach," she said in a strangled whisper, horrified by the sight of O'Neill's gun jammed into the back of his head.

Zach stared at her, a thousand conflicting emotions rushing one after the other.

They'd been trying to frame him. All those years ago and now. Using the one thing, the one thing, Zach gave a shit about. Using *her* against him.

Once, he'd had a death wish. Once, he'd physically welcomed any pain that could even reflect the pain he'd had inside him. But at this moment, when he had never in his life wanted to live so badly, he was stunned by the force of his fear. Fear of failing her, fear of losing her, fear that after O'Neill shot him, she was next.

"Drop the gun."

Fuck.

His Glock clattered to the floor.

Sue Ellen jumped to her feet, shaking her head as she clasped her hands to her chest. "Please, no! Larry, you said no one would get hurt!"

"Sue Ellen, yes. This can still work." O'Neill shot the distraught woman a desperate smile. "He did it. He has no alibi, and we caught part of her testimony on tape. His car was used to run the judge off the road. Tangible evidence. I know where that sucker is hidden. He killed the judge, and when she remembered, he shot her. I had to shoot him to defend you and myself. It can work!"

Sue Ellen cried, "Larry, you said you only wanted to know how much she knew, for me to help confuse her, nothing else!"

"They can *talk,* Sue Ellen."

"So what if they *do*!" Anguished, Sue Ellen covered her face with her hands, her cry muffled by her palms. "It's gone on long enough!"

O'Neill pressed the barrel of the gun harder against the back of Zach's head. "Nice and slow, Rivers, lean over and take out the backup piece and drop it."

"Ease up, asshole," Zach growled as he leaned down and slowly withdrew his backup piece from the ankle holster.

He could dive and try to shoot O'Neill as he rolled. He could swing around and knock the fucker down, but dammit, he could not risk Paige getting hit in the crossfire.

He let the weapon fall on the plush taupe carpet, his eyes flickering to hers. Her face was a mask—surprisingly contained. Christ. His brave, sweet Paige.

"Drop everything else," O'Neill instructed.

Zach reached behind him. He extracted the tape recorder

and gingerly pressed REC before he dropped it. A small pocket knife followed. His cell phone. Dropped it.

"Now, turn around and back away. It won't do for you to get shot in the back."

Zach did so with gradual, prolonged steps that kept Paige firmly out of view behind him. In his crisp gray suit, O'Neill remained thin-lipped and stoic, completely emotionless except for the determination in his eyes.

"Away from her!" he barked, waving the weapon. "Off to the side."

Zach docilely moved to the side. And kept moving. Dragging that piercing brown gaze with him and away from Paige. Searching for calm. Calm. Calm. So he could fucking think.

O'Neill picked up Zach's piece from the floor and aimed it at Paige with his left hand, keeping his other weapon trained on Zach.

Paige's cell phone bleeped and O'Neill's eyes shot to her.

"Detective Nordstrom is on his way, Lieutenant," she said in a tremulous but defiant voice, her chin up at an angle. "He knows about the papers. I just sent a text."

Amazed, Zach looked at her. She was holding up her cell phone, waving it in the air, and the screen was lit. And she appeared . . . damn, quite haughty and rebellious all of a sudden.

"You're bluffing." O'Neill's voice was adamant, laced with bitterness. "You just wouldn't die, would you? Oh no, you had to come back, didn't you!"

Zach said, taking a step in his direction spreading out his arms, "No way out, O'Neill. Nordstrom may already have those papers in his hand."

"Is that a fact?" His smile was sharp and cutting as he took a step forward, his aim holding. "The last man who got his hands on those papers died, Detective."

"Larry, no!" Sue Ellen screamed, sliding behind her fancy carved wood chair, gripping its back until her knuckles were white. "You can't do this! Not in our house!"

Zach met Paige's concerned expression for a moment,

trying to send a message that said . . . hell, he didn't know. *Hang on, baby.*

This bastard had already hurt Paige more than Zach could bear. And he hadn't been there to hold her, help her, save her. But he was here now. Fuck it, he was here *now*.

Hot, heady adrenaline flooding his veins, he gauged the distance between him and that bastard. Five steps. One second. Still not fast enough, dammit. His backup gun was on the floor, but it was no match for two guns already drawn. Even if he could avoid getting hit, Paige might die. No choice but one.

Stall for time.

"So the judge was on to you," he said, fishing for answers.

Sue Ellen bit.

"His work is his life . . ." she choked, tears streaming down her face. "He would not hand in his badge for anything."

"Shut up, Sue Ellen," O'Neill said desperately.

"No!" She glared at him before looking at Zach again. "It's been going on for years. Car theft . . . robberies."

"Does it bring you comfort, Sue Ellen?" Zach pressed, arching his brow. "That your husband killed a man so you could continue living like this?" His arms spread to encompass their lavish surroundings.

"Silence! Rivers killed the judge, and that is that!" O'Neill roared, glowering at his wife. "He'll either meet with his maker or meet up with his dad in prison. Like father, like son. The old man was reckless. Vehicular manslaughter, killed a whole family."

Zach could envision his fingers quite clearly pressing into the bastard's trachea, wrapping around his throat, squeezing, squeezing, squeezing the air out of his lungs.

"You're right," Zach said in an even, casual tone. "Dad's in jail for reckless vehicular manslaughter. Now try me for reckless, Lieutenant."

O'Neill narrowed his eyes on him. "Leave the room, Sue Ellen," he crisply commanded.

Gasping, Sue Ellen pushed away from the chair. "Larry, I won't let you do this."

"Goddammit, woman, leave!"

The instant O'Neill's aim on Paige strayed and his angry wife started toward him, Zach took his chance. He yelled, "Get down!" and charged. He slammed into him with his entire weight, grappling to unarm him, but before he succeeded he heard the blast of two gunshots.

He jerked violently on impact. Pain seared his shoulder, and an eerie opaque light exploded in his eyes. He stumbled back a step. His vision blurred. The room faded into shadows. *Motherfucker . . .*

His legs gave. He sucked the air for oxygen as a sticky wetness began spreading across his shirt.

"No." O'Neill scrambled away. "Sue Ellen!"

"Paige!" Hissing in frustration over not being able to see, Zach found the cold metal of his backup and curled his fingers around the grip as he got up to his knees, attempting to focus. "Baby, talk to me. You all right? *Fuck.*"

"Sue Ellen!" O'Neill screamed.

"I'm fine . . ." Paige whispered. But she did not sound fine; she sounded shaky and frightened and far away.

Panic ate at him, his sight a black and gray blur. But his hand was steady, his gun ready, aiming at . . . just aiming all over the place. Hot in his hand. "Paige, talk to me. Where is he? Twelve o'clock? Two o'clock? Where?"

"One o'clock! I think. Dammit, I *don't know.*"

Forcing his gaze on the blurry figure merging with a smaller one and straining to focus, Zach finally managed to hone in on O'Neill.

"Don't shoot!" Paige cried. "He's unarmed. He . . . he has her in his arms. He shot her." Her soft, sweet voice traveled from a different direction. Coming closer to him. Tearing up into a sob. "Zach, you're bleeding."

It took a moment to bring her to focus.

God, no, she was *crying.* Her cheeks were flushed, her lower lip quaking uncontrollably. What he saw in her eyes—so damned beautiful to see once more. *She still loves me.* For a moment he thought he'd pass out when she slowly folded to her knees before him. His world tilted.

"Yes, shoot, Rivers!" O'Neill sobbed. "Do it."

Zach jerked his attention back to him, his finger hot on the trigger, lips pulled back into a fierce, teeth-gritting snarl. "I'll do it, asshole, don't fucking invite me!"

"No!" Paige cried. "He killed his wife! She's . . . she's dead. He's going to jail." Weepy blue eyes sought out his, and her hands shook with indecision as they hovered above his chest. "Zach, you're . . ." She made an awful little sound. "You're *shot*!"

Screaming with rage, O'Neill dropped the limp figure in his arms and charged for Paige. "Bitch! It was supposed to be you, not her!" He lugged her up by the hair with an angry grunt and violently smashed her forehead against the wall.

Blood burst across the tapestry.

Stumbling to his feet, Zach roared, "Son of a . . . !" In a breath-clogging move, he wrapped his numbed, blood-caked arm around O'Neill's thick neck and wrenched the bastard's shiny bald head around. He pressed the weapon to his temple. "Let go of her!"

O'Neill growled and pulled Paige's head back for another slam. The instant Zach heard her terrified scream, he gave a brutal jerk and pulled the trigger. Pop!

O'Neill crashed to the floor. Paige landed flaccid under him.

Cursing, Zach rolled the man's lifeless body off hers. Pain exploded along his shoulder and arm as he gently eased her away from the bastard's prone body. He dragged her limp figure across the floor, leaving a trail of fresh blood across the carpet.

He lifted his cell phone painfully from the floor and called 911, code officer down. See if the cruisers didn't come *screeching*.

Blood continued soaking his left shoulder, hot and wet and never-ending. Clasping Paige's limp body against his right side, he shifted until he reclined on the wall, grunting at the pain. "Paige." He gathered her closer with his one good arm, his trembling hand awkwardly searching for pulse. He found it. Quick and sure, pushing into his fingers.

She was unconscious. A bright red gash raced up her forehead and her nose was dripping. A trail of blood streaked down the corner of her mouth. He rocked her, making a strange, animallike noise. "Baby."

"He's dead?"

His breath tore out of him as her lids opened. "Oh sweetheart, yes. Hang on. Hang on."

Her warmth seeped into him, and his chest flooded with something other than blood, something not mushy but strong and steady and loyal and hers. Always.

Hers.

Her eyes shone with tears as she gazed up at him and he could feel his own burn with emotion. If he'd lost her . . .

If he'd fucking *lost* her again . . .

She reached up to gingerly caress his jaw but her hand fell, her face scrunching up at the sight of his crimson-soaked chest.

"Zach," she murmured. A sigh shuddered out of her lips. "Zach Rivers. I knew . . . I saw you and I knew . . . you were my love."

"Am I, Paige? *Am I?*"

"Yes."

"Oh Christ." He was afraid to hurt her, tried to be careful, but he could not stop holding her, rocking her, smoothing her hair away from her damp, pale face. "Everything you said." His fingers shook on her face. "It tore me apart listening. I love you. I want to have babies with you, baby. I want to buy you a house." He kissed her lips, rocked her harder. "Would you like that? Hmm? To be with me? To be my wife? I promise we'll do everything we couldn't do before and more of what we could."

She murmured, "How lovely," and drifted away, her lashes resting on her cheekbones.

Sirens wailed outside and his brows shot up in surprise. That was even faster than he'd expected. Within seconds,

Cody and his tie crashed into the room, gun drawn, eyes bouncing the walls, settling finally on them. "You two okay?"

The rest of Zach's team burst onto the scene. A dozen detectives, all of them homicide, guns drawn, badges flashing. Within seconds they found the corpses, prone on the blood-soaked carpet. Not looking as fine as their surroundings.

As Cody maneuvered to where he and Paige were slumped against each other, Zach gazed into her face. "I thought you were bluffing."

"So did O'Neill." She grinned weakly.

"An ambulance is on its way," Cody said, eyeing them both with grim solemnity. "Rivers, you're a lucky man."

"I know." Zach closed his eyes, then stared down at Paige Avery and placed a kiss on her blood-soaked lips. "I know."

CHAPTER 8

HER NAME WAS . . .

Beep.

Paige Avery.

Beep.

Her name was Paige Avery and she was twenty-five years old. Daughter of Thomas and Leticia Avery. Born in Phoenix, Arizona. Had a cat named Whiskers who ate nothing but tuna, and a degree from the Art Institute of Seattle.

Her name was Paige Avery and she was terribly in love.

"Sir, you can't be in here! You should be in your room. Where's your IV?"

The bed creaked, and suddenly she was surrounded with the scent, the solidness, the delicious familiar heat, of one Zach Rivers climbing into her hospital bed.

Her lashes fluttered open.

She gasped at the mesmerizing sight of him, shifting to his side so he didn't fall over the edge of the tiny bed. He held her against him with one arm and drew her gently to his chest. A bandage covered his left shoulder. Vaguely she wondered why he got to wear his clothes, and *she* a plasticky blue robe.

He'd been shot and he was still so gorgeous, his expression terribly concerned and his eyes . . .

They shone down on her like beacons.

"Zach, your shoulder," she whispered.

He smiled a bit, squeezed her. "Bullet's out now." He gazed guardedly into her face, bringing the back of a folded finger to graze a sensitive bump at her forehead. "Look at this boo-boo," he said.

Her eyes filled with tears, and her chest with love, with gratitude that he hadn't married some pretty police officer, that amnesia or no, he had not forgotten Paige when he could have.

She leaned into that broad chest, gloried in the strength of that arm around her, while every lost memory danced across her mind. "I know what I thought that day," she whispered, a tear streaking down her cheek, "when I first saw you."

He swiped it with his thumb. "You do."

"I do. I do. I thought, 'God, if he's in my class, I'm going to flunk.'"

He smiled faintly, preoccupied by wiping the tears again. She tucked her wet cheek into his chest and rubbed it dry with his shirt. "Did you mean what you told me? About wanting to marry me?"

"God, yes, will you?"

She could not speak, her throat was locked, her vision blurred, but quickly she nodded against him. Yes yes yes. She was in a hospital bed. Her head banging. Dizzied by the continual beeps. And yet . . . "I'm so happy."

His arm firmed around her body. "Christ, Paige, don't ever leave me."

"No no no, never." She grasped his face between her hands, and it was a beloved face. "You just found me."

He made a sound—the kind he did that made him sound tormented—and covered her lips with his, kissing her with all the love and passion and tenderness in the world, and she kissed him back with everything she had, ignoring the wild sound of her excited heartbeats.

Beepbeepbeep*beep* . . .

Her name was Paige.

TEMPT ME

Alexis Grant

CHAPTER I

"GET OUT!" THE crystal vase left her hand at the same time the high-pitched shriek left her mouth, crashing against the wall.

"What's wrong with you, 'Nita?" Antwan leaped from his bed dragging the sheets and his two angry bedmates with him.

"You better tell your crazy sister something!" one tall, cinnamon-hued groupie said, scowling at Anita.

"And you'd better tell this heifer that your sister can fight—goes to the gym and works out eight hours a damned day to make it look easy onstage!" Anita shouted, advancing on the woman who'd wisely jumped behind her brother. "That's right! And she needs to know that I'm not too Hollywood to punch her in her plastic face and then pay the fine . . . I'm from Philly. Got it?"

The other beauty clung to Antwan with a scowl, finger-combing her long, blonde tresses. "All of this drama is unnecessary."

"*You* do not speak—because you don't pay any bills here, I do. Now get out!" Anita rubbed her moist palms against her back jeans pockets and then balled up her fists. She placed her feet in a boxer's stance, her Chuck sneakers holding firm against the carpet.

"They're right," Antwan said, pushing the naked women behind him as he took a stance against his sister. "I'ma tell you something real important—all of this is totally unnecessary this morning!"

"Tell me something?" Anita said quietly, coming deeper into the room and taking out her diamond earrings to shove them into her pockets. Oh, it was so on! Fury-induced perspiration made her tank top cling to her body. Her ears were ringing and she was sure that insanity was glittering in her eyes; it was the way her brother stopped advancing for a moment and backed up. "Unnecessary?" She yanked the envelopes out of her back jeans pocket and thrust the stack of hotel bills toward Antwan, and then threw them at him when he refused to take them from her hand. "Get these video hoes out of my suite!"

"Who you calling a—"

"Chill!" Antwan said, whirling on the women for a second and gathering up his sheet to follow his sister. He slammed the bedroom door behind him and crossed the room to grab her arm. "What was all that back there, huh? Why you trippin'?"

Anita shook off her brother's grip, now so angry that she feared passing out. "No more, Antwan! You, Derrick, Dad, your boys—I'm done!"

"Whatdoyou mean, *you're done*? We family!" Antwan shouted back. "Listen, you can run that Queen B mess for the public, but I'm your brother, so is Derrick, and Pops—"

"You all have been sucking off me like big fat ticks," she said so quietly that her brother was momentarily stunned. "I got into this music industry with hard work and to you all it's just a game—but this is my life."

"We all are supposed to stick together, you know Mom said so before she died," Antwan stammered. "When one has, all have."

Anita shook her head as tears came to her eyes. "Still running that same old tired bull, huh? It's sad, 'Twan. Well, it's not going to work anymore."

The siblings looked at each other for what felt like a long time. Anita drew a weary breath as the tears fell from her eyes. Resentment roiled within her like a silent storm. Instead of bodyguarding her and protecting her from the sick bastard who was stalking her, her brothers were laying up with women and so high they couldn't do the job she was supposedly paying them for.

Not to mention that, listening to their advice, she'd moved from soulful R&B to attempting rap as a way to make fast money, more money—because of them. But that had only been to pay off spiraling debt that they'd created. The result had been disastrous to her reputation and career. Now she was given a chance to do a comeback tour of sorts, her big break back into R&B, and they were acting like this?

"I bought you all houses—"

"Oh, here we go," her brother said, blowing out a breath of exasperation and beginning to pace. "Wait, let me guess . . . We're supposed to be grateful till the day we die because you bought us some cheap-ass, three-hundred-and-fifty-thousand-dollar houses in Philly and—"

"I bought us all houses that we could afford to keep up in a normal, suburban community, if my career tanks. Me, you, Derrick, and Pops—and the only reason I got those so inexpensively was because the bottom dropped out of the housing market. Same with the cars. I couldn't go buying Maseratis and Lamborghinis; I got you guys something fly but moderate—like a Lexus, a Benz, and not some mess you see on *Access Hollywood*. Do you know what the insurance alone is on a Bentley, not to mention the maintenance? Be serious. I don't even drive that kinda car. And for the record, it cost me almost a cool *one-point-five* for four homes, by the time I loaded on taxes, titles, and insurance, okay? Be clear—there was nothing *cheap* about what I did for you guys!"

Fury made her walk a hot path between the sofa and the love seat, talking with her hands as she spoke. She couldn't believe her brother was so naïve and so terribly ungrateful.

"You know how fickle this music business is, 'Twan," Anita snapped, stopping to place her hands on her hips. "How many artists have tax problems or have these big mansions that they can't afford to maintain or heat after their careers crash and burn, huh? You wanna go back to living in Bartram Village Projects in Southwest Philly, if say, next year, my new R&B album doesn't go platinum? That's why I got us all something we could manage after the music dies. So don't *you* start trippin'."

She needed her brother to understand that the gravy train was over, and so was all the waste and partying at her expense. Common sense told her to diversify, invest in a potential future that didn't involve strutting on the stage half-naked and belting out scandalous lyrics. The money was great, but the grind was wearing her down and wearing her out . . . and after Jonathan walked out on her, she knew her days in the industry were numbered. Nobody crossed Jonathan Evans and had her career survive more than a season. When her brother simply rolled his eyes at her, she pressed on.

"Listen," she said, more calmly. "I have paid off all your debts at least two or three times. I've even taken care of your baby mamas . . . and all you do is run up bills like I'm Santa Claus."

When he only grunted a response, she glanced at the duplicate stack of hotel check-out folios on the coffee table that she'd requested, the ones that now more accurately separated out all the expenses by room instead of putting everything under her name, and then just stared at her brother. "I came to the Trump Plaza to work. While you guys were ordering champagne and having a grand ole good time, I was doing back-to-back concerts, working my tail off. I *have* to work to keep all this going."

Antwan tied his sheet in a knot around his waist tighter and then folded his arms. "You act like nobody else works, 'Nita . . . like, I'm on security with Derrick, your so-called driver, and Pops is—"

"Oh, save it," she said with a wave of her hand, cutting her brother off. It was all a sham and she flopped down hard on the white sofa and closed her eyes. "You're on security? Right . . . smoking blunts, running women, and drunk at every one of my shows. I might as well call a cab, waiting on Derrick to bring the car around because he's always got some hoochie in there and not where he's supposed to be when he's supposed to be. We already know somebody is stalking me, leaving things under my hotel room door, in the hallway of my apartment building, just to let me know he can. *That scares me.* You'd think that would scare you too, as my brother." Her voice broke as she pressed her hands to her chest, truly feeling the heartache of loving people who were so callous in the way they cared for her in return. "If somebody wanted to do me real harm—"

"Me and Derrick would be all over it, just like when we was kids, 'Nita," her brother argued. "Just like Pops is handling your business."

She laughed and it came out as a sad, hollow sound as she opened her eyes and looked up at her brother, shaking her head. She remembered the time when they had nothing, and she and her brothers stood as a united front against anything going down in the old neighborhood . . . but that was so long ago. Now she didn't know who to trust.

"You really think I'd let Pops know about all my contracts and what I'm working on? Do I look crazy to you? After the way he mismanaged my transition into an area of music I should have never gone near, not to mention the public relations insanity that he got me into just to create controversy and media attention, as he put it . . . why would I *ever* let him handle my reemergence into R&B?"

"So you've been holding out on the family?" Antwan said, sounding indignant and completely missing her point.

"Pops can't manage his way out of a paper bag, and it's disgraceful the way he's behaving—all the women, all the scandal . . . now I know why Mom left him while she was alive. Me, like a dummy, I fell for the 'I'm your daddy and I need you back in my life' scam. I only did it because I missed Mom so much—but she never conducted her life like this."

"*Conducted*, well, ain't we high siddity now?" Antwan said, mimicking her in a high-pitched voice. "You can take the girl out of the projects, but you can't take the projects out of the girl, 'Nita. You need to be real and stop trying to be somebody you're not! Using fancy words and—"

"I'm trying to educate myself! Trying to get better! Trying to grow! Why don't you try to do the same with your free time?"

"Why don't you stop judging people, especially me, D, and—"

"Who? Our father?" Anita popped off the sofa like a bee had stung her. "I'm tired of hanging around people who get up in the morning high, continue the day with liquor and don't even remember the names of who they've slept with the night before! Do you know their names?" Anita pointed toward the bedroom door and when her brother didn't immediately answer her, the words just rushed past her lips. "I'm tired of being around big kids—who play video games all day long, and . . . and . . . why am I even talking to you?"

"You need to go smoke a blunt and chill out is what you need to do—it's too early in the goddamned morning for all of this," her brother said, waving her off.

"It's eleven-thirty, a half hour before noon," Anita said flatly, crossing her arms over her chest.

"Whateva," her brother said, heading back to the bedroom.

"My bags are packed and I've checked out—on time."

"So . . . what's that got to do with me?" he muttered, reaching for the bedroom door.

"You'll be paying for whatever expenses you and Derrick ran up in this hotel—so will Pops."

Antwan Brown turned and looked at his sister, his gaze narrowed. "It always comes down to money . . . you always trying to hang that over everybody's head. Okay, fine, so whatchu want, you spoiled little brat? Want me to send the ladies home and drive your ass to New York right this second for your awards show tonight—is that what all the drama is about? *Damn,* I *swear* you get on my *last* nerve, girl. It's not even twelve o'clock yet. If we leave here by four, we can all get up the way by seven, change, head out to the—"

"I have to be there *by* seven!"

"Aw'ight, aw'ight, relax. Damn."

"I want those hussies off my tab, so whatever you ordered

for them, you are paying for," Anita said as calmly as possible. "Wherever Derrick is, and wherever Pops is, you can tell them the same thing."

"Aw'ight, fine! I'll pay for the dinners and the bubbly, you done?"

"No," Anita said, folding her arms over her chest. "I have hired a legitimate limousine and security firm to pick me up in the lobby *today*, as well as to take me to the awards tonight—since I knew I couldn't count on you. The label will have security when I get there, as per normal, but I'll hire a *real* bodyguard, since you're too busy."

"Yeah," she said, pressing her point when her brother appeared momentarily speechless. "I've been up for hours taking care of things I should have handled years ago. I might even hire that SWAT International, the firm that's sending the limo, to go overseas with me on my USO tour, because I'm changing my life, and there can be no screwups there . . . it can't be like the disaster that was the U.S. rap tour last year. My name is still in the tabloids from that and the drama you guys got into. Never again."

"Oh, so now we can't go on the plush trips with you because things got a little wild in Vegas and in the dirty south? It wasn't my fault that things got crazy in L.A., and you know that was all Derrick."

Incredulous, Antwan stalked back toward her to get in her face. "So now we gotta stay home because I had some chicks in the spare bedroom in your suite and you might be a little late for some stupid awards show? Is that it? All because I got a little tipsy and forgot which room was which and came in here—so? Why you got beef over silly shit all the time, 'Nita? That's probably why your man left you almost a year ago and don't no other man wanna deal with your high-maintenance ass. Look at you," her brother shook his head, glowering at her. "Fine as hell . . . pretty hazel eyes, nice shape, thick long hair that ain't a weave, men falling all over you and can't keep a man—why? Because you're picky as hell and drive every man who gets with you crazy! You're mad because you ain't getting none, so now—"

"That's not fair," she said quietly, outrage and hurt making her voice tight as she held up her hand to make him stop hurling insults.

"So you heard me bouncing a coupla babes and ain't had nobody in your bed, now this morning you come busting in my room throwing vases. You need to get your head shrunk, go get some therapy or better yet, get you some d—"

"I would have definitely preferred that you took them into *your* suite, the one *I* had paid for, but this doesn't have anything to do with that. I got angry when I saw the bills, okay. Then I got even angrier when I looked at my watch, saw what time it was, and heard you starting up in there again when I have to be at an awards show in New York tonight—don't get it twisted. Then I called the other rooms, trying to get my so-called driver, trying to get my father, somebody to take me back home, and couldn't raise a soul on the so-called payroll . . . even you, my supposed handler and security guy was more concerned about getting tail than making sure that I'm back home, rested, and on point for the gig I have to do tonight—a gig that helps pay all of these bills."

"Aw'ight, my bad, so I lost track of time," Antwan said with a shrug. "But you ain't have to come busting in there going off. This is all about your ego, be honest . . . because we've still got time to get to NYC, if you put on your makeup and stuff in the limo—how long does it take to put on a dress and some heels?"

Anita looked up at her younger brother, wondering where the love had gone, where the responsibility had gone, knowing that her mother had to be turning over in her grave. "This has to do with you all getting your lives in order, not my ego," she said more quietly.

"You ain't our mother!" Antwan shouted and then walked away from her.

"No, I'm not," she said quietly, moving toward the LV luggage that she had stacked by the door.

"So, what you trying to say?" Antwan stammered, once he'd realized that this time she meant business.

"I am saying that you all have homes that were outright

purchased. You all have nice cars that are paid for and insured for the year. You all have credit cards, with no balances on them—except for whatever you ran up last night. You all have closets full of really nice designer clothes, and last I remember I had left you with several thousand dollars in the bank."

"Okay, like I asked you before, whatchu trying to say?" Her brother lifted his chin and folded his arms over his chest.

Anita nodded toward the dining room table. "There's an envelope over there for each of you . . . it has a check for two weeks' severance pay and a formal termination of services letter. You'll be eligible for unemployment, as my accountant made sure that we paid all of the necessary payroll deductions and I will continue your medical and dental benefits for a year—which should be long enough for you each to find a real job."

"Severance? What? Are you serious?" Antwan's eyes held a dangerous combination of fear and outrage.

"Completely." Not waiting for the bellman who was on his way, Anita hoisted up her gold Louis Vuitton bag on her shoulder and then picked up a matching suit bag that held her gown and shoes before she reached for the door. She had already hired another limo and while she waited in the vehicle, the hotel staff could bring down the larger pieces of luggage, but right now she needed air.

"You ain't doing this to us, 'Nita!" her brother shouted behind her as she slipped out of the door. "Now I know why everybody calls you Queen Bitch!"

IF THERE WAS anybody he'd do this emergency job for while home on leave, it was his best buddy, Lowell. The call had come in early this morning according to Lowell, who'd been trying ever since he'd started his security escort business to land a contract with this particularly difficult VIP—and the lady finally made up her mind when every good man that Lowell had was otherwise engaged with previously booked corporate clients.

Regardless, how did one say no to a man who'd saved your life by losing his leg, and then had to rebuild a military career by chauffeuring and protecting spoiled CEOs and stars? Men of Delta Force were meant for so much more than this and it tortured his soul that Lowell had to choose this as a way to feed his family. Still, it was honest work and he'd honor his friend's call to arms.

Zachary kept his gaze sweeping the hotel lobby of the Trump Plaza. This wasn't a hardship detail though; the worst part of the job was probably going to be putting up with a megastar attitude and wearing a suit, but he'd survived a whole lot worse. Time wasn't a problem, although he'd probably keep this off his commanding officer's radar so it wouldn't be viewed as a conflict of interest. He wasn't going to let Lowell pay him; that's what Lowell didn't know. Besides, if he didn't get paid then what he did on his time off was his business, as long as it was legal. It wasn't like he was working a second job or moonlighting while in uniform.

But, if anybody asked, he was off-duty for six weeks and had time to kill . . . and this was just an in and out. Go in, pick up the package—one spoiled diva, deliver her to New York, drive her to an awards show, and then return her home. From there, Lowell's other men would be off their previously committed details and could cover her building. Simple. Clean. Just the way he liked it.

Just the way . . .

Zachary's thoughts trailed off to a dead stop. He'd seen the woman before on television and had a file pic that Lowell had sent to his BlackBerry—but seeing her in person was something entirely different. It took him a second to get his bearings before he could finally admit the fact that he'd been a man starved of the basic American pleasure of seeing a gorgeous woman maneuver on her own and uncovered in public.

Sure, he'd enjoyed the eye candy on his way home from overseas and on his way here, but damn . . . some of the garden spots he'd been in, just looking too hard at a woman could get you caught up in an angry mob, stoned, or worse, could cost an innocent woman her life.

Over the past year and a half of sensory denial, he'd learned to divert his gaze and only keep a passerby female in his peripheral vision as a potential suicide bomber. Although Anita Brown wasn't carrying C-4, what this lady walking across the lobby had detonated was blowing his mind.

He'd expected to see her surrounded by an entourage of security and for her to be wearing some outrageous outfit. But she walked off the elevator like a normal person, alone, carrying her own bags, no makeup on, wearing jeans, a sexy orange tank top, and sneakers.

For a moment he couldn't move. She was so naturally pretty that it didn't make sense. Her skin looked like a piece of caramel satin—not a flaw on it . . . and her thick chestnut-brown hair was swept up in a simple ponytail. The orange color of her tank top drew him right to her rack and he was thankful for the aviator sunglasses that helped him keep a poker face as he began to walk toward her.

Instinct made him spot potential threats in the lobby. One small group of weekend gamblers started to move in on her, but then thought better of it as they caught his stare. True, it wasn't a part of his detail; he was just the driver. But the lady's expression seemed tense, like there was no one there for her to keep the public back. Not on his watch.

Huge designer sunglasses hid what he knew had to be a pair of drop-dead gorgeous eyes, and the entire package of her five-foot, seven-inch frame was so built that jeans on her ought to have been against the law. He felt his body begin to react, but gave it a swift mental *down boy*, and kept walking; he had a job to do. More importantly, her expression seemed so lonely that it made her seem vulnerable. He knew he needed to get to her before others in the lobby recognized her and then tried to accost her for autographs and invade her space.

"Ms. Brown?" he said, trying to remember to breathe. There was no way in the world that his buddy could have prepared him for her. The light scent of a delicious female fragrance instantly surrounded him, making it hard to form complete sentences. "I'm Zachary Mitchell, your driver."

Her pretty mouth remained tight as she stared up at him and then began to fumble in her handbag for her cell phone.

"May I take that for you?"

He wasn't prepared for her to jerk away from his reach for her luggage.

"I need to be sure you are who you say you are first," she snapped and then whipped out her phone. She studied him as though he were a felon while she waited for the call to connect. "Mr. Lowell Johnson? Yes, well, it's Anita Brown—tell me what this guy Zach Mitchell looks like."

"I can produce ID for you, ma'am," Zachary said calmly as she listened to Lowell's description of him.

"Okay. Fine," she said into her cell phone, but kept her eyes on him. "I'm being stalked, so I have to be careful. Thanks." She ended the call and released a weary sigh, then glanced over her shoulder at the elevators before turning her back toward the crowd that was beginning to gather. "The bellman is bringing the rest of my bags. Just show me your ID and then get me out of here."

He gave her space as he dug in his suit pocket for his wallet. "Here's my driver's license—and you're right, you do have to be careful."

She let out another exasperated breath. "It's been a really rough day already . . . I didn't want it to end with me being abducted from a freakin' parking lot."

"Neither do I, Ms. Brown," he said, reaching for her luggage again. "Let's get you to your limo and back home so you can relax."

CHAPTER 2

OF ALL THE days for a tall, semisweet chocolate hunk to be her driver. Anita climbed into the backseat of the limo as the man identified as Zachary Mitchell held the door open for her and then closed it behind her.

Even the man's driver's license photo looked good! But now was not the time to be having a hormone flashback. Abstinence kept her mind on her money and her money on her mind. She was nobody's fool—at least she wouldn't be again. So what the man was fine? But he did have a swagger that couldn't be denied. Just a look had backed up a bunch of autograph seekers.

His entire vibe was no-nonsense, and when she'd seen him coming toward her, she had to admit to herself that she'd freaked out a bit. The first thought that came to her was, if this was her stalker, she was a dead woman walking. Everything about the man seemed like he could make a swift decision kill. But then she'd found out he'd been the one sent to drive her. Anita briefly closed her eyes and tried to allow the tension to drain from her shoulders.

Now that the unsettling feeling of danger had passed she could really appreciate all of Zachary Mitchell's many attributes. Peering through the window, she tried to get discreet glimpses of him through the darkened glass while the bellman put her luggage in the trunk. He was *definitely* someone who could make her go off her man-fast, she thought.

But he was her limo driver, for God's sake. Hired help always sold your last shred of personal business to the tabloids. The finer the man, the more dangerous—because it was easy for the most sensible woman to lose perspective. She sat back with a frustrated huff and peered at Zachary Mitchell from a sidelong glance, watching him round the vehicle to put away her garment bag last. Yeah . . . he was the type who probably had a string of women, no doubt, with a build like that. Smelled too good, too. No cologne, no fancy anything, just basic male, clean-shaven . . .

She jerked her attention forward and tried to appear nonchalant when he came back to check on her and tapped gently on the window.

"Excuse me, ma'am . . ."

She pressed the window button and tried to remain bored by his presence as the darkened glass lowered. But it was impossible not to stare at his handsome face or drink in the way his full mouth moved as he spoke . . . or look at his white, white even rows of teeth.

"There is spring water in the refrigerator, juice, wine, champagne, a small salad, fresh fruit . . . in case you haven't had time to eat. If you need me to open anything for you, just let me know before we head out on the road."

He had a fabulous baritone voice that resonated in her belly, but he sounded like he was speaking from a memorized script.

"I'm all right," she said, not looking at him.

He nodded and she raised the window. When he rounded the vehicle, she slumped back in relief, glad to momentarily be out of the man's gravitational pull. But his stride and the way his suit fell just so from his broad shoulders made her follow the straight line of his back all the way down to his spectacular ass. She could only imagine what that glorious part of his anatomy would look like in a pair of jeans or leather pants.

She had to stop; she demanded that of herself. Most days she was all right—and simply worked herself hard enough that thoughts like the ones Zachary Mitchell conjured up

simply faded into the background of her psyche. But for
some odd reason, today this guy wasn't fading . . .

Anita leaned her head back and closed her eyes, blotting
out the ugly highway landscape of the Garden State Parkway.
How was someone like her supposed to meet a decent guy,
anyway? She hated what her ex had said . . . arrogant, smug
bastard. He'd predicted this day—telling her that without
him she'd be subjected to wannabe fame seekers, strivers,
thugs, and groupies. That sooner or later she'd get lonely
enough and horny enough that she'd make the ultimate human
mistake that all stars made; she'd do somebody she wasn't
supposed to do and that would have severe career consequences. Jonathan had actually laughed in her face, casually
telling her that it was still a man's world and the double stan-
dard was completely in his favor. He could do whatever he
wanted, whoever he wanted, and he'd recover; she couldn't.
She hated that he'd been right.

She swallowed hard, tasting tears of outrage and wishing
that the new security company had sent over a short old man
with a beer belly as her driver. Her body had betrayed her; it
had to be the stress. She didn't do out of control. Anita
pressed her thighs together tightly and took several deep
breaths. She hated feeling like this.

Between the industry sharks, the guys who were married
or otherwise living with a woman and lying, to the ones
who'd have a hidden camera posted in their apartments to
sell her image into Internet porn, what was a girl to do? The
horror stories were rampant; the lengths people went to in
order to make a quick buck on somebody else's back were
notorious.

That still didn't stop the dull throb that had taken over
her clit or the sudden ache that prickled across her skin. It
had been so long since she'd been touched . . . Zachary
Mitchell had great hands. Clean, long, well-kept square fingers, but not manicured in a metrosexual way. Just remembering his mouth made her part her lips and pull in a shallow
sip of air. She could only imagine what his kiss could do,
and her mind began to feel the hot daydream play out across

her belly, flowing down over her navel as her valley plumped and spilled liquid heat into her panties.

She smoothed her moist palms down her jeans legs, envisioning him pulling her jeans down over her hips. This didn't make sense, but her mind was on fire just thinking about the way he'd crossed that lobby like a man on a mission—it seemed like a little more than a job. It seemed personal somehow. It made her wonder what a kiss from him might taste like . . . what his mouth against her shoulder might feel like.

To have a man like him want her . . . to trail kisses down her body until he discovered her mound, to find that sweet spot between her thighs . . . *to take his sweet time, sweet Jesus* . . . to lick a slow, lazy trail along her slit, gently parting the fat, engorged lips of her flower with his tongue. Sucking her bud just right . . . a gentle finger finding her rim, finding the beat, finding the tight circle.

Anita squeezed her legs together tighter; she had to stop. This was pointless she told herself firmly. But right now would be so perfect to feel skin-against-skin, the simplistic beauty of human touch. In her daydream, she didn't need a condom . . . she could let the tip of her tongue travel up his shaft to revel in the spongy texture of its head, then she could envision sliding her hand back down his thick, heavily veined shaft.

Stop it, stop it, stop it, girl, you've been watching too much late-night TV.

Her brain wouldn't turn off. Each time she tried to jettison the images out of her head they came back with a vengeance. Her mind seized on that one part of his anatomy she'd become fixated on until she couldn't help fantasizing about how his excitement would release pearling fluids that would make his wondrous male organ glisten. Then her attention would release the pumping motion of his hips in anticipation, would release that fabulous baritone she'd just heard outside the limo window . . . but this time he'd say her name, "'*Nita*."

Soon that impossible-to-replicate part of him would be

inside of her, welded deep within her flesh, opening her thighs, opening her lungs, making her see stars, making her weep. Her girlfriends had all lied; a pocket rocket or a full-sized battery-operated boyfriend could never replace that natural male resource . . . if the man knew what he was do-ing . . . if he were gifted and talented. Zachary Mitchell seemed like he was both.

Oh, yeah, it had been way too long, if she was thinking about this. Anita stared at the divider glass that separated her from pure sin—Zachary Mitchell. No. The last thing she needed was to get caught getting all hot and bothered. She'd be at the penthouse the label had leased for her soon enough, alone, and in her own space that she trusted. Anita sat up and fetched a bottle of spring water from the fridge. This limo was sent and could have been wired, for all she knew. A tiny camera could be anywhere.

She placed the cool, wet bottle against her throat and closed her eyes again, stifling a quiet moan. Her canal begged for penetration, needed more than what a finger or daydream could provide—but she wasn't about to let her ex laugh at her. She could just see the front page of a tabloid now: STAR FINGERS HERSELF IN HER LIMO JUST BEFORE THE R&B MUSIC AWARDS. *Never happen.*

So what if she had to go to the awards solo and come home that way? It didn't matter that her nipples had now be-come so hard that it felt like little needles were grazing them each time she inhaled and exhaled. Anita popped the seal on her water and drank it down greedily. It wasn't just about raw sex—that was easy to find. She was searching for a real rela-tionship anyway. Good-looking men were a dime a dozen. She just needed to calm down and shake this fine specimen out of her thoughts.

Still, the condition of being alone was not the preferred option—that she couldn't deny. But if a person who'd al-ready reached her status of fame was suddenly single, then how was one to trust that a man just cared for her because of who she was inside, not because of her fame and fortune? Add that issue to wading one's way through the booty-call players. Anita stared out the window, not sure whether to laugh or cry.

It wasn't like she could just go out to a club and meet someone, or even use an online dating service. Anyone she met and slept with had to be checked out eight ways from Sunday, and then they could always write a tell-all book after it was all said and done. Paparazzi would scare off anyone decent, and the only reason they probably hadn't shown up in the hotel lobby this afternoon was because she'd had the foresight to ask her label, as a condition of her tour, to always send a drone limo away earlier with a look-alike in it, and the cameras probably chased that up the highway like a pack of rabid dogs.

Her head hurt and her body hurt. Frustration was making her crazy. Anita slumped back against the seat and considered the champagne. She needed to focus on the show she had to do tonight.

"Damn . . ." she whispered to herself and then became mute again. All she could do was put on some soft music and shake her head. It was going to be a very long ride to New York.

IT WAS ALL he could do to focus on the road. He hadn't been this messed up by a woman in a very long time. Come to think of it, he really couldn't recall a time when a woman had dissected his brain like this one had. He was never so glad in his life to see a Central Park West building.

In and out, he told himself. Just come around the vehicle, get the package out, get her up to her place, sweep it, bring up the rest of her bags, and be out.

Zachary squared his shoulders and came around the side of the limo and then opened the door. This time she reached for his hand and the buttery softness of it connected to something within him that ignited in his palm. She looked up, and he could really see her gorgeous hazel eyes for the first time as she peered over the top of her huge sunglasses.

Graceful and light, she glided out of the limo with ease

and offered him a half-smile as she bit her bottom lip. It was the sexiest thing to watch . . .

"I'm sorry I was such a trip when you first picked me up," she said quietly. "Like I said, it was a bad morning. That wasn't your fault."

"No offense taken, ma'am." He closed the car door behind her and tried to keep his tone professional.

"Are you from the south?" she asked as he went to the trunk to get her luggage.

"No, ma'am, why do you ask?" he replied, ushering her toward the doorman.

"You keep calling me ma'am."

He tilted his head as the uniformed doorman greeted them with a smile and opened the door. "Guess it's force of habit."

"Makes me feel old," she said and then smiled broadly.

He'd kept walking, but he was the walking wounded. Her smile had hit him in the chest like an RPG round. The way her lush mouth turned up in earnest joy to expose perfect pearl-white teeth, made her already pretty face absolutely angelic. There was no possible way for him to sync up the image of the woman he'd picked up in the limo to the shrew portrayed in the rags on the newsstand. This could *not* be Queen B—the diva, the scandalous heartbreaker, and stage vixen who'd gone from R&B to rap, back to R&B again in a tumultuous path.

"You're definitely not old," he said after an awkward moment, standing by the elevator and adjusting his hold on her multiple bags.

From the corner of his eye he saw her swallow a smile.

"We used to call my mama and grandmama, ma'am."

He had to smile. "Yeah," he said with a slight chuckle. "I guess you're right . . . but it's just respect, Ms. Brown."

"Anita, since you're driving me to the awards tonight and will be the closest thing I have to a date."

He gave her a quick glance, glad that the elevator had arrived. "Yes, ma'am," he said in reflex, and then wanted to kick himself when she smiled and simply shook her head.

She stepped in and he followed her, not knowing how to

process her statement. *This woman* didn't have a date? How in the hell . . .

Okay, maybe she had issues. Maybe the stuff in the tabloids was true. He just needed to stay in character, do the job Lowell had asked, and keep his mind from wandering. He was Delta Force—*Hoorah.*

They rode up in relative silence, and when the elevator doors opened, there was only one other door on her floor. Her apartment took up half a city block . . . whoa. Okay, now it was time for a reality check. This woman was loaded, he was military and did all right by normal folks' standards, but this was over the top. Anita Brown was way out of his league.

She walked ahead of him digging in her purse. He told himself that he had to stop studying her delicious posterior. But his training kicked in when she reached for the door.

"Please, ma'am, let me go in and sweep it for you first," he said in a low, firm tone. He set her bags down by the door, then took her keys from her hand, managed the locks and entered her apartment, senses on full alert.

Anita placed her hand over her heart and leaned against the small crescent table that was littered with mail, almost taking out the large vase of calla lilies. The way that man said ma'am just ran all through her. It was the way he dropped the end of the word, had an interesting Midwest something to it that was mixed into his New York sound, and was all male. Up close, he was a presence that could not be denied . . . and the way his hands felt—good *Gawd.* Had just a slight callous to them, like a guy who labored for a living. But the strength in them . . . when he'd helped her out of the limo she thought she'd faint dead away.

Fanning her face for a moment, she peeked into the apartment, listening to him go room by room and suddenly trying to think of anything she could to get him to stay for a little while longer.

"All clear," he finally said, coming back to the door. "Where would you like your bags?"

"My bedroom," she said as quietly and sexily as possible. She watched the muscle pulse in his jaw as he gave her a curt nod, extended his arm with a sweep to invite her in, and then did what almost looked like an Honor Guard three-point turn before collecting her bags and heading toward her bedroom. Never in her life had a suit looked so frickin' good on one man's body. She generally didn't go in for the Wall Street-banker style, but this guy made a plain white Oxford button-down shirt and a basic rep tie transform into something exotic by any woman's standards.

"I will be back at nineteen hundred hours, sharp, ma'am," he said.

"In plain English, *sir*," she said with a wide grin. "And will you cut the ma'am and just call me Anita?"

"Six pm, Ms. Brown." He smiled.

"Okay, I'll take Ms. Brown for now. Wouldn't wanna get you in trouble with your boss," she said, glimpsing him over her shoulder as she turned to walk back down the hall toward the front door. "It's black tie, I hope Lowell Johnson told you."

She chuckled when she heard Zachary's footfalls hesitate behind her. "Guess he didn't," she said turning to face him. "That's cool . . . I'll give my stylist a call and see what Javier can rustle up."

"Ma'am, you don't have to—"

"It's part of the job, we expense that kinda stuff all the time," she said quickly and then folded her arms over her chest. "So, how tall are you?"

"Six-four," he said in a low rumble and then looked out of the expansive bank of windows.

"Shoe size?"

"Fifteen."

"Are you serious?" she said and then covered her mouth, laughing. "TMI!" Laughing harder as he shifted uncomfortably, she waved her hands and then hugged herself. "I'm sorry, that was inappropriate and really bad . . . all right, all right . . . what's your inseam?"

"Now you're really getting personal, ma'am," he said, beginning to chuckle with her. "I take a forty-two long, all right?"

"Six o'clock," she said, walking away from him and fanning her face with a way-too-big smile.

She opened the door and closed it still laughing. He couldn't kill the half-smile that was permanently etched on his face.

As he waited for the elevator he had only one question—what the hell had Lowell Johnson gotten him into?

CHAPTER 3

ZACH WAITED ON the huge St. Marks Avenue brownstone steps juggling supermarket bags along with his suit bag and waiting for his three godsons to open the front door. He had questions for his buddy Lowell and a short two-hour window to shower at Lowell's apartment, shave, change into the fresh suit he was gonna wear, before he had to be back on his post at Anita Brown's apartment by nineteen hundred hours. Now Lowell was sick and possibly couldn't do the security detail? That cell phone call while he was driving almost made him veer off the road.

This wasn't like Lowell and this whole thing was spinning off course, he could feel it. The first problem was the tux thing. Now he'd have to get there fifteen minutes early to change into whatever Anita Brown's stylist had found, which had never been a part of the program—he was just a driver.

Truthfully he'd planned on staying in Manhattan, grabbing something to eat there, and just looping back to pick Anita up. What was this tux thing? Now he was an escort? Although he had to admit that wasn't a completely bad thing, he didn't like sudden itinerary changes. And if he was going to add security to his list, then he really needed to sit with Lowell, see the layout of the exits at the Apollo, figure out how to maneuver Anita through the crowd, then there'd be paparazzi to contend with. This was not a simple thing, especially if she was being stalked.

He was just glad he'd had the foresight to bring enough clothes with him and stuff for the kids that he was able to stash in the limo before he'd left for AC to go get Anita, which saved yet another stop to go pick up his gear at some hotel somewhere.

But there was no getting around the fact that he didn't like how this woman had totally jacked him up—he couldn't stop thinking about her, couldn't stop picturing her walking through her apartment in the buff . . . which was like something out of a magazine. Yeah, stop thinking about her body and think about the apartment. That would keep wood at bay.

Floor-to-ceiling windows on three sides, a breath-taking view of the park like he'd never seen. Insane art, flowers all over the place. The joint was spotless, seemed like a hotel, like no one ever really lived there. Baby grand piano, pieces of furniture that looked like one-of-a-kind pieces—this was how she lived? What man could compete with that? It was so-bering and definitely a wood killer.

But the sound of children dragged him away from his careening thoughts. He laughed as he heard the commotion of three sets of impatient little feet running down three flights of stairs to greet him.

Sure, Anne Marie had buzzed him in, but there was a ritual to be observed; the kids wanted to jump him and hang all over his body like extra appendages as he trudged up to their apartment. The ten-year-old would be on his back, the five- and seven-year-olds clinging to his already overburdened arms, with their mother standing at the top of the stairs yelling for them to get off their uncle while he made wrestling growls—much to the children's delight.

Junior, LaVon, and Terrence were a handful. He didn't know how his buddy, Lowell, and his wife, Anne Marie, handled it all. They made raising a family look so easy—but to his mind, being in Delta Force was a much less scarier prospect. Being there for kids to provide for their every emotional, physical, and even spiritual need . . . making sure they grew up right in a crazy world, making sure that no one hurt them in the thug-infested streets; that was the war that his buddy and his wife fought every day. And they fought it admirably. It was a helluva challenge, one that took discipline, courage, steadfastness, and honor . . . and earned his ultimate respect.

Bringing some groceries to a friend's house when he had the flu was the least he could do. He'd already gotten the toys before he'd even thought about getting on a plane yesterday, but he would have come sooner, flown in a few days earlier, if he'd known that Lowell was seriously sick.

Zach stared at the door, the sounds of children flowing into the background of his mind. Lowell had to know he couldn't cover even his basic clients. There was something in Anne Marie's voice the day before—she never called him out of the blue the way she did without Lowell being on the other line. That's what had prompted him to come for a visit, to just follow his gut and get a flight that same day. His plane had landed that same evening, but it was too late to stop by—then this morning his cell phone rang. The only thing that his buddy had said was that all his men were busy with other jobs, he was a little under the weather and was going to try to cover this important client, but then asked if it would be possible for him to get to New York by tomorrow. Zach shook his head. He was already there and Lowell had given him the job. That's how he knew how bad things really had to be.

It wasn't until he was back in the limo that the second call had come in from Lowell, who didn't sound good at all. Lowell hadn't told him that he'd need him to be more than a driver until late this afternoon—then again, that was just like Lowell to tough it out till he was at the point of no return.

Three small brown faces with wild, woolly hair filled the glass panels of the massive brownstone doors. They reminded him so much of himself and his older brothers that it felt like he was looking into a twenty-year-old Coney Island fun house mirror of the past, rather than the heavy leaded-beveled glass doors of the present.

"Uncle Zach!" the eldest of the boys cried out through

the glass, managing the locks and then flinging open the heavy door.

Two smaller versions of Junior dashed out and barreled right into Zach's midsection, and he rewarded them with a grunt as though they'd knocked the wind out of him.

"Whatcha got?" Junior said expectantly, trying to glimpse in the bags as Zach elbowed his younger brothers off him, making them giggle as they play fought.

"Groceries for your mom," Zach said laughing. "That's all. And my suit bag—hey, watch the threads!"

"Aw . . . maaaan."

"Here," Zach said, thrusting a plastic grocery bag at Junior and then roughhousing him a little. "You carry the bag; I'll carry you—c'mon up, but don't damage the suit."

He gave the two smaller boys a bag each as he stooped down to allow Junior to scramble up his back and then laughed as their faces grew long.

"Oh, you think I can't handle you two small fries with the bags, huh? Here, one of y'all hold my bag *carefully* and I'll show you what time it is."

His smile widened as their faces lit up.

"I told you Uncle Zach was stronger than The Rock!" Terrence exclaimed.

"I bet he's stronger than—"

"All of 'em," Zach said laughing as he scooped up LaVon, making him giggle. "And don't drop your mom's groceries or my suit, small fry—drop the bag, and I drop you, got it?" he said, releasing the five-year-old for a second and then catching him before his feet touched the marble flooring. Zach jerked LaVon up close in a bicep curl and then snatched Terrence who'd tried to run, but had allowed himself to get caught. "That goes for you, too, pipsqueak."

"Who you calling a pipsqueak?" Terrence said, laughing hard, struggling to no avail. "I'm a monster—a wrestling maniac."

"Uh, huh," Zach said, "we'll see," and then let out a big roar as he dashed down the hall and bounded up the first flight of steps.

"Lord have mercy!" Anne Marie shouted from the stair-well. "Zachary Mitchell, put those boys down—y'all get away from your uncle beating up on him like that! They'll give you a hernia, man—they aren't babies anymore."

"Arrrrgggghhhh!" Zachary growled, laughing and stomping up the stairs like a trapped monster, allowing the boys to think they were finally getting the better of him. "Anne Marie, they almost got me this time, I think I'm going down!"

He staggered, making the boys think he was falling backward down the steps and then all of a sudden started running, taking the steps two at a time.

"You're going to give me a heart attack one of these days, Mitchell," she said, covering her heart with her palm, and then swatting her boys as they fell off their uncle onto the hall floor. "Go in the house and keep the noise down, your father is asleep!"

"I thought I told you guys if you dropped your mother's groceries, I was gonna drop you? Hang up my suit bag, would ya?"

Kids ran and little boy voices hit a decibel that could have awakened the dead. Zach leaped over the fallen groceries and tackled three children who whooped in utter delight.

"Sorry, Anne!" he yelled over his shoulder as the boys piled on top of him, showing off every move they'd seen on television. His suit was in a luggage heap on the floor.

She just chuckled and shook her head, collecting up the grocery bags and picking up his suit bag as she re-entered the apartment.

"You didn't have to do this." Anne stood in the doorway and then looked down into one grocery bag that had produce on the top of it, disguising Wrestlemania figures from Toys "R" Us. "You spoil them rotten."

Instantly the children sprung up off the pile they'd been in on the floor to run to their mother.

"Oooohhh, ooohhh, lemme see!" LaVon shouted, making it to his mom first.

"I told you Uncle Zach always brings cool stuff!" Terrence said, elbowing his younger brother.

"Wish you could be here all the time, Uncle Zach," Junior said, running to see what was in the bag.

"Hold it, guys!" Zach said, getting up off the floor with a grunt. "Two conditions of getting those," he said, eyeing the boys. "One—you listen to your mother and keep it down . . . your dad doesn't feel good, all right?" He waited until they nodded, watching Anne swish the bag behind her back with relish and then hold her head up high. "Two—you help around the house and pick up all your stuff until your dad is feeling better, so everything isn't all on your poor mom. Deal?"

"Deal!" Junior shouted and then covered his mouth with his hand.

The two smaller kids giggled and covered their mouths, mimicking their older brother, simply nodding. But everyone laughed when the littlest in the group whispered "deal" and then made the sign of a zipper going across his lips.

"In this household, bribery will get you everywhere," Anne said, giving the boys the bag, but yanking out her lettuce first to save it.

Zach swept up the rest of the groceries and followed her into the kitchen, setting the bags down on the table.

"But, seriously, you really didn't have to do all of this." She kept her back to him, slowly putting away the food, and he watched her open half-empty cabinets, knowing that he did.

"It was nothing," Zach said, leaning against the wall.

"Yeah, it was," she said quietly. "God bless you."

Doris Mitchell would have said that, if someone had cared enough about her to do something as simple for his mother and her brood. There was no comment he could make and nowhere comfortable for him to rest his eyes. He soon found his gaze drifting to where the boys played in the clean but modest apartment. For a moment déjà vu rendered him mute. The holidays always conjured up the past, being on leave was a hardship that he admitted to no one, and coming to what he now considered his brother and sister-in-law's home was the only thing that jettisoned the eerie loneliness of it all.

He had a decision to make, whether or not to re-up and stay in for several more years . . . if he had something like this of his own, the decision would have been clearer. Sad truth was, he didn't. Reenlistment papers were calling his name. It was easier than trying to figure out what to do with his life beyond the military family.

His mother had once had a small, clean home like this one in Detroit and had kept it up even after their father died, until the mortgage fell too far behind. Yet even having to move them to New York to be near her sister and into the projects, she had rules, church, and clean floors . . . just like Anne Marie did.

Zachary started taking canned goods and pasta out of the bags and lining the items up on the table, lost in his own thoughts. Who looked after widows and women in need, women with children, women with men who've fallen on hard times, or have fallen into disrepute? he wondered. He would never allow that to happen to his best friend's family, not as long as there was breath in his body. But there was no doubt in his mind that Lowell Johnson was a lucky man indeed, wealthy beyond measure. Zach watched his best friend's pretty wife with her thick-bodied curves and good soul unpacking groceries in an immaculate kitchen. This was a home and his buddy was generous enough to share it with him whenever he needed a taste of one.

Watching the mêlée of happy children, the television blaring, a good woman putting up food so reminded him of what had been long ago . . . long before drugs and the streets took his elder brothers, and that loss broke his mother's heart till it gave out. If he'd had this, he would have maybe come home like Lowell—retired when his commission ended. He smiled as Anne Marie smoothed the front of her hair back toward the synthetic ponytail she wore and walked into the living room with her hands on her hips. The volume of boys roughhousing instantly lowered.

"Don't make me come in here again," she said, not even having to raise her voice.

Chuckling, Zach winked at the boys behind their mother's back. The boys were wild but well-mannered in public—Anne Marie had the same laser beam "eye" that his mother used to have, and it tickled him as he watched her employ it on her brood.

"Toys *and* food," she said in a weary tone, coming into the kitchen and stopping in front of the sink to stare at him in disbelief. A combination of appreciation and worry haunted her dark brown eyes and creased her normally smooth, walnut-hued brow. Anne Marie lowered her gaze and went to the fridge to put away apple juice and butter and then sighed at the gallon jug of milk.

"I don't have a bunch of growing boys to feed, and it wasn't much . . . the way they eat, this little bit will be gone in two days anyway." He tried to make a joke but was confused when she turned and glanced at him, tears in her eyes, holding boxes of cereal in each hand.

"Lowell . . . he'll be upset if he thinks you're . . . he's so proud, Zach. I don't have to tell you that."

For a moment, silence eclipsed the sounds of kids' laughter coming from the other room. He understood what she was trying to say; his buddy was proud and stubborn, no less than he was himself.

"Then don't tell him," Zach finally said. "He's in bed with the flu, and the kids are just interested in the action figures that came in the bags."

Anne Marie held up a roast. "Zach . . . a ten-pound pot roast, chicken, a ham, burgers, hot dogs, a Butterball turkey, collard greens?" She set the roast down on the counter, turned away, and sucked in a huge inhale that sounded like it contained a repressed sob.

"Okay, maybe I overstepped my boundaries a little . . . but I'm a single guy, I don't know how to family food shop, so I was following this old lady around the store putting in my cart the kinds of stuff she put in hers. Then I just ran through the aisles like I was on a game show, because I really didn't have a lot of time."

Anne Marie wiped her face and then allowed a laugh to escape. "Stop lying, Zach."

"Well, I did." He shrugged and leaned against the wall. "I'm a bachelor and normally do takeout."

"It's almost Memorial Day . . . she was probably shopping for her entire extended family or a family reunion, man."

He was glad to see the strain slip away from Anne Marie's expression to be replaced by her warm smile. "Oh, well, I hadn't thought of that—I'm just glad the old lady didn't think I was stalking her and try to cut me or something."

That made Anne Marie laugh in earnest and it took a ten-pound weight off his shoulders.

"But what are you doing here?" she finally said, glimpsing him over her shoulder. "Not that you aren't always welcome, but . . ."

"I was in the neighborhood." He took a toothpick out of the holder on the table and popped it in his mouth.

"You live in Detroit."

He pushed off the wall and went to the fridge and grabbed a beer. "Technically, I live all over the world, wherever they send me—Detroit is just an address I use to vote, pay bills, and file taxes."

She watched him turn the beer up and guzzle it. "I just spoke to you yesterday and you were in Detroit." She placed her hands on her hips and smiled when he smiled around the bottle.

Zach swallowed with a wince. "Yesterday I didn't know that my boy was down hard with the flu and had been battling it for the last week until we talked. I followed my gut and got on a plane to put my eyes on him for myself . . . and to see if I could talk some sense into him about going to the hospital like you'd asked me. This morning he called me and asked me to do a simple driving job—so it's all good."

"Lowell actually called you and told you he was too sick to do a driving job . . ." she said carefully, her smile fading.

"Ain't it a little late in the season for the flu, the regular kind, anyway?" Zach rubbed his palms down his face. "This isn't like Lowell to call me with something like this—but I want you to know that I've got his six . . . and he needs to go to the hospital. That's the primary reason I'm here, to make sure he does."

Again quiet stood between them as a silent observer.

"He's been going through . . . a lot of changes, right now, Zach. The business isn't doing as well as he'd imagined it would, not a lot of people are hiring unless you already have an in . . . and he swears it isn't that bad—he just needs some rest. I've tried to get him to go, but you know Lowell."

"Yeah, I know Lowell. That's why I came to see what was going on with him for myself. You guys are the only family I've got," Zach said in a quiet tone. "The man saved my life, least a brother can do is put his eye on the man, make sure his family is straight while he's going through a lil' something . . . make sure his boys are okay, you know? But I will get him to the hospital if I have to carry his ornery behind there myself."

"Thank you for that," Anne Marie said softly and then looked down at the floor. "I don't know if it's physical or emotional or a combination of both? After he came back, I never could be sure." She looked up at Zach and then toward the kitchen door as though making sure the children were out of earshot. "He just won a major contract . . . one that could set him and his business partners straight for a long time. He got the bodyguard job for Queen B when she goes on her USO Tour this weekend—so I know it has to be the flu. She called this morning, and when that didn't get him out of bed I knew he was bad."

"You mean he *just* got the overseas tour contract, too, for Anita Brown?" Zach said, shocked.

"The one and only Miss Scandalous herself."

Zach opened his mouth and closed it, and then smoothed his palm across his close-cropped hair. What could he say? It was clear that Anne Marie had the same opinion as ninety percent of the general public, thinking of Anita Brown as an off-the-hook music vixen who was notoriously in the news.

Her family was wild and word in the media was that the woman was as crazy as a bedbug. Everything that was ever written about her portrayed her as a waste of raw beauty— that seemed to coincide with her fleeting rap career. After meeting her it was impossible to think of her that way. He now wondered if it was all PR hype.

But he tried to keep a poker face after the initial outburst while Anne Marie went back to her task of stashing groceries.

"You know, Zach, the 'B' in Queen B's name isn't just for her surname Brown. I know this contract pays good money, but I swear I wish Lowell didn't have to take it from her. By that hussy's own admission and even in her lyrics, the so-called 'B' was substituted for a very unflattering term for a female dog. Lowell is supposed to guard *her*? Puh-lease. That chile is straight ghetto, and now she's trying to crawl back to R&B on her hands and knees and hope folks forget about her wildness." Anne Marie shook her head.

"Maybe she isn't as bad as she seems," Zach offered, not wanting to get in the middle of an obvious husband-and-wife dispute over a pretty woman. "Maybe it was all for publicity that went very badly."

"Yeah, that would be the hopeful thought, I doubt it though," Anne Marie said, sighing. "But I didn't fight him on it because it could change all of our lives. Lowell worked so hard on getting the right in, greasing the right palms, meeting the right people . . . and this is their big chance for SWAT International. If this tour goes well, and they get high-profile paparazzi coverage with it, then maybe other entertainers will also ask for them by name. The only way he'd been able to convince Queen B's people to let them have this one tour was because she was visiting U.S. military bases over where you guys have been . . . Iraq, Kuwait, Dubai, Oman, Yemen . . ."

Anne Marie blew out a long breath. "He's sick and even sicker that he can't personally oversee this ten-day mission—or whatever you call it. The whole deal could unravel for something stupid like the bug. I think that's half of why he's refusing to go to the hospital, afraid that they'll confirm that he *has* to lie down and take meds."

She put a fist to her mouth and turned away from Zach for a moment. "It would have been a thirty-thousand-dollar-a-day job for them, with all expenses paid. Each of the ten hired security men were supposed to get five hundred dollars a day, plus meals, flights, lodging, all covered by Queen B's label. Lowell was supposed to be the logistics man, the boots on the ground—whereas his other two partners handle the marketing of the firm and the administration of it . . . but Mike Epps and Vernon Knox aren't ex-Delta Force like Lowell. They don't know squat about anything like that and can't do what has to be done."

"It's gonna be all right, Anne," Zachary heard himself say without allowing the thought to consult his brain first. He downed his cold beer and set the bottle on the kitchen table.

What was there to think about, really? Each partner, after expenses, would have a little over eighty thousand dollars at his disposal. After taxes, who knows what would be left, but it had to be a far cry better than doing some mall security detail or trying to get a contract to do security for corporations that were falling by the wayside like dominoes.

Anne Marie turned and stared at Zach for a moment. "It has to be all right," she said quietly. "We're real late on the rent . . . Lowell sunk everything into this business venture and how could I argue with him after all he's given and all he's lost?"

Zach just nodded. There were no words. He knew better than anyone how much his buddy had given in the line of duty to his nation, so a little latitude to start up his own business was well in order.

"You're a good woman, Anne . . . to have his back like that without any drama—even though I know it's gotta be hard sometimes."

"I love the ground he walks on," she said quietly. "But I'm scared. He's getting so desperate for work that he's thinking of trying to get contracts with the large mercantile shipping companies—the ones that make sweeps from Saudi Arabia around the horn of Africa . . . or—"

"Being on pirate watch as a hired mercenary?" Zach ran his palms down his face again. "Maaan . . ."

"He'll be away from me and the boys just like before, but only worse, maybe . . . it's not like he's with the U.S. government, this is him going solo up against whatever is out there. I'd rather see him reenlist, if he was going to do all of that."

"Let me talk to him," Zach said, chewing harder on his toothpick. "I'm home for a coupla weeks, and if he gives me the logistics on the Anita Brown job, then maybe I can fill in for him. This way, he'll still bring home the bacon, and that'll give him a little time to regroup without having to do something rash. I don't need a cut, I'm cool."

"I couldn't ask you to do anything like that, and if he thought I—"

"You didn't ask me to do anything; I'm telling you what I'm okay with." Zach smiled and headed out of the kitchen. "Besides I'm single . . . what's not to love—being on tour with a bunch of video vixens, making sure ardent fans stay back," he shrugged. "Piece of cake."

CHAPTER 4

ANITA SECURING HER towel breezed past her stylist with a bright smile while she ignored his fussing. "Can I put on a robe at least, before you start?"

"Don't try to act like I'm the one who is getting on your nerves, boo. I'm not early; you're late. You know I'm punctual." He waved the mail he'd collected off the small crescent table in the hallway at her in a mock threat. "Look at you—you're a complete mess. You need somebody to take care of you." He tossed her mail on the glass coffee table and made a little ticking sound when he saw her wet footprints against the hardwood floors. "This makes no sense, darling," he added, singsonging the words behind her.

"I'll get a mop, and then I'm all yours."

"Oh, puh-lease." He walked into the kitchen and carefully set down the Ferragamo men's shoe box and gently laid the matching suit bag across her kitchen stool to hunt for the mop.

"See, did that take long?" she asked, laughing when Javier twisted his mouth into a combination pout and scowl. She took the mop from him and quickly dabbed the floors and returned. "There."

"Humph," he exclaimed and then put away the mop in her small utility closet. "I know you'd better keep NextStarz's floors clean and everything else. How long they gonna keep you here, boo?"

She shrugged and let out a sigh. "I only got put up here until the police find this stalker . . . I dunno. I doubt they'll let me stay beyond the tour. They're spending a lot of money on relaunching my career."

"After your father and your stupid brothers tried to tank it, but you didn't hear that from me."

Anita nodded. "I so do not want to talk about them now."

"You're right—tonight it's all about you, honey. So, let me wash those troubles out of your hair."

"I love you, Javier," she said, going to him and giving him a big hug.

He hugged her back and then held her away from him. "The pink silk looks good on you, girl—you been losing weight? But don't you get too skinny on us."

"See, why you always have to say something nice and then—"

"Because I'm nosy," he said, swishing away from her to go hold up the shoes. "Tell me, who for the love of all that is manly, is taking you to the awards tonight wearing a size *fifteen* shoe, girl!"

She laughed so hard that she fell against the granite counter and it took her minutes to recover. "No, I don't have a date—this is for my limo driver, but I had the same reaction."

"Oh, now that's sad," Javier said, sucking his teeth. "Your limo driver." He shook his head and put a hand on one hip. "Girl, you're supposed to have a limo driver, a security bodyguard team, *and* a date, and not necessarily in that order. Who is going to strut you down the red carpet? You need a real publicist and to get away from Jonathan Evans's organization. That man is still playing you."

"That's the best I could do on short notice," she said, trying not to lose her smile. "I got the security coming for the tour . . . as well as I got NextStarz to honor their contract to provide me emergency housing," she added, sweeping her arms around the kitchen. "Jonathan would have been my date but he liked teenage groupies, soooo, what do you want?"

"Well, is this limo man fine at least? I mean, since you're dressing him up?

Anita winked. "Make me beautiful and I'll tell you all about him."

ZACH POKED HIS head into the bedroom, needing to talk to Lowell, but not wanting to disturb his sleep. His gaze scanned the darkened room, and fixed on the prosthetic leg that was resting against the overstuffed chair in the far corner of the room. Memories turned a blade in his gut— nothing would ever erase that day from his mind.

Sleep deprivation had made him oblivious to a camouflaged improvised explosive device. Lowell had seen the IED in time to pull him back, shoving him far enough away from the deadly shrapnel it contained. But the vibration of his falling triggered it just as Lowell dove away, costing him a leg. He owed Lowell more than his life . . . he owed him the quality of life. How did one even begin to repay a debt so deep?

"Hey, man," Zach said, tapping on the frame of the bedroom door as Lowell stirred. Force of habit wouldn't allow him to walk up on a sleeping, combat-ready soldier without announcing himself—it was a good way to get snuffed.

Lowell opened his eyes and tried to smile. "Glad you brought your sorry ass to the Big Apple?"

Zach tried to smile and entered the room but didn't put on the light. The shades were drawn but he could still see. "Came to check on you."

"There goes Anne Marie running off her mouth again. She tipped you off before I called you, right? Sounds like too much of a coincidence that you just so happened to be in the city when I went down." Lowell closed his eyes.

Zachary stood very, very still. The tone his friend had used when referring to his wife concerned him. The stench in the room was definitely that of a sick man . . . vomit, sweat, and a lot of self-pity. Lowell's normal caramel skin tone was off and his eyes almost seemed jaundiced. He'd lost weight since the last time he'd seen him, but Lowell also seemed puffy in the face and hands.

"She meant no harm," Zach said carefully. He shrugged,

trying to seem nonchalant and then leaned against the wall, not wanting to go near the chair with the prosthetic. "She just said you had the flu—hey. No biggie."

He watched his friend relax a little, but that didn't mitigate his concern for Lowell.

"All right . . . Thanks, man. I just don't like Anne Marie trying to treat me like I'm an invalid or something." Lowell's tone was suspicious, and his gaze was hard and unrelenting. "Everything go okay with the driving job today?"

"It was easy, no sweat. I'm ready for tonight—just gotta shower and change, then I'm out. But, uh, listen . . . I have to thank you. I'm getting to see a beautiful lady do her thing on stage . . . getting a backstage pass. Wouldn't be a bad way to spend my leave keeping her safe."

Zach knew the ruse was lame, but he needed a way to open the discussion with his very defensive friend. For a moment he didn't think Lowell would buy it, and then all of a sudden his buddy laughed.

"Are you serious?" Lowell shook his head and simply closed his eyes again, wheezing.

"What?" Zach said, joking around. "Have you seen that woman? She's seriously fine, man."

"Yeah, I've seen her," Lowell said without opening his eyes. "But you know what the B stands for."

"Yeah, yeah, I've heard," Zach said, forcing himself to laugh. "Still, you can't believe everything you hear in the tabloids."

"Fortunately I don't have to read the tabloids . . . I've got a contract to bodyguard her at the awards event and don't have another guy that I can just pull off a standing job. These stars are so fickle, I can't afford to jeopardize a steady corporate contract and then have her decide on a whim to go back to having her dumb-and-dumber brothers being her bouncers. That's why I've gotta get up and outta this bed." Lowell struggled to sit up but then summarily gave up the fight. "I feel like holy hell, though . . . who gets the flu in May?"

"You know, if you give that poor woman what you've got

and she can't perform, she might sue you." Zach folded his arms over his chest. "I damned sure would."

"I hadn't even thought about that—and she's just the type who would do it, too, man."

"Why don't you have a stand-in go . . . one of the guys from the—"

"Never happen," Lowell said, cutting him off and coughing. "Those guys follow orders well enough, but aren't good at strategy, making logistical corrections and doing maneuvers on the fly, or anticipating best-case, worst-case scenarios. They've got good enough resumes in security, but not up to Delta Force standards, you know what I mean."

"I hear you," Zach said, nodding. "That's why we do what we do."

"Yeah. That's why I've gotta get out of this bed so I can feed my family."

"I thought we were boys . . . best friends, man," Zach said with a fake frown.

"We are—what are you talking about?"

"You have a gig with Queen B . . . you have the flu . . . and you can't think of another soul who might be able to step in and give you an assist? Okay, man. I'm hurt, but I'll let it slide."

"Oh, hey, Zach . . . I thought you wouldn't be interested and were just joking around. I know you said you'd go, but I really wasn't going to impose on you after this morning. Besides I know how you hate chaos, plus I didn't know your schedule. Hell, I didn't even know you were stateside and available until we talked."

"I'm on leave for six weeks." Zach folded his arms and stared down at Lowell and then smiled. "And what did I tell you on the phone when you called me back this afternoon?"

"Anne Marie told you about the ten-day tour, didn't she, asshole?" Lowell chuckled.

"That's on a need-to-know basis, soldier," Zach said, smiling wider.

"My wife probably poisoned me to keep me from going overseas alone with that fine babe anyway."

"Wouldn't blame her," Zach said, chuckling. "So, let me take the weight."

"If you do this, your cut—"

"Hey, hey . . . don't insult me, all right?" Zach paced away from the bed. "I get an all-expenses-paid, first-class, backstage pass with *Queen B* and you want to pay *me*? Be serious."

"Oh, yeah, I forgot, this is a vacation in paradise for the consummate bachelor. But you're giving up your leave and you'll definitely be working. This chick is high maintenance—"

"Aren't they all?"

"True, when you put it that way." Lowell smiled and nodded toward the chair across the room. "Grab a seat; throw that phony leg on the floor. If you're gonna do recognizance for me, then at least you need to know the basic terrain." He cocked his head to the side with a wider grin. "By the way, brother, when are you gonna finally give up the lone-wolf routine and come to work with me?"

HE STOOD IN the large hallway in front of Anita Brown's door with a suit bag slung over his shoulder, waiting. He'd called up in advance and the doorman had known to let him in. But this whole stalker business deeply concerned him. It could be an old boyfriend, disgruntled ex-employee, pissed off family member, or just a general regulation nutcase. There were so many variables that he didn't like. Although he wouldn't upset her tonight, if he was going to be her primary bodyguard during her tour, she'd have to sit down with him and revisit everything she'd given and told the police.

And if she didn't open the door in the next thirty seconds . . .

"Well, hello," her stylist said, looking him up and down. "I have your tux and I'm still working on 'Nita. Can't rush beauty—but *please* come in."

"Thank you, sir," Zach said, remaining formal.

"Uhmmmph, uhmmmph, uhmmmph—and *you're* her driver?"

"Yes, sir," Zachary said, keeping everything in his tone strictly military as he followed the slender male into Anita's apartment.

"Well, my name is Javier. That's French, by way of Haiti," he said over his shoulder with a smile. "Your things are in a guest room in the back."

Zach followed him without a word and stepped into the empty room. As soon as he closed the door he heard Javier's voice ring down the hall.

"Hurry up, 'Nita—GI Joe is here!"

A FULL TWENTY additional minutes had passed and he was determined not to pace. The endless windows gave him something to do as he looked out at the park and the little ant-like dots of people on the sidewalk. He ran the entrance and exit sequences through his mind that Lowell had given him, glad that there was a truck delivery entrance in back of the building as well as an underground lot so he could get Anita past all the fanfare that was beginning to gather at the front door.

But the moment her heels hit the hardwood floor, everything he'd been training his mind on evaporated. He turned away from the window and simply gaped.

She came out of the hallway clutching a small gold purse in her hands and was sheathed in a honey-brown fabric that looked like it was wet. He had no concept of how Javier did it, but he would definitely give the man due respect for his profession.

Anita's hair was twisted up and held as if by long crystalline magic pins . . . her gorgeous face was dusted in shimmering gold and her lashes were thick and lush—eyes absolutely breathtaking. But her mouth . . . it held the same wet quality of her dress, and good *Gawd*, it seemed like she was poured into her gown as though she were liquid flesh herself. The deep plunging neckline made him need to check his pulse, and the slit that ran up the front of the gown exposed her shapely legs that seemed to go on forever.

"So, how do you like my creation?" Javier said, preening and gesturing toward Anita.

"Stunning."

Javier bowed. "I see you are a man of few words, but I will take that as a high compliment coming from you."

"Thank you," Anita said, smiling as she air kissed Javier. "The tux looks great on you, too." She favored him with a lingering glance and then looked at Javier. "Thank you for always making everyone look so nice."

"I make it do what it do, that's all, love," Javier said. "You kids have fun."

Zach nodded and then had to remember how to cross the room and open the door. But he managed to do so without letting on just how much her transformation had fried his brain.

"Javier is going to let himself out," she said as he closed the door behind them. "And the tux really does look great on you."

"Thank you—"

"Don't say, ma'am," she said quickly, finally making him smile.

"Anita," he said, wondering if she knew just how much her compliment coated him with a new warmth he couldn't explain.

"Good, finally," she said, stepping into the elevator in front of him. "You don't have to wait in the greenroom, you know, or hang in the wings, unless you want to . . . uhmm . . . you can sit in the reserved seating in the front and just dip back to the greenroom during breaks—if you want."

"I thought the reserved seating was for your guests," he said carefully, giving her a sidelong glance.

She shrugged one delicate shoulder. "Why can't you also be a guest?"

He nodded but then caught her gaze as he stopped looking at the elevator numbers descending. "I'm no PR person . . . and I thank you for such a kind offer, but . . . if the paparazzi see me drive you and get out of the limo as your driver and then I show up in the reserved seating, that might look like—"

"I know, I know," she said, waving her hand. "I have no

right to intrude on your private life. Your girlfriend or wife could take things the wrong way, then there'd be drama and whatever."

"No," he said flatly. "There wouldn't be drama on my end. My concern is that the tabloids started up some nonsense about your reputation, signifying that you had a limo driver and a paid escort. You deserve to be shown in a much better light than that. I would be a distraction. I think it would be best if I stayed in the background."

She looked at him with a completely open gaze. "Thank you for that—for caring how things might look for me. I wasn't really figuring all of that out . . . I guess I just hated the fact that Jonathan Evans would be there flaunting his latest conquest and I'd be sitting there by myself." She turned to look at the elevator doors. "It's amazing how alone you can feel even in a room of thousands of people all screaming your name."

The elevator doors opened and she'd left him speechless. His mind immediately latched onto the task at hand as a diversion. He exited the elevator first, keeping her behind him as he navigated them toward the limo. But what she'd said and the sad timbre of her voice haunted him. So the head of NextStarz was her ex? That arrogant SOB had just cast this woman aside like refuse? What was wrong in America?

Zachary opened the limo door and helped Anita in. He was about to close the door and keep his opinions to himself, but her forlorn expression made him stop and lean in as he held onto the door frame.

"If Evans shows up there with anybody but you—he's a fool. I hope you win tonight, and I don't care how many people are there, just because I'm not in the VIP seats, doesn't mean I'm not watching . . . you're not alone, all right?"

She rewarded him with a slow turn of her head, an open gaze, and a slow smile that broke on her face like new dawn. "Thank you," she murmured. "Knowing that will get me through the night."

"Let's get you to your big event," he said in a softer tone

than he normally employed. He had to close the door; this woman was fracturing his skull, breaking his concentration, and about to make him cross a line that in the end could cost Lowell a contract, if things went poorly.

Butterflies swirled in her belly and exploded in a cloud of dancing tremors the moment he shut the door. He'd declined because he cared? Wasn't seeking a front row and the lime-light, and actually cared about appearances for her own good? Then there was the way he looked at her, oh, my God. The man smelled so good, too . . . and the tux just set off every chiseled feature in his handsome face and phenomenal bod.

She kept her gaze directed out of the window as the vehicle began its slow egress out of the lot and onto the street, wondering if Zachary Mitchell had someone special in his life.

IT WAS AN experience of a lifetime to be backstage at the famous Apollo Theater, brushing elbows with the glitterati. But his focus was singular as he waited for her in the wings; to be sure nothing happened to Anita Brown. She'd selected one of her soulful ballads from her new album, *What Happened to Us*, and as the sad anthem dipped and swayed, he watched her move to the lyrics of heartbreak, mesmerized by hers and remembering his own.

However, nothing could have prepared him for her bright expression as she exited and came into the wings breathless, greeting him and blotting her forehead.

"How was I? Was it good?"

He didn't know what to say for a moment, but found the words before her face fell. "It was . . . beyond awesome."

Her spontaneous hug blew his mind, almost blew a gasket, and then she left his embrace to dash back to get her makeup retouched. He waited, trying to stay detached in the flurry of backstage activity, and then quickly escorted her to her seat. He felt her tense on his arm as she passed her ex, but remained in character—then gave her a wink and a discreet thumbs-up to make her smile.

Anita kept her gaze forward. She would not even glance at Jonathan and his new conquest. They were becoming increasingly irrelevant anyway. If she could just watch her fellow performers do their thing that was good enough for her. Zachary's wink, his support, meant all the difference in the world. But that made no sense; she'd just met the man.

Suddenly as they began reading off the nominations for best R&B Emerging Solo Album, she understood why she'd surrounded herself with so many negative people. Her family wasn't there, her friends were mostly surface people she'd met along the way coming up, and now at a moment like this there was no one to sit on pins and needles with her . . . no one to hold her hand and cheer with her.

When they called her name, electricity shot through her, along with a numbing pang of loneliness. But she held her head high, put on her best star smile, and walked to the podium to accept her award in honor of her late mother.

CHAPTER 5

NAVIGATING ANITA THROUGH the throng of well-wishers, fans, and cameras made him feel like a salmon swimming upstream. He waited patiently in the background of the after-party, watching her schmooze and politic with all the right people, and knowing she had to be exhausted. But he also monitored the tension within her as her brothers approached; the conversation did not look like it was going well. He caught Jonathan Evans's smug expression. That's when he moved in.

"I told you it was all settled," Anita said in a low voice, glaring at her brothers. "Why can't you all just be happy for me? I'm not about to discuss any of that here."

"Is there a problem, ma'am?" Zachary leaned in calmly, but had positioned Anita slightly behind him.

"This is family, rent-a-cop," Antwan said. "So step off."

"If you're bothering the lady, you're bothering me—back away from her personal space."

"What the fuck?" Derrick said, and then nodded to three men across the room.

"Do not start in here, please," Anita said. "I'm ready to go, Zachary. I don't need this."

Unfortunately, Antwan grabbed her arm and jerked her back toward him.

"I said we are gonna discuss it now, because you ain't—"

It was reflex. Zach spun backward and caught Antwan in

the temple and dropped him where he stood. Derrick rushed him, but in a lightning-fast jujitsu move, he'd caught Derrick's arm and had it twisted behind his back at a precarious angle without even wrinkling his tux.

"The lady said she was ready to leave," Zachary said in a low, quiet threat. "I suggest that you do not cause her or yourself any further embarrassment tonight." He flung her brother away from his hold, smoothed his lapels and then took up Anita's arm. "You stay with me," he said quietly, ushering her through the crowd at a rapid pace. "The cameras are going to be all over it and you don't need to be near it."

"Thank you," she said, dipping out of the door behind him, and then held his arm tighter as he guided her through a back hotel exit.

"I want you in the car," he said, opening the limo door and quickly ushering her in. "If it gets really crazy, use your cell and call 911, but do not open the door."

She didn't have time to respond as three men entered the underground limo valet port, and Zachary took a stance.

"That was our boy," one of the combatants said and then looked at the limo. "'Twan and Derrick, us—we all go way back, and that's his sister—so you'd better tell your boss that we do her security detail!"

"Bing? Is that you?" Anita opened the limo door and got out.

"Please get back in the vehicle," Zachary said, glancing at her and then at the men who were slowly approaching him. "Gentlemen, I suggest that you don't do anything stupid tonight. Trust me, this will not end well."

"You fuckin' A—right it won't end well," the leader identified as Bing said, and then pulled out a nine millimeter.

Before he could brandish it, he was on his back, weapon stripped, coughing up blood. Zachary had a knee in his chest, his arm outstretched, weapon dead aim.

"On the ground! Now!"

The two men that had been with Bing slowly got down on the cement garage floor. Zachary jumped up keeping the gun trained on them. "Call 911," he said to Anita.

The heavy guy with the fade haircut spoke up first, trying to compromise, even though his skinny little friend glared at Zach with hatred.

"C'mon, 'Nita, have a heart—it ain't registered, Bing's got outstanding warrants . . . you know we all grew up to-gether . . . damn, my suit is all jacked, c'mon, girl."

Zach pulled the gun back and then unloaded the clip. "If I see you assholes anywhere near this lady again, I'm gonna oops and accidentally pull the trigger . . . and explain to the cops later. We clear?"

Two heads nodded as Bing rolled over, holding his throat and groaned. Zachary tossed the clip across the lot and wiped the gun off with his suit before dropping it at his feet. The cameras would find them soon and valets who'd seen the whole thing go down were craning their necks to get a glimpse of the aftermath. They had to get out of there.

"Please, ma'am, don't make me ask you again . . . get back in the limo."

Anita sat in silence, staring at the divider glass. Damn . . . But if body language was any indicator, Zachary Mitchell was so pissed off he probably couldn't speak. Her brothers had ruined her evening—adding drama like they always did, and Jonathan had aided and abetted them in their shenanigans by even allowing them a pass in. Her father hadn't even come up to congratulate her, being too busy with the women he was chasing. She sat back and closed her eyes. Still it felt good to have someone stand up for her. The hangers-on from the old neighborhood were history after this last fiasco. They'd pulled a gun? Were they high? Then she saw it . . . her award. Zach had had someone bring the award to the car for her, rather than let them ship it?

She leaned forward and picked up the box, extracting it carefully. Her fingers played over the engraving and she clutched it to her chest trying not to tear and mess up her makeup. If only her mama was still alive—she'd been the one who believed when no one else did.

The moment Anita felt the limo come to a full stop she glanced around, glad that NextStarz had at least kept her temporary location secret—but that's when she saw the mob of cameras rush the vehicle. Zach had maneuvered it into a space, but they were now boxed in from all sides.

The divider window lowered. "Are you ready?" Zach said, without looking at her.

Anita took a deep breath. "Yeah . . . are you?"

He didn't answer, just got out of the vehicle, but she noticed that after the first reporter caught a severe elbow to the jaw, the others backed up and gave him enough space to round her door.

Bright lights flashed creating a miasma of light as she exited and grabbed Zach's hand.

"Back up and give the lady space," Zach said in a sonic boom, and one cameraman who hadn't gotten the memo took a flat-palm blow to the chest that instantly put him on the ground.

Voices screamed out a cacophony of insulting questions, and suddenly a strong arm was around her waist as a stone-cut torso was body-shielding her, lifting her, hurrying her without effort.

"Is it true your brothers have beef with your new security company?"

"We heard you've made a police report about a stalker, Queen B! Talk to us, have you seen him?"

"Is it true you cut your father off and left your siblings high and dry?"

"Who's the new limo driver—any romantic connection?"

"How's it feel to come back so strong in R&B after a disastrous year in the rap game?"

She wanted to yell out curses for them to leave her alone, to tell them all to get a life—to tell them that it felt like she'd exited hell and entered a peaceful new world the second the doors shut behind her. But she said none of those things, just kept her head down as she held onto Zach, slumping now from relief.

However that relief was short-lived as they made their way to the elevators. She was just about to thank him when he whirled on her, frowning.

"Do not ever pull a stunt like that again," he said in a low warning and then stared at the doors.

"Wait a minute," she said, beginning to take offense. "First of all—"

"What, you pay me?" he said, looking her dead in her eyes. "And this is what you pay me to do—keep you safe. When you're with me and on my security detail, you do as I say. We clear?"

"Yeah, and all you forgot was the ma'am at the end of that sentence," she snapped.

"In public, you are ma'am at all times. Period." His arm came away from his body in a hard point toward where the paparazzi had been. "You saw those sharks out there. I heard their questions. You did not deserve or need that on your big night."

He turned away from her and kept his gaze focused on the elevator doors until they opened.

"I don't know how they found me," she said quietly as the doors closed behind them.

"Your ex or your family probably fed them your new location; that would be my first guess. Only one guy showed up from the new firm—me. They clearly want their old contract back and aren't happy with the new arrangement."

"That is so low . . . damn, you think they would go there?" she said, shaking her head as the elevator let them off on their floor.

Zachary stopped walking. "A man had a gun in your face, Anita. If they'd do that, and this is the so-called posse your brothers are still running with, do I need to fill in the blanks?"

"That was just Bing from the old neighborhood," she said, handing him the keys.

"Would you listen to yourself?" He shoved the door open and walked through the apartment, fury measuring his every step. "All clear!"

"Yo, what's your problem?" she said, closing the door behind them and walking over to the coffee table angrily to set down her award and her purse.

"What's *my* problem?" he said evenly. "You sound like a person who is used to settling, used to accepting unacceptable behavior as a norm."

"Oh, you just need to get out of my house with that bull." Anita placed her hands on her hips as he crossed the room. "You don't know me. What do you know about where I came from anyway?"

"I know a lot about you and where you came from—my mother came from the same place you did. Different location, same state of mind!" He pointed at her hard and his voice was like slow, rolling thunder. "She allowed herself to be around people who meant her no good, treated her any way they wanted to, and in the end, it killed a beautiful, classy woman—made her go home to glory long before her time. So, if you want to hang around thugs, give them a free pass on the things they do wrong, and squander all your beauty and brains and talent, then be my guest. I don't have to like it; I'm just the hired help. But while you're my charge, oh, hell, no! The next time a fool you know from the old 'hood puts a gun in your face I will break his punk arm off. We clear?"

"Yes, sir," she said, and then bit her lip hiding a tiny smile. "Okay . . . then, can I extend a peace offering?"

"Not necessary," he muttered. "I just need to get my suit and put this tux back in the bag for your stylist. I'll call in the next shift and will leave when my security detail replacement gets here." Zach looked down at his suit and noted a missing cuff link. "Please let your stylist know that I'll pay for any damages."

"Javier won't require all that, if I give him the blow-by-blow recount of how your suit got damaged . . . and you don't want to be on the hook for designer diamond and onyx links—we'll work it out."

"No, I insist," Zach argued and folded his arms.

"How about a cup of coffee, since I'm pretty sure you won't have a drink while on duty—you just seem like the type."

"I wouldn't mind a cup of joe; it's been a long day."

"How about a hot shower to go along with it?" She smiled wider when he simply stared at her.

"There's towels and stuff in the guest bathroom. After all the drama, I don't know about you but I'm ready to get out of the heels, get this makeup off my face." She shrugged and walked toward the kitchen. "I'm gonna start the coffee, shower, and put on some sweats—you can do as you like."

It was an offer he couldn't refuse. Just a little time to decompress and find his way back to center was in order. The hard spray and warm water unkinked his tight muscles and felt like a sedative. Until he'd stepped into the multihead spray, he hadn't realized how much he'd been running on fumes.

That didn't change the fact that Anita Brown was the most exasperating woman and at the same time she had a heart of gold. He'd quickly jumped in and out of the warm water, and to his surprise, she'd beaten him to the task. When he met her in the kitchen, her face was scrubbed clean and she had on an oversized tank top and a pair of soft grey yoga pants. The only evidence that she'd been at the awards gala was her hair was still done up in crystal pins.

"Hey . . ." he said quietly as he entered the kitchen and leaned on the center counter. "I'm sorry I yelled back there. Still had a lot of adrenaline in my system and was worried about what could have happened to you."

"Don't worry about it. At least you were fussing at me for a good reason . . . and I've been thinking a lot about what you said. I do tolerate a lot of mess I shouldn't." She brought him a coffee mug and leaned on the counter. "I like the change . . . the shirt with no tie, sleeves rolled up, no jacket. You look a little more relaxed. Cream and sugar?"

"No . . . just black . . . and you were right about the shower," he said, accepting the mug from her and taking a sip. "And right about the coffee. Thank you. Anita," he added with purpose.

She smiled brightly and took a sip from her mug.

"You have a really beautiful smile," he said. "If you don't mind me saying."

"I don't mind you saying," she said and then nodded toward the coffee table. "Thank you for getting that put in the limo. It can take days before they ship your stuff sometimes."

"You worked hard for that award and should be able to look at it tonight," he said quietly. "Your performance was outstanding."

"So was yours," she said, lifting her mug to him in a small salute. "I didn't feel like I was by myself tonight—I knew there was somebody there, for once, who even if it was part of their job, gave a damn about whether I . . . I don't know."

"It wasn't just because it was a part of my job, Anita," he said, abandoning his coffee as he stared at her. "You deserve to have somebody treat you nice, that's just basic."

"So, you don't believe the tabloids?"

"Why should I? That's not the person I've seen."

She made a little tick with her tongue against her teeth. "Everybody thinks I'm some kind of—"

He held up his hand. "I'm not everybody."

She looked at him, watching how the small appliance lights of the kitchen mixed with moonlight played across his handsome face. "No, you're not everybody at all."

For a long time neither of them spoke and finally he looked away.

"I should call in."

She shook her head no. "Not yet."

"You have an early flight I'm told."

She rounded the counter and came to stand in front of him. "I know." She rested her palms against his chest and looked up.

"This could get really complicated."

"It already is . . . don't you feel it?"

"Yeah . . . I do."

He nodded and leaned down to take her mouth and closed his eyes, breathing in her fresh showered fragrance, tasting cream and sugar and coffee all at the same time this soft woman melted against him. He could feel his hands tremble;

she was so delicate, like a piece of living art that breathed into his mouth, exploding sensations in his groin. It was a sensory indulgence that had been denied for too long, he had to allow his hands to flow over the satiny texture of her skin, then intermittently hit fabric, following the rise and swell of her body's curves while her tongue hunted his.

Delirium began to shred his formality, began to jeopardize his mission not to take things too far. Common sense peeled away swiftly; it happened as her graceful fingers gently traced the planes of his cheeks and slid down his neck, as though memorizing his face by sheer touch, then they found his back.

Flat palms, a woman's gentle press, sent sensual Morse code into his shoulders down the valley of his spine and finally over the ridge of his ass . . . oh, God . . . Roger that. He understood and deepened the kiss. Her body replied with a gasp and an arch. The crystal pins had to come out of her hair; he removed one and she began removing the rest.

Held captive by her touch, by her kiss, he remained her hostage as she slowly sucked on his bottom lip until her hair finally fell into his palms and then through his fingers in silky waves. Deftly managing his buttons, she opened his shirt and began tracing his chest through his T-shirt, her fingertips having some extrasensory perception about whether or not they should proceed. The only way he could reassure her was to take away his kiss from her warm, delicious mouth to spill it over her shoulders as he slowly lifted her tank top.

Hot hands slid up her back and made a tender sweep around her torso to cherish her breasts. Anita let her head drop back. Everything that she'd daydreamed of was fulfilled in his kiss as his warm mouth pressed against an angry nipple, suckling it softly, the wet sounds as erotic as the actual touch. Friction begat more friction which begat instant heat. Her Venus pushed hungrily against his length, her fingers gliding over an indomitable eight-pack, trying to wrest him free as he sought the other neglected nipple in a way that made her breath staccato.

He stepped out of his shoes; she stepped out of her yoga pants and clasped his hand. Their eyes met and he followed her lead to the sofa where she picked up her purse. There was no judgment in his gaze as he stared at her.

"I had hope," she said quietly.

"I didn't even dare to dream that far," he said, capturing her mouth.

"If I had known," she whispered, "you wouldn't have made it out of the elevator."

He kissed her harder, splaying his hands over the full lobes of her ass as he yanked her tighter against him. "I'll remember that when we're in the limo."

She couldn't hold onto the purse as she fumbled to get it open and collect the contents. Papers that Javier had left spilled to the floor as Zachary pulled her down on top of him. But as she picked up the condom, she froze.

"What's the matter?" Zachary's breathing was shallow, coming in short bursts.

She snatched up the unmarked envelope that had a smiley face on it and scrambled back from him, folding her body into a tiny ball.

"Baby, what's the matter?" he said slowly, watching her wrap her arms tightly around her shins as the letter fell away from her hands.

He snatched up the letter and opened it. A single page with cutout letters from various magazines made him become very, very still. The message was simple but menacing: *I know where you live again. You cannot hide from me. Soon you die.*

"I want you to go put some clothes on, I'll pull myself together—then we have to call the police. All right?" He picked up her purse and handed it to her, putting away the condoms.

Anita nodded but still seemed in shell shock. She hadn't moved and had begun rocking as moisture swelled in her eyes and then flowed down her flushed cheeks in two large tears. He knelt down in front of her and kissed her face, wiping away the tears with the pads of his thumbs.

"Don't leave me," she whispered hoarsely. "Spend the night after the police go . . . and just hold me, okay?"

"I'm not going anywhere. I promise."

TWO MEN IN the lobby, two in the limo, five already at the airport sweeping the private jet and at the ready for crowd control . . . Zachary ticked off the logistics of the job as he pressed the elevator button within the expansive lobby.

One of Lowell's other men had picked up his luggage, and he'd filled the squad in about the discovery of the stalker's latest note. Now he just needed to do one last pass through the building routes while Anita worked out logistics with her management. It was vitally important now that he remain focused. He couldn't allow his mind to flex back to what almost happened but didn't. Keeping 'Nita safe was his only goal. It wasn't about taking advantage of her when she was frightened and vulnerable . . . the look on her face replayed itself over and over again in his mind. She'd snuggled into his spoon and slept like a baby while wrapped in his arms.

Memories of the fiancée he once had stabbed into his brain—and he quickly jettisoned the thoughts. Betrayed once, never again. It was probably a good thing that they found the letter when they did, this way things hadn't gone too far, hadn't gotten complicated. This was best. He'd be her driver, her primary bodyguard. He was never destined to be her lover; it would never work. This was situational attraction; that's what he had to remember.

Zachary stared at the elevator doors and then ignored the shudder that the memory of Anita's words produced. "In the elevator . . ." He could just imagine it.

No. Think about something else. Okay, mission-related: He liked being early for the flight, but hated wearing a suit and having a wire in his ear. After last night, his white, Oxford button-down shirt and rep tie felt totally confining, just like the boring lace-up wing-tip shoes did. Men in black; Zachary shook his head. Black jeans and a T-shirt would have made him feel more comfortable, even fatigues would have been okay by him. But Lowell had them all looking like a Secret Service detail.

The elevator sounded and shook him out of his thoughts. He stepped into the elevator car alone and pressed the button, watching the numbers light up as he ascended. Mild adrenaline coursed through him, wondering how he was going to handle being around her for ten days, especially after tasting her kiss, her skin, feeling her against him. With any luck, things would be fairly routine; he'd do the job, his buddy would get paid, and then he'd get back to base. Simple. He had to disengage from the personal. He was just glad that he was able to convince Lowell that he was doing him a big favor, and not the other way around. His buddy was way too proud to have it any other way.

But as Zach exited on his floor, all his hopes of an easy morning following practically no sleep last night were dashed. The first thing he heard was Anita's voice yelling expletives so loud that she might as well have had the suite door open. What the hell had happened now?

Taking his time, he approached the door and then knocked, glancing at his watch. Whatever the problem was, his only concern and responsibility at the moment was to safely get her from point A, the building, to point B, the airport, and aboard her private charter. If her family had started some drama, he'd break both her brothers' faces.

The door swung open with a bang and for a few seconds he was at a loss for words. Today she wasn't the scared little girl or a victim. Something had clearly pissed her off to the point where she was ready to fight even a potential stalker.

Anita Brown stood with a challenge in her stance, five-foot-seven worth of stunning gorgeous female teetering on gold stiletto heels, a graceful hand on her hip, sunglasses masking her lovely eyes but not hiding her frown. A belted, ivory linen pants suit hugged her fantastic curves, a gold bra showing in the deep plunging neckline. Chestnut brown hair cascaded over her shoulders and a glistening mouth pouted as she finally crossed her arms.

"These people get on my last nerve, Zach."

"Yes, ma'am," he said, peering around her at the man in the living room and trying to keep the personal nature of their relationship off radar.

"They're trying to pull a contractual fast one, saying your firm is too costly, and denying me security—and I'm not having it," she said, full of attitude then turning away and walking back to the man she'd been arguing with.

Zach stepped just inside the door and closed it, manning an observation post by the door.

"I don't care what Jonathan said and I don't even know why you're here!" she shouted, pointing at the poor man who'd obviously been sent to deliver a message she didn't like. "This could have been done over the phone and the security detail is part of my contract. Tell him to read page thirty-five, section G, paragraph five, all right? It says that he has to pay for them when on tour for *his* label, and since the USO tour was booked on his label, not mine, then this is his dime."

"You never used to go here, 'Nita," the nervous man said, glancing at Zachary, who hadn't moved a muscle. "This isn't good business, it's pure feminine spite. You used to be fine with Jon paying your brothers and your father to do your security detail. Why all the changes? Why all the drama? Don't you want them to benefit from your success?"

"Don't try to play me, Ron," she said, circling him and making him turn to keep her in front of him. "The good cop/bad cop thing isn't working this morning. You had a lot of nerve trying to get my brothers up to my temporary apartment this morning, like nothing would be wrong and I'd change my mind. You set them up to get stopped at the doorman, not me. Who told you it was all right to hire them and try to void my contract with SWAT International?"

"I can't believe you actually did that to your own blood, girl . . . damn . . ." Ron hung his head and fingered his baseball cap. "You're really still that mad at Jon?"

"You tell that sorry son of a bitch boss of yours that he's done taking advantage of me. I deserve real top-notch security—and going into freaking Baghdad, that's what I want!"

"But we could get two or three outside hires to go with your brothers and—"

"What did I say? Are you deaf? I don't want my brothers or my father siphoning another penny off me. I'm also not going to make it easy for Jon to do anything on the cheap like he had been doing—skimming expenses because I'm his so-called woman. News flash, I'm not! So that's what's business, Ron. Take a memo. The cosmetics endorsements, TV appearances, new clothing line I'm launching, and every movie script I'm reviewing all come under *my* new label; he still owns the recording deals, and with that comes the guaranteed coverage of promotion and security."

She smiled a beautifully wicked smile and took a breath. "Fool did that when he thought I was still in love, I suppose—and thought I'd never wise up like the others he'd run in circles. That's not my problem. So, no, I'm not using some company he chooses—which will probably be some jackleg goons he knows from his old thug life. Tell the bastard to read the contract, and if he reneges, he can talk to my ass, and to my attorney! I am not afraid of him."

Zachary stood at attention at the door, watching the argument, watching the beauty before him rip into the messenger. He liked her fire, but it also made him wary. He was glad she'd found her fight, but having seen the lioness in her, he was now also aware that she had claws and teeth. The transformation was both alluring and unsettling. That was the thing he was never quite sure of—a woman could be one way when she was trying to enter your heart, and then could flip and crush your heart right under her stiletto heel the way Anita was carrying on now.

"All right, 'Nita," Ron finally said, and released a long sigh. "I'll let Jon know . . . there's no reasoning with you when you get like this. I'm out. But, just remember, Jonathan has a mean streak, too, and there will definitely be consequences, if you keep pushing him like this."

"Yeah, well, life has consequences—I guess Jonathan learned that lesson, too," she said addressing Ron's back.

Zachary stepped aside and opened the door for the man

who was leaving. He didn't even acknowledge him with a nod, which was cool, because what was there to say? The man had been humiliated in front of a complete stranger. Zachary listened to the door close.

"My bags are in the other room," Anita said, walking over to a small side table that held her Prada purse. "I'm sorry you had to see that."

For a moment he didn't move, just watched her fidget with her handbag and then extract a tube of lip gloss. After she quickly applied it, she tilted her head to the side. "So, where's the Delta Force dude . . . is that the last person we're waiting on?"

"There has been a slight personnel change that I thought you might want to be aware of before we went down to the limo."

"No more contract flubs today, Zach . . . c'mon. You just heard me light into Ron and company." She shook her head. "There was supposed to be some ex-Delta Force dude with all the medals and whatever. Please tell me this isn't some bait-and-switch bullcrap, because I know Jonathan will dig into your company's paperwork and try to sue your company into—"

"I appreciate the concern, 'Nita, but it's no bait and switch," Zachary said, carefully coming closer to her. "The primary came down with influenza—"

"In May?"

"In May," Zachary said, using his most practiced monotone military response. "It's going to be fine."

Anita snapped her purse shut. "Jonathan Evans believes everybody's got game, so why not you. I just don't want to see you take the fall if your firm isn't completely airtight."

She had a right to be worried; Lowell or someone from the firm should have informed her before now. But he also understood why no one had. His buddy couldn't afford to lose this contract, and it was evident now just how complicated Anita Brown's business relationships were. Zachary dug into his vest pocket and produced his security stats sheet as well as his passport.

"Evans can't touch Lowell Johnson for breach of contract. Current Delta Force, still employed by the U.S. military—on leave and on assist, ma'am."

To his surprise after a moment of reading and scrutinizing his documents, she laughed and then handed him back his papers, looking him up and down.

"You'll do," she said with a mischievous half-smile. "I just have one question though."

"Ma'am?" he said, teasing her while trying to stave off the electric current that her flagrant assessment produced.

"You married?"

He gave her a quick wink. "No."

CHAPTER 6

NO MATTER HOW one prepared oneself, there was simply no getting used to going through all the security checks and documentation required in the private charter area with the amounts of equipment and firearms they had to carry. An interminable flight was ahead of them with refueling stops in London, Cairo, and then eventually they'd get to Baghdad some seventeen-plus hours later. From there, they'd practically be living on a plane and moving around the Middle East.

The small talk with staff was wearing her nerves thin—right now she didn't want to talk to the band members or backup singers, didn't want to chitchat with the stylists, or dish the dirt with her personal assistant, Megan. In all, she had a full crew of audio techs, lighting techs, dancers, set designers, photogs, plus a band that, when adding everyone together and not including security, amounted to a forty-person entourage . . . and all she could think about was Zachary Mitchell.

Her mind wouldn't turn off; there were so many things about him that she wanted to know. She'd just learned that he was Delta Force, which completely explained how he handled himself in the parking lot. It also explained the way he used the words "sir" and "ma'am" as though the words themselves were sentence punctuation. From his outburst she'd learned that he was also from the 'hood and wasn't born with a silver spoon in his mouth, which she now understood was that indefinable thing that gave him a little swagger that was oh so sexy.

After last night, she knew she needed to know more, experience more; she wanted the whole package and was looking forward to unwrapping it a little bit at a time. There were things to learn like what was his family like, what did he believe in . . . he wasn't married, but were there kids or someone special?

Right now she felt like being lost in her own thoughts, lost in the conversation they'd begun last night before everything went wrong, lost in his arms that had brought her a little comfort and a little piece of home . . . but Zachary Mitchell was seated with the other security guys—so she sat alone.

The huge, comfortable leather seat threatened to swallow her up as she kicked off her shoes and allowed the deep pile carpet to massage her feet. Megan brought her a chilled glass of champagne and a legal pad.

"You look like you're in an artistic frame of mind," Megan said with a wink, her corkscrew rust-colored locks bouncing as she spoke.

"You know me," Anita said with a smile, accepting both offered items with deep appreciation.

"There's some fruit, good stuff for lunch and dinner . . . shrimp, the works. They stowed everything you like—just signal when you want some company or something to eat."

"Thanks, lady," Anita said, allowing her gaze to inadvertently drift toward Zachary Mitchell.

Megan glanced at him from the corner of her eye and then leaned in. "Who the heck is *he*?"

Anita smiled and shrugged. "He came with the security contract."

Megan slid into the seat next to Anita and leaned in to whisper. Her melodious island accent was filled with mischief. "Are you serious? The stylists have been buzzing ever since he did the walk-through, and if you've laid claim on him, you're gonna have to stab every woman in your backup section—maybe even a few of the guys."

"Tell 'em I'll cut 'em," Anita said, laughing.

"And I so don't blame you," Megan said, her gaze now riveted to Zachary. "Want me to tell him to come over?"

"No, no," Anita said quickly. "I don't want him to think . . . uhm . . ."

"Listen to you," Megan said giggling quietly. "I don't believe I've ever heard you sound like this over some man, not even Jonathan."

The mention of Jonathan stole Anita's smile.

"I didn't mean to go there," Megan whispered, her smile quickly vanishing. "Aw, lady—sore spot, I'm so sorry . . . I was just glad to see that somebody sparked your interest."

"I'm just being silly," Anita said. "Lemme work it out on paper."

Megan nodded, kissed her forehead, and stood. "Call me if you want anything, all right?"

"I've got bottled water, grapes, bubbly, paper . . . a pen, what else will I need for the next seventeen hours?"

Megan smiled. "You so don't want me to answer that."

Anita shooed Megan away with a wave of her hand, laughing quietly to herself. It would have been nice to have Zachary Mitchell sitting beside her, talking about anything, everything, just sharing the long ride . . . sharing his life. But that would cause a whole big to-do on the plane, rampant speculation, and a bunch of crap that she didn't have the stomach for right now.

Her fingers picked up the pen as her gaze found the horizon and she allowed her heart and mind to bleed all over the pages.

Placing her pen down carefully on the walnut fold-in table, Anita tucked her legs under her body and picked up her glass of champagne. She stared into the golden sparkling liquid hearing the melody and driving refrain inside her head. She closed her eyes, allowing the artistic process to take over, throwing herself down into the pit of the emotion, wallowing in it until tears wet her lashes and her hand reached out to pick up the pen again.

"Tell me when did you know?" she murmured, eyes

closed, head back, the melody drifting in her mind and in the small private space she'd created for herself. "Tell me, tell me, just be honest, baby, tell me . . . I need to know, right now, just—"

A presence looming over her gave her a start and made her open her eyes, jolting her from the creative process. Her initial scowl mellowed and gave way to excitement and curiosity.

"Ms. Brown, I'm sorry—but Megan said you wanted to discuss logistics for when we touched down . . . and I wouldn't have interrupted you if I'd been aware that you were working. I'll come back later."

"No, Zach, it's cool," she said, motioning to the seat beside her. "I was just picking away at something new. No big deal." Her heart felt like it was pounding a hole through her chest. *He'd come over.* His eyes said he wanted to sit with her, but his formal tone told her how private a person he was and how hard he'd work to keep the more personal aspects of their relationship on a strictly undercover basis.

He nodded but his entire body felt tense. This wasn't right. He'd wanted to come up with a ruse to sit by her without causing a stir, and he thought she had beaten him to the punch. But then he saw her glance at Megan with an arched eyebrow . . . so her personal assistant was playing Cupid. Just great. Clearly he'd interrupted the woman while she was working on something important. Her new hits were definitely a big deal, the stuff of platinum. Never in his life had he seen a songstress at work, seen a true musician craft a song from the depths of pain, never witnessed the birth of a song, and now, despite all his resolve not to be starstruck, he was.

"Listen," he said, carefully sitting down next to her and glancing at the paper she'd shunted aside. "We have hours to go before we land and have to disembark. I really wouldn't have interrupted you for the world. What I have to say is fairly perfunctory and can wait. There's no need to impact your creative process."

She stared at him with a sad smile, wishing they could

get back to where they'd been last night. Her hands ached to touch him, to reach out and cradle his face. Last night he'd surrounded her entire body with his like a human shield just so that she could sleep in that safe cocoon he'd created. Now, because of other people, they had to act almost like strangers. But his eyes said it all, told her not to go there as they searched her face. The slight flare of his nostrils was enough to let her know, oh, yeah, he felt it, too.

She bit her bottom lip and held his gaze. "Who knows," she finally murmured. "Maybe you're part of my creative process right now. I really enjoyed our conversation last night, which made me connect to some things I was trying not to deal with . . . just talking to somebody who missed home, knew what it was like to be alone in a crowd . . ."

He didn't know what to say. She had no idea what her statement did to him. Anita Brown connected all the dots, connected his heart and soul to his libido for some strange reason that he could barely fathom. Someone he'd initially thought was a spoiled star was a deeply profound woman fighting against a tough industry all by herself, and like any kid from the projects, was apparently holding her own, even if it wasn't always a flattering picture. Then he'd realized that she wasn't only fighting for herself, she was fighting for him—fighting to keep SWAT International, and she'd gone to war with her management for the sake of someone else she cared about, for the sake of a principle.

That reality rendered him mute. He'd been there, seen it, and done that, too. But she opened up more than his head, she opened his ears when she leaned back and quietly sang the words of the new song she was working on.

"That's good, uh, positive," he said, feeling like a complete idiot.

The timbre of her voice ran all through him, the soulful, begging quality in it, just asking a man to be honest and honorable—to love her with his complete heart—stole the air from his lungs. Jonathan Evans was a fool. He didn't care how many millions the man had or how much access he had to women he could exploit, what man in his right mind could walk away from the one sitting beside him now?

Anita smiled. Her expression telegraphed that she seemed to know that he was choking on incomplete sentences. Somehow she seemed to also know that he had no idea where to begin.

"You're right," she said after a moment, placing a finger to her lush mouth. "It is very positive, good vibes . . . and we do have hours to discuss the logistics . . . mind if we just eat a late lunch and talk about home, life, whatever?"

"All right," he said, hedging, not sure.

She chuckled. "You are so . . . I don't know . . . military." Then she lowered her voice. "In public," she said in a near whisper, before returning her voice to a normal conversational volume. "One word answers—I'm gonna call you the Spartan, if you don't loosen up. Like those guys in *300*. Now *they* were gangsta."

This woman was definitely messing with his head by carrying on a conversation in code on two levels at the same time; one private, one public. The way she looked at him and dropped her voice to give him some mention of last night, and making references to their encounter was giving him wood. Plus she'd seen one of his favorite movies and liked it. He couldn't help smiling, and a lopsided grin tugged at his cheek.

"I'm on duty, and shouldn't be imposing on your personal space."

"Are you hungry?"

He shook his head. "I ate a couple of hours ago, but don't let me stop you."

"Champagne?"

He shook his head and smiled wider. "No thank you, ma'am. I have a cranberry juice over where I was seated."

"Oh, my God . . . okay—right, you're on duty." She let out a long breath and began picking at a bowl of grapes on her foldaway table. "So, does this mean when we get to some of these really plush Middle East hotels, you're going to stand by the pool in a suit with a wire in your ear the whole time?"

"Affirmative. That's the plan; those are my orders."

She closed her eyes and slumped back like a forlorn child. "Dang . . ."

"That's what you hired me to do—to be boots on the ground and to make sure that you, your staff, and your assets are completely covered." He winked at her and chuckled.

She opened her eyes with a brilliant smile. "You don't want me to comment on that, do you?"

"Your equipment, your luggage," he said, chuckling.

"Oh, just checking, because I don't mind you covering my assets."

He looked down at the floor and felt his face warm as he laughed. "That's also in the contract . . . to make sure nothing happens to you."

"Ah, nice recovery. You are indeed a gentleman." She raised an eyebrow with a wider smile. "So, what's wrong with you?"

"Pardon?" He tilted his head, it was a throwback reaction from his old roots, and then he caught himself.

"Ooooh, I made the neighborhood come up out of you, after all."

She doubled over laughing and he found himself chuckling quietly. She was right; it had leaped to the surface without warning, and the fact that it tickled her so was hilarious to watch.

"You were ready to square off on me and run the dozens, don't lie."

"Ma'am—"

"Anita, remember," she corrected, touching his arm. "I'm really getting to the point of not caring about formality."

"Anita . . . I was just going for clarity, but you did take me back to Detroit for a minute."

"Uhmmm, hmmm."

She hadn't removed her hand and the warmth of it radiated up his arm.

"What I meant was, how come a fine, educated gentleman like yourself is still available?"

He shrugged, his smile fading. "My lifestyle leaves a lot to be desired, I guess."

"Lifestyle?" she said, panic suddenly filling her eyes as she jerked back her hand.

"No, no, I'm not—"

"Whew, okay . . . no problem with anyone who is . . . a lot of my best friends are, but that would have been a real disappointment if you told me that."

He smirked. "That's the least of your worries."

"Okay, Detroit, now you're on the verge of talking trash."

He had to laugh.

"So, what's the deal?"

He let out a long breath and his smile faded. "I travel too much, I'm on long assignments overseas, and can't be contacted in some of the places I go. I don't make what some of the guys who've chosen high-profile corporate professions make . . . and the person I had in my life decided that was too much to deal with. It would've just been nice if she would have told me, rather than allowing me to walk in on a very bad situation."

"Shut up!" Anita said in a low murmur. "Is she crazy? Didn't she know you know how to kill people with your bare hands?"

He smiled. "When you know how to do that, losing it like that is the last thing you wanna do. I value my freedom; doing time in prison isn't in my career plans."

"So *what* happened?"

He shrugged. This was not at all the direction he'd ever thought a conversation with Anita Brown would take. He hadn't even gone into full details with Lowell, just said that Monica had cheated and found someone new.

"It was what it was."

"Spill . . . you have gotta tell me—I have always wanted to know what a man thinks when he rolls up on a situation like that. Normally it's the other way around."

His outrageous client sat forward so eagerly, like an entranced child, that he felt himself almost becoming hypnotized, wanting to purge his soul and tell her just to get it out of him once and for all.

Zach let out a long breath. "Not much to tell, really. I stood there for a couple of seconds . . . tried to get my mind to make sense of what my eyes were seeing, then turned around and walked out. She sent me a text message to follow up and bring closure."

"Wait . . . she sent you *a text breakup message* after you walked in on her?" Anita opened and closed her mouth. "Now that was cold, dead wrong."

"I was gone for six months—she had needs, what can I say?"

"Then what did you do?" Anita stared at him slack-jawed.

"I went right back to the base and asked to decline my leave . . . went to Afghanistan to get it out of my system. Did a lot of damage there."

"So, you just threw yourself into work and never looked back?"

"Something like that."

Anita blew out a long breath that made a low whistle.

This was *definitely* not the conversation he'd wanted to have. Not the topic he'd ever wanted to revisit.

"Did you love her?"

He stared at Anita. "Enough to let her keep the ring . . . sometimes money doesn't matter."

"Oh, my God . . . you were engaged and she did that?" Anita murmured. "I know what you mean about the money not mattering, but, brother, you should have gotten the ring back, for real."

"Did you love him?" He figured it was a fair question, since she'd burrowed way deep into his psyche—it was an unauthorized security breach.

Anita turned the paper around toward him. "Read it and weep . . . you heard me humming that crying-ass love song. But, trust me; I am so over Jonathan Evans . . . still, what I'm not over is wanting to be with someone special—does that make sense?"

"Yeah." Zach looked at Anita and then looked away. It made more sense than he could articulate.

"I don't even know why I'm wasting time on some dumb song." Anita let out a resigned sigh.

"What little bit I heard was beautiful," Zach said, truly meaning it. Then more unauthorized words pushed past his lips too quickly for his brain to stop them. "Whatever inspired it . . . the man is insane."

"Thank you," she said with a shy smile, "for both observations. I'm glad you wound up being on this detail," she added, gathering up her papers.

"So am I," he said quietly. "I promise that you won't be disappointed that I'm a stand-in for Lowell Johnson—he's a good man, the best, but I'll try to approximate his skill to keep you and your entourage safe."

"I'm already impressed," she said very quietly and then looked around to be sure the others weren't listening in. "I think fate made sure it was you, and after last night . . ."

He leaned in and dropped his voice. "'Nita . . . I can't talk about last night and sit next to you on a seventeen-hour flight—all right? That's why I keep backing off that subject. You're messing me up."

He'd expected her to smile or tease him but her expression remained stone serious.

"I'm already messed up . . . maybe that's why I keep going there. I'm sorry."

"You've gotta stop," he said in an urgent whisper. "Your condition won't be obvious; mine will be."

"Okay," she said and then sat back for a moment. "But I have to ask another personal question."

Zachary smiled. "Do I have a choice?"

"No," she said with such a serious expression that he wanted to kiss her hard. "Okay, how long ago did this chick burn you?"

"Last year," he said, losing his smile, suddenly feeling every minute of his self-denial.

"*Last year* . . . after you were already gone for *six months*?" Anita's eyes were wide and she covered her heart with the palm of her hand. "So, you've been running women since then—you know, the lone-wolf type?"

"No. I've been busy working. That causes too much drama and I like to keep my life uncomplicated."

"Wait . . . you mean to tell me . . ." Her words trailed off as she shook her head.

He shrugged and then laughed self-consciously, not having meant to reveal quite that much detail about his life or his circumstances. But Anita was street-wise and read into his statement the subtext that was there; it was true, he hadn't slept with a woman since his breakup with Monica, and hadn't been with her six months prior to that while in Kuwait. Now staring at Anita Brown and answering her outrageous questions made him acutely aware of his personal drought.

"Okay, just tell me, is it because of some serious religious convictions, because I can respect that. If I was in foxholes and avoiding bombs, I'd probably get saved again, too."

"I do take my personal religious convictions seriously, but I can't lie on that," he said smiling. "Don't want to bait fate by doing that, especially at thirty thousand feet in the air."

"I heard that," she said with an easygoing smile. "So, why didn't you just hit a club?"

"Well . . . I was stationed in Muslim countries," he finally said, still smiling. "You don't roll like that unless you wanna get someone stoned to death or get shot by somebody's father or brother. There are also health risks and I'm already in a high-risk profession where I get shot at—so why add to the odds? When I got home, I just didn't have the energy for the games . . . so I focused on other things. No big deal."

"Oh, wow . . ."

"Yeah," he said shaking his head. "You get used to it."

"No, you don't," she said, sucking her teeth and folding her arms over her chest. "What you mean is, you deal with it, but you don't get used to it. Ask me how I know?"

She had a point and he glimpsed her from the corner of his eye, making them both start laughing again. The woman was truly outrageous. No one had ever asked him anything so personal in his life. The whole conversation was crazy, and yet, here he was having this conversation with, of all people, arguably one of the most beautiful women in the world.

"You learn serious self-discipline being stationed in foreign nations—it isn't worth dying for," he finally said in self-defense.

"I feel you," she said, nodding and taking a sip of her champagne then popping several grapes into her mouth.

"By the way . . . you're going to have to cover your head when we disembark in the Middle East . . . you don't technically have to, but it would sure make our security detail easier . . . so we're asking the ladies to cover up their arms and not have on shorts and deep plunging necklines. What you wear on the base and for the show is one thing . . . but while we're in country, if you go into the city away from the hotel—which I strongly advise against . . ."

"I'm not trying to have any problems" Anita said, raising her hands in front of her.

"Thanks," he said, growing serious. "I really appreciate it."

He had thought she would argue with him and take a stance just because she could. But she didn't. Something about their interaction had changed since he'd held her all night long and something within her overall demeanor had seemed to mellow. Urban instinct told him it was that hard-to-define thing called respect.

"I really appreciate you," she said quietly after a moment, staring at him without blinking.

He watched the light play against her satin-textured, cinnamon brown skin, wishing for a moment that there weren't thirty-eight other people on the plane. His palm ached to reach out and touch her face; his fingers tingled with the need to trace the delicate line of her jaw. Stupidity made him fantasize about watching her turn her lush mouth against the palm of his hand when he cradled her cheek. But in reality all he could do at the moment was keep a professional distance and hope that his eyes conveyed nothing but respect.

"I should probably get back to the other men," he said after a moment. "And, uh, you know . . . nail down logistics."

"Do you have to?" she said quietly, totally catching him off guard.

Anita bit her lip and looked down for a moment. Her face burned. That didn't come out right at all. She didn't want him to think of her like that, somebody playing him fast and loose. But the fact was, for some reason, this guy had her wide open and she wanted to be with him in the worst way. They shared a common bond, a common hollow in their hearts, and this man clearly had honor—which was the sexiest thing about him . . . something she hadn't seen in a long time, if ever. And she definitely wasn't big on trusting the male species, but for some reason Zachary Mitchell gave her hope.

"I mean . . ." she stammered, trying to recover her dignity. "Talking to you has really been chilling me out . . . takes my mind off the gig and problems, just joking around like we used to back home on the stoop, you know?"

He nodded. He did know. That was the one thing he couldn't share with Monica. Everything with his ex had to be about appearances, what people thought, mingling with the right social set, advancing his military career with Pentagon soirees. Hooking up with a Washington socialite had been a nightmare. But as he looked at Anita Brown he admonished himself for even going there . . . the societal gap between him and Anita Brown, aka Queen B, was leagues apart.

That reality tempered his libido and crushed his ego. The thought was sobering, no matter how forlorn her expression was. Right now she was just reeling from what was obviously a recent breakup, trying to cope with being stalked, maybe had performance jitters, and was possibly just playing with the hired help. He had to go back and sit where he was supposed to, away from her.

"I really enjoy talking to you, too," he finally said, choosing his words with care. "We'll be able to do that more over the next ten days, I hope. But right now you've got some music you're working on . . . I've gotta be alert when we touch down, and have to make sure we're all in sync . . . so, maybe I should go find Megan to bring you something to eat and you know . . ."

He stood before he changed his mind and made a fool of himself. Seventeen hours next to Anita and wanting her as badly as he did was more than a distraction, it was possibly something that could send him to the hospital.

"Okay," she murmured, and then looked out the window. "I understand."

No. It was clear in her bereft expression that she didn't get it at all.

CHAPTER 7

ZACH HAD IGNORED the knowing smiles the other security personnel gave him as he returned to his seat, and he was thankful that they were seasoned enough to not say a word. It was all in their eyes when he'd returned to their section, and innuendo about him being one lucky mofo was interspersed through dealing decks of cards and supposedly talking about the mission. But sleep eventually took them all, until their synchronized watch alarms sounded.

Thankful for the few hours of shut-eye, he still had awakened tortured. Sleep hadn't given him the respite he'd hoped for. Two international stops later and Anita Brown still invaded his dreams just like she'd invaded every cell in his body. But he had a job to do.

It was sheer pandemonium on the plane as they got close to touching down in Baghdad. Stylists were flitting between the wide aisles, dancers and singers were changing into costumes. The band members trudged to the bathroom, waking up and drumming on seats as they passed them.

He'd never seen the backstage commotion that took place before a show, much less seen it happening on a private jet. No one had the least bit of modesty as they stripped and got into their performance gear. Anita just turned her back to the aisle, stripped down to her underwear, no bra, and allowed her stylists to dress her—he and the security squad tried their best to seem nonchalant . . . like they were looking at anything but her. But that was impossible. Zachary finally forced his gaze to the floor as the captain announced that everyone had to take their seats and buckle up.

This job was in and out. Baghdad was too dangerous, so the brief show would be held right at the airport for military personnel in a hangar. While they did the show, the plane would be refueled, half of his team would stay with it to be sure there were no issues or anything suspicious loaded onto it, then they'd all get back on board and head to Kuwait—a much less hostile location.

The moment the flight crew opened the hatch, Zach was out, surveying the steps and then held out a hand for Anita. He watched her transform into Queen B for the swarm of paparazzi who had been allowed on the tarmac. She now wore a red, silver, and blue metallic halter that looked like a flag, red stilettos, and a tiny sequined white skirt. He kept his eyes forward, gaze roving behind his shades, but had he not been in front of a crowd, he would have been tempted to salute her . . . red, white, and blue never looked so good.

Backing her up were three burly guards, and the four of them cut a swath through the cameras after the plane exit photo op. The USO had rolled out a red carpet for her; he kept his gaze sweeping, moving her forward, and getting her through perfunctory security and into the hangar to the applause and cheering of hundreds of appreciative soldiers. The others had been escorted in by the balance of his men, and they rimmed the stage in dark suits, taking strategic positions.

Zach was in a backstage position, on post closest to the hangar's rear entrance—but in this environment, Anita Brown was probably the safest woman in the world. With more than two hundred arms-bearing servicemen and servicewomen who adored her, the biggest worry was getting her out of there on time, because he could tell the moment she hit the stage that she was going to sign an autograph for every enlisted person there . . . which only endeared her to him more.

Her voice was down-home, warm, and welcoming, and he listened to her thank the men and women in uniform for all that they did. Her compliments of their service and the real respect that filled her voice made him and all the others stand up taller. There was no fraud in this woman, she was the genuine article. Then she broke out into her dance routines that put soldiers on the feet.

Taking the opportunity to connect with Lowell, he switched on his satellite phone to let him know the first leg of the job was going well. As he waited for the connection to go through, he also turned on his BlackBerry and watched it boot up—glad that he and his squad also had gone through the necessary measures to allow for international access. Several voicemail messages came up on the touch screen. No one was answering the satellite phone, which was odd. Anne Marie should have picked up. He went into his voicemail and listened hard. Anne Marie's voice was ragged.

Words that made no sense poured into Zachary's ear. Lowell had gone into a convulsion and they'd found benzene hexachloride in his system?

Immediately he dialed the cell phone number that Anne Marie had left in the message. Eight rings and she picked up the telephone, sounding groggy.

"Anne Marie, it's Zach—what happened?"

"Somebody poisoned him, Zach," Anne Marie said, her voice gaining strength as she woke up. "I'm in the hospital now. That's why he was so swollen and looked jaundiced . . . this stuff is what they use for flea-and-tick powder and it affects the liver and kidneys—but looks like the flu. Vomiting, diarrhea, the same as the bug, but it takes like three to six hours before symptoms hit."

"How is he now?" Zach clutched the phone, almost unable to hear with the loud music behind him.

"He's in the cardiac ward—my mother has the boys; I'm in a family lounge, because I can't take my cell phone up on the ward where they're working on him and I have to stay in touch with Mom, if anything changes." Anne Marie's voice hitched. "He went into a mild convulsion, Zach . . .

they said he could get pulmonary edema from this so they're trying to get the toxin out of him now. If I hadn't come in, he could have died at home and it would have looked like a heart attack—and the poison would have been untraceable . . . totally gone from his system before anyone knew."

"You hold on, all right, honey." Zach closed his eyes and raked his fingers through his close-cropped hair. "When you can, I want you to give me a list of who he was with three to six hours before he started coming down with the so-called flu. Can you do that for me?"

"Yeah . . . I can look in his appointment book, and check his BlackBerry, too."

"Good. Call the police and give them everything you know, and call me any time, day or night. I want you to keep the boys with your mother—don't you go home alone, either. Make sure you take somebody trustworthy in there to get some things and then stay away from the house until I can get back there, all right?"

"Okay."

He heard Anne Marie sniff and anger imploded within him. Someone had gone after his family and he was sure it was related to the contract.

HOURS PASSED LIKE minutes; they always did when she was performing and working with a crowd. This gig, unlike many of the others she'd been on recently, felt like it gave her more than it gave the adoring fans. She'd signed every black-and-white glossy photo that her PA had passed out, as well as took pictures with everyone who'd presented a digital camera, even the brass.

On a natural high, she and her entourage tumbled back onto the plane, exhausted, giddy, and without a care in the world. If this was how the rest of the tour was going to go, then she couldn't wait. But Zachary Mitchell seemed more aloof than usual; all she could chalk that up to was he and his men having their game faces on.

"So, how did I do?" she said happily, accepting a shrimp salad platter from Megan.

"You killed!" Megan said, beaming, and gaining whoops from the rest of the plane. But Megan's smile only widened as she glanced over her shoulder. "Terminator is on the way, girl—might want to ask him what he thought of the performance, hmmmm?"

"Ssssh," Anita said, shooing Megan away. She looked up but her smile instantly faded as she stared up at Zachary's expression.

"May I sit down?"

"Sure," she said carefully, worry lacing her brow. She dabbed her throat and forehead with a towel. "What's wrong?"

"Earlier . . . when I came for the job, I heard you arguing with a man named Ron."

"Oh, that," Anita said, with a dismissive wave and then began eating her salad.

"I need to understand what that full argument was about . . . what is going on with your brothers, who used to be your security, the ins and outs of your contracts regarding that with Jonathan Evans—"

"Whoa, whoa, whoa, soldier—fall back."

Zachary leaned forward and his intense gaze paralyzed her.

"My partner didn't have the flu. You were right. May is a little late in the season for the flu. He was poisoned."

Anita started choking on the salad she'd been chewing and Zach pounded her back, handing her a bottle of water that he'd taken from her tray.

"I need a food taster now?" She wheezed. "Oh, shit."

"I don't think you'll be harmed directly from whomever you have beef with, but this was clearly designed to make the firm I'm working for void the contract. I'm also suspicious now of an inside job, as far as this stalker is concerned . . . how the hell did the guy always know where you were? Think about it."

"You actually think they'd try to get out of their contract

with me by putting a hit on me?" Anita's voice came out as a strangled whisper.

Zachary kept his voice low and spoke calmly, needing to convey the severity of his point without causing panic.

"No. You're a revenue source for them, Anita. But I don't put it past them to scare you to try to make you think that no other security can keep you safe but theirs. From what I gathered from the parts of the argument I heard, we're simply competition, thus expendable."

"There are a few people I can think of who are thug enough to do something like that . . . for one, my ex. He's as foul as they come." Anita closed her eyes. "And as much as I hate to say it, my brothers and father are certainly capable, too."

Zachary let out a long, weary breath. "I'm sorry to hear that . . . but it means that we're going to have to really tighten our ring around you. If these guys want to discredit SWAT International, what better way than to have an incident happen on the road, where you would naturally fire us? The label paying for this has our entire itinerary."

Anita stared at him, hugging herself. "Jesus . . . I never thought about that. Never thought Jonathan would be so stupid."

"We don't know who's behind the poisoning . . . Lowell Johnson is in the hospital as we speak, and we'll be trying to find out who he met with as soon as possible. We'll need hard facts before we go accusing somebody—you better than anybody know that's a recipe for a lawsuit. Meanwhile, when we get to the hotel in Kuwait, I want to move your rooms around, make some changes on the fly, all right? I know it might not be as comfortable as you're used to, but I don't want anybody knowing where you are. Go with me on this. My gut is rarely wrong."

SHE WAS NEVER so glad to get to the Hilton Kuwait Resort in all her life. After a harrowing flight pocked by extreme turbulence and the horrifying news she'd received, all she wanted was a hot shower and to hide from the world for a little while.

As instructed, she didn't even let Megan know what room she was in. Her bags were stashed in the huge suite, along with Zachary Mitchell—who was taking up residence on her sofa.

Anita slowly lathered on the creamy suds as the hot water pelted her body. Some hot tea for her throat with lemon and, despite it all, she would sleep good tonight. Her bones were weary, just like her heart. She turned around in the spray, wondering how her life had gone so terribly wrong. Jonathan was a real bastard, but she'd never really thought he would hurt someone—break them or her financially, yes . . . try to murder someone with poison? Never in her wildest dreams. But that just went to prove what her mother always told her; you never really knew what a person was capable of.

Stepping out of the shower, she wrapped her hair in a towel, dried and lotioned her body, and then pulled on a thick terry robe. Exhaustion claimed her as she padded across the bathroom floor and out through the bedroom in search of tea.

Zachary was standing in front of the tray, scrutinizing the hot water, and just seeing him do that made her smile.

"I can toss that pot out and brew some in the room," she said, motioning toward the coffeemaker.

"I'd feel more comfortable if you did."

He set down the porcelain teapot and then looked up. He was glad that he'd set down the china first, for he surely would have dropped it. He remembered so vividly how she looked without makeup, her face fresh scrubbed and damp. She was breathtaking. It brought back the flood of emotion and desire that had been bottled-up since their first kiss. Momentarily at a loss, he went to the glass coffeemaker and then headed to the sink behind the dining area.

"I'll just fill this up with water."

"You don't think they would have poisoned my honey, do you?"

He held the pot midair. "Do you need honey?"

Her shoulders sagged. "Maybe not. Just some lemon is fine."

Zachary paused, staring at her forlorn expression and then glanced at the glass coffeepot in his hand. He had to get a grip. They were not going to poison their money-maker, and his nerves had been so bad since he'd spoken to Anne Marie that he was losing perspective. The only meeting that his play sister-in-law had been able to uncover was the initial meeting Lowell had had with Anita over a month ago, and he'd have to wait until he got state-side to see Lowell to learn more. In the meantime, he needed to be cautious, but unnecessary paranoia served no purpose.

Anita walked over to the massive glass windows and stared out at the white sand and turquoise sea. Zachary set down the coffeepot and went over to the tea service and poured her a cup, adding in some honey and lemon.

"I'm sorry," he said, quietly, causing her to turn. "I guess I'm not doing a very good job as your bodyguard . . . I let it get personal, and I have definitely lost perspective." He came up to her and offered her the tea, which she slowly accepted.

"You're trying to keep them from harming me, and got a tip . . . I'd say that was doing a good job . . . and for what it's worth, I've definitely lost perspective, too."

He shook his head. "No . . . I'm also supposed to guard your head—I assess the threat levels, make them go away, and keep you safe while you can continue to do what you're used to doing."

She took a delicate sip of tea but never took her eyes from his. "I've never had anyone guard my head . . . or ever want to. It feels good." She rolled the warm teacup between her palms and then reached out and touched his face. "I bet you've never had anyone guard your head either."

He stood very still, barely breathing, almost closing his eyes to the sensation of warmth that she'd sent through his cheek. "Never in my life," he said in a hoarse murmur.

"Why don't you go take a shower?"

They both stood together quietly, her hand on his cheek, the other balancing her cup of green tea. For a moment all he could do was swallow hard.

She inclined her head toward his duffel bag and suit bag on the floor. "It's late, all the rest of the guards are in their rooms, catching some Zs . . . that's what you'd be doing now, if the unfortunate incident hadn't occurred." Her fingers found the edge of his jaw and then traced his eyebrow. "You have to unwind and go to sleep, even if it's on the couch . . . and get out of that suit you've been wearing for two days . . . and take off the gun."

"All right," he finally said, glad that his larynx had decided to work again. "But don't open the door for anyone while I'm gone."

"Where are you going?" She tilted her head ever so slightly but her expression was completely serious.

"You said to go take a shower."

A half-smile pulled at her cheek. "There's one in the other room, plus towels."

He didn't move, dared not blink, fearing that if he did he might awaken from this desert mirage.

"Are you sure?" he asked quietly, needing to hear her say the words.

But rather than answer him she simply closed the gap between them and stared up, then took his mouth.

It was the gentlest of offerings, a porcelain teacup between them; her warm palm on his cheek. When she drew her lemon-honey sweetened mouth away from his, it left an ache. He turned his lips into the palm of her hand, kissing the center of it as his eyes slid closed.

"Go take a shower," she murmured, slowly dragging her trembling fingers away from his face, but her body still brushed his, teased his, causing gooseflesh to pebble their skin.

"I won't be long," he said softly, slowly stepping back from her.

She didn't move, didn't blink, just took a very slow sip of her tea.

CHAPTER 8

A COLLAGE OF emotions pummeled his brain as the hard jet spray of the shower pummeled his skin. Desire, guilt, trepidation . . . as well as a few additional emotions that he wasn't ready to name.

There was no doubt that he wanted this woman; Zachary looked down and winced. His body had a mind of its own and had quickly made that fact obvious to both of them. But there was still a matter of professional conduct—Lowell had trusted him with this job, and once again, Lowell had taken the weight.

Sobered by the thought, Zachary turned the water to cold and stood under the blast of it for thirty seconds before turning the shower off. Jesus H. Christ, he had to keep his mind on point. This was undoubtedly the toughest assignment he'd ever had. Mud, cold, sleep deprivation, danger . . . nothing had shredded his resolve like Anita Brown.

Shivering, he quickly toweled himself dry, and pulled on a pair of sweatpants and a T-shirt, and then went to the sink to roughly brush his teeth. He'd brought three suits with him, the one he'd just shed could go down to the hotel cleaning service tonight. He had to keep his mind focused on logistics and not allow it to slip into the personal, into the areas of the forbidden.

Anita Brown was a client. Anita Brown was just feeling frightened . . . rightfully so. Like him, she was lonely—but for her, the mood would pass. Soon another well-heeled suitor would be on the red carpet escorting her somewhere. He needed to find out who'd gone after Lowell and who was trying successfully to scare his client.

Zachary set his jaw hard, looked in the mirror, and then shoved his toothbrush and toothpaste into his sweatpants pocket. Yeah . . . he needed to keep it real and not mess up the only permanent thing he had in his life—Lowell, Anne Marie, and his godsons. The last thing he needed to do was to sleep with that gorgeous woman in the other room.

Balling up his discarded clothes, he tucked them under his arm and opened the bathroom door. Anita was in the bed, curled up like a sleeping baby. He turned off the bathroom light and crept into the adjacent room to toss his dirty clothes in a plastic hotel cleaning bag and to unload his toiletries into his duffel, then came back to gently pull the covers over her.

Zachary stood in the doorway for a moment, just watching her draw in and out slow, peaceful inhalations and exhalations. In the semidarkness the light played across her soft cheek and long pretty eyelashes. To him she seemed like an angel, to hell with what the tabloids or anybody else said. He gently shut the door behind him and sat down on the sofa, staring at his gun on the coffee table, wishing like hell he didn't need to carry one around her.

HER INTERNAL CLOCK was all screwed up, and she sat up in the dark trying to remember what city she was in, what country she was in, what concert she was doing—panic tore through her until she looked at the clock radio and realized that she hadn't overslept a show. Then it all came back slowly.

Anita stared at the perfectly smooth bed and the blanket that had been pulled over her. Quietly getting out of the bed, she went to the door, hoping that Zachary Mitchell was still there.

As she peeked through the door, she smiled. He hadn't touched her, hadn't woken her up, and was asleep sitting up on the sofa, head back, facing the door and his weapon. A true officer and a gentleman. For a moment, all she could do was stare at the handsome man who'd restored her belief in honor.

Anita wrapped her arms around herself wondering why it had taken her life getting so far out of control that she'd had to hire security. Why did it take all of this for an average guy to come into her life to put back together all the shattered pieces of it? But, then, Zachary Mitchell was no average man. Far from it.

Aside from owning a decent soul and a sense of old-school values, he also had a stone-cut chest and a ripped abdomen that simply took her breath away. In a suit, or even in an Oxford button-down and slacks, she had only been able to imagine the definition covered by fine fabric and then allow her hands to roam over it. But seeing all that in a T-shirt that strained against chocolate-covered sinew, nothing was left to her imagination.

Steel-cable biceps stretched his sleeves as slow, easy breaths lifted his rock-hard chest. She bit her bottom lip as her gaze slid down his torso and stopped at his groin. Damn . . . even at ease and in a pair of sweats, the man was gifted. She remembered feeling all of that pressed against her pelvis, making her want to savor every inch of it, but that had been a dream deferred.

Her line of vision traced his thickly muscled thighs and finally came to rest on his mouth. Zachary Mitchell had a wonderful mouth, his kiss was so gentle, yet she was sure it could turn primal in a heartbeat. It *had* turned primal for a few glorious minutes until a letter stopped everything and turned the white-hot moment ice-cold.

Desire pulled her through the door, across the room, and toward the sofa. She wasn't sure what she'd say or how she'd approach him, but the burn for him had eclipsed any shame. She wanted this man, needed him in her life. She knew he thought they came from two different worlds and saw how much that mattered to him in his eyes. But they'd both been products of the same urban experience.

That had to count for something, it meant everything to

her. It had been the only reason she'd stayed with Jonathan as long as she had—needing someone from that familiar background to understand her; being so lonely, so tired of men looking at her fame and wanting her as a conquest or being too intimidated to stick around for more than casual sex. But Jonathan never had the honor, never had the values to go with all the money he'd made. And this man, who could have had her from the moment they'd entered the suite, had showered, covered her up, and gone back to his post.

Tears of appreciation stood in her eyes as she bent to kiss Zachary's forehead. But before her lips grazed his skin, he'd flipped her and pinned her flat on her back with a nine millimeter at her temple.

She stared up unblinking, not breathing. He quickly sat back and cocked the gun.

"Jesus—I'm so sorry!" He put the gun on the table pointing away from them. "You okay?"

She didn't move, just sucked in two strangled gulps of air and slowly placed her hand over her heart.

"Baby . . . I'm so sorry," he said, trying to help her up.

Trembling, she sat up slowly, closed her robe around her more tightly, then bent over until her forehead touched her knees, hyperventilating.

"Anita, I . . ."

She just held up a hand to make him stop talking.

"I'm going to get a bag and I want you to breathe into it slowly, all right?"

He jumped off the sofa as she nodded and quickly returned with a bag. He held it out for her and she took it with trembling hands and placed it over her nose and mouth, huffing into it for a few moments.

"You feel better?" he asked, taking it from her and trying to help restore her disheveled towel.

Still numb, the towel fell away, leaving a cascade of damp hair to cover her shoulders.

"You called me baby," she said, looking up at him. "Nearly blew my brains out, but you called me baby."

Zach closed his eyes. "Anita, I'm really sorry."

"About almost blowing my brains out and body-slamming me against the sofa or calling me baby?"

He just looked at her. "Both. I was on post and—"

"What if you had kids? What if a toddler came and jumped in the bed with you?" She shot up off the sofa. "Is this some kind of disease or condition? Tell me now—I need to know."

He looked confused, didn't seem to understand, but she could see that his mind was seriously trying to process her request.

"No, no, no," he said, standing and beginning to pace. "When you have a family, when you're with somebody, you know their sounds, unless you're suffering Posttraumatic Stress Disorder, you don't bug like that . . . it's when you're in a hostile terrain, expecting—"

"You were in a suite with me," she countered, folding her arms over her chest as total shock now gave way to indignation.

"The last place I ever thought I'd be," he said quietly. "I admit it—I was disoriented when I got startled awake and the last thought I went to sleep with was, protect her. I didn't expect . . ." He looked toward the window as his words trailed off.

She nodded, feeling foolish for walking up on a soldier unannounced, and still slightly shaken. "Okay, now I know better."

"You came to wake me up," he said, clearly trying to change the subject. "What did you want? I can order—"

She held up her hand. "I can't remember what it was."

When she looked out the window, he briefly closed his eyes, knowing exactly what it was that she'd wanted. He might as well have put the nine to his own temple and pulled the trigger. Damn!

The sound of his BlackBerry vibrating against the coffee table drew their attention. Zach paced over and picked it up, listening to Anne Marie's distraught sobs.

"What's happened?" he said quickly, trying to make sense of what she was telling him.

"I did what you said, Zach. I told the police." Anne Marie's voice filled the receiver in shaky bursts. "But now they want to take me in as a suspect saying that I could have tried to poison my husband—because his business is slow, he's an amputee, and his life insurance would make him worth more dead than alive!"

"Call Lowell's attorney immediately. You stay calm, Anne Marie, you hold it together now, okay—I'm going to get to the bottom of all this. You've got three kids to be there for, so you can't fall apart, all right?" Zach walked in a circle. "How's our boy doing?"

Anita watched the surreal conversation, knowing that too many innocent lives had been touched by the corruption in hers. No matter what, she made herself a silent promise to help right this wrong.

Zachary nodded as Anne Marie filled him in, his gaze fixed on Anita.

"Good, good, well at least he's fighting to stay alive, and you fight too, okay? Are the boys all right?" Zachary nodded. "Good. You tell them to hang tough . . . okay, call Mike. Call me back when you can."

Anita watched Zachary hang up and rake his scalp with his fingers. "I'm going to help you find out who did this, okay?"

He looked at her and shook his head. "This is so not your fight and you're paying good money to be protected—you shouldn't even be involved in any of this."

"I want you to lie down on the sofa," she said, going to the bedroom. When she returned she tossed him a pillow and a blanket. "I want you to get a good night's sleep—if you can. In the morning, I want you to eat a decent breakfast. We have a long day ahead of us, and a bunch more travel stops to make before it's all over . . . and if I get any more bright ideas about, uhmmm . . . waking you up with a kiss, I'll just call out from the doorway. All right?"

FIVE OF THE longest days and nights of his life had passed. Every day, Anita had wowed U.S. troops, and each night he'd spoken to Anne Marie, he was encouraged that Lowell was coming along better as time passed. Soon Lowell would be up for police questioning and maybe something would jog his memory. It was a godsend that his buddy's wife wasn't being held, even though she was probably still being watched as a potential suspect.

But he knew in his soul that the only reason poor Anne Marie was allowed to go free without charges was because he and Anita Brown had called New York's finest from Kuwait. Celebrity did have its privileges, and Anita had cashed in a favor on his behalf that could well land her in the tabloids, if someone at the precinct decided to play hardball. Regardless, he felt somewhat better that a police investigation was under way. It just wasn't right that Anne Marie should take the fall for something like this, and he'd do everything he could to protect Anita's name, too.

Still, there was that quiet, unspoken thing that stood between them every night when he took to the sofa and Anita went to her bedroom. It had followed them on the plane and then from Baghdad to Kuwait to Dubai to Oman, and now it had tracked them all the way to Yemen.

Ignored desire was the constant companion that slid in and out of their conversations, slipped between them, licking at their emotions and straining their bodies over a cup of tea and cranberry juice. This thing they couldn't talk about bled into their dreams, tossing and turning them about, threatening to spill onto the sheets.

Refusing to be denied, it softened voices and increased pulse rates while they were only laughing about the day, or when they'd delve into their collective pasts to get deep and philosophical . . . talking politics and world religions, and discussing cultures without borders. Conversation became foreplay, raging debates were heavy petting that left them both spent when it was time to say good night.

The more he got to know her, the more it was hard to deny just how magnetic their pull was on one another.

Long days of frenetic activity and an entire entourage helped keep things at an appropriate professional distance. Group dinners and Anita being out on the town with her band and staff kept things from ever becoming too intimate. He and nine other men still had a job to do standing guard, standing watch.

But it was the nights when all the hotel room doors had closed and the crowds were gone, that's when the unspoken thing screamed the loudest and stomped its feet to demand attention. Tonight it was doing the cha-cha, dancing the salsa in the middle of the suite floor, and all he could do was stare out the window.

"Do you want some tea?" she said, towel drying her hair.

"Sure," he said, knowing their ritual was always the same.

It was an invitation to sit up and talk, to keep her company and listen to her beautiful voice. It was a private audience that was evaporating day by night, one that was making him sad because he knew it would end.

She chuckled softly and he heard her filling the coffeepot with water to heat. "You always say sure, when you really want something else."

"You have no idea," he said under his breath, staring out at the blue-black velvet sky.

"Uh, huh, cranberry juice, he mutters," she said, rooting around in the minibar.

He was glad she hadn't heard him and his body tensed as she neared him.

"One cranberry juice," she said with an easy lilt.

She smelled so good, the shampoo and lotion, all things female collided with his senses as she came beside him.

"Thanks," he managed to get out and then took the glass from her without fully turning around.

She gave him a quizzical look; he took a sip of his juice and almost choked on it.

"Aren't you gonna take a shower? Road dust and heat—"

"Yeah, okay," he said, pacing away from her. He set down his cranberry juice and grabbed his duffel.

"You okay?" She looked at him with a slight frown but her tone was gentle.

"Yeah," he said, hustling past her.

He closed the door and leaned against it, dropping his bag on the floor. He was living the life of a crazy person. It had taken nearly two days to get to this side of the world, would take as long to get back. He was safe from himself on the plane—but five days of this was living hell. One more day, one more night . . . he could keep everything in perspective.

Zach pushed off the door and then froze when he heard her. Anita's voice floated on the air, her soft melody wrapping around him in a sweet caress. She was singing and making her tea . . . and driving him crazy.

He turned on the shower, almost wetting the arm of his suit and his watch. If things were still cool once they got back state-side, once he got to the bottom of things, once they were out of this surreal tour mode, then, yeah, he'd be game to see how far this could go. But right now, while she was in potential danger, Lowell was lying in a hospital bed, Anne Marie was under suspicion for attempted murder, his godsons might—oh, shit . . . he might become an instant father, just add water, if the worst happened to their parents . . . no. Now was not the time to have a discipline lapse that could mess everything up.

Determined to hold fast to his mission, he yanked off his clothes and stepped into the freezing spray and almost yelped. He could do this, he could do this. Zach soaped his body, willing away the painful erection, rinsed off and then stumbled out of the tub. Not sure why he was rushing, he hurriedly dried off, threw on some sweats and collected his items and cleared out of what now felt like a too-intimate space.

Cool water was still streaming down his neck, chest, and back when he went to hunt for his suit bag to stow his watch and shoes. Fumbling at the task, he didn't look at Anita while he brought order to his possessions. But when he finally looked up, she held a teacup midair and was staring at him.

"What?" he asked quietly, not sure what was wrong. Then suddenly he realized that he hadn't grabbed a T-shirt in his haste. "Oh, wow—uh, my apologies," he said, grabbing his duffel, and turning away from her to ransack it for a clean shirt.

"No complaints," she said quietly.

He heard her sit down but that only made him rush all the more and yank a shirt over his head backward, then only have to pull it off to fumble with it to get it back on again.

"You know, it's been a really long day . . . and maybe we should get some shut-eye early tonight, you know?" he said, his words coming out in fits and starts.

"All right," she said calmly, with a smile, looking at the duffel bag he held in front of him. "But can I ask you a question?"

"Yeah," he said with a resigned sigh but didn't move.

"Do you find me attractive?"

"What kind of question is that?"

She shrugged and sipped her tea. "Figured you had opinions about me, maybe things you'd read . . . or have seen in my show and decided that maybe I'm just a little too over-the-top for you, so . . . I don't know."

"It's not like that at all," he said, slightly lowering the bag. "I know you're none of the things they've said to sell magazines, and we've talked about too much stuff for me to think you're only the performer . . . but I'm trying to do what I was sent here to do, without taking advantage in any way or . . ."

"You're not taking advantage," she said, releasing a long sigh. "And I'm not on the rebound, if that's what you're worried about . . . or trying to play you." She patted the sofa next to her. "Can we just talk and be real? Nothing has to happen, but there is chemistry, okay, and I don't wanna go back to the States and never hear from you again, unless that's what you want."

"That's not what I want, but it's probably what'll happen," he said in a low murmur. "It's bound to. I'll get deployment orders, you'll be traveling and doing things where you'll need an escort, and I won't be there."

"So, you're not trying to get caught up," she said in a sad, faraway tone. "That's about the most real thing we've said to one another." Her sad brown eyes studied him. "I just didn't understand what I had done to turn you off so badly."

He shook his head no and dropped the duffel bag. "Does it look like you've turned me off?" He briefly closed his eyes. "Anita, I'm just trying my best to be respectful, because I know this has a very short shelf life given our careers."

"Thank you for at least letting me know that you feel the same way," she murmured, "and that I haven't been the only one tossing and turning all night."

"No, you haven't," he said thickly.

"Timing isn't always perfect," she said, standing up. She opened the sash of her white terry robe and allowed it to fall open. "Sometimes you have to invest in what you want to work out." She stepped around the coffee table and held his gaze. "But I know what it's like to be on the road and be betrayed. There are some things I'm willing to wait for. That's my pocket change for the rest of this trip."

He couldn't move as she walked up to him, kissed his cheek, turned away, and murmured, "Good night." He listened to the bedroom door click shut and the sound rocketed through his spinal column, the vibration imploding in his groin. One more day and there'd be hours on the plane that would stretch nearly two days. Zach turned off the lights and then sat down on the sofa and leaned his head back. There were so many things he wanted to say to her, and this time if he waited, time was going to run out on him.

Somehow he found himself at the bedroom door, knocking on it lightly. He heard her sniff, but didn't hear her invite him to open it.

"Can I talk to you for a minute?" he said, talking through the wood frame.

"Yeah . . ." a small voice replied and he cracked the door, surprised to see her blotting her face with a tissue.

At a momentary loss, he moved into the room and sat on the edge of the bed. She looked up at him, twisting the tissue in her hands, and it simply made him cover them with his own.

"You are so beautiful it's frightening," he said. "Everywhere we've stopped, there have probably been a thousand guys who would kill to have you . . . but I'm not interested in bragging rights." He hung his head and spoke to the floor while grasping her hands and then finally looked into her eyes. "Sounds so foolish, but over the last few days, I've laughed more than I have in so long, 'Nita . . . I've reconnected with my past, felt what it was like to come in from a long day and just sit with somebody who gave a damn about me. I got to know the real Anita Brown, who is just as gorgeous on the inside as she is on the outside—someone who is real, caring, giving, loving . . . the stuff you did for your family, man . . ."

Zach shook his head and released her hands, pushing wet strands of hair behind her ear. "If I go this next step, this soldier is going to be in too deep to get out. Black Hawk down, do you understand? We shouldn't start this if we're not going to finish it. I don't want a fling."

She touched his hand covering it where it cradled her cheek. "I've never had a man tell me no for such a beautiful reason." She closed her eyes and two big tears ran down the bridge of her nose. "Nobody has ever taken the time to get to know who I am, to talk to me, to try to protect me, to think about the future with me . . . and to rack their brains to figure out how that might all work in their life. I was always their eye candy, a trophy, or a toy."

Zach softly kissed away the tears that had slid down her nose and then landed a soft kiss on each of her eyelids. "'Nita . . . when I was a child, I played with toys . . . and spoke like a child and thought like a child," he said quietly, tracing her cheek in the dark with trembling fingers. "But when I became a man, I put away childish things."

"Corinthians," she said, resting her palm against his chest. "You knew the quote, and it's my favorite."

"Mine, too," he murmured, coming to lie beside her, "because when you really care about somebody, really love them, you'll put away childish things . . . and I've been watching you try to take care of me while I'm supposed to be taking care of you." He shook his head, drawing her into his arms. "I can't remember when somebody cared enough to try to take care of me."

He found her mouth, brushing it with gentle sweeps, and then testing for deeper acceptance with his tongue probing hers until she consumed him. What began as slow exploration against satiny skin with gentle caresses became a struggle to remove clothing.

Impatient, she pulled at his T-shirt, her hands splaying across his bare chest as she suckled his nipples. Every place her mouth landed drew a moan up from his depths . . . it had been so long, his desire for her had been so repressed that as she tongued his navel he almost wept.

Her robe hung off her shoulders, his hands reveling in her damp, tangled hair to slide down her arms, shedding the terry obstruction so that her breasts could finally be freed. For a moment, he allowed his gaze to drink her in and then gently pulled her closer. She didn't understand that he needed to pay homage to her beauty, and right now the only way he knew how to do that was with his mouth, nuzzling her breasts, drawing in the taut nipples between his lips to flick against his tongue until she arched and cried out.

Giving never felt so good. He wanted to give her so much pleasure that his shaft throbbed in agony. Their foreplay had become feral, tenderness ebbing as she yanked his sweatpants down over his hips; she clearly had the same idea and it buckled his body the moment she held him, her palm slicked by his need. Someone had to yield and he was glad that she was gracious enough to do so, rolling over on her back so that he could continue his trail of kisses to the place that would make her call his name.

Sweet sticky essence of woman covered his face as she writhed beneath his attention. There was no extraction from this once he'd entered, there was no way to walk away from her or make something this profound casual. He felt her shudder as her thighs clamped against his skull, her hand stroking his hair, and her sighs a melodic refrain, "I need you inside me."

"Not yet," he murmured against her bud, and then kept time to her thrusts with the tip of his tongue.

He wanted her wild, crazy, out of control. Needed to feel her arch and release until her knuckles turned white holding the sheets. One finger entered her in a lazy stroke that made her strain against his hand, demanding a second. She tasted so good, was so wet that he was losing his mind. Her body spilled pleasure into his mouth as she bucked her hips, need and frustration making her moans more insistent. Then suddenly she gasped hard and thrust hard against him, beginning to convulse. *That* was what he'd been waiting for . . . for her voice to become a series of pure gasps, high-pitched moans, her rhythm lost to violent shudders. He wanted her to feel the way he was going to feel: head back, insane the moment he entered her . . . and she rewarded his patience by begging him, "*Put it in.*"

Yes, ma'am, *anything* the lady wanted. A condom was the last thing on his mind. But as he lifted his head to plant deep kisses against her belly, she murmured a truth that almost made him slide against her.

"In the drawer," she said quietly scooting up to reach across the king-sized bed. "Every night I was hoping you'd come in and stay like this."

He remained paralyzed on his hands and knees as she reached over and tore open a foil package. Too close to the edge, he couldn't even help her as she put it in her mouth and slid down the bed to sheath him. Warm, soft hands, her mouth made him drop his head back and bottomed out his voice, "Oh, 'Nita . . ."

Female wisdom, female mercy guided him with shapely calves wrapped around his hips, then his waist, bringing him deeper, sinking him into a place he could never leave—a point of no return. She'd gone there, too, had fallen, slipped into the abyss of passion, her hands scrabbling at his back as her voice rent the air. His chasing her soprano like a sonic boom, bottoming out on "Oh, baby," creating music on the fly, riffs, and solos, the applause a standing O of feminine convulsions.

Every thrust sent beads of perspiration rolling down his back, his temples, and his chest. A phalanx of contractions jolted his sac so brutally that he cried out and lifted her under her waist. One hand against the headboard, one tightly gripping her back, a year and a half of denial, the near miss, the long flight, and five days of agony all became one thunderous release.

Breathing hard, they both rolled over on their backs, and then slowly came back together, him pulling her against him.

"Wow . . ." she murmured.

He was still catching his breath and could only nod with his eyes closed.

She kissed him, petting his erection. "Now I know why you said we shouldn't start this if we weren't prepared to finish it."

He opened his eyes and smirked. "Oh, I'm hardly finished, ma'am."

CHAPTER 9

THE HARDEST THING now was to get the genie back in the bottle. He didn't want her to end up in the tabloids for doing her bodyguard, or for him to wind up in trouble for moonlighting—and then exhibiting conduct unbecoming an officer on leave. But after two nights of insane lovemaking, it was physically painful to sit apart from her and act aloof for nearly two days' worth of flights.

There was a chemical difference that anyone around them with half an ounce of common sense picked up on. Sly looks, raised eyebrows, inquiring minds wanted to know. The fact that they were both dog-tired was a dead giveaway, but his lips were sealed. The main thing was to get her back to her penthouse, make sure she was secured, and then get to Lowell and Anne Marie.

Zachary stretched and casually walked over to Anita—as nonchalantly as he could make it seem at this point. She beamed up at him and turned so she could face him when he sat down.

"We've created a scandal, I'm afraid," she said, laughing behind her hand.

He wasn't amused but still found himself chuckling. "Yeah, I think it was that last go 'round that woke the neighbors.

"Uhmmm-hmmmm." She leaned over and kissed him. "And I don't care." She lowered her voice to a sexy decibel.

"Meet me in the bathroom . . . I need more of what you gave me last night."

He could feel the muscle in his jaw pulse; the temptation was so great that he almost lost his game face. "Stop messing with me."

"I'm not messing with you," she said, growing completely serious. "I'm so turned on right now that I'm about to slide out of this chair."

Her comment made him swallow hard, hang his head with his eyes squeezed shut, and then speak to her in a low, pleading murmur. "Baby, you've gotta stop."

"I can't help it," she whispered in a near moan. "I might have to go in there and get started without you."

The image of her graceful fingers sliding into her slick opening, one hand on her breast, kneading a taut nipple, almost made him grab her by the elbow and drag her down the aisle. Anita's naked, caramel-hued skin started a flash fire in his mind, all the way from her gorgeous eyes to her clean-shaven nether lips . . . she had the prettiest . . .

"So you wanna?" she murmured, touching his leg and making his entire shaft contract.

It was only after she'd touched him there that he realized his leg had been slightly bouncing. "Of course," he said, breathing out the words. "But we have to pass everybody, you know . . . and have to maybe wait until they go to sleep."

"I don't know if I can wait that long," she said in a quiet rush and then sat back and closed her eyes, breathing deeply through her nose as she traced her collarbone.

Impulse would have made him just take her mouth right then and there, just pick her up and carry her to the restroom, and kick the frickin' door down. But this wasn't his contract; it was Lowell's. It wasn't his reputation; it was hers. It wasn't his staff; wasn't people he'd have to work with day and night. Discipline took over, just like the stabbing pain had in his scrotum.

She opened her eyes and leaned forward. "Baby, please . . ."

He held up one finger discreetly to stop her words. "'Nita, you're killing me." When she opened her mouth to protest, he motioned toward the aisle with a swift nod, then let out his breath when he saw Megan do a little jig in the aisle and slap a stylist high five. "When we get back—"

"I know, I know, we're going to have to talk . . . but I was hoping that wouldn't be all."

"Yeah, me too," he said quietly. "I miss you already."

"You do?" She hugged herself and bit her bottom lip and then glanced toward the bathroom again.

"No," he said, laughing to keep from crying.

"All right . . . dang."

"Not with Lowell's guys here, you know." He studied the bathroom and then shook the thought. "No."

"Be honest, thinking about the mile-high possibilities are wearing you out." She laughed and poked him with a bare foot.

He shook his head, chuckling. "I admit it—but I want to talk seriously for a minute."

Her smile faded with his. "Okay . . . guess this is where you dump me, right?"

"Wrong," he said, taking up her hands, no longer caring who saw. "This is where I tell you that I want to check out your penthouse and make sure you're okay."

"Oh," she said stroking his cheek.

He turned his mouth into her palm and covered her hand with his own, kissing it hard. "They still haven't figured out who's stalking you or who put pesticide in Lowell's food. We don't even know exactly what happened." Zach held her hands within his, trying to get her to listen. "You met with Lowell little more than a month ago, right?"

"Right," Anita said, leaning closer and lowering her voice. "I had been looking around because my brothers were getting on my nerves, and I casually asked Ron Epps—the guy I was arguing with the day we met, and—"

"Epps?" Zach said, now almost whispering. "You never said his last name before."

"Well, I never really thought about it. He works for Jonathan . . . is his everything man—walks his dogs, runs his errands, they go way back to when they grew up." Anita looked at Zachary. "Why?"

"So, this guy gave you the name of SWAT International?"

"Yeah . . ."

"But when I came back from sweeping the route to the limo, he was really trying to talk you out of using Lowell's firm, right?"

Anita nodded. "I guess he thought I'd never go through with it."

"Not to get into your past business . . . but did you ever discuss any of this directly with Jonathan?"

This time she stared at him without blinking.

"No," she said, quietly, "by the time this all went down, we were on the outs."

"Okay, then I need you to do me a favor and lay low for a couple of days when we get back to the city. I want to make sure your place is secure and get you tucked in there, then I have to do a couple of things. Something about this doesn't smell right."

EXTRICATING HIMSELF FROM Anita and allowing another bodyguard to stand in for him was a challenge, not just because she wanted him to stay, but it was such a core need of his too right now. However, he had to get to the hospital. Lowell was up and talking. The only person he'd met from the client side was Anita, and she definitely hadn't poisoned the man.

Zachary passed through the minimal hospital security and found Lowell's floor, reading the numbers until he found his room. Anne Marie was sitting in the chair watching television with him, and she jumped up with a squeal as soon as Zachary poked his head into the door.

"You are a sight for sore eyes!" she exclaimed, hugging him and pulling him into the room.

"Hey, man, how'd it go?" Lowell said, his voice still a little weak.

"Without a hitch," Zach said, coming over to give him a man hug.

"Did that Queen B give you the blues for ten days, man?" Lowell laughed and coughed, but Zach bristled.

"She's not that way—is really good people, Lo. And I need to talk to you about what probably put you here."

Lowell and Anne Marie gave each other a look.

"I'm serious, man," Zach said. "You met with her, and then the same day you got sick, you only had an in-house meeting with your partners—Mike Epps and Vernon Knox, right?"

"Yeah," Lowell said slowly. "Mike had been to Philly and had brought back some Philly cheesesteaks for me, him, and Vernon . . . that's probably where I got that mess from—food poisoning . . . cops are thinking that maybe some pesticides they were spraying at the store or some flea-and-tick stuff they had around there for the guard dogs got in the food . . . those places are filthy and just my luck, I got the steak with some bull in it."

"That's why it was so bad, the doctors said," Anne Marie interjected. "They said it doesn't dissolve in water or liquids, only in oil and fatty solutions . . . so if some got in a cheesesteak, Lord have mercy." She fanned her face and shook her head. "Probably had them nasty pit bulls as guard dogs running around in the back of the store, folks don't wash their hands, and whatever was on the dog or near their grills got in my Lowell's food . . . but at least they're not trying to blame me and tear our family apart. I told 'em I'd take a lie detector test. They know I'd die for that man, puh-lease."

Lowell smiled. "But I'm cool, now—after what you did, man, we're on Straight Street. Can't thank you enough."

Zachary pounded Lowell's fist, but didn't smile. "Let me ask you this. How did you get to Anita Brown? Who was the contact? It's not every day you can run up on a heavy-weight celeb like that."

Lowell's smile widened. "I told you. Mike had a contact inside her organization . . . and it was through him that we got the hookup. Everybody's got some family from the old neighborhoods, man—Mike had some that came up with the big boys and worked us in."

Zachary nodded. "Cool. You get some rest."

ZACHARY'S VIBE WORRIED her. It was what he didn't say as much as what he said. Anita reached for the telephone and called the number that she swore she'd never call again in life, and then opened up the other extension and began recording when Jonathan Evans answered the phone.

"So, ten days helped you clear your head?" Jonathan murmured, trying to sound sexy and failing miserably.

"A little," Anita said. "I just wanna make sure we're cool since we have to work together."

"Why wouldn't we be cool, baby? I know we went through a thing about that chick at the last awards ceremony, but you know that didn't have anything to do with me and you, right? That was purely physical . . . what we have is deeper than that."

Anita just looked at the telephone, wondering how she had allowed herself to stay with a man like him for so long. "I figured the money problem would have pissed you off though."

Silence crackled on the line.

"What money problem?" Jonathan finally said, his tone instantly all-business.

"The three hundred large it cost you to lay out for security on my tour." She waited, expecting him to flip—but he laughed.

"Baby, now why would I stop paying for your basic expenses, just because we had a little altercation? I pay that kind of money every time you go out on tour—it's the cost of doing business. It's in your contract, love. Ten men while out of the U.S. at thirty large a day to cover you and your entourage; three men for local coverage at five hundred a day."

"You do?" she said quietly.

"Of course. Ron handles all that mess and makes sure my paper is straight—runs it through legal. What's the matter

with you, girl? You high or something? Now that shit I'm
not dealing with, because then you'll mess with my
moneymaker—your voice." Jonathan Evans let out an impatient huff. "Okay, so you want some attention. Fine. If you're
done having tantrums, we'll go to dinner tonight if you want,
but right now I've got business to handle. Tour was good?"

"Tour was excellent."

"That's my baby. Knock 'em dead. See you tonight, your
place. We'll get back to the way it should be, then go eat
late."

"Yeah."

Anita put down the telephone gently and then went in the
adjacent room to stop the small recorder. It was time to call
family.

"SOMETHING FUCKED UP is happening, man," Derrick said.
"I can feel it in my bones."

"If Anita wants to talk, then we need to listen," Pop
Brown said, looking at his boys.

Antwan sucked his teeth and folded his arms, looking out
the window. The eldest Brown went back to the phone, eyeing his sons as he spoke.

"We each got a thousand dollars a week—wire transfer,"
he said, glancing at Derrick and Antwan. "I got all the papers, bank statements. So whatchure problem now?"

ZACHARY CHECKED HIS BlackBerry, walked up to the Brook-
lyn brownstone, and leaned on the bell. He waited patiently
for Lowell's partner to buzz him in. He knew they'd both be
there, anxiously waiting on the signed off contracts with
Anita Brown's signature—the one thing necessary for them
to invoice Jonathan Evans.

The moment the door buzzer sounded, he pushed open
the heavy door and followed the hall to the offices on the
first floor. Mike Epps opened the door with a wide smile.

"Hey, Zach, what's up, man? Who knew you'd be in town
and could go stand in for Lowell? How was the bitch tour?"

"Yo, Zach," Vernon called out.

It wasn't planned, but it was reflex. Zach threw the round-house punch without needing time to think about it. Mike Epps hit the floor and Vernon Knox backed up.

"The tour was fabulous," Zach said, looking down at a stunned Mike Epps. "And although I can't prove it, I know you and your cousin, Ron Epps, poisoned my boy Lowell . . . just to throw him off the job. Wasn't supposed to kill him, just back him off so you could switch around the guard slate, get a bunch of jacklegs in there at a couple hundred bucks a day—same way you've been skimming off Anita's brothers and father—charging Evans the full rate, paying them half. Dude has so much money he can't watch it all, so a lot falls through the cracks, huh? But I wasn't supposed to be in town, so I messed up the party. You probably sent the stalker notes, too, you rat bastard!"

Mike Epps spit out a tooth while Vernon gaped at him.

"Is that true, man?" Vernon said, coming around the desk.

"I'll fucking sue you for assault," Mike sputtered, spit-ting blood and picking up his tooth. "You need to take your Rambo ass out of here before you get hurt. You think you can roll in the big leagues, run with the big dogs, and not have to pay some dues? Lowell is so damned stupid, thinks if you do an honorable job and run a tight ship, you'll get noticed." Mike pushed up and dusted off his suit.

"Tell me you did not poison our partner, man," Vernon said, grabbing Mike's arm. "And tell me you didn't send ter-ror threats to that woman!"

Mike shrugged away from Vernon's hold. "So his cheese-steak was a little tainted—was only a little bit of the meds that Evans makes Ron put on his precious dogs . . . damned dogs eat better than most people I know. Wasn't enough to kill Lowell, just to make him sick enough to stand down and get out of the way for a minute. I didn't have jack to do with the letters. For that, go see her brother Antwan—he dropped them, and had every reason to cover his ass with a little job security, just like Ron and I had every reason to keep the Brown brothers on the job. Lowell was about to fuck every-thing up."

"You are out of your goddamned mind!" Vernon shouted, pointing at Mike. "I want it on the record that I didn't have anything to do with this foul madness."

"This partnership is dissolved anyway, because that Queen B bitch is acting crazy and erratic . . . by this time tomorrow, Evans will have another one, and me and Ron will be back in business."

"You know what, man?" Vernon said, shaking his head. "This is beyond fucked up. I'm out."

"It's about who you know at the end of the day, and I was the one who knew somebody. My cousin is on the inside; that means I am, too. Don't get it twisted," Mike shouted, pointing at Vernon.

"Yeah, it is about who you know," Zach said, holding up his open Blackberry and then pressing the buzzer to open the front door. "I know a couple of people in the Department of Homeland Security . . . Anita knows a few cops who wouldn't mind a Police Athletic League donation—not sure whose jurisdiction it falls under, but some of this could have had international implications." Zachary leaned on the wall as the door opened and three burly suits came in wearing wires in their ears.

They nodded at Zach; he nodded back and glanced out the window as the police cruiser pulled up with Ron Epps in the backseat.

LOVE ME 'TIL DEATH

Lorie O'Clare

CHAPTER I

CHASE REED SQUATTED over the victim. There was a thin roped bracelet around her left hand. Interesting.

"Sir, you can't be here right now."

Chase straightened, ready to pull out his badge. At least they'd finally turned off the strobe lights on the dance floor.

"I'm a special agent." He paused, staring into dark green eyes. The woman pursing her lips didn't blink as she focused on him. If he weren't face-to-face with her he'd have missed the quick once-over she gave him. Too bad none of the ladies here in the club tonight came close to looking as good as this one did.

"I don't care who you are," she began, pointing to the other side of the yellow tape they'd just set up. "Wait. What did you say? Special agent, as in what?"

"FBI. I'm off duty but happened to be here."

"Uh-huh." She marched away from him, pulling her phone off her hip.

Chase watched her shift her weight, but looked down when she glanced over her shoulder, more than likely asking her supervisor if FBI were assigned to this case. He knew what the answer would be before she did. Taking advantage of the moment, he squatted again, getting another good look at the thin, twisted rope bracelet around the young girl's wrist. He would swear it was the twin to the bracelet found on the dead girl last week.

"Look here," the woman announced, standing on the other side of the dead body, glaring down at him with her hands on her hips. "FBI isn't on this case, which I'm sure you know. Please leave."

"Don't want to see my credentials?" He reached into his back pocket.

The officer instinctively backed up, putting her hand over her gun and unhooking the clasp that held it to her belt. He'd be amused but knew she was serious. She didn't know him from Jack.

"It's okay," he told her, holding one hand out to her, palm up, while easing his wallet out of his jeans and then flipping it up as he brought it around slowly for her to see. "Don't get nervous on me."

"Don't talk to me like I'm a fucking horse," she snapped, eyeballing his identification. Then she took it from him, again walking away, this time with his entire wallet. Damned good reason to follow her in his opinion.

There were two other officers on the scene. The bartenders remained on their side of the bar, all of them appearing to be in shock. They'd finally cleaned out all the customers, who less than an hour before had filled this popular nightclub to where he wouldn't be surprised if they exceeded the fire marshal's code for capacity. Another man, ten years or so older than Chase, stood to the side of the scene and glanced at Chase's wallet when the lady cop brought it to him.

"If you don't mind," he said, stepping around the hot investigator and meeting the older guy's pensive stare. "That has all of my money in it."

She held her grip on the leather wallet, scowling at him when he tried retrieving it.

"Chase Reed, Special Agent, huh?" She sounded disbelieving. "How come I don't know you?"

"Did you get a good look at the body brought in last week from the club down the street?" he asked, ignoring her condescending tone. "And I live here. I decided to go out tonight."

"I know every field agent working in Wichita. You aren't one of them."

"I said I live here. I didn't say I worked here," he corrected her. "Last I heard, enjoying downtime wasn't a crime, although I know some supervisors who might argue that fact."

Her badge was hooked to her front belt loop, making it impossible for him to see her name. Light red streaks ran through her blond hair, a shade he would bet was natural and explained her fiery redhead's temper. Her cheeks flushed as she studied his face and then dropped her gaze to scrutinize his identification.

"An FBI agent, on or off the clock, would know enough not to interfere with a crime scene," she said blandly.

Maybe one who followed the rules. "You're right. I know that. I couldn't get a good look at her bracelet from the other side of the yellow tape, though." He wouldn't point out that a good law enforcement team wouldn't have allowed him to cross the tape. She didn't look as if she were in the mood for insults.

"I'm sure you don't mind if I run this in." When she looked back up at him, she'd pressed her lips into a crooked, rather triumphant smile.

"I'm going wherever you take that wallet," he told her, nodding at it.

"Why do you care about the bracelet?" the older guy asked, speaking for the first time. His badge was also attached to his belt, a convenient trick every detective used to keep anyone from knowing their name unless the officer wished to offer it.

"Are you two assigned to this case?" Chase asked.

"Maybe. Tell me about the bracelet," the guy insisted.

As one law enforcement person to another, he had a right to ask. Chase had an obligation to share what he'd noticed, or so some would say. Protocol had never been a strong point with him. The lady detective walked away from the two of them, once again on her phone.

Chase held up his index finger. "One minute," he told the guy, who immediately looked put out. Chase strolled after the lady, really liking how her blue jeans hugged her narrow waist and showed off one hell of a nice ass. She wore a loose-fitting blouse that was a thin, pale pink fabric. Her blondish-red hair tapered past her collar. His gaze lingered on her bra strap, visible through the shirt, before he stepped around her.

"This is Detective Ashley Jones," she said, her soft, sultry voice adding to the hot little package she made up. "I need to run a check on an ID," she continued.

Chase crossed his arms over his chest, glancing over her shoulder when the ME showed up. If it were his case he'd take a few more pictures of the body before moving her. He committed her position, the expression on her face, the skimpy outfit she wore all to memory before the ME blocked his view. Detective Ashley Jones was watching him when he returned his attention to her. She had compelling dark green eyes.

"I see," she said, running her thumb over the indentions of his badge that she'd slid free of the small leather case he usually kept it in. "Oh really?" Her cheeks flushed an attractive rose shade, making her blonde hair around the sides of her face stand out more.

She was getting the scoop on him now, and he was grateful for the fact that computers only offered the facts. Whoever the pretty detective spoke to had looked him up on the system but didn't bother placing a phone call to hear his supervisor's opinion of him. Chase gave thanks for small favors.

"Here's your badge and wallet," she said, handing it to him when she hung up the phone. "And if you wouldn't mind stepping over the yellow tape," she added, giving him a harsh look although she probably knew now she couldn't force him anywhere.

Chase accepted his badge, nodded to the sexy detective, and let her do her job. Stepping over the yellow tape, he paused at a nearby table, which hadn't been wiped off since the young girl, who'd been sitting at the bar, slumped off the bar stool to her death thirty minutes before last call. The nightlife alcoholics were pretty pissed when the bar closed down earlier than usual in order to allow PD to do their job.

Avoiding the stickiness on the tall, round table, he slid his badge back into its leather case and then put it back in his wallet. He checked to make sure the hot little number of a detective hadn't lifted any of his cash before he slid his wallet into his back pocket.

"May I ask you a couple questions?" Detective Ashley Jones asked, stepping over the yellow tape and then walking up to him.

Her blouse buttoned down the front and the top two buttons were undone. He could see the slight outline of what looked like a lace bra through the thin material. A hint of cleavage could be one hell of a distraction during any interrogation. Chase lifted his gaze to those compelling green eyes, more than aware she watched him while he took in her figure.

"Only if I can ask a couple questions as well," he told her, and when her expression turned guarded, he decided he liked how she looked better when she was on edge. He wondered what else would put that pretty blush on her cheeks. "I'm Chase Reed," he offered, extending his hand.

Her smaller hand was warm, soft, and her handshake firm. "I know who you are. We just went through that, remember?"

"So am I going to have to rely on overhearing a phone conversation to know who you are?" he asked.

"I'm Detective Jones," she offered, sliding her hand out of his. Flipping a small notebook open, she glanced at the table next to him, but then looked farther on at the other tables. "Care if we have a seat?"

Chase liked how she was soft-spoken. He imagined more than one guy might make the mistake that she was gullible, or easily manipulated. Her blonde hair and distracting figure were more than a distraction. Chase didn't make assumptions about people that easily, though. He pulled a stool out opposite Ashley Jones when she chose a table and sat. This one didn't appear to be sticky.

"Would you mind telling me why you were investigating this crime scene?" she asked, scribbling something on her pad and then looking up at him with a hooded gaze. Thick long lashes fluttered over her dark green eyes.

He lifted one shoulder lazily. Last thing he needed was his name going on file as having offered a tip to local law enforcement. He was home on downtime, but not necessarily by choice. "I'm an investigator. If a crime happens in front of you, wouldn't you check it out?"

She put her elbow on the table and rested her chin on her hand, studying him. A small smile he bet meant anything but amusement appeared. "It would depend on the situation. So this girl was murdered right in front of you?"

"She was murdered in front of a few hundred people," he pointed out. "People you sent packing."

"That wasn't my doing," she muttered under her breath.

Detective or not, she must not have a lot of rank. Possibly the older gentleman he saw headed up this investigation. He glanced around, no longer seeing him. The ME was securing the body on a gurney while two uniforms spoke with the staff behind the counter.

"Look," he offered. "Your girl over there was drugged, slipped a Mickey. She collapsed off the barstool. A few people tripped over her until a bouncer noticed she was down. When they couldn't revive her, they called 911. You've got the rest."

"And I knew all of that before I came over here," she said tightly. "You noticed something and you're holding out on me, why?"

Maybe she was a better cop than he originally thought she was. "Yes, I noticed something. And it's something you should have noticed, too." Chase sighed. He wasn't here to judge her. And maybe if he hadn't been FBI for most of his adult life, he could actually be a normal citizen when taking time off. "Look. It's late. You know who I am and I'm sure you can find me if you need to."

"Give me contact information," she said, her pen poised. "And then tell me why you're holding out on me," she added, glancing up at him through her thick lashes. A long strand of hair drifted over the side of her face and she tucked it behind her ear.

Chase lowered his gaze to her cleavage, which was more visible now with her sitting and hunching over her notepad. "I don't want to go on record as helping you with this case. And trust me, you don't want my name involved with your investigation."

"Why is that?"

"Because I'm not a good FBI agent," he told her simply.

Detective Ashley Jones cocked one eyebrow, raising her pen and chewing on the end of it, her full lips puckering around the narrow tip. Yet another distraction. He couldn't help wondering if she knew how sexual her act appeared, and if she did, why she was using such tactics on him? To get him to open up to her? Hell, he'd been tried, used, and abused by much better manipulators than this pretty little cop.

She wrote something on her pad, tore off the bottom half of the page, and slid the paper across the table to him. "Thanks for your time, Special Agent Reed," she said, standing and closing her notebook.

Chase glanced down at the piece of torn paper without touching it. *We'll keep it off the record then. Call me. 314-840-9334. Ashley.*

He slid the piece of paper off the table and then into his back pocket. Heading for the door, he ignored the curious looks the uniforms gave him and didn't look at Ashley. And to think he'd doubted he'd head home with any phone numbers tonight. Looked like he'd scored after all, and with the hottest woman he'd seen in that club all night.

CHAPTER 2

"CRAP!" ASH SLOWED when she turned onto her street, hesitating when she saw her ex's car parked in front of her house. "Not now," she moaned.

Danny was the last person in the world she wanted to deal with right now. It had been a long day, preceded by a really long night. She didn't have enough energy to take him on.

Her cell phone rang and she picked it up out of her cup holder on her dash, staring at the word "unknown" on her small screen. Her gut tightened. This was her personal phone, her private number that only her closest friends and her parents knew. There wasn't any reason for anyone to block their number and call her. And she was pretty sure it was next to impossible for anyone to track the number down.

It rang a third time and then a fourth while she crawled down the street, practically coasting, and nearing her home. As it quit ringing, going to voice mail, Danny turned in his driver's seat and then opened his car door. She had half a mind to accelerate and lose him before he could follow her.

Ash pushed the button to roll down her passenger window as she pulled up alongside Danny. "I've had no sleep. I'm tired and I'm grouchy. So if you've come over to fight, we're going to have to reschedule."

"I'm not here to fight." He sounded uncharacteristically passive. Which made her even more leery of talking to him.

Rolling her window up, she turned in front of his car and

pulled into her driveway just as her cell phone buzzed, indicating voice mail. If she pushed her garage-door opener on her visor and pulled in to her garage, Danny would walk in behind her. It would be hell getting him out of her house. And she didn't want him inside. She didn't want to leave her car parked in her driveway, either.

"Double crap," she groaned, resigning herself to putting her car away. She was too exhausted to have to come back out and pull it into the garage later.

Danny stood alongside her car in the dark garage as she grabbed her purse and phone. Whoever had blocked their number and called had left a voice-mail message and in spite of her ever-growing exhaustion she wanted to hear the message.

Would it be the FBI hunk she'd run into at Club Toro?

"You look like hell," Danny said, closing in on her before she could shut her car door.

"What do you want, Danny?" She didn't stop him when he reached around her and closed her car door for her.

The garage door closed, engulfing them in darkness. Ash made her way to the door leading into her kitchen, punching in the security code for the alarm, and then opening the door to her home.

"I wanted to talk to you about . . ." He hesitated, leaning on the doorknob just inside the kitchen. "Mindy Simpson."

Ash dropped her purse on the kitchen table and stared at her ex. In the four years since their divorce, he'd put on some weight. She'd heard he was dating someone now but did her best not to keep up with his life. With no kids, and not much property shared, their divorce had been as amiable as could be, and there had been little reason to keep in contact since. Danny usually seemed to find reason though, especially if he needed to take advantage of her being a cop. She should have guessed tonight's visit wouldn't be anything different.

"Why are you asking about her?" she asked.

"She was killed last night."

"I know. I was on scene."

"That's what I heard." He let go of the doorknob and ran his hand over his closely shaved head, his entire body seeming to deflate when he exhaled loudly. "Can you tell me . . . I mean. Hell," he groaned, looking absolutely tortured when he lifted his watery eyes to her. "Did she suffer a lot before she died?"

"Oh hell, Danny. Don't tell me you were seeing Mindy Simpson. She was twenty-three years old." No one she'd interviewed who'd claimed to know Mindy had mentioned Danny.

She wasn't sure she remembered him ever looking so upset. Danny was all man, the macho, never-let-them-see-you-cry type of guy. Yet the man who stood in her kitchen looked like he'd just lost his puppy, or worse, someone he really cared about.

"I'm sorry, Danny," she said, hugging herself and refusing to hug him. If he came over thinking she might crack and feel sorry for him, he'd learn soon enough she was made of tougher stuff than that. "How well did you know Mindy?"

"I've actually known her a couple years. We were on the same bowling league together. I took her out six months or so ago and we've been kind of on again, off again ever since."

"So were you on again, or off again as of last night?"

"We were going to go out last night but got into an argument. Hell, Ash, some of her stuff is at my house right now."

"You were supposed to go out last night but got into a fight? Did you know she was at Club Toro?"

"She went there to spite me," he growled.

"Goddamn, Danny. You get in a fight with your girlfriend who then goes to one of the largest meat markets in town to spite you and ends up dead—murdered," she stressed.

"Wait a minute." His anguished look disappeared and Danny straightened, narrowing his gaze on her. "Don't you start playing cop with me, sweetheart."

"I'm not playing cop. I am a cop," she stressed. "And I told you I was too tired to fight." Regardless of what he might have thought coming over here, what he had just done made him a stronger suspect than anyone they had right now. Pointing that out to him would start one hell of a fight, and one she was most definitely not in the mood for. "Why are you here, Danny?"

"I want you to tell me what happened. Who the hell did this to her?" he demanded.

"If I knew I wouldn't tell you." She glanced at her phone, ready to hear her voice-mail message but needing Danny to leave so she could do so. "But I don't know who did it. I'm sorry for your loss, but Danny, I've had a hell of a day, and night. Will contact you tomorrow and take your statement." If she said "question him," he'd clam up and not talk about Mindy.

"Mindy didn't do drugs. No one will tell me shit since I'm not a relative. How could she just have died?" he demanded, ignoring Ash's suggestion to discuss this tomorrow.

There wasn't any getting rid of him until she appeased his tortured curiosity to some extent.

"I tell you what, once the reports are in on her death, I'll tell you what I can, okay?" She nodded toward her living room. "Let me walk you out. I haven't had any sleep in over twenty hours and I can't think straight to help you now anyway."

They got as far as her front door. Ash opened it, but then Danny turned on her, his expression fierce. "I want to know what motherfucker drugged her. You got that, Ash? I have a right to know who did this to her."

There wasn't any point telling him he didn't have a right to know shit. Ash nodded, opening her screen, and willing him out of her home. Tomorrow, once her head was clear from much-needed sleep, she'd question Danny further, see if possibly her dunce of an ex-husband had any connection to Mindy Simpson's death, or not.

After locking the front door, Ash didn't bother making sure Danny left. She hurried into the kitchen and plopped down in the chair at the table then pulled up her voice-mail messages. Her hunch was right and her gut twisted while a warm feeling swelled inside her as she listened to Chase Reed's rough baritone.

"I'll be at your house at nine tonight, unless that is too off the record for you." If there was a challenge in his tone, she ached to know what it meant. "If it is I'll meet you out somewhere, but my guess is you're too exhausted to drive." He rattled off his number and Ash wrote it down, repeating the message to make sure she got it right.

She glanced at the wall clock as she laid her phone down on the small notepad where she'd written Reed's number. "Lovely," she moaned. It was going on eight. Barely enough time to shower before her FBI man showed up, and one with a mystery wrapped around him. The funny feeling in her gut swelled and became an annoying pressure between her legs as she hurried upstairs to find clean clothes and hop into the shower.

It was going on nine when she rushed back downstairs, her hair still damp. Exhaustion was replaced with trepidation and something else she didn't want to put a label on when she reached the kitchen and there was a firm knock on the front door.

There wasn't any point asking how he'd figured out where she lived. She'd only talked to Chase Reed for a few minutes but already she guessed he was the kind of guy who didn't reveal his secrets.

Ash hurried to the front door, opening it just as Chase raised his fist to knock again. "Impatient, are you?" she half teased. Anything else she might have said dissipated as she stared at the incredibly sexy man filling her doorway.

"Care if I come in?" Chase didn't move, but stood facing her wearing faded blue jeans and a black, plain T-shirt that hugged his muscular torso. A perfect six-pack, long powerful-looking legs, and well-defined biceps were only part of his sex appeal.

"Sure. That's fine." Ash managed to speak in spite of how dry her mouth suddenly was. She stepped back without tripping over her own feet as she allowed him to enter.

His hair was a shiny, coarse black with slight waves that covered his ears and almost made it to his shirt collar. But it was those intense blue eyes, a sharp, focused gaze, that made her feel he looked past her face and saw deep into her soul, and immediately knew all her darkest secrets. Chase walked past her, allowing her a moment to drool over buns of steel, and wipe her palms against her jeans.

"You got my voice-mail message." He didn't make it a question. When he turned and faced her, making no qualms about giving her a slow once-over, his dark, brooding expression gave her the chills.

"Yes, I got it." At the same time, heat swelled inside her to distraction. She told herself it would be impossible not to react physically to a man who redefined the definition of the perfect male. "I take it there is something you want to tell me?"

Keep it professional. If all they did was discuss the murder last night, she might be able to keep her mind from wondering what he looked like without his clothes on.

"Several things, actually." He glanced around her home, taking his time inspecting the living room.

When he walked farther into her home, pausing in the doorway that led to the kitchen, she stayed a few paces behind him, trying to keep her focus on the way his black hair curled under at his neck. She could find no faults. His shoulders were broad and muscular. Her fingers itched, and she knew if she touched him he would be as hard as a brick wall. He wouldn't catch her staring at that hard ass of his though.

"Do you have anything to drink?" he asked, disappearing around the corner.

"Make yourself at home," she muttered, following him into the kitchen but making it to the refrigerator before he did.

"Thank you," he said, his expression still dark and unreadable when she shot him a quick glance to see if there was any apparent sarcasm. He appeared to take her offer seriously.

"I haven't had a chance to go shopping lately," she began, telling herself there was no reason to apologize for not being a good hostess. He'd invited himself over. "It's water or juice."

"What kind of juice?"

"Apple."

"Sounds good."

Ash poured two glasses of apple juice and turned, feeling as if her kitchen had shrunk with him standing in the middle of it. Handing him his glass, she moved around him to the table.

"So what was it you didn't want to go on the record as saying?" she asked.

"Did you investigate the deaths of Mary Harcourt or Daphne Sullivan?" he asked, holding his glass to his mouth but not sipping from it.

"I did Mary, but not Daphne." She ached to know what he knew about all three deaths. Three girls being killed by a date-rape drug in the past week was definitely a pattern.

"Maybe you should look at all three deaths a bit closer."

"Why? Do you think they're connected?" she asked.

For the first time since she'd met him, he smiled. And holy crap! Dimples appeared in his cheeks and his teeth were straight. Bad Boy FBI man had an all-American good boy look about him, as well. Maybe she shouldn't have let him in her home. Lawman or not, Chase Reed looked dangerous as hell; maybe not in the way of a criminal would, but if he had seduction on his mind, she was in serious danger—of losing.

Or would it be winning?

"I'm not trying to insult you as a cop," he offered, crossing his arms over all that brawn and muscle. "You don't know me, but if you did, you'd gather the same impression you're probably getting right now. I'm a purebred asshole."

"I'll remember that." Keep it on the case, she told herself, making it a mantra and fighting not to smile back at him and get sucked into the sensual magnetism that he'd just turned up a notch. "Okay. Three girls have been murdered. Obviously they're connected in more than one way. Tell me what you know and then we'll see if I know anything you don't."

"I don't know anything you don't." Apparently he wanted to prove the asshole claim. "But there was something you didn't notice last night. I was watching you."

"I know you were." That just slipped out. She opted to sit

down, which only created a bit of distance between them. But picking up her pen, which was still on the pad where she'd written his number, she started clicking it, staring at the way she'd written his name above his number. Chase—a rather unique yet fitting name for this man hovering over her.

"Did you notice any jewelry?"

She shot him a pensive look, and he cocked one eyebrow, as if willing her to remember the scene. When she'd first spotted him, stepping over the yellow tape as if he had permission, he'd squatted down next to the victim and looked at her wrist.

Ash hated missing something at a crime scene and later having the obvious pointed out to her. Call it her damnable pride, but she really got off on solving a case without anyone's help. She struggled with the image, fighting to remember what he did when he reached for her wrist.

"That's it. You remember," he encouraged, his soft baritone too damned seductive.

It snapped her out of her concentration and she glared at him. Ash didn't realize she'd been brainstorming, staring at him the entire time. He probably saw her face twist in an effort to remember what had been in front of her the entire time. But then it hit her; when he'd walked up to her and Charlie Madison he'd told them he couldn't get a good look at her bracelet from the other side of the crime tape.

"What was it about her bracelet that impressed you?" she asked, ignoring his words of encouragement.

"The other two girls were wearing the same bracelet."

She stared at him, searching her memory for details about Mary. She'd been in a bar and grill in the downtown area, not too far from Club Toro. Mary had looked like one of the hippies, a college girl, which was proven when her backpack was found where she'd been sitting before she collapsed and died. Mindy, on the other hand, was decked out in a miniskirt, wearing lots of makeup. Danny's type of girl. The two women were young, both early twenties, but the two were very different types. She remembered that Mary wore diamond stud earrings because they'd reminded her of ones her grandmother had given her when she'd turned sixteen.

"Mary and Mindy were nothing alike," she told Chase.

"You're right. All three women were very different in where they hung out, how they dressed, giving every indication that the same man wouldn't be attracted to all of them. Yet they all had the exact same bracelet on."

"It couldn't be the exact same bracelet," she pointed out.

Chase made a face. God, he was gorgeous. "I stand corrected. They were all wearing a similar bracelet, a thin rope bracelet with knots on it."

"I'll check it out." She fought not to write down what he just told her, remembering he wanted to be off the record. For some reason, she wasn't anxious for him to go. She should be. She needed to sleep. Although now she was all wound up and had half a mind to head back down to the station to confirm his facts.

Ash took a long drink of her apple juice, suddenly wishing it was coffee, and then forced herself to stand. "Thanks for stopping by and telling me that," she said, edging around him, then moving to the doorway leading to the living room. "Maybe I'll see you around sometime."

"You will," he said. "And I'm not ready to leave yet."

CHAPTER 3

CHASE NEEDED to get the hell out of there and leave Ashley Jones alone. If his supervisor got wind of him working with local law enforcement when he was supposed to be home, taking time off, and doing anything but searching for murderers, he'd hand him his head on a platter.

"Do you have any idea who is overdosing these girls?" he asked, when she turned around, appearing surprised and more than a bit leery after he'd informed her he didn't want to leave. His supervisor would have a field day if he knew what Chase was doing right now. Hadn't the reason for sending him home been to give him time to think about his actions, to understand that he couldn't jump into situations without considering protocol, rules, and regulations?

"If I did, I wouldn't be here anxious to crash." Her hair was damp from her shower and the red highlights were more obvious. She wasn't wearing any makeup, but her rosy cheeks, probably from her hot shower, provided enough color. Ashley Jones didn't need makeup. She was gorgeous without it.

He couldn't count how many nights he'd gone without sleep, surviving on pure adrenaline and determination to catch a killer. "Do you want me to leave?"

When she didn't answer at first, he knew he'd guessed right. Ashley was hot as fucking hell. The comfortable, worn-looking jeans she wore hugged her narrow hips and flat tummy. But it was her tank top, the spaghetti straps with no bra, that intrigued the hell out of him. If he didn't know better he'd swear she'd put those clothes on intentionally, opting for no makeup so she wouldn't appear obvious. He wasn't the only one aware of the sexually charged energy between them.

"What else do you know about these three girls' deaths?" she asked, instead of answering him. When she tilted her head, studying him, a strand of blond hair brushed over her cheek.

He stepped forward, reaching for it to see how she'd react. "The same man killed all three of them. They were all alone in a bar, a nightclub, or bar and grill," he continued, doubting he told her anything she didn't already know.

Ashley stepped backward when he lifted his hand to her face, wrapping her arms around her waist and hugging herself. She shook her head to move the strand, which only managed to make it outline the contour of her cheek. "They were alone as if they were waiting on someone." Ashley turned, crossing her living room quickly and stopping at her front door. She was going to throw him out. Instead of opening it, though, she leaned against the door handle, her dark green eyes smoldering as she let her gaze travel down his body. "That, or maybe they were out alone because they were mad at someone."

"Mad at someone?" He hadn't considered that angle, but he imagined a woman might head out on the town alone, going to a place she might consider a prime pickup joint for whatever type of man she was looking for. "So each one of them was out on the town alone because they were looking for someone? Is that what you would do?"

"This isn't about me," she said firmly, pressing her lips together and frowning.

He really liked her pouty look. Chase also enjoyed how her eyes widened when he cleared the distance between them, trapping her against the front door. "Let's make this about you," he suggested, and continued when she opened her mouth to retort, looking surprised. "Let's say you've got a boyfriend, someone you're close enough to that he would give you jewelry, or a bracelet. But he's pissed you off for some reason. Would you go out to a bar and let a stranger buy you a drink?"

"If I had a boyfriend and he pissed me off I'd kick his ass and get it over with," she told him, puffing out her chest when she sucked in a breath.

Her nipples turned into hard peaks, stabbing against her shirt. It was cut low enough to give him a mouthwatering view of the swell of her breasts.

"That doesn't surprise me," he growled, again reaching for her.

She raised her hand to block him and he grabbed her wrist, holding their hands in midair between them.

"What if you weren't the confident woman that you are?" he whispered, stepping closer and holding her hand before him in spite of her trying to release it. "Maybe you're seeing a guy and the relationship isn't stable. So you go out to drink him off your mind. You're distracted, not paying attention, when someone slips something in your drink."

She searched his face, not saying anything for a moment. Then her gaze dropped as she sucked in her lower lip and chewed on it, as if something just occurred to her.

"If that's the case," she said slowly, focusing somewhere on his chest. "Then the only way to know who drugged these girls is by interviewing those who would have been around them that night."

"There's no way of knowing who was in those bars each of those nights."

"True." She relaxed her hand, fisting it but no longer trying to get free. "But there is a way to talk to the bartenders who were working those nights."

Her eyes glowed like rare jewels when she lifted her gaze to his.

"We need to get you to bed then, so you can start your interviews tomorrow," he said, his voice lowering to a rough growl as he pictured her stretched out in bed, naked, with her large breasts exposed above the covers.

"You need to leave," she whispered, and ran her tongue over her lips, moistening them and making them look even fuller, a feast for a starving man.

He let go of her hand, but when she tried pressing it

against his chest, pushing him away from her so she could open the door, he grabbed it again. Ashley tried yanking her hand back, but he was faster. Moving with a speed that matched the need he couldn't restrain any longer, Chase gripped her arm once again, this time pinning it to the door next to her head, and pressed his body against hers.

"This time," he whispered, lowering his head until his lips were a fraction of an inch from hers. "Next time I think I'll stay."

Whatever words she planned on spewing at him turned into a groan when he pressed his mouth over hers. Her lips were soft, moist, and full. He dipped inside, taking advantage of her parted lips, and delved deep into her heat.

She moved against him, rubbing her body over his like a cat. Chase growled, impaling her mouth with his tongue while letting go of her hand and grabbing her shoulders. Her skin was smooth, soft, yet she was toned and firm. He slid his hands down her arms, feeling the small bulge of well-defined muscles. She kept in shape. But then he'd already noticed her quick wit, her sharp tongue, and it only fit she'd be just as fine-tuned physically.

Chase put his hands between them as he tilted his head, moving his mouth over hers and then nipping at her lip as she grabbed his forearms. He doubted she was a tease. She wanted him, and if she did, she would have all of him. He wasn't a chaste-kiss kind of guy.

When he gripped her breasts, her nipples stiffened, growing and rubbing against his palms, making his blood boil and immediately drain to his cock. Ashley hissed in a breath, every inch of her stiffening and her fingers digging into his arms, before she exhaled and moaned into his mouth.

She definitely wanted this as badly as he did. And that knowledge would torture both of them, as well as provide him with an insurance policy. He'd already told her he was an asshole. Hopefully she would never find out to what extent.

"Goddamn, sweetheart," he growled into her mouth. "I sure hope you have sweet dreams."

"What? Huh?" She blinked, licking her lips, when he

ended the kiss and straightened, enjoying watching her recover. "Oh, okay, fine."

He'd give her this, she was quick at bouncing back. Stepping around him, and he didn't stop her this time, she yanked at her tank top, allowing him an even better view of ripe cleavage. Her nipples were hard as stones when she cleared her throat, looked down, and then tucked a strand of hair behind her ear.

"Are you always this nonchalant when a man kisses you?" Chase knew he was pushing her, but he liked the way her green eyes glowed a dark, alluring shade when emotions ran strong in her.

She shot him a look to kill, her long dark lashes hooding those glowing orbs. "I don't have a set behavior for something that doesn't usually happen," she snapped.

"Good. I like knowing other men aren't kissing you." He tapped her nose before she could slap his hand out of the way, and then reached for her door. "Keep it that way," he told her, then let himself out before she could utter a crude comment in his direction.

ASH PARKED HER car in front of Club Toro, opting for door-to-door service instead of pulling into one of the many empty stalls in the large parking lot in front of it. Her mind was spinning after a day of discovery, and although she'd received all the credit, it nagged at her that she didn't deserve any of it.

After comparing notes on each case down at the station with her captain, they'd confirmed all three girls wore thin, rope bracelets, each with several knots in them. The knot pattern didn't match, but they were all hand designed out of hemp, and each girl wore hers on her right wrist.

Otherwise, each victim was as different as night from day. The autopsy on the first two confirmed the drug that killed them was the same, and of a very high dosage. ISIS, the street name of the drug put in each drink, otherwise called "Instant Slut in Service," was not only incredibly illegal, but not easy to find. It was a despicable drug, and just thinking about the kind of people who would create such a life-threatening concoction, and then give it an even more disgusting name, brought bile to her throat.

Men who viewed women as objects, who cared nothing about life, and who were willing to drug a woman and use her as they pleased, knowing she'd been poisoned and would die, such men needed to be shot on sight. No, they needed to be tortured and abused as they had done to their victims, their cries for mercy ignored, until they met a painful death.

Shaking the unpleasant thoughts from her head, she parked and shut off her car. Ash had several leads to follow up on; the first was talking to the bartenders who were working the night each girl died.

Climbing out of the car, she squinted against the afternoon sun at a dark SUV idling ahead of her alongside the building. Dark-tinted windows made it too hard to see if anyone sat inside. Ignoring it, she headed to the club doors. Once these interviews were done she needed to figure out how a killer could have gotten his hands on a not-so-accessible drug.

"What are you going to ask them?" Chase's deep baritone did a number on her insides.

The driver's side window wasn't rolled down the first time she checked out the SUV. Approaching it, making note that Chase Reed drove a black Navigator, she also made a mental note to research this guy further. The average FBI agent didn't make the kind of money it would take to drive one of these babies.

"Probably the same thing I asked at the last two clubs," she told him, stopping when she stood inches from his car door. "Do you want to come in with me?"

"Nope," he said, not hesitating. "I'm a ghost and we're going to keep it that way."

She hadn't mentioned him to anyone down at the station, but didn't tell him that. "Maybe you should have told me that last night."

"I knew last night you wouldn't bring up my name." He lifted his arm off the rolled-down window and ran a finger down her arm.

Ash had half a mind to back up out of his reach. She didn't want him torturing her and making it hard to stay focused. Nor did she want him thinking she would be his piece of ass while he decided to hang around. He'd told her he lived here and didn't work here. FBI wasn't assigned to this case. And neither of those facts explained why he was suddenly coming around.

"I've got a job to do," she told him, taking a step backward.

He let his hand fall back over the open window of his car. "I'll be by your house at seven."

"No," she told him. She'd be insane counting the minutes until seven and that wasn't how she planned to spend her early evening.

"Fine." He turned from her, grabbing a pen and jotting something down. It crossed her mind to walk away from him, but he handed her a business card before she managed to move. "Meet me at my house at seven. I want to hear what your bartenders have to say."

"I'm not sure about this," she mumbled, staring at the block letters. He'd written down a street address and phone number.

"I am," he told her.

She shot him a quick glance and his sober expression didn't reveal his thoughts. But his dark blue eyes held her captive, stealing her breath with silent promises of more than discussing a case. Men didn't just saunter into her life with hints of sexual rendezvous and erotic experiences she'd never have otherwise. Her life was full, her job keeping her so damn busy that eight hours of sleep was a rare commodity. And she loved it like that. No man around simply meant no drama.

Ash opened her mouth to tell him she wouldn't be there. But Chase accelerated, raising his hand in good-bye, leaving her standing there watching him drive off.

"Son of a bitch," she complained, glancing down at his card.

There wasn't time to dwell on him. Stuffing his card into her pocket, she entered the dimly lit nightclub, which at this time of the day was empty, and headed over to the bar. An hour later, having heard answers from the people working at Club Toro similar to those she got at the other two establishments she'd visited today, she headed back to her car feeling frustrated. No one remembered anyone in particular, and none of the people working could ID anyone who sat next to her victims.

Learning who might have gained access to ISIS would be an even harder task. Ash got out of her car back at the station, and slid her hand in her pocket, fingering Chase's card without pulling it out. He said he didn't work in Wichita, which meant he wouldn't have any connections here. Damn shame. She needed a really good street source. Someone who would know the drug deals, how they went down, and where. Maybe one of the narcotic cops could help.

"The last big bust we had was Phillips," Dan Hartman, one of the detectives who'd been on the force about as long as she had, explained. He slouched in his chair, his thick long legs stretched out in front of him, with one cowboy boot crossed over the other. Hartman did a lot of undercover work, and as a result, he got away with the shaggy, unshaven look. Possibly he was a good-looking man if he weren't so loyal to the lazy-bum look he'd been affecting for years now. "That was almost a year ago, though."

"All three of my victims died from an overdose of ISIS," she explained, fiddling with her ballpoint as she sat across from him in one of the upright wooden chairs that faced his desk. "My perp got his hands on the shit somehow."

"Bad stuff, too." Hartman shook his head. "I'll keep my ears to the ground for you, Ash," he promised.

"Where did Phillips do most of his trafficking?"

"Inner city mainly. It's possible one of his runners could have tried picking up where he left off. But Phillips dealt heroine and coke, some pot and pills, but nothing like what you're looking for. Believe it or not, most drug dealers have some level of ethics. ISIS is a lowlife's drug. I couldn't see Phillips messing with it."

"Well, someone is," she said, grunting and feeling a hot shower was in order. Just thinking about the kind of person who would purchase such a piss-poor drug premeditatively made her skin crawl. "And I need to know where he's getting it."

"I'll let you know if I hear anything."

She nodded, pushing herself to her feet and forcing herself not to look at the clock on the wall to see what time it was. Ash prayed it was after seven, that way she wouldn't feel antsy waiting for that hour to arrive.

Maybe talking to Chase would help. He was FBI, after all. Even if he didn't work this town, he might still have some connections. And right now, any lead at all would help. The more time that passed, the colder these cases would get and she'd never find her perp.

"Ash," Hartman called after her when she reached the door.

She turned around, certain her exhaustion and stress showed on her face.

"I'll put out some feelers for you," he offered.

"Thanks."

"Phillips did some of his business at the downtown bowling alley," Hartman suggested, shrugging. "He's out of the action now, but if there was someone picking up where he left off, they might be trying to slip into his shoes. I can sniff around if you like."

"Anything would help," she admitted.

Ash remembered Danny telling her Mindy Simpson bowled on a league, which was how they'd met. From what she'd gathered on the other two victims, though, they never bowled. It was a weak connection but more than anything else she had right now.

She reached her car and flipped through her notebook where she'd jotted down notes from her interviews with bartenders and waitresses who worked at the three clubs. Ash pulled the reports filed by the officers who worked the first crime scene and compared notes from what the employees had said then to what she'd been told today.

Daphne Sullivan was killed at Aaron's Bar and Grill, a sports bar in a nice part of town. It was the only murder not anywhere near the college scene, although Daphne was a third-year student, working on her bachelor's degree in fine arts. She was majoring in dance, and according to her parents, she had a scholarship lined up for the following year. Her parents paid her room and board. A free ride with a bright future. Now all of it was gone.

Mary Harcourt and Mindy Simpson were about the same age as Daphne, all of them in their early twenties. Mary and Mindy weren't in college, though. Mary worked in a factory as a secretary, made decent money, and her coworkers said she'd been saving to buy a home. Mindy worked in a grocery store and lived with two roommates in an apartment.

"Young, single, paid their bills," Ash mused, heading out of the parking lot. Mindy's roommates had little to offer and neither knew about a bracelet. She barely remembered her drive home as she pulled into her garage, hitting the button to raise her garage door. "Nothing unique about them other than the rope bracelets they wore. That's got to be a clue, but what does it mean?"

It was six-thirty when she stood in her bedroom, naked and ready for a shower. She wouldn't make it anywhere by seven, which was a damned shame. The case occupied her thoughts and she needed to keep brainstorming until some other connection became clear. Standing in front of her dresser, she stared at her jewelry box, thinking about the bracelets the girls wore.

Her jewelry was a hodgepodge collection at best. Ash fingered a locket Danny gave her years ago, before they'd married. It hung on a hook next to her jewelry box along with the few other necklaces she owned. Flipping open her jewelry box, she stared at the earrings she owned. There was the small velvet box that held the diamond earrings her grandmother gave her and that reminded her of the earrings Mary Harcourt wore.

"What?" she whispered, as she flipped the box open and her jaw dropped. The earrings were gone.

CHAPTER 4

CHASE AIMED HIS remote at his TV, all too aware of the time and fighting to stay put when he ached to jump up and pace. It was almost eight and not a word from Ashley. He almost lunged at his cell phone when it started vibrating and then chirping on his coffee table.

"Reed here," he growled, after glaring at the words "unknown caller" on his phone.

"How would you like to take me bowling?" Ashley's soft purr in his ear sent his heart racing in his chest.

Jumping off the couch, he forced himself to take a slow breath and then stretched, scratching his bare chest. "Why did you block your number?" he demanded.

Her alluring tone didn't change. "You blocked your number when you called me."

"My number is always blocked, company policy," he explained.

"Would you like to take me bowling?" she repeated.

"Why do you want to go bowling?" He'd take her anywhere she wanted to go, and realized that as he bounded through to his bedroom, ready to change clothes.

"It's a weak hunch at best."

"I'm listening." He put the phone on speaker and set it next to his computer in his bedroom as he searched for a shirt.

"I spoke with one of our narcotic cops today," she began. "I need to know where someone could buy ISIS."

He opened his mouth to ask why she hadn't come to him asking for help with that. Ashley sounded pumped up when she continued talking, her voice animated. Chase didn't want to interrupt her; just listening to her soft, sultry tone did a mean number to his equilibrium. He was getting semihard in spite of the despicable subject matter she was discussing.

"He couldn't really help me," she added.

He could have told her that. ISIS wasn't sold by the average street drug dealer. It was hard-core stuff, moved in circles that went beyond what most city cops dealt with.

"He told me the last really big dealer he took down, less than a year ago, did some of his work out of the bowling alley."

"Now, Mindy Simpson was on a league," she added. "My ex was spending some time with her and told me that's how they met."

Chase pulled a shirt over his head and stopped, facing the phone, his interest piqued. If Ashley's ex was dating Mindy, that made him suspect.

"There's something else, and it's nothing. Seriously nothing. I shouldn't even mention it because I know it's just coincidence."

"What?" he asked, grabbing the phone and taking it off speaker.

"When you first mentioned the jewelry each victim wore, I remembered Mary Harcourt wore a pair of diamond earrings. I specifically remembered them because they reminded me of the diamond earrings my grandmother gave me when I turned sixteen. They are an old family heirloom and have been passed down from daughter to daughter in my family for several generations."

"Why did your grandmother give them to you and not your mother?" Chase doubted it had anything to do with their case, but he wanted to know everything about Ashley. She'd been under his skin since he first watched her go over the crime scene at Club Toro. After kissing her at her house, she'd singed his system, leaving him hot and hard. Anything about her mattered to him.

"My grandmother and mother didn't get along with each other very well," she said quietly, without elaborating. "But Chase, when I got home tonight I was looking through my jewelry, and my diamond earrings are gone."

"When's the last time you wore them?" He headed into his bathroom, glancing at his reflection in the mirror as he applied deodorant and opted for a small amount of a cologne he couldn't remember when he'd last applied.

"Yes, I would have asked someone that question, too. I told you it was a weak hunch. The fact is, I've never worn them. I didn't appreciate my grandmother giving them to me and skipping my mother. It really hurt my mother and my wearing them would have hurt her, too. They've always been right here in my jewelry box. More than once I've thought about giving them to my mother now that my grandmother is dead. She wears jewelry like that more than I do."

"So do you look at them often?" He headed back to his room, grabbing socks out of his top drawer and then reaching for his boots.

"No. I don't have a clue how long they've been missing," she snapped.

Chase smiled. She was right. It was a weak hunch. He wanted to see her and wanted to talk about this more with her in person. It was a hell of a case, and one he'd jump on the opportunity to work, because there were no clues. Chase wasn't a glory seeker, though. Hell, if he were, he wouldn't have fallen knee deep in shit with the FBI. He knew how to be a ghost, though. He didn't have a problem helping Ash with the case and allowing her to take all the credit for solving it.

"I'll be over there in thirty minutes and we'll head to the bowling alley," he told her.

"I'll meet you there," she said without hesitating.

"Why do you want me to go with you?"

There was silence for a moment but when she spoke it was with confidence. "It would look less obvious if I show up there with someone," she explained. "I'm pretty sure it's league night and if my ex is there he won't be suspicious if I'm not alone."

"Exactly." He didn't miss a beat. "And if you've got a date it's only right that he brings you to the bowling alley. Guys check that sort of thing out. Your ex will see what I'm driving when we leave. Mark my word."

She sighed, and again he smiled, knowing she couldn't argue against riding with him. "Fine," she grunted. "Be here in an hour. I need time to get ready."

"Take all the time you need, darling," he growled.

Ash snorted, but didn't argue. "See you in an hour."

He doubted she'd needed an hour when he picked her up an hour later. Her hair wasn't wet, and although she looked hot as hell in hip-hugging blue jeans and a tube top that showed off her firm, flat belly, something told him she had put him off an hour simply to try and maintain the upper hand. She wasn't wearing makeup but her dark, forest-green eyes were bright and attentive when she greeted him at the door and then closed it behind her, turning the knob to insure it was locked.

She slung a sweater over her shoulder. "I haven't been to the bowling alley in ages, so if we're asked, you like bowling."

"Can you bowl?" he asked, opening his passenger door for her and managing not to touch her when she slid into his SUV.

Her blond hair looked exceptionally soft and wavy tonight. "I used to be able to, but it's been over four years since I've bowled."

"Since your divorce?"

She shot him a pensive look. "Yes," she said, and then reached to close her door.

The bowling alley was crowded and noisy, not too different from how he remembered it when he used to come here in his early twenties. Slipping his arm around Ashley's bare shoulders, he paused just inside the entrance, noting immediately there weren't any free lanes.

Ashley stiffened when he pulled her against him. Chase lowered his mouth to her ear, breathing in the soft smell of lavender. "You want to make it look like we're together, darling," he reminded her.

She looked at him, her face inches from his and her eyes dark as she blinked and continued watching him through thick, long lashes. "What would you tell someone you do for a living?" she whispered, her lips moist and full as she searched his face.

"Keep a very close eye on you," he growled, and enjoyed the hell out of her surprised expression.

"Do you date often?" he asked.

"Not at all."

"So your ex isn't accustomed to seeing you with another man." He didn't make it a question, wondering how possessive her ex-husband might be.

"No. We were together since high school."

"Why did you divorce?"

"He didn't want a career wife," she said matter-of-factly, not giving him any indication she regretted the fact that she was one.

"His loss," he muttered, continuing to whisper so those around them wouldn't overhear their conversation. But he was overly aware that people moved around them as they stood several feet from the door in the main walkway behind the lanes.

"Men want a woman waiting at home for them when they come home."

"Some men enjoy their woman at their side when trying to nail a killer." It didn't bother him when her mouth parted, surprised that he might consider pursuing her for more than she probably thought he wanted from her.

Before she could think of a response, he took advantage of her being off guard and pulled her closer to him. Then gripping her neck with his free hand, he tipped her head back slightly by pushing his thumb under her chin. When he kissed her, she didn't fight him. If anything, as she sighed into his mouth, and touched his arm with her warm hand, it was all he could do not to devour her right there in front of everyone.

Chase ran his hand down her back, loving how smooth and warm her skin was. She was trim, with perfect angles and curves. He gripped her ass, pushing her into him and then moved his other hand through her soft, silky hair.

"Are you ready to look around?" he asked, his voice rough as he gazed down at her.

Ashley's lashes fluttered over her eyes when she licked her full, wet lips. "Yes," she whispered.

He didn't want to let her go. Sliding his arm around her waist, he inserted his thumb in her back pocket, keeping her next to him as he took in the people around them. More than one man focused on Ashley and then gave him a wary look, but for the most part everyone milled around them without paying any attention to them. There were families, kids, and couples; the bowling alley hadn't changed much over the years.

"Do you see your ex?" he asked, after handing her a beer and taking his.

"No, but I'd think he'd be here. It's definitely league night."

"Keep an eye out for any rope bracelets," he told her, and she looked up at him quickly, holding her beer in midair, her surprise at his comment obvious.

"Do you think whoever is giving the girls those bracelets would be here?"

"I think it's too early to rule out any possibilities."

Ashley nodded and then sipped from her beer. It wasn't the best beer Chase had ever had. It was barely cold and slightly flat. He didn't remember the beer being this lame years back. Apparently his taste was a bit pickier now than when he was younger.

Not that he didn't already know that to be the truth. As much as he noticed the guys checking out Ashley as they worked their way through the mingling crowd above the lanes, he didn't miss the ladies who gave him the once-over. None of them held a flame to Ashley.

She moved with a calm confidence next to him, her ass

swaying perfectly as he rested his finger in her rear jeans pocket. He shifted his attention to one of the lanes when several people looked their way and then waved.

"Old friends," she offered, but didn't elaborate. She turned and descended the several steps to the lane where a group of people now looked their way expectantly.

"Ash!" A stocky man moved around the grinning girls, arms extended, and ignored Chase when he pulled her into a bear hug. "Why aren't you out saving the world?" he asked, his deep barrel laugh causing the ladies around him to giggle.

Ashley hugged him but then let him go, returning to Chase's side. He draped his arm around her protectively, all too aware of the curious stares from the group as they checked him out.

"Hey, Davie, Chris, Angie," she said, sounding cheerful and more energetic than she usually sounded. "Everyone, this is Chase. Chase, this is everyone," she offered, laughing.

The group laughed along with her. The stocky man, apparently Davie, held his hand out. "It's good to see someone could get Ash out of that uniform long enough to take her out," he bellowed, his tone sounding a bit forced. "I started worrying my brother had ruined your ability to get out and date again."

"Hardly," she offered easily. "Is Danny here?"

"Nope. Don't know where he is." Davie's baritone grew quieter. "I hear he's pretty messed up after Mindy got killed. You find the guy who did that to her, yet?"

All faces sobered and looked at Ashley expectantly.

"I've got some really strong leads," she answered, lowering her voice to almost a whisper, which caused the group to sober further and lean closer to hear anything she might say. Ashley pointed at one of the girls, who stood next to Davie. "Chris, where did you get that bracelet?"

Chase tried not to look too interested as he glanced at the thin rope bracelet around Chris's wrist. She held out her wrist and blushed, although when she lowered her head, thin, long blond strands covered her face.

"There's a lady down at the Crossing who makes them," Chris explained, shooting Chase a furtive look with pale blue, watery eyes. Maybe she was pretty, but her baggy clothes did a good job of hiding any figure she might have. Black eyeliner and dark lipstick distracted anyone from seeing what she really looked like.

Ashley fingered the thin rope wrapped around Chris's wrist. "What do the knots mean?"

"It's kind of personal," Chris whispered, blushing even further.

"It means how many times she's had sex," said the lady next to her, a chubby, dark-haired woman who had dimples when she chuckled. She nudged Chris, apparently indifferent to how furiously Chris blushed. "Come on, you two, join us for a beer," she said, grabbing Ashley's arm.

"We already were commenting there wasn't room to bowl," Ashley said, trying to back out of the invitation.

Chase was curious about the bracelet, and didn't have any problem hanging out with these people in an effort to learn more about Chris, as well as hear any comments about Mindy, who at least the brother of Ashley's ex seemed to know.

"We can stay for a beer," Chase said, grabbing Davie's attention when he spoke. The stocky man gave him a shrewd once-over, possibly feeling a bit protective of his ex-sister-in-law. "Ash wanted to bowl but I told her league night would make it iffy."

"Bring her down tomorrow night," Davie told him, his jovial smile disappearing as his tone turned serious. "I'm sure my brother will want to meet you anyway."

"Do I need his consent to take out his ex?" Chase asked.

The women sobered and he ignored the glare Ashley shot at him.

"Of course not," Davie said, never looking away from Chase. "It's just Ash here hasn't dated in the four years since she and Danny split up. We want to make sure she's being taken care of."

"You have my word," Chase told him, again draping his arm around Ashley. He grinned into her dark, stormy green eyes. "One beer and then we'll head out," he said so only she could hear.

"Behave," she mouthed, pinching his waist hard enough to make it hurt.

Chase lowered his mouth to her ear, holding her firmly against him. Ashley placed her hand against his chest, but didn't push him away when he nibbled her ear.

"Learn more about that bracelet," he instructed her, whispering in her ear.

Ashley didn't nod, or acknowledge what he said. But turning in his arms, she sipped her beer. "We'll stay for a few," she announced, stepping away from him. "But you're a packed house tonight. We can definitely come back and bowl another night."

Chris and Angie moved in around her, whispering and shooting him curious glances. They wanted all the details on him and he didn't worry about Ashley coming up with a convenient story to appease them.

"So how did you and Ashley meet?" Davie asked, his body stiff as he stood, chest puffed out, and prepared for a testosterone showdown.

"Grocery store," he offered easily. "Our carts bumped into each other and it was love at first sight."

Davie's narrowing gaze was proof enough he didn't believe Chase for a minute. Not that Chase cared. "How long have you known Ash?"

"Since high school when she started dating my kid brother."

"Her ex?" Chase asked, nodding and making it rhetorical. "I hear he didn't like her being a cop, wanted her at home having babies."

"Danny adores Ash," Davie growled, crossing his thick arms over his even thicker chest. "He didn't want her hurt. It's one thing being a crossing guard, but completely different racing down dark alleys after men with guns."

If his rather chauvinistic attitude was a family trait, it wasn't a wonder Ashley split up with his brother.

"But all he's ever wanted for Ash is her happiness. I've always predicted they would work out their differences and get back together. See them together and you'll see the chemistry is still there." Davie rocked up on his heels, but then turned when his name was called out to take his turn bowling.

A lot less than an hour passed before Ashley was hugging the girls and then Davie good-bye. Chase watched her whisper something in his ear and the stocky man glared at Chase. Then she was whisking Chase out of there and into the refreshing night air.

"Why in the hell did you have to get him so worked up?" Ashley demanded, marching toward his car as she threw her hands up in exasperation.

Chase kept in stride, enjoying how her large breasts bounced under the restraints of her tube top. "It sure didn't take much, did it?"

"You could have been nice," she hissed, moving to the passenger side and then holding the handle and waiting for him to unlock her door.

Chase pushed the button on his key holder and his lights blinked. Ashley yanked open her car door and slid in, slamming it shut a lot harder than necessary. Seeing she didn't expect him to be the gentleman and open, or close, her door, he moved around to the driver's side and slid in next to her. He put the key into the ignition, but then didn't start it, and instead faced her, taking in her pouting profile.

"Do you want to get back with your ex?"

"No," she said, not hesitating.

"Why would he say that?"

Ashley looked at him, shoving her hair behind her ear and then exhaling softly. "I didn't hear him say that. So I don't know. There hasn't been anything between my ex and me for years."

"Could there be on his end?"

"What would it matter?"

"If there is, your ex might have reason to try and grab

your attention. Some men will go to an extreme to try and get a woman back, especially if they feel she's still theirs."

"That isn't how it is with me and Danny," she said, her expression tight as she continued glaring at him. "At least one good thing came out of tonight. I know where those bracelets came from and tomorrow I can pay the Crossing a visit."

CHAPTER 5

ASHLEY WORRIED her lower lip as she stared out the windshield, more upset by Davie implying something still existed between her and Danny than she wanted to let on. It didn't surprise her Chase picked up on that. And she didn't flatter herself thinking he did because he was interested in a relationship. There was a strong physical attraction between her and Chase, but he was an investigator, trained to analyze a scene and pull what clues might exist out of it. She'd never felt Danny wanted to rekindle anything between them. That Davie would suggest such a thing meant either he didn't like seeing her with another man, or Danny had said something to his brother that he hadn't revealed to her.

She wasn't convinced any of this had anything to do with the case. But it showed her it wouldn't hurt for her to date a bit more. Obviously Davie, and probably Danny too, needed to see her with other men once in a while. Maybe they needed closure. God knows, it wouldn't hurt her to put work aside from time to time and enjoy the company of a man.

She glanced sideways, taking in Chase's brooding expression as he relaxed his hand on the steering wheel and started across town. "Chris wouldn't tell me what the knots in her bracelet meant," she offered, breaking the silence between them.

"We'll ask tomorrow at the Crossing."

"We?"

Chase looked at her. God, he was fucking perfect. His hard features, the way his black hair contrasted with his bright blue eyes. Her insides grew uncomfortably warm watching him as he took his time staring at her face. When his gaze dropped lower, she was suddenly acutely aware of how her tank top hugged her breasts, more than likely showing them off. She reached for her sweater, feeling more clothing would be in order before the conversation drifted to dangerous territory.

"There's no reason we can't go shopping tomorrow."

"I thought you were a ghost," she muttered, struggling with the sweater.

"Are you cold?" he asked, and adjusted the climate control on the dash. "And do I look like a ghost to you?"

"Your words, not mine," she told him, ignoring his comment about being cold.

Chase reached over and took her sweater, sliding it out from behind her and placing it on her lap. She was ready to snatch the sweater and put it on when he took her hand and brought it to his lips.

"Do I feel like a ghost to you?" he growled.

Shivers rushed over her when he nipped at her knuckles and she was positive her nipples were so hard they probably threatened to poke right through the stretchy tube top she'd been a fool to wear.

"Chase," she sighed, willing herself to tell him to stop. They turned the corner, entering her neighborhood. All she needed to do was get out of the car and into her house without inviting him in. Shouldn't be hard. "If you want to meet me at the store tomorrow that's your deal. It's a public place."

He continued driving with one hand and pressed his lips over her fingers, his breath scorching her flesh when he spoke. "Have you been to the Crossing before?" he asked.

"No, I haven't." She really should pull her hand away from him.

"So you don't know what kind of establishment it is?"

His discussing business while rubbing a day's growth of whiskers over her fingers was making it damn hard to answer his questions. A pressure swelled inside her, distracting

her and making her ache to squirm in her seat. Chase would
be on to her in a minute if she did. And she didn't doubt for
a moment he intended to get a rise out of her. Ashley prayed
he was torturing himself as much as he was her.

"I can guess but I can also Google it and see if they have
a Web site."

"It's an old hippie store run by a woman who claims to be
a witch. Do you know anyone into that sort of thing?"

It irritated her that he already knew about the Crossing
but questioned her, forcing her mind to stay focused as he
slowly drove her nuts. "People buy things from stores like
that all the time and don't necessarily view themselves as
hippies or Wiccans." She yanked her hand out of his when
he pulled up in front of her house.

Chase cut the engine and climbed out on his side as Ashley almost leaped out of his SUV on her side. She gulped in
night air, wishing it were just a few degrees cooler. Wadding
her sweater into a ball, she hugged it against her chest and
slung her purse over her shoulder. If she stormed across her
yard, running to her house for safety against his incredible
male magnetism, Chase would probably tackle her. Somehow that image got her even hotter.

Damn it! Would it be so terrible to just invite him in and
fuck him?

Chase came around the front of his car and took her arm
when she reached her driveway. "I'm coming in," he announced, his low growl leaving nothing to the imagination
as to his meaning.

Nor did it surprise her that he didn't ask. What did surprise her was that his demanding nature made her so damn
hot for a moment she just stared at him.

"Why?" She wouldn't let him believe he could just as-
sume he would fuck her and she'd lie down and spread her
legs like a good little submissive bimbo.

His hands snaked around her waist and he yanked her
against him with enough force it almost knocked the air out
of her lungs. She slapped her hands over his shoulders, star-

ing up slightly and into dark sapphire eyes that devoured her right before his mouth did.

When his mouth covered hers, he moved one hand up her back, his callused fingers digging into her hair and then tugging, drawing her head back and deepening the kiss.

Ashley's world spun out of control. The pressure swelling inside her hit a point of no return and she felt her pussy grow soaked as a throbbing began between her legs that made her weak with need. Chase didn't ask, he took. But even more so, his demanding nature controlled her, molding her body against his just the way he wanted it. He poured the need he felt for her into her mouth, allowing her to taste, to experience, the intensity his cravings had reached. Ashley couldn't think, couldn't react, but through the fog of lust quickly enveloping her brain one thing rang clear. If she took him inside he would fuck her until the pain from her lust, from the knowledge of what could be, was satisfied.

How long had it been since she'd known hard-core carnal, raw sex?

"That's why I'm coming inside," he growled, moving his lips over hers.

Ashley blinked, fighting to regain control and not letting him see the lengths to which he'd just taken her. "If it was so you could kiss me, you've just gotten that out of the way." She pushed against his shoulders, creating a bit of space between them.

"No, sweetheart," he said, his voice gruff. "Because if we stand out here the neighbors might not appreciate me fucking you in your driveway."

"Do you always just do what you want and believe it's okay?" Ashley turned from him, walking out of his arms and to her front door. Her jeans rubbed against her pussy, spreading the moisture and torturing her. When she fumbled with her purse to dig out her keys she realized she no longer carried her sweater.

Chase came up behind her, holding it in his hand. Damn

him anyway for affecting her like this. She didn't even notice dropping it.

"When I know it's the right thing to do, yes." He didn't hand her sweater to her, but focused on her purse.

Ashley dug out her keys and unlocked her front door. "It will be the right thing to do when I say it is," she told him, already arguing with herself to let him stay. There wouldn't be any getting rid of the need boiling out of control inside her no matter how long she masturbated.

He reached over her, pushing her door open and moving into the house alongside her. Instead of continuing to press his argument, he was suddenly alert as he searched her dark living room. "Did you set your alarm?" he asked, the gruffness in his voice gone.

Ashley tensed, positive she would never leave her home without setting it. In her line of work there was always someone who might hold a grudge, and she lived alone.

"Stay there." She pointed to the doorway as she flipped on the lamps in her living room controlled by the light switch at her front door. Everything appeared to be in place. Walking over to the end table next to her couch, she opened the top drawer and pulled out the small handgun she kept there. Quickly checking to see if it were loaded, she then pointed it toward the ground and turned, putting her finger over her lips to tell him to be quiet.

Chase had closed her front door without her hearing it, dropped her sweater on the floor inside the door, and barely glanced at her before taking in the surroundings. He also held a gun in his hand. Where the hell had he stashed that thing?

Arguing with him to let her search her own house would be pointless. Not to mention, he was as trained as she was, if not possibly more, to handle situations like this. In spite of her nature telling her she needed to protect him, Chase didn't appear to need protection. If anything, holding the gun in his hand, aiming it at the floor, he looked even hotter and more dangerous than he had all evening. There was no way she should be so fucking turned on when there might be a burglar in her home.

Chase reached behind him, locking her front door, then nodded at her to move through her home. Her back door opened and closed, sounding as if someone just slammed it behind them. Ashley hurried into the dark part of her house, almost running into her kitchen without saying a word, her gun aimed at the darkness surrounding her. She wasn't sure if her door was slammed, or if it was just her heart exploding in her chest. Although she didn't doubt she had serious enemies among those she'd arrested over the years and put in jail, not once had her house been broken into since she'd been living here alone.

Chase was right behind her when she yanked her unlocked back door open—there was no way she had left it that way—and hurried out.

"Over there," Chase hissed in her ear, his gun aimed at a figure racing away to a running car in the alley behind them.

Ashley grabbed his arm, shoving his gun toward the ground. "Wait," she ordered, anger replacing all the trepidation that had coursed through her veins a moment ago. "Son of a bitch," she growled, turning back to her house and stalking through her kitchen.

Chase was by her side, securing the safety on his gun when she pulled her cell phone out of her purse. "I take it you know who that was?" he asked, his expression guarded as he studied her.

"My ex," she seethed, punching in the numbers to his cell and then putting it to her ear as it started ringing. Danny answered on the second ring. "What the hell were you doing in my house?" she yelled, adrenaline attacking her with a vengeance.

"Who did you bring home with you?" Danny demanded.

"Answer my goddamn question." She walked away from Chase and put her gun back in the top drawer of her end table. "You damn near got yourself shot."

"Sorry, sweetheart," Danny drawled. "I didn't know you were bringing home company."

"Why were you in my house?" She stressed each word, blowing out a silent breath so she wouldn't loose her cool with Chase standing silently behind her, more than likely able to hear Danny through the phone. "And how did you turn off my home security?"

"It was your birthday backward." Danny laughed as if he were proud of himself for figuring it out. "I guessed it on the second try."

"Danny, tell me why you were in my house right now before I call the police on your ass, or worse yet, come after you and beat the crap out of you myself."

Danny laughed. "Sounds kinky."

Ashley swore she heard Chase growl behind her.

"But I stopped by because I swore my old pool stick was upstairs in the attic. When you weren't home I tried letting myself in but forgot about your security thing. Damn good thing I was able to turn it off, huh. I got filthy crawling around upstairs looking for that damn pool stick. I swear it's up there. But I ran out of the house when you came home and I realized you weren't alone. I didn't want to ruin your night, darling."

"Don't ever enter my home again without my being here."

"Okay. Okay. I'm sorry. Don't shoot." Danny started laughing.

And she hung up on his ass. Then tossing her phone on her couch, she blew out an exasperated breath, running her fingers through her hair.

"Change your code," Chase instructed.

Ashley spun around, ready to take all her frustration out on him simply because he stood there. He didn't approach to console her, which pissed her off. And he appeared completely calm and relaxed, which annoyed her even further.

But he was right, and that irked her even more. She needed to reset her password on her home security immediately. If Danny, who was a numbskull, could figure out how to get into her home when she'd paid damn good money for a home security system, a real thief with a lot more skill and determination could also. Her heart still pounded in her chest when she fisted her hands and marched over to the panel alongside her door.

"Make it 1275." Chase moved in alongside her and leaned against the wall next to the panel, crossing his muscular arms over his steel chest. "No one will guess that. It's my birthday. You can change it again later so I don't know it if you wish."

"I don't remember how to change the password," she grumbled, having stared at the panel for a moment and knowing that if she messed with it and pushed the wrong button, it would contact the service with the security system. She didn't want the embarrassment of telling them she didn't need the police called. "The directions are in my filing cabinet."

She thought about telling Chase to leave, and more than likely, after the incident that just happened, he probably would. In spite of anger still trying to make her grouchy, the swelling between her legs hadn't subsided. She was acutely aware of him following her silently into her bedroom where her filing cabinet stood next to her computer desk.

"Is this how you get into your attic?" Chase asked.

Ashley pulled open the top drawer to her dresser and reached to the back where the keys to her filing cabinet were. Glancing at him, she saw he stood just outside her bedroom door pointing at her ceiling.

"Yes," she said, finding the keys and locking her cabinet. She flipped through her files until she found the one labeled "owner's manuals." Thank God the instructions to her security system were where they belonged. Chase would take over and secure her house for her if she wasn't able to do it herself. And she wasn't some weak female who needed a man making sure the boogeyman couldn't hurt her.

"I thought I heard him tell you on the phone he crawled around looking for the pool stick and got dirty."

"That's what he said." She walked toward him, flipping through the pages until she found password reset instructions.

"It doesn't look like anyone's been up there."

Ashley had to stand within inches of Chase, since he didn't back up when she walked out of her bedroom, to look at her ceiling. The panel that would need to be pushed to the side definitely looked untouched. There was a chair in her hallway, which was there specifically so she could stand on it to get into the crawl space she used for storage. Stepping around Chase, she dragged her finger across the leather seat cover. Chase found a light switch in her hallway and flipped it on, making it easy to see the line she created from moving it over the layer of dust that had built up on the chair.

"How hard is it to see things up there?" he asked, returning his attention to the attic door.

"I keep a large flashlight right inside the entrance up there. If I need to get anything down, or put something up there, it's pretty easy to do."

Chase dragged her chair under the panel and stood on it. Ashley swallowed when she stared at his cock, which appeared semihard in his blue jeans, and was now at eye level. His legs were muscular and brown cowboy boots added to his bad-boy appearance. Ashley let her gaze travel up his body as he reached and moved the door in the ceiling to the side. Roped muscle flexed in his arms as he exerted a bit of effort before the door gave way. Again she swallowed, her mouth going dry at the incredible view he offered of his damn near perfect body.

But as easily as he re-created the need that surged to life and pumped through her eagerly, Ash didn't miss the obvious. Danny hadn't been in her attic any time recently.

Chase stuck his head in her attic, finding her flashlight and turning it on. A minute later he stretched, his shirt rising up his torso and revealing a taut stomach with a line of dark hair that disappeared under his shirt and into his jeans. God, she loved chest hair.

"Is this your ex's?" he asked, lowering a pool stick, in its case, down to her.

Ashley took it and leaned it against her hallway wall. "Yup. I forgot it was up there. But why would he tell me he was up there when he obviously wasn't?"

"He's an idiot?" Chase suggested, replacing the crawl space door, then jumping to the floor.

Ash stumbled backward so he wouldn't land on her. This

time he grabbed her, pulling her into his arms. "Reset your alarm," he whispered, kissing her forehead. "I'll check your back door."

"So you know, a man who thinks I'm helpless is a serious turnoff," she informed him, heading into her living room and resetting her password.

Chase was right behind her as she finished and closed the panel by the front door. "And so you know," he growled, wrapping his arms around her waist and pulling her back against all that rippling muscle. "A woman who grabs a gun when there is danger and doesn't panic makes me hard as stone."

He raked his teeth over her earlobe, creating goose bumps that rushed over her flesh. Chase brought his hands up, squeezing her breasts, then lowered her tube top, exposing her.

"I don't want a door mat," he growled into her ear as he pinched her nipples. "I want you, Ashley."

CHAPTER 6

WHEN ASHLEY shivered in Chase's arms, he knew it wasn't because she was cold.

"Is it me you want?" she asked, her voice rough as she spoke softly. "Or is it that you want to get laid while you're home, before heading back to wherever it is you're going."

Ashley tried stepping out of his arms, grabbing her tube top as if she'd cover herself back up. Chase understood she needed to hear where they stood, create a foundation for what might develop between them from this point forward. He flipped her around, pushing her against the wall and grabbing her arms, preventing her from covering her breasts. Seeing her naked from the waist up, her full, round breasts absolutely perfect, and large puckered nipples creating a mouthwatering view damn near robbed him of his ability to tell her what she craved hearing.

And Chase didn't take a woman without there being mutual understanding of where they stood beforehand. He sucked in a breath, forcing himself to meet her fiery gaze as he held her pinned against the wall.

"You've got a craving to solve a mystery, a fire inside you that rages anytime you feel someone is doing you wrong. You're strong and gutsy."

Ashley pursed her lip, her breathing coming harder the longer he kept her against the wall. Although there was no way she'd get loose until he decided to let her go, and he knew she knew that, she struggled more when he told her she was strong.

"You make it sound as if you were attracted to more than my body," she purred, flashing her long lashes over her dark, enticing green eyes. "I can't imagine an FBI man wanting a relationship, especially when he isn't planning on sticking around."

"You have no idea what I want," he growled, stretching her arms along the wall as he moved in closer and bit her neck. "But you're going to find out, my dear. I promise you."

"Don't play games with me," she hissed, almost panting as she shifted her hips against him.

Chase's cock grew so hard he ached to strip out of his clothes and throw her down right now. "This isn't a game. But there are rules."

Her bare breasts rubbed against his chest, and even though he still wore his shirt, her hard, puckered nipples scraped across his chest. Every ounce of blood in his brain drained straight to his cock. God help him if Ashley ever found out the power she could hold over him with that hot, sensual body of hers.

"Why do I get the feeling any rules you don't like you'd break or change?" she whispered.

Chase dragged his tongue along the length of her collarbone, tasting her and craving more. He breathed in her soft, musky aroma and felt her soft, silky strands brush across his face. He wouldn't be able to hold her here much longer before ripping the clothes off both of them and fucking her senseless. At this rate, he'd be the one unable to make sense. Ashley would lay down any rules and he'd agree to them in a minute. But as much as she claimed she didn't want to be viewed as helpless, he doubted she'd be impressed with a man who wasn't in control.

He dipped his head to her breast and lashed the nipple with his tongue. Her cry seared through him like a burning sword, tearing into his soul. Chase realized how hard he gripped her arms, more now to hold on than to keep her in place, and let go, running his fingers up her arms and over her shoulders. When he cupped her breasts, moving from one to the other and feasting like a man deprived for way too long, Ashley grabbed his head, tangling her fingers in his hair. She tugged, pulling his hair hard enough that he raised his head, barely able to focus.

"Remember, FBI man," she whispered, the slightest of smiles appearing on her face. "I'm a cop. There are rules and you won't break them."

"Oh yeah?" He tried pulling her hands from his hair and she tugged harder, the pinch strong enough to almost make his eyes water.

"Oh yeah. I don't submit in life and I sure as hell don't submit when fucking a man," she growled, and let go of his hair but moved her hands fast enough to pull out of his grip. Then shoving him with her hands against his chest, she pushed hard, exerting a fair amount of strength.

Chase allowed her to move him backward, holding on to her gaze. Her green eyes smoldered, her lips were parted, and her full, large breasts moved just enough to distract him when she shoved him to her couch.

Ashley straddled his lap when he sat in the middle of her couch. He reached between them, feeling how soft her flat tummy was. She was perfect, toned in all the right places yet not to the point where she wasn't feminine. In her line of work, which was predominantly a man's field, it was too easy for women to buff themselves out in an effort to fit in. The tougher they were, the more likely they were to nail the bad guy. Yet Ashley held on to being a lady, sexy and so damned beautiful. But she didn't hesitate to get tough when necessary. He never would have guessed he'd meet such a perfect package, and in his hometown.

She moved her hands around his, unbuttoning his jeans when he unzipped hers. Not once did she look away from him, or appear to go shy on him. He'd known when he kissed her last night she wanted him as badly as he wanted her, but knowing her craving matched his made his blood pressure soar dangerously high. Fire burned in his veins, the heat tightening his balls and creating a swelling that turned into a pressure as he throbbed, swollen and stiff and dying to be inside her.

"The only way these jeans are coming off, my dear," he told her. "Is if my boots come off. And I can't kick them off."

When she tilted her head, giving the matter thought, a long strand of blond hair fell over her face. She blew it out of the way, her lips puckering and causing his dick to dance eagerly in his pants.

Ashley's gaze shot to his, her dark green eyes growing wide. One corner of her mouth turned, her sly if not incredibly ornery grin showing him she liked seeing that she could control him with her actions. Some ways of being controlled might not be that bad.

"Take my boots off, Ashley."

She licked her lips but then slid off his lap to the floor. Her unzipped jeans and tube top creating a belt around her waist looked so damn hot. Light from the floor lamp across from them reflected in her hair, showing off her red highlights. Her hair was tousled and her lips pouty when she knelt at his feet. The quick look she shot him told him he'd be wise not to comment on her kneeling before him.

"This is the only time I'm going to do this," she muttered, yanking one boot off his foot and then reaching for the other.

"I've always been partial to my boots." It was too hard not to tease her, not to mention how fucking hot as hell she looked kneeling on the floor, half-naked, her hair tousled, and her nipples so hard his mouth watered. "Watching you grip them is making me like them even more."

She tugged the second boot, yanking it off his foot and then tossing it at his crotch, her smile and the glow in her eyes showing how willingly she would spar with him.

Chase dodged the boot and grabbed her, not caring when the boot fell off the couch with a loud thud. He dragged Ashley over his body and then turned, pressing her back against the couch and moving between her legs.

"My turn," he drawled, yanking her jeans down her hips. "I'd never ask something of you that I wouldn't do myself."

"You aren't kneeling at my feet," she howled, coming up off the couch and pushing his shoulders.

"I'd be a fool to turn down an invitation like that." Chase slid off the couch, taking her with him.

"This isn't what I meant," she cried out, but her laughter made it too hard to fight him.

Chase pushed her to the floor, then knelt at her feet, or alongside her legs, and peeled her jeans down her legs.

"Oh my God," he whispered, pausing for a moment when her jeans were at her knees. She was shaved, her skin smooth without a tan line or anything to distract him from the sweet view that appeared before him.

"I'm not going to lie here naked with you dressed," she griped, coming up in a perfect sit-up that showed off her tummy muscles as she leaned forward and grabbed her jeans.

When she kicked them off her, the only thing left on her was her tube top, which was twisted into a belt around her waist. Ashley came up to her knees and grabbed his jeans at his waist. Chase stood, helping her out, and shoved them, along with his boxers, down his legs and stepped out of them. He doubted she realized she was on her knees once again, before him. Her lips turned into that pouty circle he was growing to love on her as she stared at his cock.

Chase wouldn't profess to being the largest guy out there, but he knew his dick was decent. The look Ashley gave it, though, made him feel she thought he was the best she'd ever seen.

"Oh yeah," she whispered, and dragged her fingers down the length of his shaft.

Chase hissed in a breath, determined not to move and to allow her all the time in the world to get to know him. He couldn't remember the last time a woman had knelt before him like this, other than one he'd paid. But Ashley remained on her knees, all declarations of being in charge and not submitting vanished, as she ran her index finger over the swollen tip of his cock. When she wrapped her fingers around him, and brought him to her mouth, Chase was positive he'd pass out from lack of blood in his brain, or explode in her mouth.

"Fucking crap," he growled, grabbing her head and holding her firmly with both hands, partially to keep himself balanced, and partially to prevent her from stopping. "Goddamn, Ash," he hissed, using every bit of strength he had not to thrust his cock down her throat.

Ashley hummed, lapping her tongue around him and then stretching her lips, enclosing them around him. Her mouth was paradise, moist heat dragging him deeper as she teased him with her tongue. She glanced up at him through long, thick lashes and sucked more of him in until he wondered where the brazen, determined-to-be-dominating woman had gone.

Ashley had skills, and damn good ones. He'd be the last to mention that, for a strong-willed lady, her submissive side was equally hot. He was moving, slowly fucking her mouth, before he realized he'd taken over the act. And still she sucked and licked, taking what he offered and moaning delightfully.

It was easily the best blow job he'd ever had in his life. And probably because it was obvious she was enjoying herself. Her hair streamed past her shoulders and her slender back curved into round hips he couldn't wait to hold on to when he fucked her. Her breasts swelled into perfect, round mounds, her nipples brushing against her legs as she moved slightly with his rhythm. But when she moved her hands, cupping his balls as she sucked, his world about exploded in front of him.

"Crap, Ashley!" Chase yanked her to her feet, grabbing her under her arms and lifting her so fast her gaze was still very fogged over when she stared at him. Her mouth was swollen and wet, her lips parted. She was so fucking hot, more than he ever imagined her being. "I need inside you," he growled.

"Not until you return the favor," she whispered, her voice rough, her green eyes smoky with lust.

Her words surprised him, not that he minded her suggestion at all. But as completely submissive as she'd become for him, that she still had it in her to administer a command somehow impressed the hell out of him. He was more than eager to fulfill her wish.

Lifting her into his arms, he gripped her bare ass as she wrapped her legs around him. Chase turned to her bedroom, moving into the dark room with his cock pressed against her warm flesh. Her smoothly shaven pussy was soaked. It made him swell and throb even more knowing that giving him head turned her on.

Chase let go of Ashley and she started to crawl across the bed. He grabbed her tube top, liking how it made a convenient "leash" although he'd be damned if he'd tell her that.

"I don't want you that far from me," he informed her.

"I want the lamp on. I want to watch." She grabbed her tube top, pulling it over her shoulders, and then left him holding it when she turned, giving him one hell of an ass shot as she reached and flipped on the lamp on the far side of her bed.

Chase was on her bed, grabbing her hips, before she could turn around.

"Oh no, mister!" she howled, flipping on to her back and wiggling, trying to get him to let her go.

Chase came down on top of her, smashing her large breasts against his chest, and seized her mouth, devouring her with a hungry growl until she relaxed underneath him. He was quickly learning her feistiness lasted only as long as he didn't touch her, or she touched him. But the moment he engaged in any act, she surrendered her cocky nature, willingly wrapping her arms around his shoulders and deepening the kiss.

She wrapped her legs around him, bringing her pussy up and rubbing it along the length of his shaft. Colors exploded in his brain, rendering him incapable of doing a thing other than continuing to feed off the incredible woman who enjoyed torturing him as much as she appeared to love being tortured.

He left her mouth, loving the sound of her groan, as he kissed her soft skin and worked his way to her breasts. Ashley writhed underneath him, rubbing against his body and scraping her nails down his back as he suckled one breast and then the other.

When he moved lower, dipping his tongue into her belly button, she squealed, grabbing his shoulders and bringing her legs up so she could wrap them around his arms. There was strength in her inner thighs and she squeezed, pushing against his shoulders until he obliged and moved lower.

"God, Chase, please," she begged, pushing hard to get his face exactly where she wanted it. "Now, damn. Please, now," she cried out, shifting and wiggling underneath him until he breathed in the musky aroma of her soaked pussy.

"It's okay, sweetheart," he told her, kissing her inner thigh. "You're going to have everything you want. I promise."

"Now," she hissed, her tone turning bossy once again.

Putting what he already believed to be true about her to the test, Chase ran his tongue down the length of her wet folds.

"Oh!" she cried out, her legs shivering on either side of him.

"Relax," he encouraged, moving his lips against her smooth flesh. She smelled so good and tasted even better. "Enjoy this, sweetheart. I'm going to make you feel so good and make you come so hard."

She hummed her answer, obliging, her thigh muscles noticeably relaxed as she spread herself wide open for him. Chase adjusted himself, keeping half of him off the bed. His cock was heavy and throbbing, and his balls tight. The pressure inside him smoldered, threatening to boil over if he weren't careful. But taking his time, enjoying the perfect pussy in front of him, he once again ran his tongue along her smooth skin, lapping up the come that soaked her.

Chase focused on the swell of her breasts as he dipped inside her. They were perfectly round and her nipples hard beacons. He loved large nipples and Ashley's were pretty good sized. But then her breasts were more than a handful and couldn't be more perfect if she'd had them specifically designed for her body.

Her ribs were barely noticeable unless she sucked in a deep breath. Her tummy was smooth and flat, but not concave. Ashley wasn't skinny, but perfectly thin. Hell, everything about her was just the way he liked a woman, including her feisty nature. He'd caught a glimpse of her temper when she dealt with her ex earlier, and if he'd voiced his opinion, he would say her ex was up to no good. Since he planned on hanging around for a while, he would learn what the bastard was about, and make it damn clear messing with Ashley meant messing with him.

She might believe she could make it on her own, and Chase was sure she could. But there wasn't any harm in making his presence known, marking his territory so to speak. It wouldn't surprise him if her ex did a drive-by or two while he was here. Chase's SUV was parked in front of her house. He was off to a perfect start in making it clear he was laying claim on this hot, sexy lady.

And it wasn't just because she was easily the most enticing woman he'd ever met. Chase refused to think damned good sex was all it would take to make him want to keep her by his side. Hell, he hadn't actually fucked her yet, although if he didn't really soon, he was going to explode. There was a chemistry about Ashley, from the way she investigated a crime scene to how she argued with him over the facts of a case. He'd never been one to share his work with a girlfriend. Hell, whenever he'd had a girlfriend in the past, the term applied weakly at best; more accurately she'd have been called a fuck buddy. Getting close to a woman inevitably meant heartache, and headaches. Especially when they tried digging their claws in.

Chase impaled her pussy, feeling her soaked muscles quiver around his tongue. Ashley dragged her nails over his shoulders, purring delightfully as she moaned and mumbled words he barely understood. Her long lashes draped over her eyes, fluttering when she tried focusing on him. When she lifted her head, staring down at him, her cheeks were flushed and her dark green eyes glazed over with need that matched his own.

"Don't ever stop," she groaned, her order sounding more as if she begged.

Chase chuckled against her wet flesh and moved his attention to her swollen clit. The moment he sucked it between his lips, Ashley came off the bed, howling and digging her nails in deep enough it stung. Meeting a lady he'd be happy to see dig her claws in and fight to hold on should terrify the hell out of him. He teased her clit, batting at it with his tongue before closing his lips around it again.

"Chase! Goddamn," she yelled, every inch of her stiffening as fresh cream soaked his face. She came hard, crying and moaning and probably leaving serious scratch marks over his shoulders. "Oh crap," she wailed. "I can't . . ."

"Yes you can," he growled, his voice thick with his craving for her. His cock throbbed so hard between his legs he wasn't sure he'd be able to lift himself over her, or move at all, without exploding.

He held out until her breathing slowed. A moist sheen of perspiration made her glow. But it was the slow smile, when she opened her eyes and gazed up at him, that about undid him.

"That was so good," she moaned, and raised a hand lazily, reaching for him. "Come here," she told him. "I need you to fuck me now."

Chase didn't mind following that order. Climbing on to the bed, he gripped his cock, feeling the incredible weight of it. He was swollen and harder than steel, and her heat beckoned him. As much as he wanted to take his time, fuck her in every position possible, he doubted his ability to hold out much longer.

Ashley raised her legs, stretching them and giving him a view to die for. "Hard and fast, sweetheart," she instructed, trying to grab his cock and bring it to her. "I want it hard and fast."

"We'll see what you can handle." And what he could handle.

She made a face at him, but didn't argue when he positioned himself and then glided into her heat. Her mouth formed a perfect circle as she raised her hands, reaching for him but only managing to brush her fingertips across his chest before he impaled her. Chase wanted to take his time filling her, experience all those hot, tight muscles wrap around him. But she was like a magnet, dragging him in deeper and deeper, until he couldn't fight it any longer and gave her exactly what she wanted.

CHAPTER 7

ASHLEY COULDN'T let Chase spend the night. As worn out as she was, her body sated and sleep calling to her, she rolled out of the bed, almost falling to the ground. Opting for her bathrobe instead of her clothes, she didn't want to glance back at the perfect body sprawled out on her bed. And she wouldn't dwell on the fact that there wasn't a thing she could think of to complain about.

Chase was too good to be true. It should bother her that he was so aggressive, dominating, and controlling. But she really loved those characteristics in him. Even when he was concerned about protecting her home, and the way he re-acted to Danny's breaking in, appealed to her. And it shouldn't. She needed to send him home, bask in incredibly wonderful sex, and leave it at that.

Traipsing barefoot into her kitchen, she opened her re-frigerator, surprised to find an unopened bottle of water. She was positive she'd run out a few days ago but gave thanks for small miracles and pulled the chilled bottle out of the refrig-erator. Twisting off the top, she scowled when she heard her phone ring.

Ashley drank some of the water and almost gagged. "Shit," she hissed, spitting the water into her kitchen sink. It tasted putrid.

"What time is it?" She squinted at the digital clock on her

microwave, trying to focus, gave up and hurried to her phone. If someone was calling in the middle of the night, it wasn't good news. Rubbing the back of her hand over her lips, she fought to get the sour taste of the water out of her mouth.

Chase stood naked in the doorway to the living room, his brooding expression as captivating as the rest of him. She found her purse on the couch and pulled out her phone.

"Shit. It's dispatch," she offered, a sinking feeling twisting in her gut as she flipped open her phone. "Hello," she said, flinching at how raspy her voice sounded, as if she'd been yelling the past few hours. A warm flush heated her cheeks when she realized how much she probably had yelled.

"Detective Jones, a call came through less than an hour ago, possible suicide. But when the officers arrived on scene they asked me to call you. Sounds like another lady got hit by ISIS, and she is wearing one of those rope bracelets."

"Ten four," she groaned. "I'll be right there. What's the address?"

THE SUN WAS coming up when Ashley almost fell into her car. Chase made her promise she'd call him the moment she finished going over the scene. She almost considered not doing so, knowing he'd probably fallen asleep and hating to wake him. There was no reason both of them should have to go the entire night without any sleep. Not to mention, a scary feeling, mixed with something that excited her, created a knot in her tummy when she thought about him. Chase was too good to be true and she wasn't exactly the most experienced lady when it came to dating. Her life was her work. Divorcing Danny had wiped her out, and made men, or getting close to them, a taboo thought.

Already as she walked through the house where Chris Perkins's roommates found her dead when they came home from the bars, she looked at something imagined and, more than once, how Chase would view it. The entire time she was there she made mental notes of what she'd tell him. This had to stop. Two days. She'd known him for two days, had fucked him, and he was in her thoughts nonstop. A good, healthy case of lust had turned quickly into serious infatuation. Ashley stared at her phone, the numbers blurring while she struggled to keep the events of her evening in order in her mind.

"Just go home and go to sleep," she ordered herself.

Her phone rang in her hand and her heart slammed into her throat, the damn thing scaring the crap out of her. Since he'd entered his number into her phone before heading out, she stared at his name on the phone's screen.

"Crap," she hissed, forcing her heart to quit beating a mile a minute and yelling at herself for being so jumpy. She'd just endured a couple hours of grueling interviews with semi-sober roommates, and focused on a murder scene, yet the phone ringing in her hand sent her heart pounding and made her palms damp.

"I was just going to call you," she said as she answered, feeling disoriented and fighting to remain grounded.

"Are you done?" His deep baritone in her ear created a warmth inside her that made her pussy throb. The hell with going home. She'd go to his house and fuck him again.

"Yes, for now," she admitted, squeezing her eyes closed and willing the burn to go away. No matter how much she tried it was impossible to focus. Hell, she shouldn't be driving anywhere.

"Come on over. I'll make coffee. I want to hear about it while it's fresh in your head."

She was too tired to argue. And as she cruised down the quiet road a minute later, she didn't remember hanging up the phone with Chase. It amazed her she found his house, although she knew Wichita pretty well and he was in a fairly established community. Another time Ashley would take in his home, study his yard and the layout of the place, but when she parked in his gravel driveway and turned off her engine, she swore darkness engulfed her. It was too hard to move, let alone keep her eyes open. Apparently she wasn't as young as she used to be. And if she weren't so damned tired she might try counting how many all-nighters she'd pulled just this year working one case or another.

Ashley barely acknowledged her car door opening. Had she forgotten to lock yet another door? But when strong hands reached for her, and Chase's familiar smell wrapped around her, Ashley cuddled against his strong, muscular body. Immediately her insides swelled, smoldered, need ransacking her so hard it made it damn hard to breathe.

"Fuck me," she murmured, hearing the words leave her mouth although it didn't sound like her. It sounded like she was drunk. Ashley didn't remember the last time she'd been this out of it. Obviously she needed more sex. If fucking Chase once wiped her out this much, it was imperative she build up her stamina. Which could only be accomplished by fucking him again, right now. "Now," she uttered, barely able to get the word out.

Chase's chuckle sounded so far away. Even so, his rich, deep baritone created a fever inside her. She wanted to touch him, demand he take the incredible urge that suddenly attacked her away. But as she felt herself lifted, held securely in his strong arms, everything around her went black.

"ASHLEY?" SOMEONE asked. "She's coming around now."

Ashley blinked, her head pounding so hard and bright lights attacking her making it worse. She raised her hand, feeling something stuck to her, and covered her eyes, her brain refusing to cooperate. The sheet over her was crisp and cold, which made no sense. Where was her warm blanket? Had Chase fucked her so well that she'd passed out?

"You should let me run the show next time," she grumbled, knowing if she fucked Chase the way she'd wanted, she would have paced herself better and not be so out of it now. "You don't listen very well."

"Ashley?" the voice asked again.

She frowned, her mouth like sandpaper. "I need something to drink. Oh, not that water. It was nasty."

Wait a minute. She'd already gotten out of bed, and there had been a phone call. Ashley blinked again, enduring the painful bright light to take in her surroundings.

"What the hell?" she gasped, sitting up quickly and feel-ing the room spin around her.

"Easy, girl," Chase whispered. He ran his rough hand over her forehead, the touch enough to send her back to her pillows. "Try some ice chips."

"Give them to her slowly. Her stomach is still going to be very weak." It was another woman.

Why the hell was another woman with them?

"I don't understand," she murmured, enjoying the way Chase stroked her forehead.

"Is she awake?" Her captain, John Sullivan, appeared at the end of her bed. He stared at her with dark, warm eyes that looked almost compassionate. "How are you doing, Ash?"

"Confused." She looked around her and realized she was in the ER. Curtains enclosed her bed, and Chase stood on one side of her, the woman on the other, and now her captain at the end of her bed. "What am I doing here?" she asked, study-ing the IV tube entering the vein in the back of her hand. Her head started pounding again when she looked up at the bag hanging on the IV pole. "What are you pumping into me?"

"We're just rehydrating you right now." The nurse next to her glanced at the panel showing Ashley's vitals. "You seem to be coming around nicely though. I'll go get the doctor."

She took the cup of ice chips from Chase and dumped a fair bit of them into her mouth. Then looking from Chase to Captain Sullivan, she frowned further. Did they know each other?

"Someone mind filling me in?" she asked, glancing down at herself and then tugging the hospital gown, making sure she was covered. "I don't have a clue why I'm here."

"Your friend brought you in," Captain Sullivan told her, wrapping his large hand around the bar at the end of her bed. "Apparently he couldn't wake you up."

Captain Sullivan gave Chase a hard look. By the way he said "your friend" it appeared he didn't know Chase. His expression was hard, almost cold, the compassion she swore she saw when she first woke up definitely gone.

"You mind if I speak with Ashley alone?" Captain Sullivan growled.

Chase took his hand from her forehead, his expression tight and unreadable as he backed away from her bed. She searched his face, wishing she remembered something, anything. When he disappeared around the curtain, leaving her alone with her captain, he came up alongside the bed, moving a stool she hadn't noticed and then sitting next to her.

"What do you remember before coming here?" he asked.

"Everything is foggy." Flashes appeared in her mind, making love to Chase, him fucking her so hard she was barely able to make it to her kitchen for water. That wasn't something she was going to share with her captain.

"You worked the crime scene for Chris Perkins," he prompted.

Ashley searched his dark features. In the ten years on the force, John Sullivan had never aged. He had to have one of the highest-stress jobs in the city, yet his smooth black skin didn't wrinkle, and his brooding stare once again appeared concerned, and not stressed.

"Chris Perkins," she whispered, the flashes in her mind piecing together. "I remember." She nodded, once again trying to sit up in her bed. There was something weird about lying against pillows while talking to her captain. "It appears we've lost another lady to ISIS."

Captain Sullivan nodded. "Where did you go when you left the crime scene?"

She squinted, frowning. The fog was lifting from her brain, leaving a dull, thudding headache in its wake. "I headed over to . . ." She hesitated. Captain Sullivan hadn't acted as if he knew Chase.

"You went over to the guy's house who brought you in here?" He asked the question but looked at her as if he were reminding her that was what she did.

Ashley nodded. "I really don't remember anything after that." She couldn't even picture his house in her mind. "How did I get here?"

"He brought you here. What's his name? Is he a close friend?"

Close enough that she fucked the shit out of him. Ashley wondered how thorough an exam they did on her when she arrived. Losing a piece of her life seriously sucked. She couldn't account for anything after leaving the crime scene.

"Yes, he's a close friend," she conceded. "I guess I was more exhausted than I realized. I don't ever remember passing out this hard." She hoped her smile appeared sincere. The sooner she could get out of this hospital the better.

"You didn't pass out, Ash. You were drugged. They found small traces of ISIS in your system." Captain Sullivan's dark features turned dangerous, the white around his black eyes suddenly glowing as he stared at her. "I want to know everything about the guy who brought you in here. How long have you known him?"

ASHLEY STOOD in her living room, staring at her familiar surroundings but not seeing them. Chase had taken off after leaving the side of her bed, which made him even more of a suspect in everyone's eyes. But her gut told her he wasn't the ISIS killer, that he couldn't have been because he'd been with her when Chris Perkins died. Her reaction to the lethal drug was proof, though, that a person could ingest and not die for a few hours.

"Have you had company recently?" Captain Sullivan, who'd brought her home, walked through her living room and into her bedroom, switching on the light.

In spite of having slept almost all day, Ashley still felt exhausted. They'd almost pumped her stomach at the hospital in an effort to get the ISIS out of her system. When test results showed she'd only ingested a minuscule amount, and her reaction was more an aftereffect than being drugged, they'd let her sleep it off, monitoring her until she woke up.

Ashley walked past her captain, knowing what her room probably looked like, and headed to her kitchen instead.

"Who's been over here, Ash? Was it that guy who brought you in? What did you say his name was, Chase?"

She'd done her best to avoid giving too much information about him, although the more vaguely she was answering him, the more guilty she made him look. Ashley knew he wasn't her killer.

"Yes, Captain, his name is Chase. He's not your man, though."

"He's a suspect. You've been poisoned. Who else have you been with?"

"No one," she said quickly, spinning around but then realizing she wasn't helping Chase's case. "You're going to have to trust me on this one, John," she offered softly. "There is no way he killed any of those women, or drugged me. What I need to figure out is how, and when, I would have ingested ISIS."

"You know as well as I do people will defend criminals when they have feelings for them. Some people honestly believe a serial killer is as innocent as God when they love them."

Ashley stared at her kitchen, willing the dull headache throbbing at her temples to go away as she fought to replay every event that transpired over the last twelve hours. Wait. Make that over the past twenty-four hours, since she'd slept over eight hours at the hospital.

Her kitchen was clean. They hadn't eaten anything here. She'd had a beer at the bowling alley before coming here, but as many times as she replayed walking into the bowling alley with Chase, she didn't remember him ever touching her beer. And she'd never left his side, not even to go to the bathroom. Other than the beer, they hadn't eaten, but come home and gone at it.

Danny had called. No. Wait. She'd called him. He'd broken into her home. How the hell had she forgotten that?

"My ex broke into my house," she announced, looking at her back door and then walking over to it. It was locked.

"What? When did he do that?" Captain Sullivan stood in her kitchen, his thick arms crossed over his chest, watching her with a shrewd eye.

Another person would have been intimidated by his commanding presence. But John Sullivan didn't hold half the dominating, protective aura that Chase did.

"When we," she began, but then turned, facing him, and started again. "I came home and realized someone was in my house. The jerk damn near got himself shot," she added, forcing a dry chuckle. "I chased him out the back door and then recognized his car idling in the alley."

"You know it was him for sure?"

"Yup. I called him and chewed his ass." Her gaze fell on a bottle of water on her counter. The cap was barely on it and it was almost full. Ashley walked up to the bottle, remembering taking it out of the refrigerator. "I thought I was out of bottled water," she mused.

"What?"

Ashley picked up the bottle and the cap fell off it, rolling under the kitchen table. She brought it to her nose, sniffing the water.

"Does this smell funny to you?"

Captain Sullivan tried taking the bottle, but she wouldn't let him. "Don't touch it. Just sniff it. If I'm right, I don't want anyone else's fingerprints on it."

CHAPTER 8

CHASE PICKED up his phone, already knowing why his supervisor would be calling. "What's up, Doc?"

Harry Docking, his immediate supervisor, was calling from his private line. Whatever he wanted to say, it was off the record. Nonetheless, Chase answered with the code words he'd used for years, "What's up, Doc?," which told Harry there was no situation at his end.

Unfortunately, Chase was damn near positive that was anything but the case.

"Do you remember Big Al Crete?" Doc's tone was all business.

Maybe the events in his hometown hadn't reached his supervisor's desk. "The Greek who was shipping drugs over the border a year back? Didn't he turn evidence over to the state?"

"Yup. And walked free. Apparently he walked right back into his old lifestyle."

"Don't they usually?"

"He just got picked up down there in Wichita, apparently he moved beyond the acceptable drugs of heroine and cocaine. They busted him with a fair amount of ISIS on him."

Chase froze. He didn't realize he'd been pacing his living room until he stopped, a tightening throughout his body having him gripping his phone so hard he damn near broke it in two.

"Was he dealing here in Wichita?" Chase's mind started racing. He'd put Ashley in one hell of a position walking out on her, and it bugged the crap out of him knowing she was keeping his cover for him and he wasn't there for her.

"I'm surprised you don't have the answer to that question." Doc continued with his hard tone, which was impossible to read over the phone. "If you've been behaving, though, and not taking the law into your own hands and trying to solve cases without following protocol, I might be willing to put you on another case."

Chase didn't like being asked if he was behaving. Doc knew Chase was one of his best operatives. And if nailing a perpetrator meant breaking a few laws along the way, he sure as hell wasn't breaking as many laws as the bad guy was.

"That's up to you," he growled, unwilling to keep the grumpiness out of his tone.

"You aren't some rookie, Chase. You know how it works. I hate thinking you're burned out. You're one hell of a good agent, but you've got to follow the rules."

"Yup," he said, heading into his bedroom to get his keys. "Where did you say they booked Big Al Crete?"

"I didn't. Why do you care?"

Chase didn't care any longer about protecting who he was, not if he could help Ashley crack this case. And especially if he could see her again. From what he'd observed on the few drive-bys he'd done today since she'd come home from the hospital, her captain was hanging around too close. If she was protecting Chase, it wouldn't surprise him a bit if her captain felt she was hiding something. Which she was—his identity.

"I don't know if I care yet, or not." And he wouldn't until he talked to Big Al.

"Stay out of it, Chase," Doc ordered. "It's not your case. Stand by and I'll fax information to you there in an hour or so. I'll get you a plane ticket and tomorrow you'll be in New York."

"Uh-huh." Chase wasn't listening. He locked up his house and headed to his car. Ashley's car was still there, further proof she hadn't disclosed to anyone who he was. The longer she protected him, the deeper she incriminated herself. Both of them couldn't lose their jobs.

He got off the phone with Doc, not sure if he had agreed to anything or not, and not really caring. After knowing Ashley a few days he already saw what he hadn't seen in any other woman he'd ever met. Her feisty nature, her craving to solve a crime—and obviously at any expense since she hadn't narked him out yet—were characteristics he'd never imagined finding in a woman. Add to that her sex appeal, her distracting good looks, her commanding nature that turned submissive when he pushed her to a certain point sexually, and he knew he'd found the woman for him.

Chase flipped his cell phone open and called Ashley.

"Hello," she said slowly, the wariness in her tone obvious.

"My supervisor just told me a known drug dealer, Big Al Crete, was arrested in Wichita recently," he began, keeping his voice low in case anyone was near her who might overhear before he could say what needed to be said. "He was arrested for selling ISIS."

"Oh really?" she interrupted, matching his calm, quiet tone. "Where are you headed?"

It didn't surprise him she wanted to know about him. Ashley wanted him as much as he wanted her.

"Your house."

"I don't think so," she told him, her slow drawl giving anyone around her listening the indication she could be talking about the weather.

"I already know your captain is there. Tell him I'm on my way and I'll show my credentials when I get there. You're not covering for me anymore, sweetheart. And you're not getting a bad rap because of me."

Ashley sighed in his ear and his dick immediately responded. "I'm feeling better, thank you. I guess I'm doing things backward today. Most people work all day and then sleep, I slept all day and am now going to work."

"Where are you going?" he demanded, and at the same time heard a man speak in the background.

"Don't worry. I won't overdo it. It's really rather scary but there was a bottle of water in my refrigerator. I took a sip of it last night and thought it was sour. Thank God I spit it out. We took it down to the lab and it was heavily laced with ISIS. Danny was in my house last night and he's agreed to meet me down at the station and be fingerprinted, just to eliminate him as a suspect," she said, laughing. "He's seriously grouchy with me for even suggesting he could do something so terrible as murder women with a date rape drug. But he's the only one who was in my house."

Again the man in the background said something. Ashley mumbled a response. "And yes, I know," she continued, speaking to Chase. "I wasn't alone last night. So I guess if my ex comes away clean than I'll have to seek out the guy I was with last night."

Chase wouldn't even consider the possibility that Ashley might think him guilty. "Ash," he growled. "Your ex is going to run. You tell your captain right this minute who I am or I'll call the police station and demand to be put through to him myself."

"That really is a very bad idea," she whispered. "Thanks for calling, though. If I have time I'm heading to that store where Chris and the others bought those bracelets."

"I'll head over there now." More than anything he wanted to see Ashley. There was something she wasn't telling him, though. Chase hated not being in the loop, but for some reason she didn't want him coming over and she didn't want her captain, who he was sure was the man in the background, knowing he was on the phone. "Quit covering for me, Ash," he added.

"You'll have to trust me. But I promise not to work too hard." Again she laughed.

"And you have to trust me," he growled, his insides tensing at the thought something else might have happened that she couldn't tell him about right now.

"I do. Believe me, I do," she said quietly. "Well, I better get going."

"Ashley," he growled, but she'd hung up on him. "Damn

it," he howled and almost threw his phone at his windshield.

He had parked downtown in a stall not too far from the Crossing when his cell rang again. The moment he saw the number he flipped it open, ready to snap.

"Don't ever hang up on me again," he growled.

"Calm down," Ashley said. "Captain Sullivan is convinced you're a very likely suspect and I don't have time to waste chasing false leads."

It was nice hearing Ashley didn't suspect him. "And he wouldn't think that if you didn't try to protect me. I should have called you sooner, or told you not to keep my identity a secret."

"I did it as much for my own pride as anything else, but we can fight about this later," she said, sounding tense. "I'm supposed to be on my way to the station."

"Supposed to be, where are you headed?" Chase reached the Crossing and pushed a heavy wooden door open, getting a powerful whiff of incense the moment he set foot in the eclectic store.

"Over to Danny's. Remember I told you about those earrings? I think Danny took them. Those earrings on Mary Harcourt were mine. He showed up at my house after Mindy's death to make sure I knew how distraught he was about it, but he also admitted he'd been dating her. I know he knew Chris and now she's dead. And she was too closemouthed about that bracelet."

"You think Danny gave the bracelets to all the victims?" he asked, spotting a gray-haired woman behind the counter and lowering his voice. "Don't head over to his house without backup. He's already tried to kill you once."

"Exactly. Which is why he broke into my house the other night. He wanted to kill me. I'm not sure why he agreed so amiably to coming down to the station but he won't show, and I'm not going to let him get away."

"Don't hang up," Chase hissed. "Stay on the line while I find out about those bracelets."

"Okay." Maybe it was his imagination but she sounded

tired, or possibly scared. Chase's insides tightened as an overwhelming protective instinct damn near kicked his ass.

He reached the counter and put his phone down, the woman behind the counter eyeballing it as if it might leap up and bite her. There wasn't time to play out the scene. He needed answers now. Reaching into his back pocket, he pulled out his wallet and produced his badge.

"Hi, ma'am, I'm Special Agent Chase Reed. I need to ask you a few questions."

"Okay," she said slowly, paling noticeably.

"You sell a thin rope bracelet that has small knots in it," he began.

She nodded and gestured with her head to a table next to him. "Those," she said.

Chase looked at a table, covered with a piece of purple cloth with a variety of jewelry on it. He immediately noticed a row of thin, roped bracelets, but there weren't any knots in them.

"Yes, but these had knots in them."

"The person who buys them puts the knots in them," she explained, moving around the table and picking up one of the bracelets. "Usually the knots are made according to a series of accomplishments. They are life bracelets. If there are goals, or events the person needs to leap through to reach their meaning in life, they create the knots for each one."

Chase nodded. "Have you had a male customer come in and buy several of these in the past month?"

"They are really popular. But other than my carpenter, no one has taken more than one."

"What's your carpenter's name?"

"Danny Surrelli. He's a wonderful craftsman," she explained and pointed to a glass-enclosed cabinet along the wall. "He made this for me as well as all of the tables in here."

Returning to the counter, he pulled a pen out of a colorful cup and picked up one of her business cards. "This is you?" She nodded. "And all of your contact information?"

"Is there a problem?" She frowned at the card in his hand.

"Not anymore. Thank you, ma'am. You've been a great

help." Chase grabbed his phone from the counter and stalked out of the store. "Did you hear that?" he asked, turning and heading down the street for his car. Ashley didn't answer him. "Ash, you there?"

He climbed into his SUV, straining to hear faint background noise coming through the phone. It seemed Ashley had put the phone down, but something told him to hold off screaming into the phone to grab her attention. There was a pay phone halfway down the street and Chase jumped out of his car, digging into his pocket for change as he hurried to the phone.

"Just be listed, motherfucker," he grumbled, feeling the pain from tight muscles throughout his body. Ashley didn't have the support of her police force, probably because, although she believed she was doing the right thing, she'd become involved with him. Maybe his work ethics sucked according to every suit in the agency, but he'd be damned if Ashley came out of this case marred in any way.

He dropped the coins into the phone and dialed directory assistance. "Danny Surrelli, Wichita," he told the animated voice. Then pressing his cell to his ear, he struggled to hear what faint noises sounded through the cell phone while waiting impatiently for directory assistance on the pay phone to search for the number. "Bingo!" he hissed, when the number was repeated by the animated voice.

Writing it down on the back of the card he'd taken from the Crossing, he hurried back to his car and pressed the button on his key chain to unlock all of his car doors. There were advantages to living in an age of modern technology and gadgets. Chase pulled a briefcase out of the back of his SUV, popped it open, and slid out the flat laptop and cord to plug it into his car lighter.

And in spite of modern technology, it still seemed it took forever to boot the damn thing up, wait for the desktop to load, then dig the small gizmo out of his glove compartment that plugged into the laptop and gave him instant access to the Internet. They were tools he didn't use often, but in a pinch, it sure as hell beat trying to convince dispatch at the local police station that he was an FBI agent who had a right to know where one of their police officer's ex-husbands lived. By the time reverse lookup provided him with an address, there wasn't a sound coming through Ashley's cell phone.

"Hold on, baby, I'm coming," he whispered, squealing out of the parking stall and heading to Danny Surrelli's home.

There was a patrol car parked in front of the address he'd written down on the back of the card, and Chase pulled in behind it, cutting the engine and hurrying across the yard to the front door. He knocked firmly on the door. If the police were here, and not Ashley using a squad car since her car was parked at his house, they would open quickly. Chase pulled out his wallet, flipping it open to show his badge. No one answered. Chase turned the doorknob. It was locked.

"If you've hurt her . . ." he growled, not giving it another thought but stepping back, kicking the doorknob and breaking the lock. He pushed the door open, pulling his gun out of his shoulder holster and shoving his wallet back in his pocket as he entered the home. "Ashley?" he yelled.

"Back up, boy toy, and get the fuck out of here," a stocky blond growled as he slowly rose to his feet.

Ashley lay on the floor, her clothes torn and her face tearstained. There was a wild, frantic look in her eyes as she stared up at Chase, but she didn't get to her feet when Danny did. Next to her, on the floor, was a shot glass filled with a clear liquid.

"I said leave!" Danny bellowed.

Chase didn't hesitate. Pulling the trigger, he aimed and fired. The gun exploded and Ashley screamed.

CHAPTER 9

ASHLEY PULLED into the gravel driveway and parked. She stared at the ranch-style house sitting back from the street with the tall juniper trees scattered throughout the yard. Although she'd been here before, she didn't remember Chase's house. It looked masculine, solid and secure, just like Chase.

Two weeks had passed since he'd shot her ex, and with the case wrapped up and Danny out of the hospital and behind bars awaiting his trial, life had returned to normal for the most part. Except for the nagging yearning inside her that wouldn't go away. When she'd returned from lunch to the message that Chase had called, inviting her to dinner, she'd called him back without hesitating. All she'd been able to do was leave voice mail.

She hadn't seen him in several days, since he'd flown to New York, but it seemed a lot longer. One look at his face when Chase answered the door and stepped to the side so she could enter and she knew he felt the same way.

"You're late," he growled.

"I got off work late," she lied.

"You were off work at five." He closed the door behind her and then wrapped his hands around her waist, pulling her backside against his chest. Chase lowered his mouth to her neck, his breath instantly torturing her oversensitive flesh.

Just knowing she'd see him tonight had created a pressure inside her that refused to subside, no matter how much she dwelled on mundane paperwork. The smoldering need exploded into a fiery craving that stole her breath.

"Don't torture me and make me wait for you," he growled.

"I didn't know what to wear," she confessed, rubbing her hands down the sundress she'd opted for after changing clothes too many times before heading to Chase's house.

"I don't like your choice."

"Really?" She couldn't turn her head far enough to see his face.

"Nope. It covers way too much of you." He took the spaghetti strap off her shoulder with his teeth and tugged on it.

Ashley tried turning but stopped at the sound of fabric tearing. "How did your case go?" she asked, needing something to ground her. If they talked about work maybe they wouldn't be tearing each other's clothes off right at the back door.

"I don't know. I came home."

"What? You walked off the case?" She did turn then, and her strap ripped free from the material stretching over her breasts.

Chase's gaze darkened when he released the fabric from his mouth and stared at her chest. He reached for the other strap and she grabbed his hand.

"Tell me you didn't walk off the case," she insisted.

He didn't try freeing his wrist. "I didn't walk off the case," he told her, his dark blue eyes glowing like sapphires as he tore into her soul with a predatory gaze. "We came to a mutual understanding. I'm not going to play around with bureaucratic bullshit any longer, and they aren't going to ask me to do it."

"What exactly does that mean?" It was hard maintaining his stare with her blood pressure soaring and the throbbing between her legs pulsing so hard cream soaked her pussy.

Chase freed his hand from her grip and headed into his house, leaving her to follow him. They entered his kitchen where a glass pan filled with bubbling lasagna was on the top of the stove. A loaf of French bread had been cut on a cutting board and a bottle of wine sat on the counter. She glanced farther into his house, spotting a small dining room table, set beautifully with a white tablecloth, and decent-looking china. Two long thin candles burned in the middle of the table. Chase had a domestic side she'd never dreamed existed.

"It was an amiable parting," he explained, running his hand through his black hair and tousling it around his face when he glanced at her. Then taking the bottle of wine, he wrapped his arm around hers and guided her into his dining room. "I'm not cut out to bring in criminals who break every rule in the book while following a meticulous set of guidelines that trip me up every time I turn around. I could have busted that guy in a matter of hours after arriving in New York if I hadn't had to wait two days for a judge to get around to signing a damned piece of paper."

It was a common frustration many law enforcement men and women voiced in her line of work. Ashley didn't say anything as he pulled out her chair for her and then scooted her toward the table after she sat. He popped the cork and poured wine into two glasses.

"I've submitted my resignation," he said.

"You have? What will you do?" She spoke to his back as he strolled into his kitchen, returning a minute later with oven gloves on his hands as he placed the lasagna on a wicker mat in the middle of the table.

Chase didn't answer but left her again, returning with the bread. Then sitting opposite her, he took her plate and dished food on to it. After doing the same to his own plate, he then set it in front of him and lifted his wine glass. She lifted hers, watching him as their glasses clinked together.

"There's a man I've known for a few years out in California," he began, not making a toast but instead bringing his glass to his lips and sipping. "He's helped me out a few times over the years with one case or another. Ash, he nails the perp by his own set of rules, and it's completely legal. He's licensed, earns a decent living, and takes cases as they appeal to him."

"A PI?" She lifted her fork when he did and then sliced into what looked like incredibly good lasagna.

"No. A bounty hunter."

Ash stared at him. His eyes glowed, and she could tell he'd given this serious thought and made his decision. "It might not hurt having a bounty hunter at my beck and call," she offered, and her heart flipped when the side of his mouth curved into a dangerous-looking smile.

"Beck and call, eh?" Something darkened in his eyes and whatever silent promise he made her, she felt her body respond with a craving that made it almost impossible to eat. "Eat your food, my dear, and I'll show you what is at your beck and call."

Ashley almost choked and took a quick drink of her wine. Her heart swelled as the realization hit her that Chase wouldn't be leaving as much. If he meant what he said, there were steps he would need to take to license himself and then he'd have to set up an office. She ate the incredible meal, enjoyed his company, and felt more at home than she had anywhere she'd been in years.

When she picked up her plate and reached for his after dinner, Chase stopped her. "We'll worry about these later," he told her, taking her hand and guiding her around the table and into his living room.

A large fireplace was empty and she imagined what it would be like in the dead of winter, cuddling up with him while a fire raged. Chase pulled her down on him and reclined on his black leather couch. Before she could relax he'd pulled the zipper down her back, causing her dress to sag, held up by the one spaghetti strap.

Chase focused on it, lifting it with his fingers and toying with it while he tortured her shoulder with his slight touch. "Did you ever get a confession out of your ex?" he asked, his voice a gruff whisper.

"Actually, I didn't. One of the other detectives, Charlie Madison, interrogated him. Danny told him marriage was until death, and he was sick and tired of women entering his life and then sauntering out. But they were still alive, chasing after other men."

"Sounds like he cracked."

"I was stupid never to notice it."

"You weren't paying attention to him."

He was right. Once her divorce was final she'd moved on with her life, not giving Danny a second thought. She didn't blame herself. But she hated thinking there had been so many clues in front of her and she'd taken so long to piece them together. Too many young women had died while the evidence was right in front of her.

"I should have killed the bastard when I saw him with you on the floor."

"He wasn't able to get me to drink anything. That was something about Danny that never appealed to me, his lack of aggressiveness. I didn't realize it until I was lying on the floor, but when I attacked, verbally and physically, he balked."

Chase flipped her over him, and she landed on her back on the couch, so stunned by his quick actions she wasn't able to stop him from hiking up her dress and discovering she wasn't wearing underwear. Immediately he slid his fingers inside her soaked pussy.

"There's such a thing as too aggressive," she teased.

"Not with you, my dear," he growled, squeezing her breast while thrusting his fingers deep inside her. "Fight back all you want. I know how it turns you on."

She made a face at him, unable to argue. He was right. His dominating nature got her so hot she felt him pushing her to the edge as he finger-fucked her. But when his mouth covered hers, branding her with a kiss so hot and sensual, there was no holding on. Ashley tumbled over the edge, the pressure exploding inside her as she cried into his mouth.

He wasn't wearing boots this time and had his jeans off in a matter of minutes. She dragged his shirt over his head, loving how his dark hair tangled around his face as he stared at her with a look so intense the swelling he'd released inside her built again with record speed.

"Stay with me," he growled, kissing her again and then entering her.

She didn't know if he meant tonight, or longer, but didn't care. Her answer would be the same either way. Wrapping her arms around his neck, she lifted her legs, encouraging him deeper, and enjoyed the hell out of their lovemaking.

"I'll stay with you," she whispered, her vision blurring when she tried focusing on his smoldering gaze.

"And love me."

Her heart exploded in her chest at the same time her orgasm ripped through her. "I love you," she told him, and believed she loved for the first time in her life. And she prayed this time it would be until death.

Look for *New York Times* bestselling author Lora Leigh's
sizzling new novel

RENEGADE

ISBN: 978-0-312-94583-1

Coming Soon From St. Martin's Paperbacks

Don't miss the sizzling new novel from award-winning
author Lori O'Clare

STRONG, SLEEK AND SINFUL

ISBN: 978-0-312-94344-8

Available From St. Martin's Paperbacks

Don't Miss This Other Red-Hot Anthology
From Today's Bestselling Romance Writers

RESCUE ME
Featuring

CHERRY ADAIR

LORA LEIGH

CINDY GERARD

ISBN: 978-0-312-94842-9

Available From St. Martin's Paperbacks